You Know Better

You Know Better . A NOVEL

Tina McElroy Ansa

WILLIAM MORROW *An Imprint of* HarperCollins*Publishers*

HarperCollins books may be purchased for educational, business, or sales promotional use. For information please write: Special Markets Department, HarperCollins Publishers Inc., 10 East 53rd Street, New York, NY 10022.

FIRST EDITION

Designed by Shubhani Sarkar

Printed on acid-free paper

Library of Congress Cataloging-in-Publication Data has been applied for.

ISBN 0-06-019779-X

02   03   04   05   06   WBC/RRD   10   9   8   7   6   5   4   3   2   1

Acknowledgments

It's taken me a while, but I finally get it. Holy Spirit writes all my books, gives me all the words, themes, ideas, images.

I thank Spirit. I thank Spirit. I thank Spirit for this novel.

I also thank and acknowledge all the named and unnamed spirit guides and friends who led, helped, spurred, nudged, and wrote this work. They affect my life as surely as they affect my characters' lives. I love them and thank them all.

My family continues to be a source of love and inspiration for me. I thank my ever-widening support system: my hometown of Macon; my Macon sisters; Consuela Floyd and Kent Elmore, for continued faith; Varnette P. Honeywood for clothing all my "babies" in beautiful attire; and my faithful companion, Zora. I am grateful to my editor, Claire Wachtel, an old friend who was midwife for another of my "babies" and who still asks me all the right questions. My agent, Owen Laster, who has supported me from the beginning of my career in fiction, is a blessing to me. And as always, I am grateful to St. Simons Island, the spirit of which continues to offer me the love and acceptance of home.

Contents

part 1. FAITH

Lily Paine Pines

1.

"Miss Moses?! Is that *you?* Good God, I thought you were *dead!*"

They were the first words that I spoke to that dear old lady. And I did not merely speak them. I shouted them—from across the street—out the window of my automobile.

Can you believe it? That was the first thing out of my mouth: "I thought you were *dead!*" It was so unlike me. But then again, as my little granddaughter and her contemporaries say, "I was *stressed!*"

I rolled down the window and shouted it all the way across the street right out of the car. Of course, I was mortified. I was beyond mortified. I had spent my entire life conducting myself in an exemplary fashion. Any deviation from that role disturbed me.

In my embarrassment over that coarse slip, I almost forgot for a moment that I was out after midnight on a Saturday morning scouting around the streets of Mulberry, Georgia, looking for my almost-nineteen-year-old granddaughter, LaShawndra, my only grandchild.

That was the reason I was in what used to be downtown Mulberry, outside the local nightspot called The Club, located on the corner of Broadway and Cherry Street, looking for LaShawndra even though I knew the establishment had closed at midnight, nearly an hour before. If LaShawndra had gone there, I figured I might still be able to catch her little butt hanging around outside looking for a ride.

But the only little figure I saw on the corner of Broadway and Cherry Street that dark early morning was that of old Miss Moses, Mulberry's pioneering educator.

The clouds chose just that moment to shift in the sky, exposing a moon directly over her head that was split right down the middle, like half a pie.

Seeing that old blind lady in the middle of downtown Mulberry at almost one o'clock in the morning more than shocked me.

At first I almost thought I was having a flashback from some bad drugs I took back in the sixties.

I couldn't help myself. I was stunned to see Miss Moses standing right under one of those high-crime, high-intensity street lamps with an umbrella hanging over her arm—proudly—as if she were fully prepared for anything. I lowered the window on the passenger's side and yelled across the seat, almost expecting her to vanish before my eyes. But I knew I was seeing the old woman's face clearly. There was no mistake about it. It was Miss Moses.

The first reason I was so surprised to see Miss Moses, even in the midst of this crisis with my granddaughter, LaShawndra—besides the fact that it was nearly one o'clock in the morning—was that Miss Moses was all by herself. And I couldn't believe that Miss Moses was the kind of elderly blind person who went off on a jaunt by herself.

I knew a blind masseur I would go to sometimes. Extraordinary man. He told me that as a teenager he regularly jumped the fence of the Mulberry School for the Blind and ventured out at night to buy beer for his dormitory cohorts at the corner 7-Eleven. Imagine the nerve that took.

But I could not imagine Miss Moses jumping any fences at night to come out to The Club. My God, she had to have been ninety-five if she was a day.

Miss Moses looked like a dainty little wrinkled urban poppy growing up through a crack in the middle of all that weathered con-crete. And between the bright streetlight she was standing under and my increasing farsightedness—you know, I can see farther off now than I can close up—I could see her just as clear as day. She was dressed in this red and purple flowered voile dress that nearly came down to her ankles. And it had a high neck with some grayish-looking crocheted cotton lace around the collar. The sleeves of the dress were long, all the way past her wrists, but you know how you can see through voile, so I could see her little stick arms through the sleeves.

Planted on top of her head was a small, round, pink straw pillbox hat—I had not seen one of *them* in thirty years—with a strip of hot pink grosgrain ribbon for a band. And planted on top of the pillbox hat was a huge—I mean *huge*—lavender cabbage rose.

All of which made her gray nappy hair—kind of tucked in in some places and sticking up in other places—look like a tuft of dried but living grass sprouting around the pillbox.

You know she had on a sweater. In fact, she had on two sweaters. One on top of the other. But she didn't have either one of them completely on. Both sweaters were merely thrown around her shoulders. And I was worried about her standing out there on a street corner in the cool. Her little gray sweater with yellowed satin ribbon woven throughout was just wrapped around her bony shoulders, and the two top buttons were fastened to keep it on. And another buttercup yellow cotton sweater with pink and blue flowers embroidered on it was tossed on top of that first one. And its top two buttons were fastened, too.

The second reason I was surprised to see her there was I was almost sure I had seen the notice of Miss Moses's death in the *Mulberry Times* a few months before. I read the local newspaper cover to cover each weekday morning before I leave for work and in the afternoons on the weekend. Most mornings I'm up to hear the thump of the paper on my front porch. I could have *sworn* I'd seen Miss Moses's obituary! GRACE MOSES, LOCAL EDUCATION PIONEER, DEAD AT 95. Or something like that. The death notice had jumped out at me because I had always heard my dear father speak so highly of her.

But I figured I must have been mistaken, because there she was: standing all by herself on the corner of Broadway and Cherry in the middle of what used to be old downtown Mulberry. She was standing there just as big. Well, not "just as big," because she was just as tiny and insubstantial as a ten-cent bag of Tom's potato chips.

And it's not just because I'm five eight, a tallish woman. I *know* "tiny." My daughter and my granddaughter are both petite women. I know tiny. But Miss Moses was so teeny she looked like a little squab under a potato cage on a Sunday-brunch plate.

Well, you know I just went on and on apologizing about having informed Miss Moses I thought she was dead!

"Oh, I'm sorry, Miss Moses. I'm so sorry. How uncouth of me. Just blurting that out. Oh, forgive me."

Of course, I jumped out and helped her into my car.

Lord have mercy. She was as fragile as tissue paper.

I expected her to feel a bit cool, standing out on that corner the way she was, but she felt like a sliver of ice, chilled to the bone. I put my arm around her and took her little birdlike elbow. When I was a child, my father and his buddies used to go to the woods around Lake Peak and hunt squab and pheasant and bring them back for their wives to pluck and dress. That's what Miss Moses's limbs reminded me of. Those small birds lying out on damp newspaper on our front porch. I picked up all the bags she had around her and led her slowly slowly slowly to the passenger side of my car. She moved in increments of millimeters. As upset as I was about LaShawndra's whereabouts, however, slowing down was the best thing for me. I probably didn't even have any business driving.

"Come on, Miss Moses, let me help you in," I said. "Easy now. Take your time. It's okay. It's fine. Really. No, just watch your head getting in the car. Time doesn't matter. We've got all the time in the world, Miss Moses," I said. "All the time we need. I wouldn't rush you for anything in the world. Truly."

At first I was talking just to be polite and to cover my confusion, but after a while I just surrendered to the moment. Since I did not see LaShawndra anywhere around, you know, my first inclination was to rush that beautiful old lady into that car and gun that motor on to the next likely spot. But I was immediately grateful that I didn't. Even though I felt in my soul that I was in the middle of a whopper of a

LaShawndra crisis, I meant what I said: I would not have rushed Miss Moses for anything in the world. And, you know, the universe is generous: As soon as I did the right thing and took that old lady into my car with me at her own pace, I felt better. I felt a bit of peace right there around my gut.

In fact, for the first time since I had awakened, I felt as if the state of Mississippi had been lifted from my chest.

Then Miss Moses took a deep breath—it must have taken thirty full seconds for her to inhale and then exhale. I saw her tiny flat titties slowly rise and fall. Then she spoke for the first time. She looked toward me and said, "Well, that is better, isn't it?"

She said it nicely, conversationally even, but her soft old voice gave me a chill all over. I reached across and cut the heat up a notch.

"I was waiting for a Green and Cream," she said suddenly.

That's what she said. She was waiting for a Green and Cream because she needed to go across town.

At any rate, I couldn't leave that lovely old blind woman standing by herself in the middle of nowhere in the middle of the night waiting for a bus that hasn't come through Mulberry in twenty years.

A Green and Cream indeed!

Years ago the public buses in Mulberry were painted this awful putrid-looking color of green on the bottom and a cream color on the top.

But Mulberry doesn't even have public transportation anymore, let alone those old Green and Cream buses.

"Waitin' for a Green and Cream!" I should not have been surprised. The full moon was still glowing in the Georgia sky, and the day was already shaping up to be a strange and confusing one.

"But, Miss Moses," I persisted, "you're all alone down here by yourself in the middle of the night."

All she said was "Um-huh." Then silence.

"*Are* you all alone out here?" I asked, trying to keep the anger out of my voice. "Is one of your great-grands suppose to be taking care of you?"

I just *knew* some irresponsible teenager had not left that dear old woman out on the street corner while they went partying. They just *couldn't have.*

But there she was.

"Where in the world are you headed at midnight, Miss Moses, waiting for a Green and Cream? Why in the world do you 'need' to go across town?" I asked her as soon as we were finally settled in the front seat of my car. I bet it took twenty minutes to get her all gently in, settled and composed. I reached in the backseat and got the soft gold chenille afghan I kept in the car and threw it around her shoulders and tucked her in like a baby. She had already started feeling warmer to the touch.

I had been trying not to stare at the old woman, but as I arranged her in—she had three or four brown paper shopping bags *and* an old croaker sack; I don't know *what* she could have had in those bags, especially that croaker sack—I couldn't stop myself. I looked at her in the inside car light, and I could see she looked ancient, but in a strangely unsettling way.

As I helped her get settled, she leaned forward to check one of her bags, and her dark sunglasses—classic black-rimmed Ray-Ban Wayfarers—slipped down her nose, and I got a good look at her eyes.

I had never seen her eyes before. They looked as if she had seen all the events in the world since the beginning of time. That the swirl of life was not up ahead of her just out of her reach, something to be attained, but rather behind her a little bit, she having passed through it all.

But then she pushed the glasses back up on the broad bridge of her nose with four fingers of her left hand, and her eyes were hidden from me again.

Up close, her nose looked bigger than I remembered it. But you know, your nose gets bigger as you grow older. I know mine is growing larger.

My friend Joyce claims hers isn't. But to let her tell it, she is untouched by any signs of aging. Her nose isn't growing bigger. Her butt isn't sinking southward. She doesn't have any of those little white spots on her legs, nor any visible varicose veins. And to let her tell it, she still can go to church services in her good clothes without a bra.

Hmmmm. She's as bad as my daughter, Sandra, who thinks she can halt the hands of time.

At least I had enough presence of mind not to blurt out something about the size of Miss Moses's nose. I had already embarrassed myself enough by mistaking her for dead.

As I reached over Miss Moses's lap and adjusted her seat against her lower back, I could tell from the way she smelled that she was used to being well cared for. Not that every human being and sentient creature on this earth doesn't deserve to be well cared for, but Miss Moses smelled as sweet as a freshly bathed baby. She smelled like old-fashioned lavender talcum powder. And there wasn't a *trace* of a whiff of urine odor about her.

I tell you, the smell of Miss Moses's lavender almost calmed me down a bit. It had an herbal, not a flowery, scent, and I inhaled it like incense. I could feel my heartbeat slow down and regulate.

I asked again, "Where are you headed this time of morning, Miss Moses?" Hoping she could give me some kind of clue as to what I was to do with her.

I really didn't expect a straight answer, because I assumed—see, when you assume, you make an *ass* of *u* and *me*—I just assumed that she must have been a bit out of her head and had wandered off from the Mulberry Arms Retirement Village—I thought that's where she lived—and become disoriented.

But then I thought, She's blind! Recalling the little I knew about her, I remembered that she had lost her sight in her later years. I thought it was from an inherited degenerative disease, but it may have been from cataracts. I wasn't sure. Whatever the cause, I did wonder how she made her way the twelve or thirteen winding blocks down there from the nursing home.

You know, it's not easy even for people who're not blind to come to Mulberry, Georgia, and find their way around downtown when there's no "downtown" downtown anymore, with all the stores out to the Mulberry Mall now. And no real businesses to speak of located in the heart of town anymore.

Other than The Place and The Club, there's only the offices for Candace Realty Company. That's where my daughter, Sandra, works. Well, actually, she's a part owner of the business. All the women who work there own part of the business. Black folks in Mulberry are very proud of that. Lena McPherson—the former owner of The Place—used to own Candace, too. But she just walked away from that a few years ago.

Miss Moses answered right away, just as clear and lucid, facing straight ahead.

"Miss Moses going over to Pleasant Hill to see 'bout a young girl in trouble."

Well, you know that made me think of my little granddaughter, LaShawndra, and the mess I felt she was about to get into.

It just breaks my heart, because LaShawndra really has something to offer the world besides trouble.

She's a good girl underneath, she just has a bad reputation.

It's the way she talks and the things she says mostly that give people the wrong impression.

LaShawndra, bless her heart, will say *anything*. I know I'm a bit responsible for that. I encouraged her to speak her mind, because she started talking so early and so well. I just wanted her to excel at something—a number of things would have suited me just fine—but I may have made a misjudgment in that respect.

Also, I encouraged her to express herself because she has such a way with words. Now, if that child would just use some of those words to her benefit . . . Oh, she could easily be a writer or editor or something if she applied herself. But she seemed to get nothing out of all those beautiful books I bought for her growing up—Virginia Hamilton and Rosa Guy.

All she wants to be is a little "coochie."

"What young girl in trouble, Miss Moses?" I asked, and realized that even though we were still parked, my hands were clutching the steering wheel. I was almost afraid to hear what she was going to say. But she did not say anything, not a mumbling word. She just sat there in my car just as relaxed and comfortable as she could be, looking out the windshield at the empty blocks of Broadway as if she could see.

Well, I said to myself, I guess she's not going to answer that. So I pressed on.

"You sure I can't give someone a phone call and let them know where you are?" I asked her as I took my cell phone out of my purse on the backseat.

"Naw," Miss Moses said. "You ain't got that much money on you, sugar."

And, of course, I had no idea what *that* meant. So I just smiled and nodded my head and said, "Uh-huh."

I felt at the time a bit guilty for not pressing her about her current residence and caregivers, even though I did say once, "Miss Moses, I really should take you back to the nursing home."

She answered very sweetly, "Oh, sugar, I don't live in a nursing home."

I didn't know what I was gonna do with this old lady, who by that time was casually playing with the window buttons and the air vents on her side of the car. And to tell the truth, I was a great deal more worried about LaShawndra than I was about Miss Moses. With every minute that clicked by, I was becoming more and more sure in my bones that something was terribly wrong with my granddaughter.

I just did not feel I had the kind of time to get Miss Moses to the proper authorities *and* look for LaShawndra.

But Miss Moses solved my dilemma.

As I sat at the wheel of my Explorer parked at the corner of Cherry and Broadway the motor running, confused about why I was out there in the streets at 1:18—that's what it said on the dashboard clock—Miss Moses spoke up again.

"Why don't I just ride around with you for a while before you try to take me back anywhere?" she suggested.

She must have seen me wavering, because she added, "Don't you want some company on a night like this?"

And you know, I did. It was as if she were seeing right into my heart. For that very reason—want of some company—before I had left the house, I had almost broken down and called Charles, my ex-husband, at his home outside Atlanta. I don't know what I thought he could have done. He *is* the child's grandfather, but I guess I just did not want to be alone in my fears. However, when I picked up my small address book to find his new number in Atlanta and I saw that under C for Charles I had written "Gambling House" and a local number from years ago, I sucked my teeth and decided against it. It was probably a good decision. Charles took every little overture from me as a sign that I wanted him to move back for the third time. And even though the third time's the charm, he and I both knew it was too late for that!

The way my heart was racing, I was beginning to feel it was already also too late to help LaShawndra.

"Let's just drive around and look for the girl," Miss Moses said, as if she were reading my mind. "When you're moving with the Spirit, it's never too late."

2.

So that's just what I did. I put the vehicle into drive and pulled away from the curb with Miss Moses, her two sweaters, her four bags, her croaker sack, her umbrella, and her hat with the large cabbage rose on top safely at my side.

I know most folks would have thought, Lily Paine Pines, have you lost your mind? You find a confused old blind woman wandering around by herself in downtown Mulberry in the middle of the night, and you just pick her up and continue to drive around looking up and down alleys for your granddaughter?

And I'd have to say, "Well, yeah!"

And if someone had asked me why, I could not have told them. It's not as if LaShawndra were a child. She was almost nineteen years old.

Nineteen. Humph. When I was nineteen, I was handling a baby, a full freshman course load at Mulberry College, a part-time job, and a leadership position in the civil rights movement in Mulberry. But I try not to judge LaShawndra by my standards. She's a little individual, and she's had her own accomplishments.

She no longer lived at home.

She had a job—even if it was one as a part-time receptionist that I had gotten for her at the offices of the county school board where I'm the administrator.

She had her own place. Actually, she had moved into her friend Crystal's place. But she paid rent and was responsible for her share of other expenses. Oh, I helped her out a bit from time to time, but she was her own little woman.

But she was still my only granddaughter. It was after 1:00 A.M. I had no idea where she was. But I cannot tell you how much better I felt sitting up in that car with that old lady riding shotgun next to me.

We didn't talk for a while. To be honest, conversation just did not seem necessary. My ex-husband, Charles, and I were like that a bit. We could sit for hours and hold a conversation in our very own way without saying a word.

He would look at me, and I'd look at him. Then we'd fall out laughing. Or I'd just shrug my shoulders over something I'd read in the newspaper, and he'd nod his head in understanding. Or he'd wake me up in the middle of a late spring night and I would know what it was for even before he'd say, "Wake up, Lily. Smell the jasmine," as the sweet white scent wafted over us in bed from the vines growing on the trellis outside the window.

I do miss that camaraderie.

Charles and I have been divorced six years now, this second time. He's been out of my house for almost seven. But I still miss his presence and his ways.

My maiden name is Paine, and Charles's name is Pines. I always say, "I was born a Paine, but I'm going to die a Pines." And it looks like that's going to be the truth, because even though I do have a number of men friends, none of them is able to hold a candle to Charles, even if we couldn't seem to make it together.

But then black men as a whole are having such a difficult time holding it all together. My daughter, Sandra, doesn't think I understand about black men—bless her heart, like she does!—but I know the ponderous burden they carry around. Such *baggage!* Their pasts, their insecurities, their penises!

Charles wasn't an educated man. But he was a craftsman, a fine one, too. A master carpenter.

The first time I saw him striding along the rafters of the skeleton of a house two stories above the street, his leather tool belt slung low on his narrow hips—they were narrow then—his dazzling white short-sleeved T-shirt tucked tightly into the waistband of his jeans,

I almost lost *my* balance with my two feet planted firmly on the ground. It was the sexiest image I had ever seen. He was so manly, so in charge.

Of course, we had known each other since childhood, but I had never been to one of his father's building sites where he helped out some Saturday afternoons. Since I was a preteen, Saturday has always been my "volunteer/give back to the community" day. So I was busy myself.

I had never in my life seen a man so sure of his step. So self-confident. And at the time Charles was really just a boy still in high school. I bet I stood there on Pringle Street in East Mulberry looking at him for an hour. Even from down on the street I could hear the little tune he always hummed to himself as he hammered and measured and stroked the wood. I can still remember what he smelled like—sweat and Lifebuoy soap—when he came down to greet me, put his strong, sweaty young arm around me, and show me off to the other workers.

But even those times that Charles smelled like sweat and dirt and a hard day's work when he came home from the construction site, he still smelled good to me. It's funny how we put up with funky smells from someone we love and sleep with that we wouldn't abide from a stranger. Even grow to like the funk. Heh, funny.

Of course, I do have some male friends now who I see from time to time. We Pines women just seem to attract men. Well, some of us do. But my current relationships, even the intimate ones, are nothing like what I had with Charles.

As LaShawndra says: Annnnnyway...

I chose to drive on out Broadway, since that was the way the car seemed to be headed.

At the corner of Broadway and Jackson, I thought of Charles again. No matter how I tried, Charles played in my mind all the time. Even now with us apart seven years.

Sandra wouldn't admit it, but she is a big daddy's girl. Charles thought the world of her from the moment she entered the world. He once told me that he knew, *knew*, the only reason I decided to settle down and marry him was because of Sandra.

And, you know, he was right. Toward the end of our second marriage we just clung to each other for the familiarity. He knew what I was thinking. What I needed. What I wanted. He knew me so well. Still does. Now he just gives me room.

At first it was a scary thought. I could not remember a time in which Charles Pines did not love me. He always seemed to know we would be together. Even after we got our first divorce, he just calmly went about his life in the interim, waiting to get back together with me. It was almost eerie watching him wait for me to come back around.

When he'd call to talk to Sandra or even when he would drive down from Atlanta to visit with her, he wouldn't even ask about what I had been doing lately for fear I'd take it the wrong way.

He never wavered from his certainty. I think he's doing the same thing now. But I do believe he is wrong. I won't be back again this time around. I will not. I will not. I will not.

As we paused at the stop sign on Jackson Street, I looked in the dimly lit dusty window of the army-navy surplus store on the corner. Charles brought Sandra there to buy her an authentic pea jacket to take away to college before we found out she was pregnant with LaShawndra.

Sandra and her daddy used to do a great many things together. In the fall she and Charles would go to the fair together, and both of them would come back all sticky with cotton candy and candied apples and a little sick to their stomachs from too many, foot-long hotdogs. You know that daddy-daughter thing. It's so big you have to get out the way sometimes. And Charles always was a good daddy. I was proud of him for that. I'm sure I told him.

When Miss Moses and I passed the old train terminal with newly planted peach trees lining a garden at the entranceway, I could almost still hear the engines roaring in and out of Mulberry on the Macon-Dublin-Savannah line. Now you have to go over to Macon to catch the train going north or south. Back in the early eighties the city of Mulberry restored the old Gothic-style station and put little shops there, but it didn't take off, because the place doesn't even smell like trains anymore.

"I remember when they built that place," Miss Moses said, almost to herself. "I bet they still got up that big granite sign engraved with the word 'colored' over the side door."

I had a thousand questions about that time—I'm a bit of a historian myself. My mother was, too. She had biographies and history books all over the house. But Miss Moses didn't seem much for conversation. And she appeared to be comfortable and all buckled in to the passenger's side. So I didn't ask the questions that immediately bubbled up. I figured, why disturb her comfort with a legion of questions the answers to which she probably could not remember anyway.

I just looked over at Miss Moses and smiled.

She smiled back at me, then turned her sunglasses back to the road ahead as if she could see. I pressed on out Broadway, thinking, That was strange. I was not able to pinpoint exactly what had seemed off. The whole morning seemed off.

A little more than an hour before, I had been lying in my bed sleeping soundly—I always slept soundly—when, at the stroke of midnight, my eyes just flew open like shutters. You know how you wake up suddenly, as if someone had whispered your name and shaken you awake. That's exactly what had happened. Except the voice did not whisper. It bellowed.

And I could have sworn that I had felt an icy hand press down on my left shoulder. The thing was, I was alone in my house on Oglethorpe Street. I was still a bit groggy, but when I looked down, I did see a hand on my shoulder. It was brown and old and wrinkled, the nails clipped to a medium length, thick and grayish. I've felt and sensed things all my life. My mother used to call me "my little sensitive child" because I just seemed to feel things deeply. But you know how mothers are about their children. My mother thought I was as cute and smart as they came. It helps to have someone think that about you.

As a child, I'd say, "Grandmama's coming today." And sure enough my mother's mother would arrive for a surprise visit from the country. Or I'd warn, "Mama, be real careful while you cooking," and before the sun set that day, my mother would have burned her hand on a big hot black cast-iron skillet.

Sometimes Mama would even bring me to Grandmama's bed and ask me to lay my hands on her arthritic knees and ankles. After a while Grandmama would sigh and smile and say, "Thank you, baby. Grandmama's knees feel a lot better." But I always thought she was just saying that to humor her favorite grandchild. Or that the healing was all in Grandmama's head.

The hand on my shoulder, however, was no illusion. It might have looked old, but there was strength in that hand. It shook me awake, and a voice that sounded like Yahweh speaking to Moses in the desert said, "Get up and go forth!"

Needless to say, I woke up.

At first I tried to pretend that perhaps it had been my cat, Honey, walking across my chest, mewing in my ear, wanting me to get up and give her a dried-shrimp treat, but when I looked down toward the foot of my bed, my old honey-colored cat was curled up there sound asleep.

I yearned to ignore that cold hand and that wake-up call.

It was barely midnight, but I knew I did not want to face that day. Because I could feel deep in my soul, in that space between your breasts and your navel—that spot, your gut, your intuitive self, your knowing place—right there I could feel that this day that had not even yet dawned was going to be one that tried my very faith.

But I did not tarry there for even a moment in my nice soft, warm, freshly changed bed—I had just received a lovely rose-colored down comforter by FedEx that I had ordered for myself, and it was a chilly hour. I did not even consider if what I was feeling was real or just the residue of some upsetting dream that I could neither remember fully nor completely forget. I try to honor my commitments and my intuitions. Besides, I knew that the cold hand on my shoulder was no dream. Even completely awake, I continued to feel the chill from that wrinkled otherworldly hand spread down my left arm like a heart attack. I knew, if nothing else, that it was time for me to, as my mama always said, put my knees to the floor.

I just rolled out of bed and landed in a supplicant's position.

Kneeling there beside my bed, at my low altar, I lit a stick of frankincense. The Word still on my lips, I fervently prayed that the fragrance would lift souls up to heaven. My first mind told me I would truly need heavenly help to conquer this day.

I've learned not to doubt my first mind. You can't go wrong following your first mind. I had discovered that over the years.

My first mind was never wrong. I believe that has contributed to the sheer number of projects and accomplishments over my life— teaching, raising a family, volunteering in the community, traveling to my favorite village on the coast of Sardinia, chairing charity committees here in Mulberry, sponsoring a student at my alma mater each semester, putting in a full vegetable garden each spring and fall in my backyard. And fifty-seven isn't all that old in the world we live in now. Except for gravity lowering my butt and titties, I do very well, thank you. And I make up my mind, and I stick to my decision.

That morning as I knelt on the long narrow foam pad I had covered myself with burgundy leather, knelt there in silence at my little altar covered with a clean white cloth, my first mind spoke to me, spoke to me clearly. It said LaShawndra, my granddaughter, my only grandbaby, was about to fall into deep trouble.

I closed my eyes and prayed like Hannah or someone else from the Old Testament. I felt myself swaying and rocking on my knees. Then a little irritation like a tickle started in the back of my throat, and before I knew anything, a small guttural sound replaced the tickle there. Then, again before I knew it, a humming was emanating from beneath my throat, from somewhere near the depths of my soul.

My mouth automatically began moving. "Jesus, Jesus, Jesus," I chanted over and over. I was seeking succor and an answer to my pleas. "Help my little granddaughter. I got such a bad feeling she's in trouble. She may just be a little hoochie mama, but she's my child, Lord. And she's yours, too. You know and understand hot women like her. So save her!"

I only have the one grandchild. A girl. I only had one little ole big-eyed girl. That's Sandra. And she only had one little ole big-eyed girl. That's LaShawndra. But even so, I've always felt blessed. Many of my friends' grandchildren may have done better scholastically and professionally than my LaShawndra, but they don't have the drive and fire that mine has. Of course, LaShawndra could stand to learn some discipline, and it wouldn't hurt her to use some of the social graces I've taught her, but you can't beat her spirit.

Even though it was after midnight, I reached for the nearest portable phone and hit number one on the speed dial. I knew that Crystal and her two children would be in bed at that hour. Crystal's a good mother. She answered the phone on the first ring. I could hear the sleep in her voice, but she perked up when she recognized mine.

"Mrs. Pines?" she said. "What is it? Is everything okay?"

I knew that LaShawndra probably wouldn't be there at home. She stays in the street so much. But I had to find out. Crystal knew that my granddaughter was out when she answered the phone, I could tell by her tone, but she still got out of bed and went to LaShawndra's bedroom next to hers and double-checked for me.

"I'm sorry, Mrs. Pines, LaShawndra isn't in," Crystal said after a bit, trying to make her voice sound neutral. "I think she was planning to go to The Club tonight. And she may be spending the night with a girlfriend. Do you want to leave a message for her?"

I knew good and well LaShawndra was not hardly staying overnight with a "girlfriend." But all I said was "Just tell her to give me a call when you see her. Okay, dear?" I saw no reason to upset Crystal for no more reason than my unsettling midnight feelings.

Looking back on that morning, I wish now I had been psychic and told Crystal to grab her babies and get out of that apartment as fast as she could. But like I say, I'm not clairvoyant, so I didn't give a word of warning.

Crystal is a good girl to be a mother of two barely out of her teens. So is LaShawndra . . . a good girl . . . in her own way. It's her spirit that gets her in trouble so much.

It was LaShawndra's fiery spirit that I saw and felt in every nook and cranny of my house on Oglethorpe Street as I got ready to go look for her. She had been with me so much of her life—up until about a year ago, when she moved out—staying overnight or over the weekend or all week, or even for months sometimes, that there seemed to be imprints of her stamped all over my house.

As I quickly combed and brushed my long nappy hair, black with just a few flecks of gray, into a chignon—my colleagues call it my "signature chignon"—at the dressing table in my bedroom, I saw LaShawndra at age four, sitting there on that same sturdy wooden stool, her little bare feet, toenails painted pink, poking through the old lace cover, trying to imitate me.

Of course, her mother, Sandra, had given the child a perm already, at the age of four, to, as Sandra put it, "smooth out some of LaShawn-dra's rough edges." So even as a toddler LaShawndra wouldn't just play with the brush—getting her hair all caught up and twisted in the bristles. She would *style* her hair. Like a grown woman. She has a knack for that. Anything to do with enhancing one's looks. She even started combing my hair when she was only about six or seven. She always wanted me to wear it loose and wild. So she'd comb it into all kinds of styles—multiple Afro puffs, a nappy pageboy, hundreds of tiny braids with the ends loose and bushy. All kinds of styles. But when she finished, she'd always brush it back from my face—no bangs, no baby hair coaxed down from the edges—and then twist it back into this bun at the nape of my neck. Same way I wear it now.

Bless her little vocational-school heart, LaShawndra has always had a way with hair. She thought it was funny that I didn't straighten my hair and instead wore it long and natural.

My hair has never had a chemical in it in its life. Nothing to straighten out the nap. I was the first girl in Mulberry to wear a natural. We called it a "bush" back then in the sixties. Virgin black hair. Shoot, my hair is like a person all on her own. I read a magazine article in which Sonia Braga—you know, the Brazilian actress with all that great wild hair—she said, referring to her own hair, "She loves for me to wash her and let her dry in the sun." That's how I feel about my hair.

And that's what I do sometimes: I wash her, rinse her in rainwater that I catch in a wooden barrel at the southeastern corner of my house, and sit out on my patio off the kitchen to let her dry in the sun.

But when you're worrying about your own flesh and blood, those things—like your daily toilette—seem rather trivial. For the same reason, I didn't stop to stretch my body on my Pilates machine before I left the bedroom. I've been practicing yoga since I was a teenager, but in recent years, I've moved to Pilates training. I *love* my Pilates.

But even while I washed up, brushed my hair, and pulled on a bra, a big beige cotton sweater, and some black slacks, I continued to pray. By the time I took my soft black moccasins from the shoe rack in my closet, I was chanting to myself under my breath. But through my praying and my chanting, I was trying to get to my granddaughter before it was too late. Too late for what, I wasn't clear about just then, but that didn't decrease the urgency I felt one bit.

I didn't even take time to stop and stand in front of a full-length mirror to make sure I looked as good going as I did coming.

It was a small hint that my mama had taught me when I was about thirteen years old. So here it was, forty-four years later, and whenever I'm headed out the door, I'm still asking myself, Now, how does my butt look? Do I have any VPL—visible panty lines? Is my skirt so tight it's cupping under my butt? Is my slip hanging? Can you see my bra straps peeking over my shoulder?"

I've been doing it for so long, I do it without even thinking. But I guess that morning my mind was more on my grandchild, LaShawn-dra. I didn't care much about visible panty lines. She would have understood that.

When I had passed on the little hint of a last mirror check to the child, she said, just as seriously, "But, Mama Mama, sometimes I *want* my bra straps or my panties to show."

Lord help us all!

As I headed for the stairs, I tried to avoid looking into what used to be LaShawndra's bedroom. She had moved out all her furniture and most of her other possessions—her clothes, her CDs, her stereo, her beauty aids, which are considerable for one little girl—the year before when she had moved in with Crystal. But she still knew she could keep anything there she wasn't using at the moment and could retrieve it anytime she wanted. She dashed in and out of my house four or five times a week.

Down in the kitchen, LaShawndra's spirit was just as alive as in the rest of my house, dancing around in her baggy jeans and cropped T-shirts—she dresses like all young girls now—with her ever-present earphones on like a diadem as I fixed breakfast for her, as my former husband, Charles, sat at the table in the golden morning light of a school day. LaShawndra would mist the pots of African violets on the windowsill over the sink for me as she danced. I could still feel her spirit move next to me almost bumping me out of the way in her gyrations, *snatching* her head one way over her left shoulder, then *snatching* it back over her other shoulder. Oh, my little granddaughter is so full of life. Feeling her there so close to me almost moved me to eschew a midnight breakfast and rush on to my duty of looking for her and trying to stop whatever was going on. But then I remembered reading that Mother Teresa made it a hard-and-fast rule not to send her sisters out on the streets of Calcutta to care for the poor and hungry without first having a hearty meal themselves.

The tiny wrinkled Catholic nun said that one cannot minister to the starving while starving oneself. It sounded like wisdom to me.

Then, too, I also knew a woman in Mulberry who used to say all the time, "You cannot face this world on an empty stomach." She wasn't a saintly little nun. She was a big, hefty woman who weighed more than two hundred pounds, but she knew what she was talking about.

So I put some instant oatmeal and water into the microwave in one of the bowls that my granddaughter used to like—the china ones with botanical drawings in the bottom and along the rim. While the oatmeal heated, I peeled and sliced a banana from the fruit bowl to go on top of the oatmeal and thought that even Elijah the prophet had to eat a little hoecake of bread and some water—twice, in fact—before setting out for a forty-day walk to the mountain of God. At the same time, I had another thought. I picked up the kitchen phone and called my daughter, Sandra. Naturally, she had her answering machine on.

"Hello, Sandra, it's your mama. I was looking for LaShawndra. Is she there? I'm kind of worried about her, and I don't know where she is."

No one picked up. I figured that was my answer.

I hung up and finished slicing the banana. It's the only way I can stand to eat oatmeal. I can't stand any hot cereals, especially oatmeal. It multiplies in my mouth.

But my cholesterol count is so high that I now eat oatmeal every morning to do my part in my own health maintenance. The whole time I was forcing down that oatmeal with banana slices on top, I was praying for my granddaughter, LaShawndra. Her cholesterol is high, too, but she has the good kind. HDL. She's lucky like that. Bless her heart. The glass of tangerine juice I sipped reminded me of the tiny glass with bunnies on it that LaShawndra still liked to drink her juice from. I'm not ashamed to say I went to the flat white cabinets next to

the sink and took down that little glass and held it between my hands until it was almost too hot to hold.

I could even smell her too-sweet perfume wafting on the air in the darkened entrance hall as I went to pick up the keys to my Ford Explorer. I could see her short brown legs dangling from the tall bench and her big dark eyes scanning the Varnette P. Honeywood painting of a farmer's wife in the mirror on the facing wall.

Such intelligent eyes! Under all that mascara and liner and carefully blended eye shadow—full stage makeup—was a set of eyes that could cut to the meat of a concept. She just had not found the proper place to focus her attention. She just needs— Lord, help her, she just needs so much.

Other than the odd hour, I can't really say why this particular morning was any different from any other. I always was a bit worried about LaShawndra around the edges. When she had come into this world almost nineteen years before, bless her little heart, she had caused a stir, and she's been doing it ever since.

I had even gone out looking for her before. But let me tell you, I had *never* been awakened at midnight by a cold hand and a loud voice to go out in the night and look for her.

Getting up and out of the house a little after midnight, however, was no huge sacrifice for me. I don't sleep any more than four hours in any one given night. I've been like that most of my life. I guess that's why I seem to accomplish so much in any one day. Charles, my first husband—and my second husband—used to just shake his head and call me "superwoman" when he'd wake up in the middle of the night, reach for me, and find me up sewing our daughter, Sandra, a little dress for school later on that week—I'm a quite competent seamstress—or working on my doctoral thesis at the dining room table. So, for me, I had already had practically a full night's sleep when I rolled out of bed that dark morning and greeted the day at my miniature altar by my bedside.

I just picked up my favorite gold hoop earrings off my mama's small piecrust table in my reading corner of the living room, put them on, and hit the second outside light switch as I headed out the front door of my house on Oglethorpe Street. Just as an old lady who once lived across the street from my parents promised me when I was a child, my home would always be a blessed place, full of peace and tranquillity. Everybody who walks in the door of my home says they can feel it. But my reflection in the beautiful beveled lead-glass inset in the door didn't impart a sense of peace and tranquillity. It actually frightened me that morning. I looked like a caricature in a fun-house mirror. I couldn't believe the distorted look of distress on my face.

I knew then that I was more worried than I was even admitting to myself. But I tried not to give in to fear.

My home had belonged to my parents. They had left it to me, their only daughter. It is the oldest house on Oglethorpe Street and one of the older ones in Pleasant Hill. You know, it's a historic-preservation neighborhood, one of the oldest established African-American communities in middle Georgia. It's always been a nice community overall: two schools—St. Martin de Porres, the private Catholic school, and Pleasant Hill Elementary; more churches than true Christians; wooded areas and a couple little corner stores. At one time back in the sixties, the community was a place that black folks were trying to escape in favor of new suburban neighborhoods like Sherwood Forest. Now folks almost fight, really come to blows almost, to live here.

My daughter, Sandra, told me she had to physically jump between two prospective buyers right in her office down at Candace to prevent fisticuffs!

All you hear around Mulberry now is "historic sites this" and "preserve that."

First, the town of Mulberry razed half of Pleasant Hill for a free-way we didn't even need. Then we sat by and let them tear down just about *all* of this town's little downtown area just for the hell of it, and

now they are all into "historic preservation." Now every alley and lane
is important to somebody. I guess it always was.

My neighbors on Oglethorpe Street and I have done all we can to preserve our piece of the world: Pleasant Hill. It's truly pretty as a picture up and down my side of the street, with large dogwoods planted at intervals in the sidewalk and a clear rocky creek that runs through my backyard and meanders down Pleasant Hill to find its destination at the foot of the community in a waterfall and clear spring in the woods behind the old McPherson place that's a home for homeless young people now. "Four fifty-five," they call it.

When I got out on my screened-in front porch, where I could barely turn around for all the pots of pink and orange and purple and scarlet bromeliads I grow that had spilled over from the house, I was glad I had worn my favorite soft, thick, beige cotton sweater instead of a heavier jacket. It had felt a bit chilly in the house, but outside it was comfortable for an early April night, with a hint in the air of just how hot it was going to get later that day. It was almost balmy; the wind was blowing insistently but gently. I could hear the midnight wind rustling in the big weeping willow tree on the slope in my yard next to the garage.

The willow was just beginning to put out tiny, translucent lime-colored leaves the size of a bumblebee. It always took my breath away when trees that in winter were nothing more than sticks in the ground suddenly were transformed into living creatures covered with lush vegetation.

That morning the sound of the wind reminded me of palm trees. If I hadn't been navigating the cement steps at the front of my house for more than fifty years, I probably would have tripped on the uneven things and tumbled headfirst down the thirty-seven steps to Oglethorpe Street.

But at the sound of the wind, even in my hurry, I stood on a step midway down the incline and listened for a moment.

The wind that morning reminded me of my ex-husband, Charles.

He tried so hard to satisfy and please me. I know that. When we were married the first time, he drove his truck down to Savannah and spent all his money on palm trees he dug, wrapping the roots in burlap, and transported himself, trying to get them to grow in middle Georgia for me. He tried it three times before finally giving up.

Those palm trees just would not grow in this hard red-clay dirt of Mulberry, no matter how much sand Charles added to the soil. And he did work at it.

He knew I coveted the sound of the wind in the fronds of a palm tree. It's that lush, gentle, faraway sound that you barely notice when you are in the tropics. But it's the sound underneath all the other sounds. It crackles and whooshes at the same time, making it difficult to grasp and re-create in your head later on. Not like middle Georgia wind rushing through the leaves of a chinaberry tree. But something more subtle and exotic-sounding.

I know my former husband, Charles, felt if he could reproduce that sound for me in Mulberry, it would settle down my wanderlust and keep me with him. I know that's what he hoped. But the trees just wouldn't take. Sort of like our marriage.

The tiny white lights I had a young man from the high school string along the sweeping branches of the weeping willow danced in the midnight wind in tiny encouraging waves. My granddaughter, LaShawndra, used to say seeing the lights made her smile when she came home at night after being out "jamming." Although they were technically Christmas decorations, for the past few years I had left them up all the time and turned them on each night. On that April morning each precious light—alternately blinking, burning, pulsating, running—reminded me of a risen spirit. My daughter, Sandra, said she worried that her friends were going to call me the crazy woman who keeps her Christmas lights up all year long. But I've never been one to care much about what others thought of me. Having a child as a teenager back in the fifties in a town the size of Mul-

berry will do that for you. And being me, an on-her-way-to-being-a-
countercultural-Afro-wearing-bohemian, didn't hurt either.

Truly, the lights gave me a beat of hope, too. Even in that strange, warm, midnight April weather.

Then, as I continued down the cement steps and turned in to the garage, I caught sight of a lightning bug in the azalea bushes along the drive, and then another and another and another. The first lightning bugs of the season. The sight gave me another burst of hope. But then I heard that wind again.

And instead of calming me down the way it always had on my travels, the sound of the wind blowing through the fronds of nonexistent palm trees unnerved me even further.

As I slipped behind the wheel of my car and threw my handbag on the seat next to me, what I thought really surprised me. I thought, Please, Lord, I can't handle this by myself. Send me some help.

I felt I needed as much help, especially spiritually, as I could call on with LaShawndra out there who-knew-where doing who-knew-what.

Not that she would do *anything*! It was just that after that sudden ethereal wake-up call I had had, I did not feel comfortable in my soul not knowing just where she was and what she was doing.

Help me, Lord, I prayed again. Then I cranked up the Explorer, flipped on the headlights, and backed out into the darkened streets of Mulberry.

3.

When Miss Moses turned to me and smiled, I was struck with how lovely she looked.

Miss Moses had a beautiful face. I could see that even in the darkened interior of the car. Not beautiful like a lovely elderly woman, but beautiful like a woman in her prime. And although her face was relatively unwrinkled for a woman her age, it was not her youthful skin that made her beautiful. It was the glow of spirit underneath seeping through the very pores of her skin. Just beautiful.

The women in my family have good skin, too. But Miss Moses looked like something in an old painting. Luminous.

The glow of her skin lit up the dark inside the car like an aureole.

As I continued on out Broadway, I tried to drive with an air of confidence, but I did not know *where* I was going.

I tried to cover up my confusion.

"Oh, look!" I said, then felt stupid as I realized Miss Moses could look but she could not see. I just kept on talking. "I helped to build that house over there on the corner of Broadway and Elm Street, Miss Moses. It's a Habitat for Humanity house, one of the first ones built in Mulberry in the mid-eighties. Still looks good under that bright streetlight," I told her. "The owner, a single grandmother now, raising her children *and* three grandchildren, just had a mortgage-burning party last month. Bless her hardworking heart. It's a solid little wooden frame house painted yellow, with a white picket fence around a neatly mowed lawn. Got some purple pansies blooming on the border outside the fence."

"Um," Miss Moses said appreciatively. And it made me feel good and brought back some pleasant memories. Charles was the foreman

on the job of building the house for the black family with five
children, little "stairsteps" from an infant girl to a boy almost ten
years old.

Our whole family worked on that house: Sandra, LaShawndra, and
I, along with Charles, hammering, hauling, lifting, painting. We even
donated and helped to plant the pecan sapling that was now a tower-
ing, nut-bearing tree shading the front lawn.

I never could get the girls to work on another house. I tried to tell
them that our family had so much, we were duty-bound to do something to help others get something permanent also. But Sandra always
said she was too busy and that the Habitat houses were eating into
her business, and LaShawndra said all that manual labor messed up
her nails. But Charles and I continued to work on houses all around
the middle Georgia area until we split up the last time.

I guess I got lost there in the past for a while, just thinking about
how satisfying it was to see Charles building and directing and giving
back then, because when Miss Moses spoke, it startled me.

"Let's go down to the river," Miss Moses said as I stopped, hesitat-
ing at the corner.

"The Ocawatchee River?" I said dumbly, as if there were another
river running through Mulberry. You talk about the blind leading the
blind. I had no idea where I was going next.

I took her silence for assent and made a U-turn on Broadway and
headed back in the direction I had just come. Which is also so unlike
me. As a rule I don't change my mind and I don't break laws cava-
lierly. Now, I've been in jail a few times, but that was for following my
beliefs and my conscience. *Civil* disobedience, not just disobedience.

On a whim earlier that morning, when I left my home and headed
downtown for The Club, I had decided first to turn down Vietnam
Alley on my way.

Vietnam Alley is a little dead-end lane with no street sign at all to
mark it, adjacent to the last house on the south boundary of Pleasant

32 Hill, where I happened to know they sold nickel bags of weed. LaShawndra claims she doesn't smoke marijuana, but I've smelled it in her room and in her hair. And I've known what marijuana smells like since I came of age in the sixties.

The back alley is known as a hangout for petty drug dealers, shoplifters, and whores. I felt like a criminal myself, slowly cruising past known drug dens, but the need to find my granddaughter and perhaps prevent some disaster was intense, and it kept driving me.

I made a left turn into Vietnam Alley and pulled to a stop to gather myself before driving on. There were a couple of streetlights scattered along the dark lane, and I didn't see LaShawndra anywhere. I saw a couple of young men I recalled as students from a few years ago when I was principal at East Mulberry High School. They all looked me dead in the face, defiantly, like wage earners. But no LaShawndra. I looked again when I turned around and headed out of one of the toughest streets in town.

Not a pretty picture.

I said to myself, So here you are, Ms. Lily Paine Pines, Miss Board of Education, Miss Woman of the Year three years running until I insisted they spread the title around, Miss In-Demand Founders' Day Speaker, Miss All That, as the young ones say, out in the middle of the night scouting around Mulberry's seamy side looking for your granddaughter.

No, not a pretty picture. If we still had a News of Our Colored Community section in the *Mulberry Times*, with its gossip column, "What's Going Around," it would end up there. "Eminent Local Educator Haunts the Night in Search of Fallen Granddaughter."

But where my children were concerned, I had no false sense of pride. I asked God to forgive me for thinking of myself for a moment when I should have been putting my mind and prayers on LaShawndra.

It would have been quicker and more convenient to jump on the interstate connector one street over from Vietnam Alley, but I just

Tina McElroy Ansa

refuse to use the highway that destroyed part of my community. It's a
matter of principle.

As I headed for downtown Mulberry, I tried to tell myself that I had a plan for finding LaShawndra, because that's the kind of woman I am. I usually have a plan. Not that I did this on a regular basis, riding around in the middle of the night looking for LaShawndra. In fact, I had not done that since LaShawndra was fifteen or sixteen years old, and she was nearly nineteen now.

My "plan" really was just to drive past some of her haunts and see if I was lucky enough to run into her at one of them.

Since LaShawndra's housemate, Crystal, had suggested that my granddaughter might have hit The Club, that was going to be one of my stops.

That was indeed why I had been downtown at the corner of Broadway and Cherry Street after midnight on a Saturday morning driving past Lena McPherson's old juke joint. Well, The Blue Bird Café, Grill, and Liquor Store isn't Lena McPherson's anymore, since she called a halt to being a businesswoman—not only quit the juke-joint business but even pulled out of Candace, the top realty company, where my daughter works. Well, Sandra's part owner now. But if you know Mulberry, you know The Place. Everybody does.

It's a truly old-fashioned juke joint, located in one of the last standing buildings on the entire downtown block that urban renewal and so-called progress destroyed back in the seventies. My father used to go by there for a cold beer or two after he got off from work at the box factory.

Not the kind of place my mother would frequent, but when I was growing up, Daddy went there right regularly. Since Jonah McPherson opened it in the forties, people have called it "The Place," like it was the only "place" in Mulberry to get a cold beer. It may not have been the only place, but for the last fifty years or so it's been the most popular place.

The new management who took over from Lena McPherson built

a young folks' club up over the old Place that serves no liquor. The young people call it "The Club." They have a DJ some nights and "open-mike night" one or two nights a week. And dancing all the time. That's another reason I thought I might catch my granddaughter still hanging 'round outside The Club.

Anyplace there's dancing, you can find LaShawndra.

God help her, that's what she calls herself doing: dancing. She fancies herself "dancing" as a living. Well, she certainly hasn't made a dime dancing, I don't think, to say nothing of making an entire living out of it.

But at least it's one thing in which she's interested.

You know, sometimes, it's a good thing to have only one interest, so you can really focus all your attention on that, so you can excel in that one area. That's what I tell LaShawndra. That she's ahead of the game because, unlike me, she seems to be able to do only one thing well.

My granddaughter doesn't even drive a car.

Bless her little heart, LaShawndra has never been focused enough to learn to drive.

I'd wager that I have tried twenty or thirty times to teach her to drive and be responsible behind the wheel of a car. We used to spend a great deal of time together. But the child never could seem to focus on the task at hand or even on the road, for that matter. In the middle of a turn she'd catch sight of herself in the rearview mirror and go to fixing her makeup or finger-combing her hair.

God, she nearly killed us any number of times in one car of mine or another. Once—she must have been about sixteen—she sent us into a spin in the parking lot of the Mulberry Mall that had my life flashing before my eyes. Truly!

Before my car—a green Saab, I think (I never cared much for cars, I don't remember one from the other)—miraculously came to a stop about three centimeters from a parked minivan, just like in an old black-and-white movie, my life flashed before my eyes. I saw myself playing in my girlfriend Patricia's dusty front yard on Elm Street, giving the valedictory speech at Mulberry College, dancing in the rain at Wattstax in this baby blue halter top, my huge Afro rocking with a spirit of its own, praying in the hospital chapel the night LaShawndra was born.

LaShawndra would turn loose the steering wheel as if we were in one of those student-driving cars with two steering wheels—one for the student and one for the teacher—and she expected me to grab the wheel just as she turned it loose.

Behind the wheel of a car, she would just go to nutville on you in a minute. And you know my grandbaby is not crazy.

I had an uncle once who saw things and said things when other people didn't see what he was seeing or hear what he was hearing. They called him "Milledgeville," because that was where the Georgia insane asylum used to be located. All of us children—my two brothers and I—called him "Uncle Milledgeville."

But I knew even as a child that Uncle Milledgeville wasn't crazy. He was just different. People in my family were never what you would call plain old normal folks. We always stood out.

You have to be open to people's eccentricities, I've found. I try to tell my daughter, Sandra, that about her own daughter. But Sandra has always been a little hardheaded. Then, so was I. You know, children don't take after strangers.

I did have a brother who wound up at Milledgeville once. But it wasn't because he was crazy. Although he said they almost got him all hooked up with the crazy group.

You see, my brother, Shank—he was ten years older than I—had checked himself in again—he did it dozens of times, bless his heart, just to please his family—to a program for alcoholics, and it was located at the institution for the insane at Milledgeville. He said one day, when they let all the inmates out into the courtyard for some air, he was out there, too, with his group. When it was time to go back in, they got him mixed up with the wrong group.

"Wait! Wait!" he yelled. "I ain't one a' the crazy ones. I'm the alcoholic! I ain't crazy! I'm the alcoholic!"

It was better than any AA meeting confession. It was an affirmation from the heart. And from that day he stopped drinking and started getting better.

My family has always had a lot of heart. And not a lot of craziness in the past. No, LaShawndra isn't crazy. Just crafty. Too crafty for her own good sometimes.

But no matter what, she knows she can count on me to try to straighten out the situations her craftiness can cause.

I know I've done too much for the child. That's why she expected me to take over control of the car when she just let it go. But I had to tell her Mama Mama's not going to always be around to help her. Shoot, I've been thinking of moving down to the Georgia coast. I have always loved the beach and tropical climes.

But then I'd think, What will become of my grandchild if I move away? I worry about her so. Even though I know she's not being reckless behind the wheel of a car, it worries me how she is getting around. She is the *queen* of hitching a ride. She'll get in the car with *anybody*. And you know, these are not the sixties anymore when you could safely hitch all the way across this country.

Back when I was trying to teach her to drive and when the car spun out of control, I reached for the child to try to protect her, and damn if she wasn't reaching for her big blue makeup bag on the floor in the backseat! So I grabbed the wheel instead and saved our lives!

As my heart started beating again, LaShawndra looked at me with those big pretty black eyes of hers—just like her mama Sandra's for the world—and she said, "Oh, thank you, Mama Mama." Like nothing had happened.

Bless her little heart, that's all she's ever called me: "Mama Mama." From the day she began to speak. "Mama Mama."

LaShawndra has been with me so much of her life, especially when she was a baby, that she thought she was mine. She looked at me one day when I was feeding her strained peaches and said just as clear, "Mama?"

I was shocked. She wasn't but eight or nine months old. LaShawndra was quite a precocious child. It was the first time she spoke, and bless her heart, she hasn't stopped talking since.

She said it just as clearly. "Mama?" with a tiny question in her voice.

I was at home by myself—Charles was off at a building site or gambling—so at first I thought I had imagined it. She repeated it—"Mama?"—looking right at me. When I got over the shock of her talking and speaking so clearly for the first time, I took her baby face in my hands and said, "No, lil' LaShawndra baby, I'm not your mama. I'm your *mama's mama*." Like that.

So she looked me right in my eyes and said, "*Mama Mama*." Then she blew a little spit bubble and laughed.

And to her I've been "Mama Mama" ever since.

It is cute, isn't it?

Well, if she's nothing else, LaShawndra's cute.

But I try to tell her that she can't live off being cute. My mother used to tell me, "Pretty is as pretty does. Beauty is a gift from God." When I recite that to LaShawndra, she just raises her hand in mock prayer and shouts, "Thank you, Jesus!"

She's not even five feet tall and just as petite and dear as she can be. But she's got a nice round shape. She and my daughter, Sandra, are both little women. They get that from my mother. She was a cute diminutive brown-skinned woman, too, barely five feet tall. I, on the other hand, at five feet seven, take after my father.

I could pick out my grandchild in a lineup. The prospect of which I did not even want to consider at that time, with my heart racing like a sewing machine in my chest under the tiny gold cross I always wear on a long black silk cord.

Not that LaShawndra had ever been in trouble with the law. Other than skipping school—which she turned into an art form—LaShawndra had a relatively clean record. Oh, she was detained a couple of times at parties that got too rowdy or was stopped for taking a five-finger discount at one of the stores out at the Mulberry Mall, but because so many people know me from the school system in Mulberry, someone always called me first before pressing charges. And I knew how to deal with the situation discreetly, because this kind of thing came up quite often when I was a high school principal.

Lord knows, LaShawndra did not need to *steal* anything. Her mother or her grandfather Charles or I would give her anything she needed. But you know how young people are now. They don't seem to realize the consequences of what they do. But that's been true of young people forever. I had two friends in high school who stole some cheap dresses from a little shop in downtown Mulberry, and they never did finish high school and get their lives back on track. That was back when there *were* shops down there. I got my first pair of black high-heeled pumps at a shoe store downtown. It was right around the corner from where I found Miss Moses. But like all the other stores in downtown Mulberry, the shoe store was torn down for no reason except what the city council called urban renewal, even though nothing was ever "renewed." But that was also back when wearing your first stockings and a pair of tiny French heels was a big deal. When I was young, you couldn't wear heels until you were a certain age. My mother decided my wearing-heels age was fourteen. Now toddlers almost are wearing high heels and makeup. I've seen it in the school system time and time again.

And that's why I was glad to be around LaShawndra so much so I could at least monitor her dress a bit on the days I took her to school. I can't stand to see a pretty young girl dressed like a streetwalker.

But like I said, I didn't see LaShawndra outside The Club in one of those little put-together ensembles of hers—a tiny red skirt over orange leggings with socks and high-heeled pumps, with a patent leather bandeau tube top and a big white shirt tied over the whole thing.

Mulberry is a nice town—I personally think it's one of the best—but it is a small town. So the traffic lights were not even functioning at that hour. Every light we came to was just flashing saffron, leaving it to the discretion of any night owls to use caution and stop and go in safety.

But don't get me wrong. Mulberry isn't so small that I thought I was likely just to run up on LaShawndra accidentally. It's not that small. It used to be. When Sandra, my daughter, was young, she could go hardly anywhere in town without somebody seeing her and making sure she didn't get into any trouble. It's not like that anymore.

Truly, getting pregnant and being a little self-centered was the only real trouble Sandra ever gave me and her daddy, Charles.

I was glad Miss Moses suggested the Ocawatchee, because it was one of the places I had planned to look for LaShawndra anyway. Finding Miss Moses on the street had just thrown me a bit. I just was not thinking straight. *Another trait* so unlike me.

I turned into Spring Street and headed across the Ocawatchee River. As I drove across the Spring Street bridge, I could hear the waters of the river crashing underneath. It sounded like high tide at the beach.

The Ocawatchee River is just a red muddy southern river that turns magnificent every once in a while, running just as clear and pristine as a north Georgia mountain spring. In some parts of the state it is a mere trickle, but in the last few years, when it gets to middle Georgia, it turns into a torrent. If it weren't for Cleer Flo', it probably would not even be on the map.

I don't think anyone has figured out definitively what causes this new phenomenon—"Cleer Flo' " is what folks have called it for the last two years. But it is a marvel of nature. Once every few months or so, the river loses its ocher color, turns clear enough to drink, then a few days later returns to its original muddy state. I don't know what it was doing that April morning. It was too foggy down by the riverbank to tell.

I made the slow right U-turn on the other side of the Spring Street bridge and pointed the Explorer down the narrow red-dirt road to the riverbank. My headlights cut through the mist, and I pulled right up to the river's edge and cut the engine off.

"We're at the Ocawatchee River now," I told Miss Moses politely.

Just as politely she replied, "I know. I heard it."

It was down there by the Ocawatchee River that I realized how worried I actually was about LaShawndra, because it finally dawned on me that she could be *anywhere*!

I shook my head and thought, Lord, I'm looking for my little granddaughter down by the river like she was a bum or something.

The Ocawatchee River does seem to attract some strange characters. Not just cultist types who use the changing waters of Cleer Flo' to perform their rituals of fertility and worship, but just lost souls period.

I didn't like for LaShawndra to go there even in the daylight and when she was younger I had forbidden her to go there. Of course she went anyway.

But what could I do? I told her she ought to know better.

Through the mist I saw the form of two cars parked at a flat section of the riverbank. One was small and square, a Jeep. The other car was much larger. A van perhaps. But the fog was rolling pretty thick off the river. That's something new, too—fog. Four or five years ago there was no such thing as fog or mist down by the Ocawatchee River.

At two o'clock in the morning it's not an easy thing to find one tiny, big-eyed, nappy-headed black gal who doesn't want to be found even in a small town like Mulberry. And since she doesn't have a car that one can spot in the parking lot, I never know what car she's in. So, as I have in the past, I had to get a little hands-on.

Even though I knew it was dangerous to be wandering around down by the river all by myself past one in the morning with an elderly blind woman to look after, I felt that LaShawndra was in even more danger.

"You stay here, Miss Moses. I'm just going to step out of the car for a second," I said as I took the tiny flashlight Charles had given me out of my purse.

"How will you know if the one you're looking for is in which car?" Miss Moses asked.

"Sometimes you can see in...if the windows aren't fogged up on the inside," I answered.

Miss Moses just nodded. I thought she certainly did seem to follow a great deal for a person with no sight.

With my first step out of the car, I could feel my soft black moccasins sink into the muck of the riverbank. I cringed, because I hate to get my feet wet. However, I kept going.

I know it's not a wise move nowadays to walk up on a parked car in the dark, but that feeling in the pit of my stomach kept insisting that I needed to find my granddaughter and keep *her* out of danger. So I was willing to risk my own safety. I squared my shoulders and turned toward the parked van.

I shone my flashlight in a front window and saw no one. But there was a large black plastic garbage bag on the passenger's seat with wrinkled clothes spilling out. Over the roar of the waters of the Ocawatchee, I heard a soft snoring noise from the back of the van.

I stepped around to the rear and peered in the van's window.

There was a whole family in there: a man, a woman, and two little ones, all curled in the back of the van. Even with the windows closed, I could tell it smelled bad in there, like weeks of old food and dirty linens and unwashed bodies.

They must have been exhausted, because the light I shone in their faces didn't wake any of them.

I tell you, it took my mind off *my* problems for a while.

I may not know where LaShawndra sleeps every night, but at least I know she's not homeless, sleeping in a van that smells of urine. And I said a little prayer of thanksgiving right quick right there by the river for Crystal for opening up her home to LaShawndra. Crystal is a *good friend* to my granddaughter.

I didn't have my purse with me. I had left it in the car, but you know God is faithful. I reached into the pocket of my slacks and found two twenty-dollar bills I didn't even know were there. I folded them up and slid them through the crack in the window that the father had probably left open so his family would not all wake up dead from asphyxiation in the morning. The bills floated into the interior of the van right at the nose of the father.

I silently prayed, Thank you, Jesus, and turned in the direction of the other parked vehicle.

As I approached the Jeep, the fog rolling off the river cleared some, and I could see a bit better. As I peered into the passenger side of the vehicle, I could make out one head bobbing up and down along the side window and the other one above the seat thrown back. The bobbing head belonged to a girl, and my heart began beating harder when I saw that she had a short pixie haircut like LaShawndra's.

But when I shone my little light in her face, I saw that it wasn't my little hoochie mama.

Even with the light in their faces, they didn't stop. They didn't even notice.

I think I recognized her as one of my friends' granddaughters. She had her dress up around her shoulders. The boy had his pants down to his knees. And he was going at it so hard that the little girl's head was banging over and over again into the driver's zippered side window. Thank God it was soft plastic. Otherwise the poor girl would have suffered a concussion.

I just turned and headed back through the river mud to my Explorer.

Heaven help them—the two in the Jeep and all their peers. If I had as much sex in music and music videos and soap operas and commercials around me all the time, I would have been having sexual relations at ten. I would have. How could I not?

Well, I'm just being honest. And it doesn't get much more honest than being out in the middle of the night dragging the streets for your teenage granddaughter.

I look at the shows on TV and the movies and the commercials and the ads and know that what some ten-year-old child has seen in the course of her life is more than I had seen by the time I was thirty, and that's the truth. Sad to say.

I understand why they fucking like bunnies out there, and, God bless their hearts, they don't even know half what they doing. They don't!

You should have heard the fantasy and imagination that came out of the mouths of the young people I used to teach. I'm an administrator now, but somehow I've always thought of myself as a teacher.

Not just stupid things that my schoolmates and I thought forty years ago. You know, "If you do it standing up, you can't get pregnant" or "You'll get hairy palms if you masturbate." But truly ignorant and harmful things.

"Only white homosexual men get AIDS." "God only speaks to men." "You should wait until your children are big enough to enjoy the wedding before you get married."

I know things are different now with young people. I've been in the school system through three or four generations—with girls having babies so young now—and I thought having a child at nineteen was young. That's nothing now. Generations turn around so fast these days. But there are some things that have no business changing.

I had a young man doing some work in my yard. You know, I don't have much of a front yard because my house is built on the steep side of Oglethorpe Street and most of my front is on an incline. The only things I have growing out front are grass and my willow tree.

But I have a big yard in the back, and I need some gardening help. And this boy was somebody I knew from school, the one who strung up the Christmas lights in my weeping willow trees for me. Now, this is a boy—a young man, really—who had two children, by the same young girl. They had lived together five or six years. And every time I referred to his wife, he corrected me, *corrected* me.

"She ain't my wife," he'd say. "She my girlfriend."

For a while I would just bite my lip, continue digging in the dirt, and not say anything. But he said it so much, every time I'd mention the girl, that I finally screamed at him one day, "Stop correcting me! Stop correcting me! Hell, she *ought* to be your wife. You've had two babies with her. Why *aren't* you two married?" I asked.

"We ain't ready to settle down and marry yet," he explained, as if he were setting me straight.

"Not ready?" I exclaimed. I really was incredulous. "What in the world are y'all waiting for? Grandchildren?!"

Oh, young ones are so confused and misguided that it almost makes you want to throw up your hands and hope you can just walk out your own little walk of faith on this earth without having to have anything to do with them. And I am not a nihilist.

Joycelyn Elders got into trouble when she was surgeon general merely by saying that we should teach our children to masturbate. But I agree with her. I think we should give them an alternative to what they themselves call "Bang! Bang! Bang!"

Or maybe we should even teach them how to pet and kiss and make out instead of having oral, anal, or full intercourse.

When I was young, I used to think that I was called to do something for the world. I thought about the Peace Corps. I thought about starting an orphanage in South Africa. I considered the possibility of starting a small school on an Indian reservation in the West. I was gonna change the world in some way.

My generation was so concerned about saving the world, our rights, the environment. Now I see we'd better be as concerned about saving our own poor little children right here in this country. Heck, right here in this county. Right here in Mulberry. Right in our own homes. Shoot, I can't even trust my own granddaughter enough to give her a key to my house.

I had almost gotten back to the driver's side of my car when I decided to turn on my heels and go back to the parked Jeep.

When I got there, the children inside were still going at it. I balled

up my fist, reached around, and rapped sharply on the windshield.
Bang! Bang! Bang!

The girl—she did look a little like my LaShawndra—and the boy
both jumped about a mile. She clutched at her clothes and tried to
pull her skirt down over her naked butt, kneeing her partner in the
chin in the process. He scrambled just as quickly, grabbing his big
baggy pants at the waist and turning to me with an ugly look on his
face.

I shone the flashlight on my own face—I can only imagine what
my face looked like—so they could see that it wasn't a mad killer or
the police.

"Miss Pines?!" the girl screamed, still trying to cover herself. "Miss
Pines?!" she repeated.

"Yes, it's me," I said. "Y'all need to be more careful. I hope you're
at least using a condom."

Then, as I turned, walking through the muck, and went back to
my Explorer, I heard them start up the Jeep and race away.

I know it wasn't much. But I did feel I had done all I could to interrupt what was going on and offer some advice. I would have wanted
someone to do the same favor for my LaShawndra if given the chance.

4

"Wasn't her?" Miss Moses asked as I got back in the car. She had been playing with the vents and buttons on the dashboard again. I could tell because the caution light was flashing and her vent was partially closed.

"No, it wasn't," I replied, opened her vent again, clicked off the blinking yellow lights, and threw the car into reverse.

Cautiously, I pulled out of the muddy river road back onto Spring Street and turned to the right. I didn't tell Miss Moses what our plans were, but I was headed for the East Mulberry High School parking lot. I didn't get far.

"What we slowing down for?" Miss Moses asked, sitting up straighter and looking around like she could see.

I could barely bring myself to answer her for a few seconds as I stared straight ahead at the scene in front of us on the highway and prayed.

I swallowed hard and said, "A car accident."

You know what I thought. I could just see LaShawndra's mangled body in the flashing blue lights of the police car, torn and disfigured, laid out on a stretcher under a white plastic sheet. Especially as we rolled past and I saw that a motorcycle had been involved in the accident, too. When LaShawndra's mother was a teenager back in the seventies, I had to pull her off the back bar of a Harley when I, by pure Providence, rode up on her and a boy at a stoplight one Saturday afternoon when she was supposed to be at piano lessons with Mrs. Frazier. No helmet, no boots, no leathers. Just a little red miniskirt and sandals. It was so reckless of her. But that's about the only trouble we ever had with Sandra, other than her getting pregnant at nineteen.

As we slowed further, I recognized one of the police officers standing around the scene waving a huge moving van past with a long silver flashlight. I came to a stop, lowered my window, and called to him. I couldn't remember his name at that moment, but he heard my voice and ambled over, shining the flashlight in my face.

"Mrs. Pines, what are you doing here this late at night by yourself?" he asked before I could ask him anything about the accident. Half the young people in town who have gone through the Mulberry educational system know me. I didn't think to introduce him to Miss Moses or ask him to take her back to the nursing home. I suppose I didn't want to continue that early-morning search by myself.

"Oh, I'm just headed back from a late meeting," I lied, much too easily. I was ashamed of myself for the fabrication. It was so unlike me, but I decided I might as well go with it. "I'm on my way home now."

He nodded.

"Was anyone hurt in the accident?" I asked, still trying to see the victims and keep the panic out of my voice. I didn't think the officer knew my granddaughter. "Anyone you know?"

I heard Miss Moses ruffle one of her paper shopping bags with her feet. But I was too afraid of the policeman's answer to care about her disapproving noises over my little lie.

"I don't think so," he said. "The motorcycle has out-of-state plates on it. The boy on the bike, he took a fast turn and slid into that telephone pole. The ambulance just pulled off."

We weren't exactly ambulance chasing. But I was drawn to the city hospital by the sound of that siren off in the distance, getting fainter and fainter.

I looked in Miss Moses's direction.

"Well," she said, "we might as well check out the hospital, since that's going to be on your mind until we do."

Miss Moses was really turning out to be an invaluable riding companion.

"Good idea," I said.

We drove back across the Spring Street bridge and headed toward the Mulberry Medical Center. When the big stone building, wings jutting off in every direction, appeared in front of us, I slowed down. By now I had slowed down and cruised by so many places I was beginning to feel like part of a drive-by conspiracy.

When we arrived at the building's front gate, I decided not to stop there. I made a left turn and circled around past the parking lot to the back of the building.

I pulled up to the emergency-room entrance. An ambulance attendant, his white-and-blue uniform covered in blood, was just stepping back into the driver's side. The ambulance pulled off slowly and turned onto a ramp leading to an entrance under the building. But I could not make myself go inside. It's not that I have an aversion to *all* hospitals. Just the Mulberry Medical Center.

The medical center is the only hospital in all of Mulberry now. It's where LaShawndra was born. St. Luke's Hospital—where my daughter, Sandra, and I both were born—would have been my choice for LaShawndra's birth, too, but by the 1970s the all-black private hospital at the edge of Pleasant Hill was closed and destroyed. Like so much of what black people in the South had built and supported by themselves.

When my granddaughter came into this world, it was a hot summer night in June, and *everybody* showed up, folks on both sides of LaShawndra's family. My mama and daddy and my big brother, who was visiting from Cleveland, were there. So were LaShawndra's daddy's people. His mother and father, three sisters, and an aunt.

That's the last time we were all together, and it turned into the biggest mess you've ever seen in your life. Because, for starters, everybody was there except the baby's daddy—LaShawn. That's who LaShawndra is named for.

I had really been disgusted with LaShawn for not showing up at his own child's birth. He was only nineteen years old himself at the time, like Sandra, but I expected more of him. It was not long after Father's

Day, and I had bought him a nice shirt and tie and put "From Your Baby" on the card. And LaShawn's mother—she is my granddaughter's other grandmother, for all she ever sees her—decided that was the time she would start talking loudly to the waiting room in general about blood tests and paternity tests. And how "a person don't ever *really* know without some kind of tests."

I could not believe the callousness of this woman. Here I was worried about my only child in there in the delivery room having her son's baby, and this woman had the nerve to be implying that my child either did not know or was lying about her baby's paternity. Then one of the nurses came out covered in blood and mucus and was all upset.

I told them *all* just to shut up talking to me until after I found out if my child and my grandchild were okay. But they wouldn't, so it was on!

First, LaShawn's older sister said something. Then LaShawn's mama said something. Then *somebody* started talking 'bout how you can't ever *really* tell who a child's daddy *really* is no matter what color it comes out.

Then my own mother became a bit unglued and was screaming about the baby not having a name, not having a name!

"If that boy don't marry Sandra, my grandbaby won't have no name!" Mother kept screaming, stretching her hands to heaven and walking back and forth over the worn tile in the hospital waiting room.

And that just set off LaShawn's family. His mother yelled back, "Well, you ain't gon' rope my child into no fake shotgun wedding. You ain't gon' just *steal* his name!"

I was so angry and upset by all that screaming and hoopla, I told them all, "Hell, let her have *my* name! She can be a Pines!"

That's why LaShawndra is LaShawndra Pines. That entire hospital scene was just too intense for me.

You know, I'm not a fighting woman. Never been in a fight in my life, not even on the school grounds when I was a girl. We were the

You Know Better

nonviolent generation. But don't you know I had to invite that bitch out of the hospital waiting room to settle this thing outside when she had the nerve to imply that *my chile* wasn't good enough for her little light-skinned son. That really struck a nerve with me.

I'm telling you, I was hoping that by the 1970s we were so through with all of that. So through with that divisive, old-fashioned out-of-date, hurtful color consciousness: "He's too dark for her." And "She ain't light enough for his family." And "He may date her, but he sho' ain't gon' marry her." And "Oh, I only like light-complected boys with curly hair." And "She's just evil. Black women are just evil!"

I hate to see it come up again in LaShawndra and her peers. But twenty years later and here it comes again. It's as if we did not completely stamp it out in the sixties and seventies, so it's springing back up like weeds.

One day LaShawndra and I were shopping at the mall for school clothes. This was when LaShawndra was still pretending to go to school. She pointed out a clique of light-skinned girls who had told her right to her face that she was too dark to run with them.

LaShawndra said she didn't care, but I know her little feelings were hurt.

I thought we were through with that. So, so through.

And there Sandra was lying up there in that Mulberry Medical Center putting her very life on the line to deliver that yellow Negro's baby. Um, um, um.

Charles's mother used to say, "Don't nothing go over the devil's shoulder that doesn't come back and buckle under his belly." And it's true, because LaShawn's family has not had any good luck since then.

The way they have just ignored my LaShawndra's existence all these eighteen years, I probably *should* have jumped on LaShawn's mother back in that hospital waiting room.

And I would have done it, too. Kicked LaShawn's mother's ass! About some mess with my only child? Shoot! In a *minute!*

Of course, I know that sounds coarse of me, but it's the truth.

That's how I felt sitting up there in the Mulberry Medical Center back in the spring of '78. First, people started running down the halls. But no one said anything. I tried to tell myself it had nothing to do with my child, but I knew that the commotion was about Sandra. You know, a mother knows. Then a nurse came out of the delivery-room area, shaking her head and muttering, "I ain't never seen *anything* like *that* before!" And I guess I just lost it for a while.

The next couple of hours are *still* all a blur to me. The young nurse's exclamation should not have unnerved me so, but even though I was surrounded by my family, I felt so alone. Charles had moved out for the first time and was looking for employment on a construction site up in Macon. I knew where he was, but I couldn't get in touch with him. I called—twice—and you know I don't ever go running after anyone ... well, except for LaShawndra. I found out by mistake a while afterward that I couldn't find Charles because he was caught up in a poker game. You know, that's the kind of thing that finally broke us up, that gambling.

I felt if he really cared about me and his own reputation, he would have given it up.

I sure could have used him that night.

I think that was one of the reasons I broke down there in the hospital when they wouldn't tell me what was upsetting the nurses so. I didn't have Charles there to support me.

I found out later from the doctor that it really wasn't anything life-threatening. It was just unusual.

I never said anything, but LaShawndra was born with a caul over her face. Medical people will say that it's only a piece of the amniotic sac that encloses the baby that wasn't completely ruptured during birth. It doesn't occur as much nowadays, because most obstetricians break the sac to facilitate the birth, but the old folks believe it's a sign from God marking the child as special. I don't know why I never said anything to LaShawndra about it or explored it any more with Sandra. Even without the baggage of the veil, LaShawndra was more than enough to handle on the physical plane without exploring the supernatural.

I guess I was just grateful LaShawndra came here intact. I knew that Sandra had thrown herself down the staircase of our home on Oglethorpe trying to get rid of her baby before anybody knew she was pregnant. I heard the thumps in the night and thought it was Charles coming in from gambling a little tipsy. The next morning I saw the bruises on her arms and legs.

As she sat at the breakfast table playing with her grits and eggs, I prayed over what I suspected. Then I got up from the table and went around, stood behind her, and massaged her shoulders. I knew she had to have been sore.

When I spoke, my wisdom didn't come from me. I knew it came directly from the Holy Spirit.

"Don't throw away what God has given you," I told her. "It might be the greatest blessing you'll ever receive. Our blessings don't always look the way we expect them to."

Then I hugged her and sat back down.

I never even thought once about getting rid of my child, even though Sandra's birth complicated my life, too. However, I felt it was all for the good.

It was the sixties, and even at the age of nineteen I felt myself something of an earth mother as it was. I would have had more children if I could have. A houseful of children would have been just fine with me and Charles. But after Charles and I married—Sandra was almost two by then—I wanted to wait and make sure he wasn't marrying me merely because I was pregnant. It just never happened again.

I thought about going to a fertility expert, but the one time I mentioned it, very casually, Charles got really quiet. So instead I put all my energy into raising Sandra. I took her *everywhere* with me. She was exposed to so much, and I wanted her to know all kinds of people and experiences: civil rights marches in south Georgia, Wattstax in California, classical concerts at Chastain Park in Atlanta.

I guess that's why I couldn't understand how Sandra could let me keep LaShawndra so much when she was a child. There's no way I would have ever let *anybody*, not even my own mother, take my child while I was able to care for her. Absolutely not!

But as Sandra and LaShawndra tell me, things are different now.

Because LaShawndra is nineteen this year, I'm keeping a close eye on her. Nineteen was a pivotal year for both me and my daughter, Sandra...you know. We both became pregnant in our nineteenth year. So I'm trying to watch LaShawndra. As Jesse Jackson *used* to say, "Let us break this cycle of pain."

I guess that's why I worry a bit about my two girls and men. I don't think LaShawndra has ever had a real date, where the boy comes to the door and rings the bell and steps inside for a few minutes while she finishes dressing. Not even for the prom.

Since LaShawn, even though Sandra has had plenty of dates, she can't seem to find any man that she values. And LaShawndra picks those who don't value her.

I know they are both missing out on something important. I have to tell you, there have been many times *I've* missed that "man stuff" in my life. How a man can turn a phrase, a phrase that might seem rough or inappropriate to someone who was not intimate with him. You know...

Charles had a way of teasing me when I was in the bathtub, in the midst of my "toilette." He would be in a hurry for me to get out and come to bed, so he'd yell through the door, "Okay, Lily, just get the dirt, baby. The funk's okay with me."

And it would be funny. I'd sit in that deep old claw-footed bathtub with soapy water up to my chin and laugh. Charles had sprayed the outside of the tub a bright fire-engine red, 'cause he knew I once had a dream of bathing in a red tub. I would not be able to get out of that tub and into bed with Charles fast enough.

Charles was funny like that. That's where LaShawndra gets it.

LaShawndra has a great sense of humor. When she stayed with me on Saturday nights, we'd sit up watching W. C. Fields on videos and eating popcorn and apple slices. She always got Fields, even when she was no more than nine or ten. Charles would join us on the sofa when he came in late—from gambling, but I didn't know that for sure at the time. I thought he had just been out with some friends for a beer. We were the kind of couple that enjoyed our own private time as well as our together time. The three of us would sit there together until dawn and laugh until we cried. LaShawndra, bless her heart, cherished those times. She called them her only "family times."

As I drove around town that Saturday, I could hear Charles's voice just as clearly saying, "Lily, sugar, what you doing scoutin' 'round Mulberry in the middle of the night?"

He said he always called me "sugar" 'cause I taste so sweet. And that's how he'd say it, too. " 'Cause you taste so sweet."

When we were in high school, Charles always signed my yearbook with the same words: "Lily is my Life."

Ummm. Yes, there are times when I do miss Charles. Then I remember the things he said—well, actually, things we said to each other—in the last big fight we had. I've never been one who liked to fight. Screaming and hollering and crying in the bathroom and waking up the next morning with your eyes all swollen underneath with bags big as steamer trunks. I hate all that.

LaShawndra says I don't like all that "drama," and I guess she's right.

Charles was like most men: He would avoid a fight or confrontation with his woman at any cost. And Charles was an easygoing man anyway.

But just before he left for the last time, eight years ago last month, we had a dilly of a fight. One of those fights that starts in the bedroom, moves down to the kitchen, and then continues out the front door, down the steps, and out to the garage and driveway, where you find yourself standing in the street in your bathrobe, your fist raised in the air and you hollering at the exhaust pipe of your man's car as he screeches away. And ends with him shouting out the window that you're too damn hard and strict.

That's the kind of fight we had.

That was when we ended it for good.

It all started when he got arrested for gambling. Actually, the warrant read GAMBLING AND RACKETEERING. I can still see it as if it were still lying there on the slim silver tray on top of the television where Charles tossed it. I stood there in my work clothes: my dark business suit with a bright—probably red, I look good with red up close to my face—scarf around my neck. It was cold outside. I remember dropping my heavy black coat to the floor right there at my feet as I read again and again, with just my lips moving, GAMBLING AND RACKETEERING.

I looked down the long panorama of Charles's life, with all the exemplary things he did, and I thought, Um, all of that to come to this.

I felt I could not let him take me down with him. I had to set an example for *my* girls.

Charles had to go. For all the good it did my girls to have a male figure in the household, he had to go. Despite all the years we'd spent together, he had to go. Despite all the rough times we'd weathered together, he still had to go. He had to go.

The first time we broke up, I just had Sandra to think of. But the last time, I had Sandra *and* LaShawndra to think of.

I could not be responsible for my girls' having a bad home life.

Charles used to tell me that I didn't *know* anything about a bad home life when I complained about his gambling or when I tried to criticize Sandra, his baby girl, and her parenting skills. Now, Sandra's a true "daddy's girl." She was the "baby daddy baby" for sure!!

Charles would say, "You shoulda been brought up in a home with a real crazy daddy and somebody was always screaming, 'Lord ham mercy! He got a knife! He gon' kill us all!' Now, *that's* a 'bad' household, Lily."

Well, one thing I did like about Charles—he was a straight shooter.

So was Miss Moses. After we had sat at the emergency entrance to the hospital in silence for a couple of minutes, I started up the Explorer and circled the block twice.

"Just can't make yourself go in there, can you?" she said as we rounded the last corner.

She was right. I couldn't. As often as I had visited sick family and friends—the last time I saw my mother alive was in a bed at the medical center—taking flowers and magazines and fruit baskets with me on a regular basis, this time the terrible memory of LaShawndra's birth, even if it was nineteen-year-old memory, just would not let me move through those doors.

"You must be a mind-reader, Miss Moses," I said, trying to lighten the gloomy atmosphere in the car.

"You easy to read, sugar," she said.

I had to smile.

"Why don't you use a telephone, then, and call inside to ask what you want to know?" Miss Moses suggested.

It was a good idea. Miss Moses was being a true godsend to me. I had my cell phone in my purse. So that's what I did.

The little girl on the hospital switchboard knew me from high school, and she gave me everything I needed to know.

No one fitting LaShawndra's description had been admitted in the last twenty-four hours. And let me tell you, hearing that news at two forty-five in the morning, I felt better.

Tina McElroy Ansa

5.

In fact, I was beginning to feel so peaceful with that old lady riding shotgun with me in the car smelling like lavender that I was content for a while to just drive up one street of Mulberry and down another looking for one little big-eyed girl. If I had not been so worried about LaShawndra, I think I would have actually enjoyed the ride.

Miss Moses started humming a little tune under her breath, and it sounded so moving and old, like something from my childhood. Miss Moses sounded so content I knew she was enjoying the ride, too.

I used to have an old aunt in the country who would jump in the car with anyone who was going into town, whether she had any business there or not. She would say, "I'm just 'long for the ride." Looking over at Miss Moses as I toured Mulberry in the dark made me think of Aunt Mattie. That lovely old lady made me remember others, too.

On Elm Street I saw my best little girlfriend, Mary, playing hopscotch on the wide sidewalk in front of the shotgun house of her childhood, her thick, nappy pigtails tied in red plaid ribbon at each end hopping with each move. On one street over from Oglethorpe, I envisioned my great-aunt walking to town for her Saturday shopping, shaded from the summer sun by a big flowered purple-and-red umbrella. On the corner of Poplar and Vine, I smiled at the memory of Charles, covered in the dust of Sheetrock, sitting on a crate of nails waiting for me to pick him up at the end of his workday.

By the time Miss Moses and I had covered most of the west side of Mulberry, I still had not seen hide nor hair of LaShawndra. But I felt like I had been sitting next to my own sweet mother, who has been dead more than ten years. I was as content as Miss Moses seemed to be to sit there and drive in silence.

After about half an hour she reached down and rustled around in one of the paper bags she had brought on board.

I remember thinking, Now, where did she get one of those old shopping bags? The department store itself had been moved from downtown out to the Mulberry Mall and changed names and conglomerate owners thirty years before. But the bag, glossy chocolate brown paper with the store's name—Davison's—written in large white letters on it, looked crisp and new. Her scratching around in the bag raised the herbal scent of lavender all up in the car. I heard her take a deep cleansing breath. And I took one, too.

The interior of the Explorer was beginning to smell like the inside of this white convertible VW Beetle I had back in the sixties right after Sandra was born.

The car cost less than two thousand dollars new then. And it was less than a year old when I got it for fifty-four dollars. A man I knew in south Georgia took up with this white girl who had a nice van, so he gave the Beetle to me for fifty-four dollars and a half bag of some kick-ass smoke.

And no matter what kind of perfume I wore, the interior of that car always smelled like herbal incense—lavender.

The scent of lavender must have been what enhanced my short-term memory, too, because I suddenly recalled that I had been headed for the high school in East Mulberry when we came up on the motorcycle accident. So I turned at the next corner over from the McDonald's and headed back across the Spring Street bridge.

"Humph," Miss Moses said.

"Excuse me, Miss Moses, did you say something?" I asked. I was eager for the conversation.

"I used to be a high school teacher," she said.

"Is that right?" I asked, even though I knew that Miss Moses had taught in the Mulberry school system as well as having taught adults in her home at night after she had retired.

"I taught English and art appreciation," she said as she rummaged through another of her bags. "I got a book in one of these bags here entitled *How I Did It* that was a teacher's guide I used back in the 1920s. I come from teaching folk," she explained.

I understood that. Because I come from teaching folk, too. Not formal teachers, but teachers all the same.

My mama used to say that her grandfather was the only man on the old plantation in a settlement along the river outside of Mulberry who had a knowledge of reading and writing. At the end of a day he would come home from the fields and find a whole pack of folks waiting on his front porch to have him read their bills and correspondence and write letters to relatives for them.

The bells of Mount Calvary Church of God on Spring Street were chiming the half hour—half past three—as we drove by.

"Those are the bells of Mount Calvary, aren't they?" Miss Moses asked as we drove by the African-American church. But she asked it as if she already knew the answer.

"Yes," I answered, just as the church chimes began two bars of "Oh, Blessed Savior, Count on Me."

"Is that your church?" she asked.

"No," I told her, "my church is Emmanuel Baptist. But I don't see myself as just a Baptist. I simply call myself a believer in Jesus.

"As a matter of fact, my daughter, Sandra, is dating the pastor of Mount Calvary."

As soon as I had said it, I wanted to take the information back. Sandra told me she didn't want me talking about her fledgling relationship with the dark, handsome minister, because she was so afraid that any talk of it would jinx the whole thing.

Miss Moses ignored my comment and got on with the conversation.

"When I retired from the school system," she explained, "I taught adults in my home at night. You know, I was married briefly—my husband died ten days after our wedding—and I did not have any children. I loved children, but I didn't ever have myself any. I got plenty of nieces and nephews and godchildren, but none of my own."

"Oh, really?" I said, trying to sound casual, but I was thinking, Ten *days*!

"Well," Miss Moses said, obviously deciding to talk up a storm, "you should have seen the folks who used to line up for lessons at my home at night after they worked hard all day. Sometimes I would have to open a window in my front room, even in the wintertime, because of the way they smelled—from hard work in the fields outside Mulberry, grueling labor at the box factory, cleaning up some white woman's house from top to bottom."

That really got my attention, because although my mother worked in an insurance-company office, my father was a laborer at the box factory in town. He always was good with his hands and did odd jobs, too, in the neighborhood. But his main job was at the corrugated-box factory. I guess women in my family have always been attracted to hardworking men who used their hands.

Miss Moses kind of chuckled dryly to herself and continued.

"In the evenings after he got off work, I'm the one who taught *your* father to read," she said, calmly dropping a bomb inside the car.

"My daddy?!" I asked, shocked.

"Um-huh," she said. "You were probably in junior high school at the time."

I just knew she had to be mistaken about that and told her so.

"My father *always* was literate, Miss Moses."

"Oh, he could sign his name and recognize traffic signs and such, but Joe Paine couldn't read till he was a grown man," she said matter-of-factly, as if she were telling me what she'd had for breakfast. "And you children were almost grown."

"My father couldn't read while we were growing up?" I asked. I got a sudden image of my father listening to me recite my ABCs in the morning before school. My father was as good a daddy to me as

Charles was to Sandra. I thought about my father every time I saw a
vermilion male cardinal at the bird feeder outside my bedroom window shell a black-oil sunflower seed and drop it into the mouth of its
mottled baby redbird. Joe Paine believed in his family's eating well.

"No, Joe went to the fourth or fifth grade, but it was hit or miss
because he was needed at home all the time to help with his brothers and sisters so his mama could work. Then, when he was barely
big enough, so *he* could work. I remember him as a child. He was a
good boy."

"My father couldn't read when Mother married him?" I still
couldn't take it in. My mother did not attend college, but she loved
literature and history and learning.

"One of the things your daddy said he loved most about your
mother was she was not judgmental." For the first time that morning,
Miss Moses sounded as if she were making a point.

"He told me one evening that his wife accepted him just the way
he was, but he didn't want to embarrass his only daughter by remain-
ing illiterate, because she was so smart in school herself," Miss Moses
explained.

I couldn't form any words to say. I was picturing my father when I
was five or six falling asleep in what he called his reading chair with
an open copy of *Life* magazine or the *Saturday Evening Post* or *Ebony* in
his lap at the end of a long workday.

"Don't let it bother you, sugar," Miss Moses said. "He wouldn't
have wanted it to."

I had to swallow hard just thinking of my daddy worrying about
me judging him.

"Wasn't no worse than playing a few hands of cards," she said.

I shot Miss Moses a glance, but she was staring blindly straight
ahead.

After a few seconds of silence, Miss Moses continued speaking of
her adult-literacy students.

"And the one thing they wanted to learn to read was the Bible.

Which was kinda funny. Because they would say, 'Miss Moses, all I want to do is learn to read the Bible. I don't care much 'bout nothing else.' Well, you know, some of the hardest words in the world are in the Bible. But that's what they wanted to learn to read."

"Um," I said, trying to concentrate on the road ahead.

"You woulda thought that they would have wanted me to teach them to read so they could take care of their business and make sure nobody was cheating them in the stores and at their places of work. But no, what they were interested in was reading the Bible.

"Even some country preachers would come to me in the night after all my other night students had left to get me to teach them their letters so they could quote the Scriptures accurately and put together better sermons for their congregations."

Well, you know, that resonated for me, because I've always been drawn to the eloquence and wisdom of the Bible as well as to the stories. I had three or four translations in my home that I read every day. I couldn't help but think of my father again, this time with the big family King James Version of the Bible at his elbow on the kitchen table as he told us children his favorite biblical story of how the baby of Jesse's family, David, instead of any of his older brothers, was anointed king by the prophet Samuel, as we washed up the dishes. I was lost back there in time, trying to remember if I had ever actually seen or heard my father read when I was a child, when Miss Moses's sharp-edged question cut through my reverie.

"Did you teach little LaShawndra, your granddaughter, the Bible stories you learned from childhood?" Miss Moses wanted to know.

And I couldn't say anything but a noncommittal "Ummm," because the truth was, for most of her life, I could not *pay* LaShawndra to go to Sunday school with me, let alone sit still to hear some Bible stories. And Sandra, who goes to church all the time now because she's dating Pastor, only went for women's-day programs that embellished her community standing when LaShawndra was a young child. When LaShawndra was little, before she turned nine or ten and got so grown so quickly, I'd make sure she went to church by picking her up on Saturday and keeping her overnight with me if she wasn't already staying with me that week. Sometimes Sandra would have a date or plans with her girlfriends—ever since she was a majorette at Mulberry High, Sandra has always had a big circle of girlfriends— and would be glad for me to take LaShawndra off her hands on a Saturday night. I loved getting her all dressed up in pretty little-girl dresses and patent-leather shoes and even hair ribbons sometimes if she let me. Sandra let her dress in such grown-up clothes. I tried to bring some balance to her wardrobe when I could.

I remember for one Easter, a couple of years after my mother had died, I even pulled out the old Singer sewing machine she had left me and made LaShawndra the prettiest little lemon yellow dress for church. With her dark brown coloring, she looks pretty in yellow. Me, I can't wear yellow. It makes me look sallow. I even made a cute little white piqué jacket trimmed in the same yellow lace as the dress. I didn't even use a pattern. I just designed it and cut it out myself. I'm quite a proficient seamstress. I learned just by watching my mother. I made my first dress when I was seven.

But as she got closer to her teens, no number of cute little hand-made yellow dresses could get LaShawndra inside a church. Riding around Mulberry in the early-morning darkness with Miss Moses made me think that not forcing the issue had been a mistake.

When we crossed over the river, the waters were still raging. But all evidence of the motorcycle accident had been cleaned up.

It was 3:45 by the clock on the dashboard when we pulled into the parking lot of East Mulberry High School.

You know, it's a shame that I have been in the public education system for more than twenty years and I could not keep one little granddaughter in school enough to push her on through to graduation.

And God knows I did try my best to *push* her through. I tried everything I could think of.

She was so smart even before kindergarten age that no one said a word when I brought her to the elementary school when she had barely turned five to enroll her in first grade. And, you know, they don't allow that early enrollment in the smallest school system anymore.

And my secretary did not bat an eye when she found destroyed copies of the truancy records in the trash can in my office, showing how many days LaShawndra had missed in ninth and tenth grades.

I had been so good to my teachers that I did not even have to ask most of them to give her a barely passing grade in her junior year. When LaShawndra would stay over at my house—which was quite a lot—I'd wake her up for school singing "Hey Hey, Lil' Schoolgirl." Trying to make it lighthearted for her. And I'd have a nice little outfit ready and pressed for her with her shoes and socks laid out so nicely.

It didn't work. She had her own ideas about how she should dress. "Mama Mama, you know better than this. Don't *nobody* wear this tired old stuff no more." Then she would pull out some hoochie-mama outfit from her big red overnight bag or wait until she got to school and change. So I finally gave up.

When she just would not come to class at all or even stay the whole day when she did come, I saw that it was not fair to the other students who had to walk through Vietnam Alley and wash their own little cheap clothes and practically steal school supplies to keep on pushing her through.

By twelfth grade she had officially dropped out. It broke my heart.

As much as her mother and I loved learning—and her great-grandfather, too, I was just discovering—LaShawndra never did care if she learned anything or not. We just couldn't seem to pass it along to her.

Unfortunately, it seems that all my poor child Sandra is passing on to her daughter is shame. So much shame! LaShawndra talks a good game. To let her tell it, she's just as happy as she can be with her life. She sucks her teeth and throws her head when some of her friends' mothers are bragging on their daughters and their accomplishments, but I've seen the look in her eyes. And it isn't anything but shame I see there.

It's stupid self-defeating shame that Sandra doesn't have any business carrying around herself. I see it in my work with the school system. There seems to be so much shame at work in young girls' lives nowadays.

They're ashamed of where they live or that their parents don't show up for teacher-parent meetings or that their mother's latest boyfriend came into the bathroom unannounced and saw them naked or that some boy persuaded them to perform oral sex because it wasn't *real* intercourse. Those are the kinds of things young girls— even preteens—would sit in my office, twisting their hair around their fingers, gnawing the purple polish off their nails, and tell me when I was a middle and high school principal.

I never will forget one child—even though she was fifteen years old and taller than me, she was still just a little girl—sitting across the desk from me for disruptive behavior in the classroom. Wiping away big salty tears with the palms of her hands, she finally broke down and told me, "My mama hate me. She keep saying, 'You big, black, and ugly just like your daddy!' "

I do my best to encourage the young girls who cross my path. And I tell them the truth, too. I tell them I had a baby before I was married and that didn't stop me. I tell them I didn't get a chance to march with my high school graduation class because I was stuck out this far with Sandra.

Girls at East Mulberry High used to say, "Uhhh, Miz Pines, I can't hardly believe that about *you!*"

I used to ask them, "What part you having trouble with? Believe it!" I try to tell them that they don't have to carry around a lot of shame for making a bad decision. Oh, I know now that girls act like it's okay and the proper thing to do to have a baby at fifteen without an education, a job, a husband, or a sense of your own self and nothing to give a child but anger and frustrated dreams. But I know about the kind of shame the world will try to hang around your neck.

But now I'm beginning to think I should have kept my mouth "shet," 'cause our grandchildren and great-grandchildren seem to have gone way way too far the other way with their first baby daddy and their second baby daddy and even their third baby daddy. Now they don't seem to know the difference between shame and conviction.

I tried to do the same thing with my own children, tried not to hide too much of myself from them. I think of both Sandra and LaShawndra as my children.

They know that I haven't always been Miss Board of Education, as LaShawndra calls me behind my back. They know about my wild young life. They know I wasn't married to Charles when I became pregnant with Sandra. They know I smoked a little marijuana and experimented with some hallucinogens. They know the summer I was seventeen I traveled in one van with a bunch of local boys and girls— "hippies," "freaks," and "weirdos" they were called—across the Southeast to "find myself."

I think I did just about everything I wanted to. And some things twice!

But that was the sixties, you know.

We may have been stoned, but we weren't stupid!

In silence, Miss Moses and I cruised the parking lot of East Mulberry High School, where I was principal for six years before I became an administrator. That's how I knew that the young people hang out there some nights. You know, in a small town like Mulberry, there are only so many places open to young people late at night. Not that they should be out that late, but if they are going to hang, they have to make their own hangouts. In Mulberry, I've noticed, they choose parking lots—of convenience stores, gas stations, and the high school. By that time we must have driven past every store and gas station in Mulberry. One of my last hopes was the high school parking lot. I hoped LaShawndra would be there.

I had found her near the school once when she was fifteen and had not come home by midnight on a weekday night. She had told me when she left home at about six o'clock that she was going to the school to finish up a project that was due that week. I was so eager to believe that she was doing some schoolwork and just might stay in school that I accepted her story. I should have known better.

I simply refused to let her stay out all night while she was under my roof. I knew that she had done that while she was living with Sandra, who said she couldn't control her. But I could not sit by and condone that kind of behavior.

Just before I had turned into the school driveway, I had spotted LaShawndra leaning her back against the plate-glass window to the left of the 7-Eleven entrance on the corner. She had the sole of one of her booted feet propped up against the glass wall, with a tall, lanky boy standing over her little body with his hand draped across her breasts as he watched the other young people dancing to music coming from a big boom box on the ground.

As soon as she spotted my car, she came running up, her short black leather skirt and her lime green cropped sweater riding up even shorter and jumped in the passenger's seat.

"Mama Mama, I was just fixin' to call you to see if you could come get me. Wouldn't nobody give me no ride."

I lectured her all the way home and even on into the house. I stood in the doorway of the upstairs bathroom while she took off her clothes and put on her PJs, while she took off her makeup and washed her face, while she sat on her bed and rolled up her hair, telling her how worried I had been, that she was only a girl and how dangerous it was for her to go out and stay like that.

I didn't want to appear to promote deviant behavior, but I even told her if she was going to be all up under some boy kissing on him, the least she ought to get out of it was a ride home!

She just kept saying, "Um-huh, Mama Mama, I hear you. Yeah, you right, I won't do it no more. I don't wanna worry you, Mama Mama."

But I knew she had just been trying to placate me.

Miss Moses didn't say anything for a long time as I made the circle twice around the perimeter of the campus. She kept staring out the passenger-side window as if she could see the passing scenery, and for about the fifth time that morning I was tempted to ask, "Are you still blind, Miss Moses?" When she spoke up so suddenly, the sound of her voice in the car startled me.

All she said was, "Um, um, um, as if LaShawndra was going to be hanging around the schoolyard, even after midnight."

And, you know, I couldn't say anything in response. LaShawndra never graduated from high school. And she didn't half go when she was there.

Bless her heart, LaShawndra thinks she's gonna make it as a dancer in the music business. And she'll tell me in a minute, she doesn't need a high school diploma for that.

Oh, the dancing she does would make a shake-dancer blush, but it's the way all young people seem to dance now. It looks to me as if girls are being assaulted on the dance floor, the way boys come all up on them, humping them—like dogs mating. Unfortunately, the girls seem to hump right back. Oh, Jesus, help our children!

LaShawndra has a good job for a young woman who did not finish high school. Well, I'm certainly not ashamed of her.

I had always believed that you have to take *every* opportunity, *every possible* opportunity to teach your child something. And I've come to believe that every event in life is an opportunity for teaching.

When Sandra was a little girl, I always did that.

I know I do too much for LaShawndra, but I can't help it. She *needs* so much. And I've seen what can happen with our children when we leave them so needy. Oh, they so *needy* I could just cry sometimes.

God is going to make us pay. We're gonna be held accountable for all this mess. We are.

But it's our poor needy children who will suffer the greatest. Isn't that a shame?

I tried to do the same thing with LaShawndra as with Sandra. Sometimes we'd be driving along to shop or to the library and I'd point out people and we'd make up stories about them using the trees and flowers. Like, in the spring I'd ask, "What tree do I see that barks?" and she'd be so proud when she'd get it right and yell, "Dogwood tree!"

But, you know, after LaShawndra turned about twelve, she would have her music on so loud we couldn't have a conversation, let alone play a little brain teaser. Many times my efforts just didn't seem to *take* with her.

I don't know why, because I was a fairly effective schoolteacher back when I was in the classroom. But I haven't been in the classroom in years.

"It must have been a dagger in your heart that your granddaughter didn't finish school," Miss Moses said as we pointlessly circled the campus a third time. "You being an educator and all."

"Um-huh" was all I said.

I *know* how much all our children need education—of all kinds.

As an educator I've come to see each child, each student, each individual as a brilliant light. I know what can happen when you shine some attention on a brilliant light—it reflects glory. True glory, true splendor. I've seen it in what others thought of as a little piece a' street trash. A little piece of hoochie trash. I've seen miracles happen.

I guess that was what I had been praying for that morning: a miracle. And I *believed* in miracles.

I had had such plans for LaShawndra in high school. When I was a girl, not that long ago, high school afforded me some of the best times of my life. So pivotal to the development of who I am today. I was into *everything*! Do you hear me? *Everything.* The Debate Club, the Drama Club, the History Club—I've always been a history buff—the Band. I played the flute my freshman and sophomore years, and then I was a majorette my junior and senior years.

In my senior year, when the Mulberry High yearbook came out, some of my classmates stopped speaking to me because my name and picture were in it so much.

And I would have been valedictorian if I had not been showing by June of my senior year. I guess I was still at the head of my class, even though I didn't get to march and give a speech in the school's new auditorium.

Well, it didn't kill me. And in the long run it taught me to keep all those honors and accolades in the proper perspective. In all the hub-bub and hoopla of graduation, giving life to Sandra was more impor-tant to me than giving a speech in a new auditorium.

I guess I was just a born mama. It came so naturally to me. Until she went to kindergarten, I had Sandra with me all the time. I can see us now, back in the early sixties, riding around middle Georgia in my white convertible VW Beetle. Sandra wasn't six months old before I was tying her to my back with this long orange and tan and green swath of material the way I had seen African women do it in text-books and taking her with me to classes at the college outside of Mul-berry. I was the first black student to go there. I had a complete scholarship—books and everything else—a part-time job, and I was staying at home with my parents before Charles and I got married. So I was independent. And, you know, nobody there had the nerve to get in my face about Sandra's being a disruption in class.

There really wasn't anything to complain about. She was just as good as gold, because she was getting all that love and attention.

Everybody from the groundskeepers and the cooks to the janitors and maids fussed over that child—the only little black baby on campus. And after the older women in the dining-hall kitchen got over the shock of me "coming flouncing out unmarried with my baby to college like it wasn't nothing," as one of them told me, Sandra was hardly ever in class with me. She was somewhere being cared for and doted on and made over by some loving black woman, being taught to read before she could hold a textbook by herself, having her thick, nappy hair brushed and braided in styles folks had not seen in decades.

It just made her *crave* attention. LaShawndra's the same way. You can't give her enough attention. You know, it's true that children don't take after strangers.

As Miss Moses and I were about to pull out of the parking lot, I spied a group of three or four boys standing way over by the football field in the shadow of a big mulberry tree, out of the light. You know, I thought LaShawndra was over there. Since she's been big enough to walk to the neighborhood playground by herself, she has always been the only girl among a bunch of rusty little nappy-headed boys.

"I see some young people across the way over by the gymnasium, Miss Moses," I said, explaining my sharp U-turn. "Let's check it out."

I cut straight across the parking lot and pulled up to the group. I recognized one of the boys leaning up against a car. I knew him from school a few years before. He is about LaShawndra's age. But I also knew him because LaShawndra has a little crush on him. Oh, nothing she would talk about, but I had seen her around him once at the Mulberry Mall, and I knew she liked him in a special way and just yearned for him to return her attention.

They tried to hide their beer bottles and joints and cigarettes when they saw it was me. But I didn't pay that any attention this time. Usually I'd take the opportunity to reprimand them about the drugs, but I had just been driving up and down Vietnam Alley—the biggest drug lair in Mulberry—myself, and besides, I had other concerns that morning.

I lowered my window and asked the young man, the one LaShawndra had a crush on, "Have you seen my granddaughter, LaShawndra Pines, tonight?"

He thought for a moment and said very seriously, "No, ma'am, I don't think I even know nobody named LaShawndra."

And it just about broke my heart for her. Because I know she really likes the boy, since she first mentioned him more than a year ago, and she's still interested in him. That's a record for her. And he didn't even know her name.

I merely sighed and looked to the others in the group. They all sort of looked at the ground and shook their heads, mumbling "uh-huh" and "naw."

"Thanks anyway," I said, trying to make it sound like it wasn't important, as if me driving around asking after my granddaughter's whereabouts at nearly four in the morning was not very serious.

Then, as we pulled off, my window button jammed for a bit and I heard another boy's voice laugh and say, "Aw, man, you know that little ho named LaShawndra. She the biggest skank in Mulberry, the biggest little chickenhead ho in town." Then another boy in the group said, "Derek, what you talkin' 'bout you don't know her? You been having ho problems since you were twelve."

"Yeah, I may a' had 'ho problems,' " the boy said, "but LaShawndra Pines ain't never been one of them. Don't nobody want to be tied up with *that* trouble. Ain't no telling *what* she got!"

Well, that really *did* break my heart.

As soon as the last word of the boy's pronouncement trailed into my car, the window button clicked in and the window glided firmly shut.

I don't even remember where we drove for the next few minutes. I could hardly see straight.

I could still hear that boy's voice in my ear calling LaShawndra—

my granddaughter, my own little precious girl who calls her grand-mama "Mama Mama"—"the biggest little chickenhead ho in town."

I've tried for years to pretend that I did not hear what people said about her. I tried to ignore the fact that she never really had a boyfriend she could bring home, that she slept around with just about anybody who would give her some attention for the night and pretend not to know her the next day at school, that at age fourteen she was slipping out of my house at night to go God-knows-where.

That deep down she did not think anything of herself.

That she judged her own self unworthy of love and esteem.

That she casually called her own self a "little ho."

I had tried my best to get her to stop calling herself that. I know how powerful words are in the universe, in the mind of Christ. But she wouldn't stop. Many times I had thought it was as if she *couldn't* stop. Couldn't stop calling herself a "ho." Couldn't stop seeing herself as that.

Sometimes she would have the nerve, even when she was a pre-teen, to remind me that *I* had a baby at nineteen, out of wedlock. It broke my heart to say it, but I had to tell her, "Yes, I did, baby, but I wasn't no ho."

I've told her so many times, the only time you can get away with calling yourself a "ho" is when you're not one.

You know, back in my day, the biggest slut at Mulberry High School—the biggest "hoochie," as they call them now—did not let you call her a "ho." She didn't do it.

She would get her brother or her cousin or one of her "boyfriends" to kick your ass if you called her a "ho."

Even the hos refused to be called "hos" back then.

Now it's just another word for "girl."

And it's not only in hip-hop music or on videos, it's in regular every-day life. I can't tell you the number of disciplinary actions I've had to initiate over that word in the schools. In the last few years the school halls and classrooms just *resound* with the calls of "ho" and "bitch."

Sometimes I have had to throw my hands up to God and say, "Jehovah! Jesus, Jesus, Jesus, help us *all!*"

As I drove along, I was fighting back tears the entire time. When we passed through a thick patch of fog so soft and swirling, I was tempted to let go of the steering wheel and just drift off into the abyss. I wanted to cover my face and sob. When a couple of tears did escape and roll down my cheeks and onto my nubby cotton sweater, I was glad Miss Moses could not see me.

But she must have smelled my tears and my sorrow, because she said, "Don't cry, child."

"Oh, Miss Moses," I said after I composed myself, "just because my granddaughter thinks of herself as a little ho, and maybe other people do, too, doesn't mean she *is* just a ho. Does it? She deserves to be saved, too. Right?"

Miss Moses didn't answer for a moment. And I was beginning to get peeved with her, because all I really wanted her to do was agree with me.

Then she leaned over out of her seat very close to me. At first I thought Miss Moses was going to kiss me on the cheek, but instead she gave a deep, ancient sigh, and I felt her breath—which also smelled like lavender—on my cheek. In a flash, as she leaned back into her seat, a picture came to my mind. Sadly, I realized that it was a scene like many that had played over and over since LaShawndra was twelve or so.

I saw myself on the phone in the kitchen talking to my friend Joyce about how LaShawndra had let me down again. This time it was in the area of hygiene. The night before—a hot, steamy middle Georgia night—LaShawndra and I had decided to run out for some ice cream before the Dairy Queen closed. But we missed it because LaShawndra had spent so much time running around looking for a clean pair of jeans to wear.

I heard myself saying on the phone, "Now, Joyce, you know you a

funky ho if you can't wear your jeans but one time before you have to
wash them."

The memory of my words shamed me so, I could feel my cheeks burning in the darkened interior of the Explorer.

"Oh, Miss Moses," I said, with no explanation, "I was sure LaShawndra didn't hear me when I said it. Oh, I wouldn't hurt her little feelings for anything in the world. She got little feelings, too! I wouldn't do that to my own baby grandgirl!"

After a couple of moments Miss Moses spoke. "Lily," she said, "everybody is somebody's baby."

And even though it sounded like the lyrics to some old blues song or just the prattling of an old lost woman, it made some sense to me.

"I just don't know what to do anymore," I said honestly.

"Well, then, let's pray," Miss Moses suggested.

I thought that was a splendid idea. I realized then that I had been silently praying ever since I was awakened at midnight. Miss Moses bowed her gray head and started:

"Our Father, who art in heaven . . ."

I pulled the Explorer over to the curb and joined her in the Lord's Prayer. At the amen she prayed, "Help these young girls, Lord." All I could add was "Yes, Lord."

Then Miss Moses lifted her little stick arms to the roof of the car and shouted, "Jehovah, Jireh!"

Then "Jehovah, Rapha! Jehovah, Shama!"

From church revival services I knew that the Hebrew pleas meant "God, Provider! God, Healer! God, *there*!" We certainly needed God's presence there that morning, even more than I knew at the time.

I truly appreciated Miss Moses's being there with me, too. With the sound of "Amen, amen, and amen!" ringing in the air, I felt the veil of condemnation lifting from my shoulders as I silently vowed, I'll never call that child a "ho" again. I pulled a tissue from the box on the floor in the back and blew my nose.

"Thank you, Miss Moses," I said. And I meant it. I knew she could tell that from my voice. I even sounded stronger to myself.

"Well, sugar, what good are we if we can't pray together for one another? You know, Jesus didn't tell us to love everyone in the world. He said, 'Love one another.' "

Again she was right. It made me consider her feelings for the first time since around midnight.

"Are you hungry, Miss Moses?" I asked. "We can stop up here at this place on the corner. I know there's a McDonald's on the next block, but I don't eat fast foods."

"What I really got a taste for is some barbecue," Miss Moses offered, smacking her slack, wrinkled lips and jigging her little shoulders in anticipation.

She wants some *barbecue*?! I thought, surprised and tickled at the same time. But since we were coming up on the Dixie Pig right then, I just pulled into the parking lot of the Mulberry landmark that stayed open all night.

"Um," she said. "The Dixie Pig. I ain't had no ribs from the Dixie Pig in *ages!*"

I thought, Has this woman gotten her sight back in her old age? But I didn't question her. I could not bring myself to be that rude and nosy. So I just said, "Um."

"Smells good," Miss Moses murmured when I parked in an empty space under a metal shelter near the entrance and rolled down my window. The air was full of country-smelling oak-wood smoke.

Oh, that's how she knew where we were, I thought.

As if magically, a short, stocky man in his thirties appeared at my window wearing black slacks and a clean white long-sleeved shirt. He winked at me and asked, "What you gon' have, Miz Pines?"

I tell you, I know most of the young people in Mulberry, or they know me.

I turned to Miss Moses to ask what she wanted, but she was way 77
ahead of me.

"I'll take a rib plate with slaw and potato salad," she ordered, looking out her window at air. "And a tall sweet iced tea." I repeated it for our server.

I thought, Well, her appetite seems to be intact. That's a good sign.

As we waited for our order, Miss Moses entertained herself by humming a little song under her breath. I couldn't catch what it was, but it was a pleasant tune. And it was nice not to feel I had to make conversation.

Charles popped into my head again. I guess the smell of the oak wood burning and the barbecue sauce in the air reminded me of him.

When we were married, Charles would bring home a plate of barbecue ribs from the Dixie Pig some late nights after he had been out gambling. That was before his cards became a problem and embarrassment to me and our household. I thought then he was just playing cards every now and again with his friends, not a regular at the gambling house. After what Miss Moses had told me about Daddy and his reading, it was difficult for me to think straight about Charles and his gambling anymore.

Back then Charles and I would sit in the middle of our bed—with Sandra asleep down the hall—and eat barbecue and share a tall can of Miller High Life or Pabst Blue Ribbon or some other cheap beer. Then we'd cap off the night by making love smelling like barbecue sauce and coleslaw. He would pretend to smear me accidentally with the sauce on his fingertips, then lick it off... slowly. Ummmm.

When he wasn't gambling, Charles did know how to make me happy.

I still have scraps of paper torn off from the tops of boxes of nails

You Know Better

or some construction-supply container where he had written notes to me while he was at work.

One of my most cherished love notes from Charles was:

U R
2 sweet
2 bee
4gotten

And he drew a little smiling striped bumblebee over the word "bee."

He was a good artist, too. I have a drawer at home in the den just full of sketches he has made of me over the years. Some mornings I'd wake up early like I always do and Charles would be asleep in the big pumpkin-colored easy chair in the bedroom, on his lap a sketch pad with a drawing of me naked and a piece of charcoal in his hand.

Thinking about those nude drawings of me made my cheeks burn a little as Miss Moses's humming broke into my musing. Despite my concern for Miss Moses and for LaShawndra at the time, I could not ignore that I was feeling a bit damp between my legs at the memory of Charles and his drawings.

It made me feel as I did when we first fell in love as teenagers.

It had all been so exciting, sneaking down to the river, cutting class, just smelling each other's breath, almost getting caught in the stacks of the school library with his hand up my blouse, his fingers inside my white lace Maidenform bra.

Thirty years later I can still feel the dizzy excitement that my first sexual experiences with Charles induced, like some lightweight drug from the 1960s.

Charles was like that for me—a drug. I guess that's why he is so hard a habit to kick; I'm a little addicted, I guess. No matter how many "CA meetings" I attend, I'm still a Charlesaholic.

Through all that has happened with Charles and me getting together, breaking up, getting back together, breaking up, I've tried to

build my life as a gate of love instead of building up a wall of resent-
ment. At least, I thought I had.

I guess that was why I was out there in the wee hours of the morning looking for LaShawndra.

When the plates came zipping to the car in the capable hands of
my young ex-pupil, he leaned in and said, "I put some extra sauce in
there for you, Miz Pines, 'cause you were so sweet to me." And then
I remembered that I had found a place for him to live his senior year
after his father had put him out on the street when he had discovered
a couple of joints among the pages of the boy's social studies textbook.

As I took the heavy plates, swimming in spicy orange sauce, I
smiled my thanks at him and thought, Um, look like I can save everybody's child but my own. And I felt right sad.

However, I did think to ask my passenger, "How's your blood pres-
sure and your sugar, Miss Moses?"

"Ain't got neither one," she replied as she reached for her Chinet
plate covered in waxed paper and the tall paper cup of sweetened
iced tea.

But bless her heart, for all her show of heartiness, she couldn't eat
a thing. She just sat there smelling her rib plate and looking as if that
were just as satisfying.

I ended up taking the plate and cup from her and putting them
back in their paper bag along with my untouched smoked-shoulder
sandwich. I turned and placed the whole thing on the backseat in case
we ran across some more homeless or hungry folks.

6.

As we pulled out of the Dixie Pig exit, I looked down at the gas gauge and realized that driving around off and on for nearly five hours had left me dangerously close to empty.

"We need some gas, Miss Moses," I told my passenger, and pulled into the first gas station we came to. I asked Miss Moses if she wanted to go to the restroom or get out and stretch her legs. But she said no.

Then she added, "All I can say is thank goodness for Depends."

Even in my state of worry, Miss Moses made me smile. She really was an angel.

I could just imagine her bending over my father's shoulder gently pointing out the correct pronunciation of "immaculate" or "felicity" from the Bible.

As I pumped the high-test, I looked over at the carload of young girls at the pump across from me.

I recognized one of the girls as the daughter of a schoolteacher I knew named Sadie Tyler. A pretty girl. She was one of the girls running for the Peach Blossom Queen contest that was going on that weekend. I called to her, but she couldn't hear me.

They weren't just pumping gas, they were pumping up the jam, as LaShawndra says, and the chorus of "Freak me, freak me, freak me" was reverberating over the whole lot.

In my heart I knew I should have reprimanded them for being out so late by themselves. They had probably told their mothers they were at each other's houses getting ready for the Peach Blossom Ball. But I had another girl to be worried about that night. I felt bad about not being a better guide to them on that occasion. Our children are so desperately in need of guidance. But I guess also I was partly embarrassed and afraid one of those little hot mamas would have laughed at my reprimand and said, "It's after midnight. Do you know where *your* child is?"

I waved from the rear of my car until I got their attention. They turned down the music.

"Hey, Miz Pines," "Hey, Miz Pines," "Hey, Miz Pines," they called in chorus.

"Hi, girls, have any of you seen LaShawndra tonight?" I called back across the pumps.

"No, ma'am," one of them yelled. "You know, she don't roll with us."

I nodded. They waved again and turned their music back up. I recognized a couple of the girls as granddaughters of my friends. It broke my heart that these girls were amassing memories of preparing for the Peach Blossom Festival, sharing makeup tips with their peers, doing each other's hair, laughing and giggling, and my little LaShawndra was out somewhere in the middle of the night with God-knew-who.

I thought of LaShawndra with those earphones of hers on all the time like they were a diadem on her head, and it gave me an idea. When I returned to the car, I switched on the radio for a news report.

Since Miss Moses seemed perfectly satisfied to sit there in the passenger seat of my car and just ride around Mulberry until the sun came up, I was looking everywhere for some direction. As soon as I did, Miss Moses decided to speak again.

"All the answers, all the guidance is within you," she said, just like she said everything else: casually, conversationally. "You ain't gon' find an answer on the radio."

You know, I just had to keep myself from throwing my head back and screaming at the top of my lungs at that little piece of empty wisdom. And I am not the hysterical type. But I was at my wits' end.

I don't usually listen to the radio in the car, other than NPR in the morning and *All Things Considered* if I'm in the car later on. But I clicked it on anyway to a local station that morning as Miss Moses and I drove around to see if perhaps there was guidance on the airwaves. Although God knows the last thing I wanted was to hear something about LaShawndra on a Mulberry radio station. But it just goes to show how deeply I felt something was amiss, seriously amiss.

I could almost feel it stalking around me like a predatory animal outside the Explorer. Having Miss Moses in the car with me had kept the fear at bay a bit, but as soon as I heard the first news report on the radio—"A local businessman has shot and killed his wife in what appears to have been a domestic dispute in the suburb of Sherwood Forest"—I had to click it off again. I could hardly breathe.

I didn't want to think it. Usually I just put it out of my mind, what I knew about my granddaughter, LaShawndra.

I knew she could just as easily wake up dead some morning in some boy's bed that she didn't even know. I never ever even said that out loud to anyone, not even to my friend Joyce, but I know that LaShawndra is almost always in some precarious situation. In the last seven or so years, I just had had to turn it loose from time to time: the worrying, the continuous trying, the not stepping on Sandra's toes about her motherhood and her parenting skills, the repeating the lesson or advice or warning to LaShawndra for the five hundredth time—lessons, advice, and warnings that she paid absolutely no attention to.

I was just doing my best to stand in the gap for my girls. I believed and still do that the Lord asked that not only of Ezekiel but of all of us.

When we passed the Chuck E. Cheese pizza restaurant on Orange Highway, I thought of all the birthday parties I had held there for LaShawndra over the years. The last one I had there was when she was eleven, and only Joyce's granddaughter and a bunch of thuggish-looking boys showed up. So after that I just made her birthday celebrations family affairs.

My goodness, Sandra gets so depressed around LaShawndra's birth date that the last thing she's up to is giving a birthday party. So every year for the last eighteen years, I've tried my best to really fuss over LaShawndra and her birthday around that time. Not just the exact birthday, but also the time around the date, because Sandra's depression begins about a week before and lasts about a fortnight after. LaShawndra calls her "Drama Mama." Indeed.

I've talked with Sandra about it. I've had eighteen occasions in the last eighteen years to bring it up. The first year when I saw it happening, I just mentioned in passing that LaShawndra had a right to have a happy little birthday, too. You see, I always—well, Charles and I always—made a big deal over all of Sandra's milestones: birthdays, A's on report cards, Sunday-school recitations, band tryouts. I would buy her a pretty new dress or her daddy, Charles, would make some extraordinarily beautiful wooden chair just her size, or one time he even built a complete playhouse in back and kept it under a huge tarp for weeks so it would be a surprise. Having gotten all that attention herself, Sandra, I thought, would have understood. But eighteen years later she's still too busy going to nutville around her own daughter's birthday to make over *her*.

That's why I've always felt I had to rescue LaShawndra from her home life.

I could not help myself. From the time LaShawndra was born, Sandra would be on one of her rants about how men weren't nothing but dogs who end up deserting you, and I would hear myself talking fast as I rushed over to LaShawndra's crib—pretty pink wooden one that Charles and I had found in a secondhand store. It was an authentic antique that Charles stripped and sanded, and I painted it myself. I would bundle that baby up in her soft pink baby blanket and take her home with me for days on end.

Oh, I'd say something like "LaShawndra, baby, why don't we give this new mama a little break?" as I got her things together and headed out the door.

Charles didn't mind. He loved his daughter, and he loved his grand-daughter. We felt blessed to see LaShawndra take her first steps, to hear her say her first words, to witness her first true giggle.

Charles was a man who just liked children. Didn't mind having them around. He was comfortable with babies in that rough, unconscious man way he had. He'd change LaShawndra's diapers and toss her around while she cooed and laughed just as naturally.

I would just be praying the entire time. "Lord, don't let this man drop my child!" But I'd know what care he was truly taking of the baby.

We could not make it together, but Charles had some good qualities, still does. Sandra wouldn't say so to me, but she still calls herself mad at me for Charles's leaving. I know she thinks it's *my* fault. But then she's a daddy's girl. As far as she's concerned, her daddy can do no wrong.

"Where are we now?" Miss Moses asked as we turned onto Chestnut Street.

"We're over by where old St. Luke's Hospital used to be," I said, thinking street names would only confuse her.

She just smiled at me and kept humming her little tune. I still could not put my finger on the title even though it seemed familiar.

"What's that tune you humming, Miss Moses?" I asked.

She stopped just long enough to reply, "Oh, just a little something I used to teach to my students. I made it up myself."

"Well, you're a talented composer because it certainly is pretty," I told her. And I meant it. It was a lovely little ditty.

Just driving past the empty site of that lovely old hospital brought back a flood of memories. Of Sandra's birth, mostly.

I named my daughter Sandra after a dear friend of mine who died when we were young women. My friend Sandra changed her name to Afeni in the sixties, and I respected that. I just knew her my whole life as Sandra, and when my little girl was born, I automatically said, "Sandra Afeni!" when old Nurse Bloom at St. Luke's Hospital barked at me, demanding I give her a name for my baby.

Uh, that old head nurse nearly frightened me to death. I learned later that she was not nearly as rough as she seemed. But at that time—I was nineteen years old, unmarried, apprehensive, unsure of what lay ahead—Nurse Bloom was quite daunting. While I was there in labor, I had heard the gruff old nurse tell another girl that "y'all young gals [meaning the young unmarried mothers, not the young married ones] don't know nothing about nothing but getting babies."

I had heard about her from other women, old and young, who had had babies with Nurse Bloom at St. Luke's or at home with her as a midwife. She went way back and inspired real awe in people, even in folks like my grandma, who was pretty daunting herself.

I was pretty strong-minded, even back then, so I didn't take any offense at much of what she said. She *was* an extraordinary nurse and midwife, too.

I was still feeling pretty dopey from the delivery. So I guess I was expecting a little gentler service at St. Luke's. Charles had been adamant that his child be born in the all-black private hospital—the only hospital for blacks in Mulberry, or in the whole area, for that matter.

Old Dr. Williams, who had founded the hospital back in the late thirties, was still there then in 1960. He wasn't still delivering babies, but he was still a strong, distinguished presence at the place, overseeing every operation and procedure. Sometimes from his office. Sometimes from over the other doctors' shoulders. Nurse Bloom passed away in the early seventies. The city tore the building down in the mid-seventies to make way for the crosstown extension and "urban renewal." By then most black people in town were going to the new medical facility where LaShawndra was born anyway.

Quite a loss—both the private hospital and Nurse Bloom, who died more than twenty years ago—to our people. And our community.

We as a people have lost so much from those early days of integration in the South. Shoot, in the last couple of decades we've lost so much, period. I think the biggest loss has been just our being there for each other.

That's why it hurt me so to see Sandra hold herself off from her own child. I would see it. Even when LaShawndra was an infant, with all her sweet baby smells and adorable coos and gurgles, I would catch Sandra leaning back from her at the waist, withholding herself, holding herself a little distant from LaShawndra.

Well, it would just break my heart. For all practical purposes, the baby didn't have no daddy, nor any of her daddy's family.

Her daddy's sisters...well, they may as well not be her aunts. Actually, LaShawndra is probably better off not knowing them that much. From my experience with them, they don't like my granddaughter. And if I'm right about that, then it's better they stay away from her.

But I do wish she had more women relatives. Especially older ones.

Half the children in my school district haven't been half raised because their mamas have been too busy trying to raise themselves or running after their own dreams or some man. Most of the rest of them are so young and in need of nurturing themselves that they just don't know any better. And if they do know better, they're too caught up in themselves to care. You know I don't mean to criticize her, but that's part of Sandra's problem.

She discovered that many men didn't want a woman with a young child.

Of course, being a mother, I missed out on some things, too. And many times Sandra and LaShawndra were intrusions in my life, in my little plans, but that's the way it's supposed to be with your children. They aren't put on this earth to be convenient for us. I think that's the direction we're moving in.

Whenever I tried to explain to little LaShawndra that her mother was still a vibrant young woman who wanted and needed male companionship, she always said, "Mama Mama, you got you a man—a couple of them—and you still raised Sandra." And she's right.

Most of my generation, they didn't know any better. We just thought you had to do everything, and we just went on and did it: home, family, job, church, community work. We didn't know any better.

I looked over at Miss Moses, who was pulling an entire economy-size box of pink Kleenex out of one of her bags to blow her nose, and thought, I wish LaShawndra had somebody like this old lady for guidance and inspiration.

Somebody other than her mother and grandmother might be able to get through to her about herself and her direction and life, since she seems hell-bent on building her life around what some anonymous boy who doesn't know she's alive thinks of her.

LaShawndra says she wants a career in the music industry, but that's only because she thinks someone will notice her dancing in a music video. Truly. And give her the kindness and attention she craves and didn't get in her own home.

My mind was wandering so that morning, but Miss Moses, of all people, put me back on track.

"Chestnut Street? That's over there by the park with the big fountain in the middle, isn't it?" she asked.

I don't know *why* I continued to believe that Miss Moses was confused. She seemed to be thinking a great deal more clearly than I was.

"Uh-huh" is what I said, but what I was thinking was, "This woman can see!"

"I can't see, sugar," she said as if she heard what I was thinking, "but I have an excellent sense of direction."

I was sure now that Miss Moses wasn't any ordinary ninety-something-year-old woman. Still, I was truly shocked when she turned to me and asked, "You think she might have left town for that Freaknik in Atlanta?"

"Miss Moses," I said. I know that my mouth must have been hanging open. "What do *you* know about Freaknik?"

Looking back on it, I guess I was just fooling myself that

LaShawndra would be somewhere in Mulberry, where I could put my hands on her. I knew as well as Miss Moses, LaShawndra, and every other little coochie—I guess I need to stop calling them that if I don't want them to be like that—that Freaknik was scheduled that April weekend in 1997 up in Atlanta.

Freaknik began as a huge party for African-American college students during spring break, but it had degenerated into an outdoor sex orgy. Bad as those white students in Daytona Beach. They congregated in Atlanta, the educational ground of such stellar denizens as W. E. B. DuBois, James Weldon Johnson, Alice Walker, Martin Luther King Jr., Lois Mailou Jones, Elizabeth Catlett.

When Miss Moses spoke of Freaknik, I felt with such certainty in my very spirit that LaShawndra might have been headed for Atlanta, but in reality I knew that wherever she was, she was on a road to nowhere, a road of no return. No matter what I did.

For the last couple of years LaShawndra had sworn to me that she never went to Freaknik. She had told me she was going out with her girlfriend, Crystal. Then I heard terrifying stories circulating around Mulberry about her being groped and flashing her titties at Freaknik. My friend Joyce heard that she had to throw herself from a car at a stoplight on Peachtree Street just to save herself from being attacked. The thought of it made me frantic.

"Lord Jesus," I prayed right then, "let me find this child before it's too late."

Earlier that spring I had overheard LaShawndra telling a group of boys she was talking to out on the sidewalk outside my house one evening, "Where else a little freak like me gon' be other than Freaknik?!"

Well, of course it went all through me to hear her call herself a "freak," which is what the young people call a girl who partakes in a wide range of sexual activity. But poor LaShawndra and her generation feel no compunction whatsoever about calling themselves all kinds of vile things. If I had a nickel—no, a *penny*—for every time I've stopped her from calling herself or some other young girl a "ho," I could have *hired* someone to keep an eye on her.

They don't even know what a freak is, and here they are calling themselves that.

Sometimes I was just overwhelmed by how much of young people's lives seems so immersed in sex. I tried to talk to my children in the same way I tried to speak to my students—openly and honestly. Although nowadays you can't seem to talk openly enough with young folks about sex. They're way ahead of you in some respects—I've heard eleven- and twelve-year-old girls screaming and fussing at boys in the playground because the boys declined to have sex with them— but in other respects they're so far behind I don't think they'll ever catch up.

Most parents don't want to hear it. If you mention our children's sexual lives and experiences at a dinner party or over lunch, people will actually get so angry with you they get up and leave.

"Not my little darling," they say. "Not my little girl, she's not like that." To let them tell it, their children are the only ones immune. "Not my little so-and-so. I watch her like a hawk." I watched LaShawndra, too. I took her to the parties and came and picked her up at ten o'clock. Tried to watch the way she dressed. Tried to check her bed every night. And still here I was after three o'clock in the morning dragging the streets of Mulberry for her.

It was a hard pill to swallow. Too hard for some folks.

I think my daughter, Sandra, felt from the time LaShawndra was in kindergarten that it was just too hard. And the children end up feeling unwanted. I don't get it, but that kind of thinking is certainly screwing up our children—mine included.

LaShawndra, she doesn't feel wanted. After all our trips together to Atlanta and our personal projects and our intimate talks, she still is looking for herself in some stranger's eyes. Dancing for them. Lending them her little possessions never to be seen again. I don't know how many times I've bought that child another portable CD player. We leave our children so needy. It just breaks my heart.

And worse than that, this generation of little ones has grown up so ignorant—of just about everything. Girls graduating from law school don't know how to make gravy. Or how to say no and mean it.

Or even how to act. I used to see young women who didn't want to be trouble, who wanted so badly for folks to like them, but it was just their behavior. They don't know the right thing to do, so they do just anything. They don't know the proper thing to say, so they curse you out.

Inappropriate behavior! You know how you see a five-year-old girl in the churchyard: "Oh, look at you, you cute li'l thing. What a pretty dress!" And the child just doesn't know what to do—with the attention, with the compliment, with herself, so she just pulls her dress over her head. She spins around with her panties on display, and for good measure she says all the bad words she knows.

My little granddaughter is the queen of "inappropriate behavior." I try to tell her, "Don't be like that."

I try to tell her over and over, "Baby, put your *best* foot forward!"

Much of her behavior, it really is harmless, but people are so turned off by that kind of behavior that I know folks are judging her by these things. And it's a shame, because she has a good heart.

Underneath it all she's a good girl. She is. She's just as tender-hearted as she can be. I've seen her make a point of talking to a shy new girl down at the Board of Education office, taking her out to lunch at the Dairy Queen or the soul-food restaurant when none of the other girls would give her the time of day. When I praised her for her actions, she told me, "I know how it feel to be left out, Mama Mama."

And LaShawndra has been a good friend to her roommate, Crystal. I even heard Crystal's little girl call my granddaughter "Auntie

LaShawn," and it just warmed my heart. Neither one of them has too many other friends. So I'm grateful for Crystal for any number of reasons.

LaShawndra's so much of a people-pleaser, but of course she's always trying to please the wrong people, folks who don't care anything about her.

She's so needy.

I tried my best to give LaShawndra what I had given Sandra, which is all of myself. But I just could not do it all. I tried.

Earlier that morning, when Miss Moses and I had passed the Mulberry Hyatt Hotel, I felt a pang of remorse about how even I thought about LaShawndra. The city had my luncheon there last year around this time when I received a Woman of the Year Award during the Peach Blossom Festival. And I wanted LaShawndra to be there. I try so hard to expose her to all manner of events so she will know that the world is not bounded by her little dancing and parties and hanging out with her "homeys."

But she said she didn't want to go up there with all those "dead" people.

"They gon' have any music?" she wanted to know.

I was honest. I said, "Not your kind." So she declined the invitation.

To tell the truth, I was almost glad that she didn't go. I should be ashamed to say that about my only grandchild. But she would have shown up in one of her hoochie-mama outfits with half her behind showing. So I actually was relieved when she said no.

Of course, by that time in my search for her—it was well after four o'clock—I was feeling extremely guilty about that. About being ashamed of her and the way she looks sometimes. My own flesh and blood!

When LaShawndra was younger and living with me or just staying over some nights with me, I could keep some kind of eye on her and the way she dressed. I made sure that when she left out of my house on Oglethorpe Street, she looked decent and presentable. No see-through tube tops and big jeans hanging down to the crack in her behind.

And since I bought most of her clothes, I felt I knew what she was wearing. LaShawndra loves to shop. She got that honest.

Her mother *loves* to shop, *loves* to shop. The only things full in Sandra's whole house are her closets and cupboards.

Truly. She will buy anything. Clothes, small appliances, cleaning supplies, pots, pans, shoes, computers, televisions. As long as Sandra is buying something, she's happy. She doesn't seem to care what it is, as long as she's shopping. It's almost like an addiction. I think the only thing she and LaShawndra ever agreed on in life was shopping.

They certainly did not get it from me. Oh, I love lovely things, but I can think of a million tasks I could be accomplishing, rather than running from store to store acquiring things. I either order from catalogs or buy very good classic items that will last forever. I have a beautiful black cashmere coat that I bet is fifteen years old. It cost me more than a thousand dollars. It probably costs two or three thousand dollars now. But it's worth it. I plan to wear it till the day I die.

Now, Sandra spends a great deal of money on clothes, but she tires of them so quickly. And she doesn't stop at clothes.

She's not the most assiduous housekeeper, but her pantry is stocked to overflowing with cleaning products. Boxes and boxes of Tide. Rows of Clorox bleach. Cabinets full of Woolite and Mr. Clean and steel wool.

She almost hoards, like someone who was brought up in the Depression. The products keep piling up and piling up, because nobody uses them. I go by Sandra's house sometimes and take as many of them as I can carry out to my granddaughter and her little housemate, Crystal.

It's just a few cans of Comet and some Sunlite dishwashing liquid. And I know Sandra's never gonna use them.

Crystal keeps that house on Painted Bunting Lane just as neat as a pin. And you talk about *clean*?! Shoot, that child's house is cleaner than mine! A fly could slip up and break its neck on her floors. I know that LaShawndra took after her mama in the cleaning department, so I know she's no help to Crystal there. I like to help out struggling young folks, especially when they're tryna help themselves out. That's why I started a class in etiquette at the high school, because they're going to need to know how to move smoothly through the world, and Lord knows, most of their mamas are too caught up in their own lives to teach them the simple niceties of life.

Sandra doesn't care much about what her house looks like on the inside as long as nobody sees it. Maybe that's my fault, too.

I always tried to teach Sandra not to live her life under condemnation. Beating up on herself for some little old human failing. I just didn't want her to live her precious existence in the throes of regrets and second-guessing and a bunch of "what if I had done such-and-suchs" and "why did I do thats."

Sometimes I think I might have done too good a job. Because Sandra can't seem to take any responsibility for how her life turned out. So she blames everybody else. I, her mother, take up too much space in the world. Men are just no good, you can't find a good one—that's why she says her relationships don't last. Her daughter, whom she formed from the womb, doesn't rise to her expectations. Orange juice doesn't taste as good as it did when she was a child.

When I heard Mount Calvary's chimes playing two bars of "Just As I Am," I looked up at my location for the first time in about fifteen minutes. We were back on the other side of the river. And I didn't even remember crossing the Ocawatchee again.

7

At around five o'clock that morning, I was just about ready to throw up my hands and say, "My name is Tess, I ain't in this mess!" But I couldn't do that. Number one, because it was LaShawndra whom I felt to be in peril. And number two, Miss Moses sitting next to me in the front seat of my Explorer so serene and sure that we were doing the right thing kept me on track.

"We're just riding around in circles now, aren't we, sugar?" Miss Moses asked.

She made me feel like the Israelites, spending forty years in the desert on a trip that should have taken about eleven weeks.

I was looking for guidance from anywhere I could get it. I was open... you know. To being led wherever I was meant to be.

And even though I was thinking and worrying about my grand-daughter, LaShawndra, Charles—my Charles—kept coming up in my mind. I would push him out one way and he would seep back in another. Each time Miss Moses called me "sugar," I'd think about Charles again.

In my mind I kept seeing all the things he had done for more than forty years to make my life happy and better. Everything from trying to get palm trees to grow in middle Georgia clay to demonstrating to my daughter that all men aren't dogs, the way she proclaimed over and over to her own daughter.

I saw the tiny black patent-leather tap shoes that he took himself to the shoe shop on Broadway when Sandra was five to have taps put on them for her dancing lessons. Then I saw him proudly sitting up in the audience, his face still covered with sprinkles of white paint from a job he had just rushed through, watching Sandra perform her little "shuffle-stamp" as if she were Judith Jamison.

I also could see myself being so hard on him. All of a sudden I winced, because I saw myself being a bit put off with him the night of that recital because he didn't take the time to run by the house and clean up before coming. I didn't mean to, I didn't mean to be so hard on him. I guess I did it without knowing.

Then, in a flash, I saw Sandra running around her first apartment wearing only a black half-slip and a strapless bra, screaming and ranting and raving about some "dog" who had just had the nerve to come pick her up for a date late and not "properly dressed" for the occasion.

Oh, God, I thought, did I have something to do with that?

Just then I felt Miss Moses's leathery old hand slip over mine on the console between us and give me a tiny strong squeeze.

"How could I have been so strict and hard on the man, Miss Moses?" I asked. I knew she knew who I was talking about.

"You were doing the best you could," she said supportively.

"It wasn't good enough" was all I could say.

We sat there in silence for a while. Then Miss Moses had a suggestion.

"If you don't think you can look him in the face, maybe you could write him a letter. Folks don't write nearly enough letters anymore. Before I was married for that brief time, I corresponded by mail with my husband for three years before we even spent the evening together. Or if your Charles got one of those machines on his telephones, you could call him when you know he's not there and talk as long as you want."

Then she paused and said, "Think about it, Lily."

When she called me by my given name, it went right through me. Right then I knew that Miss Moses wasn't of this world. That she was inside my head as well as sitting on the seat next to me in the Explorer, because that's just what I was thinking of doing.

After driving around Mulberry for nearly six hours in the dark of night—well, it wasn't night, it was after five or so in the morning by then, but it was still dark. Anyway, as I had driven around town—past The Club, past Mount Calvary Church of God, past the big fountain in the park, past the Dairy Queen (now the kids call it "DQ"), back and forth over the Ocawatchee River—with that lovely old woman looking for LaShawndra, I had suspected there was something strange about my riding partner.

I guess I was growing too tired to pretend I didn't notice what I had noticed.

Then Miss Moses said something that made me pull the car over to the shoulder of the road right where we were on the west side of the river.

"Um, it's gon' be light soon," she said, looking off into the east. "I'm going to have to get out of here soon."

I put the Explorer into park and took a deep breath. Shoot, we had been riding around together for what seemed like an eternity, and I just went ahead and asked her. With my gaze straight ahead, looking out the windshield, I asked, "Miss Moses, you can see, can't you?"

When all I got was silence, I steeled myself and slowly turned to look at her.

She was glowing!

I don't mean her face was luminous and beautiful. I mean she was *glowing*! Like a glow-in-the-dark Frisbee that LaShawndra had left in the bottom of her closet when she moved out. Rays of light were just shooting from that old lady's face and body.

I must have let out a little cry, because Miss Moses reached over and put her old, wrinkled, incandescent brown hand on mine and squeezed it. At that moment I felt a flood of power, a virtual out-pouring of Spirit surge through me from that hand.

I don't know how else to explain it, but when I felt that hand on mine, I knew it wasn't the touch of anything from this world. It went all through me like a bolt of electricity and left me shaking in ecstasy.

Tina McElroy Ansa

I knew right then that she wasn't blind, that she wasn't just an old woman who had wandered off from her nursing home in the middle of the night, that it wasn't just lucky guesses when it seemed she had read my mind.

I knew from the touch of her hand for sure that she wasn't any of those things. She was a spirit.

"Miss Moses!" I exclaimed. "You *are* dead!"

And my exclamation just *resounded* in that car like the chimes of Mount Calvary Church.

Miss Moses took off her Ray-Ban sunglasses—true light was shining from her eyes, too—looked at me, and slowly nodded.

After that there was no further need for pretense.

Shoot, I knew then that she was a spirit and that I better use her while I had her. I mean, she was just a little wisp of a thing to begin with. Her aspect kept reminding me that she was not going to be around much longer. She seemed to be evaporating with the coming day.

I fired every question I could think of at her:

"Do you know exactly where LaShawndra is? What kind of trouble is my granddaughter in? Can I stop it? Can I save her? Where should we go next? Is LaShawndra still in town? Is she on her way to Freaknik?"

If I had not been so worried about LaShawndra, I would have taken the opportunity to ask Miss Moses a few questions about myself. Such as, Should I give Charles another chance? Will the third time be the charm for him and me? Should I move to the Georgia coast? What would happen to Sandra and LaShawndra if I moved away from Mulberry? Had I done the best I could with my children?

But I know it's not just a song kids sing at graduation exercises. The children *are* our future. So I stuck to queries about my granddaughter.

It didn't matter anyway. Miss Moses didn't reply to a single one of my questions.

"Miss Moses," I implored, "give me a word, give me a word. I need a word!"

All she said was "Don't worry, God gon' take care a' Crystal."

And that was it. That's all she said.

"Crystal?! LaShawndra's friend, Crystal?!" I exclaimed. " 'God gon' take care a' Crystal'?! Crystal is fine! *Crystal* is just fine! Crystal's got a home. Crystal's got a good job. Crystal's got two children. Crystal's got some *sense*! It's my little LaShawndra *I'm* worried about!"

But Miss Moses clamped her lips shut and didn't say another mumbling word. She just sat there looking at me with a small half-comforting smile, still glowing, as if she had helped me out.

I never thought I'd live to see the day when I felt that an unmarried mother of two—still practically a child herself—would be doing better than my own granddaughter.

Lord! If my little LaShawndra were anywhere, *anywhere*, as responsible and levelheaded as her friend Crystal, I'd be so happy I'd get down on my knees and paw the ground. I would!

I was just worn out. I guess I had finally gotten to the point that we all come to eventually. I just gave out and surrendered.

"Surrender is always the answer, ain't it, sugar?" Miss Moses said quietly.

I just nodded. I was too worn out to do anything else.

"You may be shocked to know it," she continued, "but when I was 'live, I wasn't a praying woman. I wasn't even a believing woman."

She said it just as naturally, "When I was 'live . . ." And I accepted it just as naturally.

"Oh, I believed in what I could do and I believed in what human flesh and blood could do when we put our mind to it. I believed everybody should try to be a good person and do what they could for each other. But after my husband took sick and died so young before we even had any time together, I just lost belief in God and Spirit and your spirit going somewhere after you're dead. Shoot! I used to just chuckle under my breath at that."

"That *is* hard to believe," I said. And I meant it. Miss Moses seemed like the epitome of belief to me. Why, she had helped *me* to believe that all was not lost with LaShawndra and even Charles, with just her quiet, nonjudgmental presence.

"I'm glad I could help you," she said. "I guess that's what I'm here for."

I was amazed. "You didn't know why you were back here in Mulberry?"

Miss Moses was amused. "Naw, sugar." She chuckled. "One minute I was on the other side enjoying myself, walking through endless garden paths, visiting with folks I hadn't seen in decades, and the next minute I was standing down there on the corner of Broadway and Cherry."

Then she sort of shook her head and chuckled again before settling back into silence. "I guess if God wasn't so merciful, I woulda been in west hell with my back broke."

"Just for not believing?" I asked. I was incredulous.

"Well, sugar, if you don't believe, then what's the point?"

It was about quarter to six and not completely light yet, but I could see the eastern horizon over the river growing the rosy hue of a springtime dawn.

"You can't do *everything*, can you?" Miss Moses asked. Her glow was beginning to fade.

"But if I'm not there for the child, what in the world is going to happen to her?" I asked. I was sincere.

"Maybe your job is just to be there, live your life, and have faith. Don't you read your Bible?" she asked, a smile playing around her wrinkled lips.

"Of course I do!" I said.

"Well, then, you ought to know: Faith moves mountains," she replied.

I just sat there beside her, stunned, speechless, because she was right. I was so full of fear for LaShawndra right then that I couldn't think at all, let alone think straight. I realized then that I had been frightened for her all her life. That when I wasn't out dragging the streets at night looking to bring her to safety, I was calling around Mulberry asking had anybody seen her. And when I wasn't doing that, I was lying in bed reading or going out to some meeting or preparing for some trip with my old college chums worrying about her.

Then Miss Moses asked, almost irritated, "Child, where *is* your courage? Where *is* your faith?"

And I burst out crying in earnest right then. It felt good to cry, really to weep, not just a few tears rolling down my cheeks the way I had back at the schoolyard but real tears like I had cried when Charles moved away the first time. I had lain awake alone in our bed night after night trying to remind myself why I felt it was best for him to go. I wept the way I had the time I had to comfort LaShawndra when she was nine and had run away from home and shown up on my doorstep with huge tears streaming down her pretty face, sobbing, "Mama Mama, Sandra, she so mean to me. Why don't my daddy want me?"

I had been trying more or less to hold it in since midnight. After I turned it loose, the tears flowed like the Ocawatchee River during Cleer Flo'. Big old *cleansing* tears and deep moaning that left me panting and gasping for breath.

I cried and screamed in that car like a madwoman, like a drunk woman. I called on the name of Jesus over and over, until I was almost hoarse. I wasn't ashamed. I wasn't abashed. I beat the steering wheel and banged my head on the padded center until I was playing a dirge with the horn.

My pitiful sobs and cries filled that Explorer and seemed to threaten to crack open the windows.

When they began to slacken up like at the end of a good hard summer rainstorm, I found my voice again and answered Miss Moses's question.

"My faith is in God," I said.

"Well, then," Miss Moses said.

I couldn't say a word. Then Miss Moses spoke again, softer, so as not to bruise me with her words.

"Maybe, if you put your faith into action and really believe, then you can have a little more space in your heart for other people."

You know, I immediately thought about Charles up there in Atlanta in his house still loving me, still wanting me, still hoping that I wouldn't be so rigid and unforgiving down here in Mulberry in my house.

And there wasn't anything else for me to say.

"Why don't you pull into this gas station and use their bathroom to wash your face?" Miss Moses suggested. But it was more like an order. I obeyed her. When we had parked in the light in front of the cashier's booth, I gave her one last, long look. She held out her hand for me to squeeze it.

I took it and squeezed it for all I was worth, trying to memorize exactly how it felt: the warmth of her blood, the creases in her palm, the wrinkles over her knuckles, the bones in the fingers, the raised veins on the top of her hand. Then I obeyed Miss Moses again and got out of the car.

As I walked away, I longed to turn and get one more look at my old ghost guide, but I did not dare. I felt I had to just keep my eyes on the path in front of me and walk the walk God had laid out for me.

When I returned, Miss Moses was gone—bags, umbrella, extra sweater, and all. Gone!

If it had not been for the scent of lavender still wafting inside my car and clinging to my sweater and slacks, even to my skin, and to the gold chenille throw folded neatly across the front seat, I would not have trusted my own memory.

I knew that the "girl" in trouble over in Pleasant Hill wasn't just me. And it wasn't just LaShawndra. It was all of us little big-eyed girls who were doing too much or not doing enough or not believing we could do anything.

And it was going to take a great deal of faith and courage to pull us all through. But from that point on I believed we would make it. I knew that was my job: to believe.

So that's why by 6:00 A.M., when I pulled back into my garage at 991 Oglethorpe Street, the passenger seat quite empty, I didn't feel quite so hopeless about my family: Charles, Sandra, and her baby girl, LaShawndra.

And that hope gave me a little strength.

As my mama used to say at the end of a rough day, "I'm kicking, but I ain't kicking high."

I was glad at that point to be kicking at all.

In retrospect, I realized I had known that Miss Moses was a ghost from the moment she got in the car. I knew it was her wrinkled old hand that had shaken me awake six hours before. And I welcomed that. I did. Because I knew that my little big-eyed girl and her little big-eyed girl were going to need something more than the physical world to get them through the next few hours. I guess I had taken them as far as I could and had to let each of them go on to the next step.

All I could do then was pray for LaShawndra. I gave her to the angels. I thought about Miss Moses and how she said she never was a praying woman on this earth. And I gave thanks that *she* was now in the hands of the Lord. I gave LaShawndra to Miss Moses. LaShawndra was in the hands of the Lord, too. And that realization made me feel better right there.

I went inside my home, dropped the keys on the marble-topped table by the door, and kicked off my damp, muddy moccasins.

The last thing I did before I went into the kitchen to make myself a cup of peppermint-green tea was pick up the phone in the hall and call Charles.

part 2. H O P E

Sandra Pines

8

Nurse Bloom seemed to appear right out of thin air. One minute she wasn't there. Then, the next, she stood in the foyer of Candace Realty Company like some solid angel of vengeance, all clothed in white.

She wore a severely starched, shiny white nurse's uniform with a short navy blue cape over her shoulders. Each tip of the cape was carefully flung back to expose the white satin lining. Her muscular, slightly bowed legs—the legs of a much younger woman—were tinted white by the silk nurse's stockings that had the nerve to have a seam up the back. And she was wearing sturdy white leather nurse's oxfords. On her head—she had a good-size head—atop coarse, steel gray hair pulled back in a low bun, perched a stiff, immaculate nurse's cap. Over her right arm hung a solid rectangular navy blue leather purse. It could have been new or seventy-five years old. It looked like Nurse Bloom—timeless.

"I'm Nurse Joanna Bloom," she announced—as if she could have been anybody else. The sound of her voice echoed off the back wall of the reception center of Candace Realty and boomed up the atrium. It was barely half past six o'clock in the morning, and I was the only one in the office that early. So her voice really rang out in the silence.

I was so taken by my new client's mien and her sudden appearance outside my inner-office door—I was almost certain that I had locked the front entrance to the building when I came in—that as I went gliding over to greet her—just the way we had all seen the founder of our realty company, Lena McPherson, do right before she closed some lucrative deal around Mulberry, her arms extended in two soft

Ls. Just as I reached Nurse Bloom—this woman all clad in white—I tripped over a crack in the Spanish brick entranceway and fell full-faced against the woman's chest, sending the papers I held flying through the air like huge snowflakes and spilling half my latte down the front of her pristine uniform.

She screamed like a banshee, and I screamed, too.

After I gained my footing, I just stood there as if I were viewing a movie of two other women—one stern, sturdy, and heavyset, the other (that's me) petite, still cute, and usually a hell of a lot more graceful. I stood there and watched the wet beige stain from the cup of mocha latte in my hand spread all over that poor woman's white nurse's uniform.

I hate for things like that to happen, because even though this one was an innocent mishap, they can ruin your reputation in the realty business. And you know I have a *good* reputation. Until recently, good reputations ran in the Pines family.

Nurse Bloom just looked at me the way my mother's friends some-times would when they saw me on the streets of Mulberry right after I got caught pregnant with LaShawndra. You could tell they were summoning up all their Christian charity and acceptance just not to be angry with me.

But they had been disappointed. I'm sure that little period of dis-approval damaged me in some way forever. It didn't last long, but I was so used to being doted on, being Lily Paine Pines's daughter and all. I'm sure it marred my personality somehow.

"I can't believe I spilled the whole cup of coffee down the front of your immaculate uniform" was all I could say.

Nurse Bloom still did not say anything. She just looked down the front of her uniform, then looked up at me.

"Oh, I don't know *what* is wrong with me this morning!" I exclaimed as I guided her through the offices' foyer, past an original collage by Varnette P. Honeywood—one of my colleagues at the agency went to Spelman with her—and the wildly colored drawings of some local grade-school children Lena had put up.

Nurse Bloom just made sounds like "Um" and "Um-huh." I think she even said "Yeah, right" one time.

"Oh, please forgive me," I implored her. What could I do? I had to say something. I can't stand for anyone to be angry with me. "Of course, I'll have it cleaned for you. As a matter of fact, if you like, I can run it over to the one-hour cleaners this minute and have it cleaned right up for you."

Of course, I knew the cleaners wouldn't be open at that early hour, but I had to say something to try and fix the mess I had made.

Oh, I rushed and fawned and apologized something awful and escorted her into my office—it's on the entrance level—and sat her on my big, soft, soft, pink-flowered tapestry sofa there. I have two Queen Anne chairs upholstered in mauve antique velvet in my office, too, as well as the matching chair I use at my desk, another antique piece. But I sat Nurse Bloom on the comfortable sofa. I probably have the most beautifully decorated office down at Candace. I should have. I paid a decorator from Atlanta enough to do it.

I expected her to smell a bit antiseptic—like a hospital ward—even though she was retired. But she just smelled clean. Like soap and water. Like freshly washed laundry hanging on a clothesline.

As soon as she was settled, I apologized again and rushed into my small bathroom to get a wet towel. I have one of the few offices there at Candace Realty with a private bath. But by the time I got back, the creamy brown coffee stain had disappeared. Completely! I just breathed a sigh of relief, put the damp rose-colored hand towel back on a rack in the bathroom, returned to my sofa, and sat down beside her.

"Well, Miss Pines," she said all businesslike. "I don't have all day."

"Please, call me Sandy," I said, trying to get the situation back on a cordial footing.

Well, my given name is Sandra. But I go by Sandy. It's more like my personality. I've always thought of myself as a Sandy instead of a Sandra. And my middle name, Afeni—a holdover from my mother's black-nationalist days—is so not me.

But I've always felt that I have been mislabeled, misunderstood in a way.

And anyway Sandy sounds younger than Sandra to me. At my age—I was moving much too quickly for me toward the "Big 4-0"— I'm always looking for youth-makers.

I don't usually share my personal business with business clients, but since I had made such a faux pas with the coffee, I felt she deserved some kind of explanation.

"Oh, I'm so sorry about my little accident," I offered. "*Que je suis bête*. I don't know where my mind is this morning."

"I *thought* it woulda been on our appointment," she said grandly and pointedly.

It was on the tip of my tongue to say, "Well, actually, you didn't *have* an *appointment*, Your Royal Highness." But I bit the sarcasm back and said instead, "Oh, of course, it is. It's just a family matter that's on my mind. It's my . . . my . . . my daughter." I just said it automatically, just pulled it out of the air. I didn't even think. I guess I was recalling Mother's earlier phone call trying to track her down. My mother says I'm always blaming LaShawndra for everything. But it is convenient, because I'm not usually lying when I blame her. She's always causing some kind of trouble. She's done that since the day she was born.

"My daughter is always the source of some consternation for me," I explained. At the time I didn't have any idea how true that really was. I thought the family angle would help me connect with Nurse Bloom. You know, woman to woman. "You know how family is," I said lightly.

Nurse Bloom replied, "Not really. I never truly had a family. Didn't have no husband. Didn't have no children."

Well, that just threw ice water on my little attempt to be nice and try to explain my clumsiness. But I forged on. I'm not Mrs. Lily Paine Pines's child for nothing.

"I just wanted you to know it wasn't because I didn't value your business or think that this appointment with you today did not deserve my full and focused attention. I promise you I am here for you."

She said nothing. Just left me hanging.

"Nurse Bloom," I continued, trying to soften her up, "you come so highly recommended—and by my mother, too."

I didn't know all the particulars about Nurse Bloom and her credentials, but I knew she was important enough for my mother to rouse me before daylight to come see about her. Still, I was a little discombobulated by the early "up and at 'em."

As if to remind me how early it was, my stomach let out a loud rumble that sounded deafening in the quiet of the empty office.

"Excuse me," I said pleasantly. "That's my stomach growling." I hadn't had time for any breakfast that morning. Just the cup of latte I had picked up at a convenience store that I had dumped on Nurse Bloom's chest. As it had spread out over her bosom, I had noted that she had what my mother called "a generous front porch."

Mother had called and awakened me that morning at six o'clock—it was still dark—to tell me about Nurse Bloom and her "appointment" with me. Well, she didn't really have an official appointment. Just a sudden early-morning phone call and my mother's expectation that I would simply clear my calendar for this "Nurse Bloom—trailblazing health professional, a legendary middle Georgia midwife, a highly esteemed personage in our African-American community," Mother said. As a matter of fact, I had never even heard of a "Nurse Bloom" before Mother's call. And besides the suddenness of it all, Mother had sounded so funny that morning.

I always have my answering machine on so I don't have to talk to just *anybody*. I can't believe that people used to let just *anybody* who had your phone number and a quarter come into your home whenever they felt like it. I tell you, I *live* by my answering machine.

Besides, I get a lot of hang-ups. I think my daughter, LaShawndra, gives out my number and my mother's number as well as her own to just any little Negro she meets on the street. So I have to keep my machine on to screen my calls.

Mother is always up before the crack of dawn getting her day started, but that morning she sounded so strange, otherworldly almost, her voice kind of singsong on the answering-machine tape. At first I thought I was still dreaming. I have always had the strangest dreams. Mother has told me all my life that I wouldn't make any mistakes if I'd just pay attention to my dreams. The old lady who lived next door to Mother when I was a child used to ask me regularly what I had dreamed about, so she could consult her dream book.

Miss Eliza Jane—that was her name—would catch me on the way to school in the morning. She'd be dressed in a fancy peignoir. From her porch to mine she would yell, "Sandra?" with a question in her voice. And I knew what she'd want and just yell back, "A horse!" or "A big old oak tree!" or "My pastor at church!" And she'd smile and wave and go on back in her house reading her little dream book with the stars and moon on it.

But that morning I wasn't dreaming. Mother didn't even give me time to get to the phone.

"Sandra, get up!" Mother had said as soon as my greeting ended. "Go down to Candace now!"

She explained that this Nurse Bloom wanted to buy some property. "She's on her way down there now. Hurry up!"

Then she hung up.

It was the second time Mother had called me within six hours. I hadn't talked with her either call. Both times she just left a message.

On her earlier message, at about midnight, Mother said she was worried because she didn't know where LaShawndra was. She had made it seem that my daughter was "missing," as if we don't know where LaShawndra made her last step many a night.

I barely opened my eyes at Mother's midnight call, but after the second call I hurried on down to the Candace offices, because when Mrs. Lily Paine Pines commands, everybody listens.

Well, almost everybody. My daughter, LaShawndra, never did. But she doesn't listen to *anybody*. That's her problem.

No matter what I said, LaShawndra insists on calling my mother "Mama Mama"—some silliness she made up when she was a baby— instead of "Grandmother" the way I wanted her to. I told her and *told her* how lovely and genteel it sounded—"Grandmother"—but do you think that little coochie listened to me, her own mother? Of course not!

Uh, "Mama Mama." Uh, I can't stand to hear her say it. It sounds so low-class and ghettoish. And I must tell you, even though she may have had a single mother, that is not how LaShawndra was raised.

LaShawndra has always gotten the best of everything: literature, music, home life, clothes, education, exposure to the finer things in life. You wouldn't know it by looking at her. All LaShawndra wants to be is a little coochie.

It's like her name, I guess. She's just acting like her name. It sounds like the name of one of those girls over in Vietnam Alley.

Why I named that child LaShawndra I will never know.

I swear! I do not know what *possessed me* to do such a thing. And of course she loves her little name. She wouldn't take a million dollars for it.

Well, part of the reason I named her that was in honor of her father, LaShawn. An honor he neither appreciated nor deserved. My girlfriends Lynda and Myra were the ones who put the idea into my head of naming my baby LaShawndra. They were practically *daring* me to do it, *egging* me on with it. We were all just teenagers. They thought—well, we all thought—that with his name attached to her, there wasn't any way LaShawn wouldn't straighten up and take on his responsibility, so he and I could get married and move on with our lives just the way I had always imagined it. Me and LaShawn and our baby in a nice new house out in Sherwood Forest subdivision with a family room and a pink nursery and a patio and swing set in the backyard. He would work, and I'd finish college. Then I would work as a French teacher at the high school, and he would finish college.

I had it all planned in my head, right down to the color of the taupe drapes and off-white sheers in the living room and the French-style furniture in the master bedroom.

I just *knew* if I named his baby LaShawndra, he would always know she was half his and half mine. And he would watch over her and take care of her and make over her and cherish her the way my father did with me.

But it didn't turn out like that. Not at all.

And, in retrospect, all it ever accomplished was to *piss me off* every time I called her name.

Truly, to this day, every time I say "LaShawndra," it's like a dagger in my heart.

I see that high-yellow Negro who was her father looking at me all big with his child as if we *both* were mistakes. Not just LaShawndra a mistake, but me, too!

I haven't even seen LaShawn Johnson more than three times since LaShawndra was born. And one of those times was not even at her birth. I had to go through that all by myself—well, except for Mother. He didn't even show up at the hospital. It almost broke my heart.

What am I talking about? It *did* break my heart.

And over the years, he hasn't called more than ten times altogether to talk with LaShawndra. That's in nineteen years! Once or twice he's sent some little useless, inappropriate gift around her birthday, like a reading lamp or a purse shaped like a panda bear when she's a teenager. Now what can she do with a toy bag at her age? It just goes to show you he doesn't even see her as a real person.

Now, with Nurse Bloom sitting there with her purse in her lap glowering at me, I felt I had to do something quickly to get the situation back on an even, pleasant keel. Sometimes you have to be kind of insincere to be a good businesswoman.

You know what they say: Sincerity is everything, and if you can fake that, you got it made.

I put a smile on my face and pointed out my Candace's bestselling record award for the year right there on the wall between the office door and my Monet print. They keep it up all month; then you get to take it home. I've got a few of them already, but I haven't found the exact right place for them in my condo yet. So they're stacked up on the kitchen counter under a pile of mail. I *must* get around to hanging them up sometime soon.

Nurse Bloom did not seem very impressed.

"When I was in the working world, a person's honest full day's work was reward enough," she said shortly.

I thought, Well, excuse the hell out of me for achieving.

But then, Nurse Bloom knew my mother, and that's what comes of being born to an achieving woman like my mother: Whatever you do is no big deal. So much is expected of you—with no appreciation or reward, because your mother already has such a spectacular record of achievement.

My mother and her friends are that kind of women. They always seem to do things so effortlessly, that the same is expected of me and my peers.

I'm less than twenty years younger than my mother, and I *know* for a fact that I will never be the extraordinary woman she is. Shit. I don't even want to be.

Oops, that slipped out. We have a "curse jar" at work that is just full of five-dollar bills that came from my purse. I put enough in there each month to pay the tab for our entire monthly office luncheon—bar bill included.

But I'm good about it. I *never* curse in front of clients.

It is the truth, though, about those overachieving older black women. Personally, I don't have the energy. I don't have the time. And I don't have the inclination to be one of those can-do-it-all black women like my mother. They just don't make 'em like that anymore ... thank God! Because I don't want the job. "If called, I will not run. If elected, I will not serve."

And with all that Mother does in a day, she has the nerve to find time to walk forty-five minutes almost every evening and not even look her age with her strong legs and her tight butt. That's what I mean: Mother and women of that generation make it look effortless.

Well, I may not be my mother, but Nurse Bloom was not going to get the better of me. I forged on.

"My mother said you were looking to purchase some property," I said, trying to bring the discussion back to my business.

"Well, I want to *look* at some property," Nurse Bloom corrected me. "If I see something I *like,* then we can talk about purchasing."

I could see that this was going to be a long morning.

"Maybe you can tell me what *types* of properties you're interested in," I said, trying to nudge her along.

"All kinds," she said.

"Well, are you looking for a residence?" I asked.

Nurse Bloom just nodded. But the whole time she had the nerve to be sizing me up. I could tell. She was really *checking me out,* looking me up and down. Openly appraising me.

I felt I looked presentable enough, even though I was not quite as together as I usually am in my personal appearance. It's not as if I'm like LaShawndra, my daughter, who thinks the only thing that matters in life is her looks. But I know that a pulled-together appearance is important in the business world. I feared I may have looked as if I had dressed hurriedly in the dark.

Actually, I just about had. I had rushed my toilette that morning. I hadn't taken the time to put any hot curlers in my short, straight hair. I just ran a wet comb and some gel through it and slicked it back

behind my ears. But it looks nice that way. And I had on my good
pearl earrings on tiny gold hoops.

I had highlighted my cheeks and put on some mascara, but I hadn't
taken the time to use the eyelash curler first the way I usually did.

The azure-and-black Versace scarf was definitely not the best
choice for the gray St. John knit. But it wasn't exactly a fashion faux
pas. If I had taken my usual leisurely hour to dress, I probably would
have decided to wear a nice crisp white shirt under a lightweight pin-
stripe wool suit and forgone the scarf. Then Nurse Bloom would not
have been shooting disapproving glances down my cleavage. I used to
have nice firm breasts before I got pregnant with LaShawndra. Each
one just big enough for a man to get his hand around. And even now
with a good Wonderbra, they were still an asset.

And I usually dressed in a way that accented my best features. At
Candace, our credo is: "We got on different colors, but we all look
good." And we take that motto seriously. But you have to understand,
I was not used to being roused from my sleep to go to work before
daylight like a farm wife.

"I lived my whole life out in the country," Nurse Bloom said. She
paused, then added, "On a farm."

That kind of unnerved me.

I straightened the jacket on my shoulders, lifting the neckline a
bit, put a smile on my lips, and reached for my personal Realtor's
guide on the glass-topped desk.

"I don't want to see any pictures," she informed me. "I could look
at pictures on my own. I want to see the real thing."

That threw me a bit, because I had laid out a nice presentation in
my head that relied heavily on the photographs in my book.

"Well, Nurse Bloom, if we sit here for just a little while and—"

"I got all the time in the world," Nurse Bloom replied, cutting me
off. "And you got until noon. I have somewhere else to be at noon.
That's almost six hours."

I didn't say anything, because I was trying to think of some way to

You Know Better

get out of all that driving around that Nurse Bloom's "plan" entailed.

"Bet you ain't got nothing in that book on Greenwood Bottom. And that's one of the areas I'm interested in."

"Greenwood Bottom? Greenwood Bottom?" I repeated dumbly. This woman was making me sound so stupid. "I don't think there is a section in Mulberry called 'Greenwood Bottom,' Nurse Bloom. It does seem, though, that I *have* read that name in a local history book."

"I see I'mo have to direct this little excursion," Nurse Bloom said with a sigh of exasperation, as she stood, gathered her cape around her, and hung her blue leather purse on her right arm, clamped across the front of her waist.

Just what I need, I thought, another one of those big bossy black women like Mother's friends to tell me what I'm doing wrong.

I forced a smile and picked up my black leather day planner, the Realty book, my croc envelope purse, and my keys. When I escorted Nurse Bloom out the front entrance of the Candace Realty building, it wasn't even 7:00 A.M. yet.

9.

I had to walk fast just to keep up with Nurse Bloom.

I locked up the front entrance of Candace Realty, and we headed for my Mercedes. I really don't care that much about cars. But for my business, so much of which is conducted on the move, I've found that customers want to be comfortable. That's why I have the Mercedes. Not for status like LaShawndra accused me, but for my work.

My dark blue Mercedes coupe was the only car in the Candace parking lot. Not that I had thought Nurse Bloom had driven herself downtown. But I did wonder how she had gotten there. However, I didn't ask. I could see that she was not one for a lot of unnecessary small talk or for a lot of questions.

Which was a shame, because I'm very good at both of those things.

So I simply assumed that relatives had dropped her off. Probably just to get rid of her officious ass for a while, even if it was six o'clock in the morning. I didn't blame them one bit.

I was going to offer Nurse Bloom a hand getting into my car as soon as I unlocked it, but she didn't give me a chance. She swung the door open with surprising strength and gusto and plopped down in the passenger's seat with a solid-sounding clap. By the time I had barely scrambled into the driver's seat, she had fastened her seat belt and was sitting there with her hands folded on top of her blue leather handbag that was resting in her lap like extra ammunition.

The day was already getting warm, so I turned on the air and adjusted the vents so it would not blow directly on her. She didn't seem to notice, let alone appreciate my thoughtfulness. She stared straight ahead.

When I accidentally bumped her with the black leather daily

planner I had placed on the seat between us, I quickly explained that I had no intention of showing her any pictures of properties. I did, however, have a plan.

But she seemed to have her own plan.

First thing, Nurse Bloom wanted me to "turn off that incessant music. It's getting on my nerves!" she said.

That really surprised me, because most of my clients don't even notice the soothing sound. You can barely hear it, I have it turned so low. I'd heard about the mildly subliminal tactic in a symposium at a Realtors' convention in Las Vegas a couple of years before. And I think it certainly puts clients in a receptive frame of mind. Nature sounds as well as gentle music.

Nurse Bloom was the first person who'd actually heard it.

"Turn it off!" she barked a second time.

I clicked the music off.

The second thing Nurse Bloom wanted to do was drive past old St. Luke's Hospital and look at some residential properties near there.

Now, that old all-black private hospital has not existed since before LaShawndra was born. And that was quite a few years ago. The city tore down the building to make way for a leg of the new expressway that came through town back in the seventies. But then they decided to go another way, and the lot still sat empty.

Personally, I thought the plans for "A New Mulberry," as the project was called, was a terrific idea. But so many people were up in arms about destroying the old white wooden building that housed the hospital—my mother included. She had been born there and so had I. So it really meant something to Mother. Apparently it did to Nurse Bloom, too.

"You know, that hospital isn't there anymore," I informed Nurse Bloom in my gentlest, most inoffensive voice.

"Don't you think I know that?" she snapped. "I just want to drive past the lot where the hospital *was*. Is that okay with you?"

I bit my lip and said, "Of course."

As we drove through Mulberry, past the beautiful old Parkinson's
Funeral Home building, past the nineteenth-century white stone
facade of the town's first library, past the corner bakery that still
baked yeast rolls and real petits fours, I had to give myself a serious
lecture.

I said over and over to myself, She's a client. She's a client. She's a
client. She's a client.

Then I had to make myself slow down and not run every yellow
light I came to. I certainly did not feel like getting a lecture, one from
Nurse Bloom, on safe driving.

I'm not what you would call a sentimental person, but I can get
almost misty driving through Mulberry sometimes. The town is more
than just property to me as a Realtor. And it's more than my hometown. Not to sound too grand—LaShawndra calls me "Grande Dame
Drama Mama" behind my back. And I know she and Mother must
have come up with that, because LaShawndra has no idea what a
grande dame is, let alone how to use it in an insult. But anyway, not to
sound too grand, I think of Mulberry as the scenery for my life story.

Many times in scouting new property or driving around clients
from up north heading back to their ancestors' homeland, I'd be
tempted to point to the parking lot of the old post office and say,
"That's where I fell when I was nine and learning to skate." Or, outside the army-navy store, "That's where my daddy took me when I
was getting ready for college to help me pick out a genuine pea
jacket." Or, across from the Mulberry Square Park, "That's where I
ruined my life making out with that long tall yellow Negro in the
backseat of his black GTO."

As we came up on the empty site of the hospital, I could hear
Nurse Bloom quieting down. Not that she had said anything much
since insisting that we drive by St. Luke's other than to derisively pick
my purse up off the seat next to her with two fingers and demand,
"Tell me, just how much did you pay for this here bag?" And before I
could tell her how much I had shelled out for the beautiful bag I had

You Know Better

bought at Neiman's in Atlanta to celebrate the closing of an impressive deal, she added, "Ain't it against the law to make things out that animal skin?"

I had just shrugged my shoulder, swallowed my indignation, and kept driving.

But as we neared the street where the old hospital had stood, it was as if her soul were resting. Despite her sharp, rude manner toward me, I felt *my* soul seeming to settle down, too. I could sense that this place had really stirred her.

"Can we pull up over here?" she asked. It was the first time she had sounded human and vulnerable since I met her.

"Of course," I said, and slipped into a space in front of the empty site.

I bet we sat there in silence for ten minutes before either of us moved. I tried not to look at my Rolex, but I couldn't stand it. I hate to waste time. So after a while I sneaked a glance as I pretended to smooth down my hair.

Nurse Bloom just sat there looking at the empty lot with what seemed for a moment like tears welling up in her eyes. I felt the way I did when I sat next to Pastor—that's the man I'm dating. He's the pastor of Mount Calvary Church of God—in his car when we went on drives out in the country to relax after last services and he would get soooo quiet I didn't dare interrupt. I knew he was meditating, and I wanted him to think I was, too.

Nurse Bloom and I sat there in silence for almost another ten minutes. Then she spoke.

"I bet I helped to deliver hundreds of babies on that very spot," she said, pointing with her wrinkled index finger to the empty lot. "I even helped to deliver your mother. Did she tell you that?"

"No, she didn't," I said, beginning to see some reason for Mother's making me take Nurse Bloom on as a client with no notice.

"Don't look like it," she continued, "but at one time half the life in this here town began right there. And when I was a midwife in the country outside Mulberry, I bet I delivered almost that many by myself without no doctor. All those lives. And I was part of it.

"Tell me about your daughter's birth," she said softly.

"LaShawndra?" I asked.

"You got another daughter?" she asked, sounding again like the Nurse Bloom I was getting used to.

You know, LaShawndra's birth was the last thing I wanted to talk about. It still makes me depressed just to think about it.

I sure thought about an abortion when my period was late. It was legal by that time. I talked to my best girlfriend about it, but I knew that my mother would find out. In Mulberry, Lily Paine Pines sees all and knows all. So I decided against it. I even thought of throwing myself off Mother's high front porch and rolling down the steep, inclined lawn to the street to induce a miscarriage, but I was afraid I wouldn't be able to stop at the bottom of the grass and hit my head on the cobblestone sidewalk and end up a vegetable. So I figured I'd try falling down the staircase in the house, where there was a soft carpet at the bottom. But I tumbled all the way to the foot without a change in my condition. Before I could think of anything else to do, the news was out—you know, back in my day, if you wore a raincoat to school just one day and it wasn't raining, then everybody knew you were trying to hide something. So what could I do?

"Oh, you know, Nurse Bloom, I don't like to talk about that," I said, thinking she might leave it alone. But she kept looking at me, waiting for me to continue. I could not *believe* how intimidating that old woman in white was.

"It was such a difficult birth that it still upsets me to think about it," I said. "All I remember is lots of blood and screaming and pain. They finally just knocked me out. I had to have a cesarean section to save LaShawndra's life and mine."

"I wish I coulda been there to help," Nurse Bloom said sadly and sincerely. "I could have at least slipped a knife under your bed to cut the pains."

"What a kind thing to say," I said. Despite myself, I was softening toward the old girl.

Then she brought me back to reality by adding, "Young girls having babies so early don't know *nothing!*"

But she was right. I didn't know anything about life or birth.

"Mother had given me all kinds of juices and concoctions during my pregnancy that she swore the old folks said would make natural birth easier. I don't even recall all the stuff she gave me. I remember the cranberry juice because I liked the tart taste of that. But just between you and me, I poured most of that other stuff down the bathtub drain when Mother wasn't looking. I didn't say anything to anyone but my best friend, Myra, but I never had any intentions of having a natural childbirth.

"Shoot, I figured. What for? As it turned out, LaShawndra's daddy didn't even show up for the delivery, so I didn't have a Lamaze partner or anything to prove. I was doing my part by just being there. Right?"

"Was there anything unusual about the birth?" Nurse Bloom persisted, no matter how upsetting I had tried to tell her the subject matter was for me.

"I don't know, Nurse Bloom. I was so glad that they finally gave me some drugs and stopped ordering me to push, that I just blocked anything else out of my memory."

Nurse Bloom did not reply. She just turned her gaze back to the hospital's empty lot. I was grateful she didn't press me any further.

I try not to think too much about my daughter LaShawndra's birth or about her in general, because all it does is upset me to no avail. I never could do anything with her because I had no experience with a fast, bad gal like her. I certainly wasn't like that.

LaShawndra's out of my house now that she thinks she's grown and everything. She never listened to anything I said anyway. She wouldn't even scrub her elbows when I told her they were getting rusty. And you know if LaShawndra doesn't care about anything else, she cares about her little looks. She's so vain. I don't know *who* she gets that from.

When I was a girl just starting to notice boys, all Mother had to do to get me to do something about my hygiene or looks was to say something like "No boy would want to kiss that nose." And right away I'd start taking greater care with my diet and grooming to get rid of the blackheads on my nose. Mother would know just the thing to say to nudge me in the right direction. I have to admit I never could bring myself to say anything cute like that to LaShawndra. And I don't think it would have done any good anyway.

You should see the kinds of messes she gets herself into now that she doesn't have any adult supervision.

The little girl she lives with—Crystal is her name, and she isn't that little either; I bet she wears a size fourteen or sixteen—isn't much older than LaShawndra. Probably named for some character on the soaps. She's got *two* children, no husband, and she can't be any older than twenty or twenty-one.

Oh, they're cute little things, the children are. But you can tell by looking at them that they have different daddies.

I only had the one child, LaShawndra. But I tell you, if I had had more than the one, they would not have been by a string of different men, the way young girls do now. The first baby daddy and the second baby daddy and even sometimes the third baby daddy.

God, I felt like my life had ended when I got pregnant out of wedlock that one time.

Sitting outside the site of the old black hospital so near the public park where LaShawn and I used to go to make out in the backseat of his black GTO made me think too deeply on the past. And I tried my best not to *ever* think about his yellow ass.

I tried never to say too much about it, but I do detest that man. He is such a *dog*!

I always prided myself on trying to keep LaShawndra shielded from so much in the world. Until she just got so wild and I couldn't do anything with her, we used to spend a lot of time together. I didn't like to be alone. I couldn't stand it—the silence and loneliness, the feeling that no one was ever going to care about me. I'd lug LaShawndra from room to room of our tiny first apartment as I heated up a frozen dinner or ironed a blouse on the bed or sat at the kitchen table and studied, just so I could hear some noise in the house, even if it was just her little-baby prattle.

And as she got older and started developing so early—she had breasts as big as mine when she was eleven—I made it a point to ensure that the men I did date were not casting an eye at my too-fast daughter. I can say with certainty that she's not a little coochie because of me. That's for sure!

The minister I'm dating now really is a fine man. He ain't no dog like so many men. Although Pastor doesn't take a drink every now and then or gamble like my father did, he still reminds me of my daddy. He's a few years older than I am. But I've always been the mature one in my group, even when I was a teenager, so I tend to gravitate toward older men.

The last man I had dated before Pastor was a good twenty years older than me. Franklin was his name. We got on okay. He had a good job and everything. But after about six months I found some of his dirty boxer shorts and shirts left in my clothes hamper like I was going to wash them or take them to the cleaners for him, and I told Franklin he had to take his old butt and his dirty underwear with their skid marks somewhere else.

And the guy before him was almost twenty years older than me, too. Now, he had a really good job with the state utilities company. Real good-looking, dark-skinned man with a little gray at the temples and a beautiful smile. But he was too happy-go-lucky for me. With him, everything was a joke. And he was from the North, Detroit originally, and he would say things like "You people down here must live behind the sun. You don't even use house numbers to give directions."

Then, the last time we went out, we were at dinner at this little French restaurant outside Mulberry on the way to Atlanta, and I was trying to tell him how LaShawn had disrespected me and deserted me with his child when I was only a child myself. He said, "Let it go, Sandy. You're nearly forty years old. What difference does it make now?"

"Nearly forty years old!" I couldn't *wait* to get home and sit by the phone with a glass of wine and watch the clock until I knew he was back in his own house so I could call his old ass and tell him not *ever* to call me again.

Come to think of it—and I rarely even think of the parade of men who've been through my life—there was this old aging thug I dated once who had made his money in the numbers when he was young and had bought up a bunch of real estate, rental property, with the proceeds.

He had had the nerve to say he saw where I could use some exercise to tighten up my butt a little. Then he had the nerve to point to the area with his bare foot. Lying on my bed in his underwear, pointing out my defects with his big old ashy foot. He didn't make it through the night. And come to think of it, he might have even been behind some very suspicious damage done to my car a few nights later.

But now Pastor. He's not old or vengeful at all. Not by any stretch of the imagination. He just turned forty and the sweetest-natured man you'd ever want to meet. And he's a well-built, dark-brown-skinned man, not thin and light-skinned and lanky like LaShawn Johnson. Of course, Pastor towers over me because I'm little, but he's about medium height, not six feet tall.

Although he's not old in years at all, he *is* old in wisdom. He's so wise. I've heard any number of his congregants say how Pastor is not surprised by *anything*! How they can tell him anything and know he won't be shocked and condemning.

From what I've seen of his ministry, he's as much of a counselor as he is a preacher. You would not believe the demands on his time. So I'm working on not being so upset when he doesn't call me all the time the way I'd like for him to. I'm working on that.

There *is* just something about a man of God that gets me hot. That personal relationship with a Supreme Being that most men don't open themselves up to fully. I mean, Pastor *talks* with God. He talks to Him as if God were sitting next to him on the other end of the sofa.

"Okay, Lord," he'll say sometimes as he flops down on the sofa in his office between Sunday morning and afternoon services, "we finished up that sermon. I thought it was pretty good. What did You think of it?"

Just that easily, he talks to God, has conversations with Him. And if I'm in there in his office or at the parsonage—a lovely old two-story bright redbrick house near the top of Pleasant Hill on Chestnut Street (I checked a comparable place out in my Realtor's guide, and with its big yard and apartment over the garage, it is probably worth a couple hundred thou on today's market)—helping out with some paperwork or pairing needy families with organizations, I'll tiptoe around, because I feel that silence is called for.

I find it very attractive, even sensual in a very spiritual kind of way, to be in the presence of a man not afraid to talk to God.

Thinking about Pastor made me remember that there was a lovely property on the market two houses down from the parsonage, not far from the hospital site where Nurse Bloom and I were sitting. Without asking for permission the way I felt Nurse Bloom expected, I just put the Mercedes in drive and pulled away from the curb.

"Nurse Bloom, I just now thought of a property not far from here that might appeal to you."

She kind of looked over her shoulder at the hospital site receding behind us. She looked so wistful as we turned the corner at Forsyth Street, I almost felt sorry for her until I remembered I might get a chance to see Pastor as we drove by his house on the way to this property.

Nurse Bloom didn't say anything to stop me, so I kept driving, making two right-hand turns—one at the old ice cream shop I used to go to as a child with Mother and Daddy after dinner and another at the tidy pink house where the crazy lady who wore pink all the time lived—and came up on Chestnut Street.

Chestnut Street is a lovely little cul-de-sac with tall crepe myrtle trees growing along its sidewalks. I pointed them out to Nurse Bloom as I slowly made the circle. They were just beginning to put out leaves, but I knew that the tight, lacy blooms would not be far behind. I notice things like that. That's why I make the big bucks. But my mind was really on Pastor's house. I just cut my eyes toward the parsonage as we drove past it, but I could have sworn that Nurse Bloom caught me looking and sort of snorted at me. I pretended not to have noticed and pointed out the generous-size side yards between the houses.

I didn't know how to reply when Nurse Bloom spoke up suddenly.

"Nice neighborhood," she commented in a sort of casual tone. Then she added pointedly, "I bet you wouldn't mind living on this street yourself."

Damn, it was like she was reading my mind.

And she was right. I sure wouldn't mind being a minister's wife, living on that shaded street in that old parsonage. Being called "First Lady." A First Lady in a nice-size church like Mount Calvary. "First Lady Sandra." Maybe "First Lady Sandy." I think it sounds nice. I can just see myself attending luncheons, going on retreats with Pastor, buying some tasteful new hats for Sunday services—I look good in hats—leading women's conferences at the church. I'm a good speaker. I got that from Mother.

Marriage hasn't come up yet in Pastor's and my discussions. But I assume that a man of God would not be dating if he didn't have matrimony on his mind.

Since I've never had a wedding ceremony, I'd truly love to have the whole thing: The ten bridesmaids in classic long beige satin slip dresses that they could wear later on and tell people, "Oh, this is my bridesmaid's dress from Sandy Pines's wedding to the pastor. Wasn't it generous of her not to put us all in some unflattering mint green or deadly mauve?" The cute little flower girls, maybe one light-skinned, one dark-skinned. The catered garden reception with streamers and a tent. The full orchestra. The white doves released at the end of the ceremony. The white wedding gown by Vera Wang. I know it's not really proper, but I still see myself in a long fitted white lace wedding gown like I imagined as a teenager when Mother and I would talk about my wedding as we went shopping out at Phipps Plaza in Atlanta.

Even though we haven't been sexually intimate in the three months we've been seeing each other, I didn't doubt for a minute that Pastor was a highly passionate man. He has a real tenderness, when he's just kissing me good night at my door, that I find very sexy.

You know, over the years, I've found that it's been very difficult to date when you already have a child. Almost every woman I know has at least one child, so it's not an unusual situation. It's just difficult.

It's not like I'm jealous or anything. For God's sake, LaShawndra is my *daughter*, my own flesh and blood.

No, there's no way I could be *jealous* of *her*. It's just that sometimes when I'm with her, it's as if I'm not even there. I'm just *invisible* to some men when she's standing next to me. And I don't mean young boys. I mean *men*.

So many men my age—I'm in my middle thirties, okay, *late* mid-thirties—seem to want girls and not women. I'm not the only one who thinks so. It seems *all* my friends and co-workers at Candace Realty have the same problem.

And I say once you reach a certain age—not that I'm old or any-thing—it's hard to compete with a firm young butt, perky breasts, and a flat stomach. It's just a fact of life.

Tina McElroy Ansa

LaShawndra's father was the first and only man in my life until LaShawndra was born. And I didn't even date again until LaShawndra was five or so. Not like the girls nowadays. Now young black girls don't think their lives have begun until they meet their "second baby daddy."

Well, at least in my day folks had the decency and the character to condemn boys who had more than one real girlfriend, more than one baby, especially by more than one girl.

Now they *lionize* men like that. "Players," they call them, men and boys who have a lot of women and take no responsibility for their actions or their children. Can you imagine wanting to emulate "players"!?

That wasn't my case. LaShawn Johnson didn't have another girlfriend when I got caught pregnant. He just didn't want me—the one girlfriend he had.

That spring, before he knew I was having his baby, he even wrote the word "Forever," with all kinds of hearts and flowers, in the front of my yearbook to keep any other guys from signing it. For a while I really treasured that gold-and-white yearbook. When I was pregnant with LaShawndra, I used to go to sleep with it folded in my arms.

But I burned that sucker one night in the backyard at Mother's house when one of my girlfriends told me she had heard that LaShawn had written his mama and said he didn't know for sure that LaShawndra was his. I think it was on LaShawndra's second birthday. Or maybe it was her third. I can still hear her crying inside while I stood over that blazing fire.

Nothing good has ever happened to me on LaShawndra's birthday.

I guess I have to take *some* responsibility for the way that girl turned out. But mostly I think it was the fact that her father was never around to give me any backup.

You know, "absentee African-American father."

In the days after LaShawndra was born, LaShawn's family stepped in and facilitated the whole thing, his abandoning me. They made it so easy for him to take off by getting him out of town so quickly and into the military.

I tried to keep it to myself how I felt about LaShawn Johnson getting me pregnant and then deserting me when I wasn't anything but a child.

I was just this very sheltered nineteen-year-old girl who got pregnant with the wrong boy's baby. One who didn't really care anything about me. Oh, sure, I had been exposed to many different people and lifestyles through my mother and her travels and projects. When I was still a baby, Mother would pick up and drive her little convertible Volkswagen Beetle to a concert in an open field somewhere in Florida as quick as she would fly the two of us to New York to attend the opera, where one of her college chums was singing. Where she got the money to do all of that, I do not know. I can barely make it myself, and I know I make three or four times as much as she ever did. But even with all Mother showed me and took me to, truly, I didn't know any more than my little high school friends who had never traveled outside of Mulberry, Georgia.

Little country girls who lived in Georgia towns as tiny as Ludowici knew more about life than I did. That's what happens when you come from the kind of can-do woman my mother is. Sure, she exposed me to a great deal in life, but she took care of so much for me. Just her being who she was in Mulberry—Mrs. Lily Paine Pines—paved the way for me in lots of instances. Her friends, too. Teachers let me slide on unpleasant assignments. I never did have to dissect a frog in high school biology lab or sew a blouse with long sleeves and cuffs in home economics class.

But I knew enough not to be asking men I didn't know for money. Oh, I hate to admit it, but LaShawndra thinks that that kind of behavior is just fine. She even came up to one of my dates when she was nine or ten and said, "Gimme five dollars!"

My daughter does not take after the women in my family.

I certainly tried to teach LaShawndra to know better, but she's a lost cause.

And I do partially blame her father for that.

Once I calmed down after I realized LaShawn wasn't ever gonna go ahead and do right by me, I tried to make sure he was a part of LaShawndra's life. I tried to put aside my hurt feelings for her sake, but he moved so far away, joining the armed services and ending up in the Philippines for a long time.

I tried to encourage him to stay in his daughter's life, to call regularly and keep in touch by mail. I did all I could to facilitate that relationship, even though I had some issues of his abandonment and denial to deal with myself. But I did the very best I could to bring some healing to the situation.

It just never worked. I did the best I could. That's all I can say. I did the best I could.

But LaShawndra's daddy is like the boys she runs after now. Her daddy just wanted some light-skinned woman to have babies with because he ended up with a woman from the Philippines who looks half white and half Japanese. He has a whole family that I guess he can be proud of out in Oregon. Could he get any farther away from us and still be in the continental United States?

I tried to tell LaShawndra that boys are just like her daddy. They just don't want no black woman or girl anymore.

I hear young men and old ones, too, saying that very thing all the time. "Don't give me no evil black woman. She'll just try to run everything. Won't even let you be a man." Especially those men who specialize in white girls and Asian or mixed women. *Anything* but a sister, you know. And every one of those men seems to have had a mother who was too big for him.

I wouldn't say it in mixed company, but these can-do black women have ruined them some sons.

The whole time I was thinking about LaShawn Johnson, Nurse Bloom just kept asking me questions. She seemed to be having her own conversation, whether or not I participated. All I remember saying was "Well" or "Um" or "I'm not sure." I'm good at that.

"Did you ever think that your daughter might be special instead of just difficult?" Nurse Bloom asked.

"Special? Special!" I nearly shouted. "She's special, all right. When LaShawndra wasn't any more than six years old, she used to tell my mother 'So?' when she tried to correct her. Now, you know you a bad-assed gal when you tell your own grandmother 'So?'

"When I was a teenager and starting on my period, Nurse Bloom, Mother always told me that if I was out and smelled something and didn't know if it was me or not, I was to drop my keys, and when I stooped to pick them up, sniff around and see who it was who was smelling."

"Did you pass on that wisdom to LaShawndra?" Nurse Bloom asked.

I tried my best to explain to Nurse Bloom what an incorrigible and unteachable child LaShawndra was. Nurse Bloom just shrugged. The old lady frustrated me so. But I pressed on.

"Oh, you can't tell my daughter anything."

There's no predicting what LaShawndra would drop anyway. One morning she dropped her purse in the doorway on her way to school, and more condoms and makeup along with a bunch of other people's house keys and a joint came rolling out.

I wouldn't *think* of giving LaShawndra the key to *my* home, even when she was living there. She's too irresponsible. She doesn't even know my alarm-system code, and I guess she should know that for emergencies. But my daughter is not the kind of person you would call in case of an emergency anyway. She's more like the emergency itself.

Even though Nurse Bloom was a medical professional, I didn't tell her that LaShawndra always seemed to have some kind of gynecological problem going on. One time after she went to the doctor, I saw a leaflet in her purse on chlamydia, and I tried to talk to her about exposing her body to diseases and how she might want to have children down the road. All she said was, "Oh, yeah, STDs, yada-yada-yada," and kept right on putting on her lip liner.

Mother used to walk through LaShawndra's room picking up her dirty clothes when she was living with her, and say "Funkytown" under her breath.

Of course, I was a very clean teenager. Not like LaShawndra. I always was having to get after her to clean up her room and not wear things three and four times before washing them in Woolite. Or always smelling under the arms of a garment before slipping it on. My mother taught me that, too. I guess, on consideration, she taught me a great deal. But, shoot, I just didn't have the kind of time my mother seems to have in a day to do all that. And I still didn't have time for any kind of private personal life when LaShawndra was growing up.

When I was growing up, Mother always seemed to find time for me. And Lily Paine Pines was already on her way to being the one and only Lily Paine Pines. She was on the Committee to Save Downtown Mulberry before they put in the Mulberry Mall. She was the first black woman on the Board of Education in Mulberry County. And she would still find time to make me princess costumes and pumpkin suits for Halloween and take me out for trick or treat.

Shoot, I didn't even *want* to be the kind of excellent mother my mother was. It was much too hard! Not that I'm not a good mother.

But my mother's generation's idea of a good mother is just too difficult.

Hell, *my mother* was named Woman of the Year two years running! By the city of Mulberry! And the only reason she didn't get it again later on is she insisted they change the rules to—in her words—"prevent well-intentioned favoritism." And *she* was the one getting the "favoritism."

Good God! My mother!

And people want me to live up to *that*?! I don't think so. Not with a child like LaShawndra.

That little ho has told me a couple of times when she wasn't older than nine or ten and I was just commenting on how hard it is to be a single parent, "Well, I didn't *ask* to be born!"

Can you imagine that? Shit, I told her right back, "Well, *I* sure didn't ask you to be born! You ruined my life!"

Uh, I guess that was kind of harsh to say to a child. But LaShawndra *pushed* me to it. She does that. And besides, I have a right to *my* feelings, too.

I know I messed up and ruined my life when I became pregnant out of wedlock with LaShawndra. But she has had such a better chance to realize her dreams. And she just refuses to have dreams. She doesn't even *try*! She certainly doesn't have to mess up, too. She ought to know better.

The day I saw my father, Charles Donald Pines, look me straight in my teary teenage eyes when I came running to him about something Mother would not let me do, and say to me, "Look, girl, let's not get too crazy. You know your mama the major breadwinner in this family...!"

Well, that was the day I knew that women like my mother just overwhelm a man. And I do not want to do that!

That's one reason I really like my relationship with Pastor. With him, there is no room for discussion about who is the head of the household. It's in the Bible. I'd *love* to have lived in a household where the man was truly at the helm.

Now, my father is quite a strong man, but he had to get away from my mother just in order to run his own household. He moved outside of Atlanta so he could be close to his family here in Mulberry and still have a little room to breathe.

Not that my daddy was not strong enough to stand up to Mother when he wanted to.

I was going to be a debutante that year when I got pregnant with 135
LaShawndra. Mother wasn't wild about the whole thing, the debutante thing, because she said it wasn't anything but a money-raising
fish-frying phony parade. But I wanted to come out with my friends.
And my daddy convinced her to let me do it.

I guess I have always been sort of spoiled by my daddy.

Not like I'm a spoiled daddy's girl or anything. I just received a
great deal of good healthy support and attention from my father.

One day right after Halloween when I was about seven years old,
Mother let me dress up in the cowgirl outfit she had put together for
me for trick-or-treatin' and wear it to school. But instead of taking me
to J. J. Masterson Elementary and dropping me off at the school door
the way he did every single morning I went to grammar school,
Daddy told me he had a surprise for me. And he drove me downtown
to Central City Park—it's not far from Candace's office building—
where there were trailers and cars and animal cages and a huge red-
and-white-striped tent and a *circus*! We went to the *circus* instead of
to school!

I'd never been to the circus before. The acrobats and clowns and
candied apples and cotton candy and hot dogs and Daddy laughing
and pointing things out to me. Just me and Daddy!

It was the best time I ever had!

But Daddy was always taking me somewhere with him. Showing
me off. Asking me to do some math on the site of one of his construction jobs and actually using my figures.

Oh, I had the best daddy!

He thought the world of me. Mother says when I was growing up,
you would have thought I was the *only* cute little brown-skinned baby
girl in Mulberry, Georgia.

"I can't tell you, Nurse Bloom, how stupid and wrong and ashamed
I felt after I was caught being pregnant. I missed out on so much.

"Of course, he never said it, but I know how I must have disappointed my daddy. And that's the *last* thing on earth I wanted to do.

"That's one reason I was never able to deal with LaShawn and his total irresponsibility as a parent. Because my daddy was such a good father."

Between the thoughts I was trying to keep out of my mouth and the conversation I was trying to keep going with Nurse Bloom, I got all turned around on a one-way street and ended up in the middle of a crowd of people. I had forgotten that Mulberry's Peach Blossom Festival was that weekend, and the "Peach Blossoms" were out early.

"I'm sorry, Nurse Bloom. We seem to have gotten caught up in all this Peach Blossom Festival parade traffic. I have tickets for the ball tonight, and a beautiful lavender outfit. It's a lovely, long, silk shantung strapless sheath with a delicate flowing chiffon duster that makes me look almost statuesque. But I'm not going. I don't have a date. The pastor is leading Bible study tonight. And I don't go *anywhere* unescorted. A real lady never does. I tried to tell LaShawndra that, and she actually laughed in my face.

"She said—and I quote—'A little ho nowadays can't be waiting around for some brother to show up and take her somewhere. I'd never get *anywhere* if *I* waited for a *escort*!' "

I felt Nurse Bloom cringe at LaShawndra's language, and I cringed, too, because I realized how bad it made *me* look.

As I tried to navigate through the traffic and get around the streets cordoned off for the Peach Blossom Run, I was on the lookout for LaShawndra in the crowd. But then I realized that unless she was coming in from the night before, 8:13 A.M.—by the clock on the dashboard—was too early for her to be stirring.

"You know, our agency, Candace, sponsors a young person—it's almost always a girl—in the twenty-five-K run. And we help a black girl who is running in the Miss Peach Blossom pageant. Buying her peach-colored gown or paying her entry fee or something. Our company founder, Lena McPherson, started us doing that. Our girl won last year, and this year our contestant was first runner-up."

"You ever picked LaShawndra for any of those events?" Nurse Bloom asked.

"LaShawndra?!" I nearly laughed right in that old lady's face. "Heck, LaShawndra doesn't even half show up for work at that little office job Mother got for her at the Board of Education! Let alone some outside community activity. Besides, never would I let her embarrass me in front of all those white folks. Coming in late and half dressed in some hoochie-mama outfit and dragon-lady fingernails."

Nurse Bloom didn't think I did, but I saw where she was going with her line of questioning. But I figured if my own mother couldn't shame me about my relationship with my daughter, damned if this uptight old lady who was practically a stranger to me was going to do it.

"All LaShawndra want to do is shake her little ass—oops, I mean butt—in front of some man's face," I explained as I saw an opening in a group of joggers trying to cross the street in front of the East Mulberry High School marching band and drove through it. "That's all."

She calls it "dancing," but it's hardly dancing. Have you seen what young people call "dancing" lately? It's enough to make a whore blush. I can't stand to even watch it on television.

And when you see them dance in real life, it is truly shocking. I used to volunteer once in a while at the schools LaShawndra attended, at the dances and events they had there, but I could not stand to go and see those young people dance the way they do.

I tried to tell LaShawndra how seductive and dangerous music can be. Music is what got me into trouble in the first place—pregnant with her.

LaShawn was a professional-caliber musician even in high school. Played the saxophone. A talented musician. When we were in high school, he would sneak his father's beautiful old restored Mustang convertible out of their garage and we would drive down by the Ocawatchee River on a Saturday night. LaShawn would bring his sax and play the sweetest music for me—jazz, R&B, standards. A saxophone is the sexiest instrument. The notes would just float out over the muddy river like flocks of geese and ducks. That was back when it was safe to park down by the river. Before derelicts and wild teenagers took over.

We would have the sweetest talks, too, about how we were going to spend the rest of our lives together. Humph, see how that turned out. Men are such liars.

I knew that his family thought I was not the right girl for him. Even though I was Lily Paine Pines's daughter, they let it be known that I was too dark-skinned for their little high-yellow baby boy. At a school picnic down at Central City Park, his ma had the nerve to say to me, "Sandra, dear, don't you think you need to be wearing a hat out here in all this harsh, bright sun?" Then she took off her big straw hat and gave it to me.

Even after Mother had him over to our house for Sunday dinner any number of times when we were dating, LaShawn's mother *never* offered me as much as a vanilla wafer, let alone a baked-hen-and-dressing dinner around their dining room table out in Sherwood Forest.

But LaShawn and I *talked* about that. He even made fun of them for being so stuck-up and bourgeois and old-fashioned. Good God, it *was* almost the 1980s. We would laugh at them as we sat down by the Ocawatchee River and cuddled.

That's what got us holding each other and being intimate without birth control in the first place. LaShawn called it "throwing down." You know, that was an expression we used back in the day for when you were about to get serious about anything. And LaShawn made me think he was very serious about me. The first time he slipped his long, tapered finger inside the front of my hip-huggers I wasn't even nervous, even though it was my first time.

All my friends were on the Pill, but I couldn't make myself bring up the subject with Mother. You see where *that* got us.

I guess the laugh was on me.

I took LaShawndra to my own "gynie" before she was thirteen to

Tina McElroy Ansa

get her on some kind of birth control. I figured three times was the charm. And so far it's worked, since she has not turned up pregnant yet and ruined her life the way I did. Well, I didn't exactly *ruin* my life, but I sure did mess it up for a while.

"Did you tell LaShawndra all of that, all your history?" Nurse Bloom wanted to know. I couldn't even remember telling *her* anything about my history. I decided to pay more attention to what I was saying.

"Now, Nurse Bloom," I replied, "how is anybody going to tell LaShawndra *anything*? But especially about dancing and music. LaShawndra has the nerve to think that she is actually going to get a *job* doing that embarrassing little butt shaking with hardly any clothes on that she calls dancing. She's always talking about her 'work' and her 'craft.'

"You know, my mother, Mrs. Lily Paine Pines, says, 'Well, if that's what the child is truly interested in, then that's what we need to throw all our weight behind and support her in that.'

"When LaShawndra started talking so early, I just *knew* she'd be a lawyer," I explained. "I just *knew* she would."

"Maybe she ain't got that kind of brain," Nurse Bloom said matter-of-factly. "You ever thought about that?"

"Oh, pssst. LaShawndra is just as smart as she can be. She is. Well, she's my daughter, isn't she? And she's Mother's granddaughter. So . . . She only uses sloppy, lazy, incorrect English just to get on my nerves. The first time I heard her say, 'I went out to the mall to get my nails *did*,' I just about lost it! She was not raised to speak that B-girl ghetto way!

"Oh, she's plenty smart. She was reading long before Mother got her into kindergarten early. She just got lazy and decided to stop reading when she was about ten or eleven.

"I think that's probably when she discovered she had a little vagina, a little coochie.

"And I'm ashamed to say she's been leading with her vagina ever since."

"Is that so?" Nurse Bloom said. That's what she said, but I could hear a whole bunch of condemnation of me in that question, too.

"I told my mother I would never speak to her again if she encouraged that little you-know-what of mine to think she could make a living dancing in music videos. Like LaShawndra has ever even been *around* the making of an actual music video. Now, where could she be making a living dancing in music videos in Mulberry, Georgia?

"Mother says we need to be supportive of her in some way. But I *refuse* to support her in some harebrained idea like that. I'd rather not be involved at all.

"Just because she is Mrs. Lily Paine Pines and LaShawndra's grandmother, she does not know *everything*. I am the mother, you know."

"Yes you are," Nurse Bloom agreed.

God, that woman could make three words a superior court jury's censure! But I forged on, trying to explain myself as I maneuvered out of the center of downtown and away from the parade preparations.

"I even found some pieces of paper around LaShawndra's room once—yeah, I searched her stuff; in these times we live in, you better!—where she had signed her name over and over with messages like "All the best" and "Keep Kool" and "We Just Like That." Like it was an *autograph*! Like somebody wanted *her* autograph. Like she was somebody!"

"And she ain't?" Nurse Bloom asked.

"Oh, Nurse Bloom, you know what I mean!"

Then I remembered she was a client and about a hundred years old. So I softened my voice.

"Doing it all by myself has been hard, Nurse Bloom. It's just hard."

"Um" was all she said.

Nurse Bloom had sat there in the front seat of my Mercedes firing so many questions at me that I told her all kinds of secrets. Things I never even said to myself.

For instance, just as we pulled onto the interstate connector, I turned to the serious-looking woman dressed in white and I said, "I'm so afraid I'm going to grow old alone."

Now, what made me unburden that load, I do not know. I just said it.

10.

Maybe, I was talking too much about my personal life. I spoke to myself the way old folks used to and said, You talk too much, you make folks hate you. It's what I'd told LaShawndra a thousand times ever since she said her first word and just prattled on and on: "Oh, be quiet for a little while, LaShawndra. You talk too much, you make folks hate you."

Me, I do this selling thing for a living, so I could tell that I was bringing the client down with my life story. I know how to sound upbeat and hopeful when I'm showing property, even when my heart is beating a mile a minute.

I picked up the phone and overheard LaShawndra and Mother talking one day when LaShawndra was still living with me some of the week and pretending to go to high school. They were talking about me. LaShawndra had the nerve to say I was phony just because I knew how to put a good face on a bad situation. I have to give Mother credit, she did try to defend me and remind LaShawndra that I was her mother. It took everything in me not to get that little heifer, LaShawndra, told right then.

Then LaShawndra said, "Even when she stressed and everything."

That's how LaShawndra talks. She ends each comment with "and everything." It drives me crazy.

Then, still referring to me, she said, "*High Anxiety* ought to be her favorite movie."

The two of them are always watching movies together over at Mother's house. I don't think they've ever invited me to join them after I turned them down the first few times. But I had better things to do than sit around all night watching some old movies.

LaShawndra's comment really almost hurt my feelings, because I do suffer from panic attacks. So I just let her comment pass. I certainly didn't want to go into another one right then listening in on their phone call. Not that I have them all the time. But I do have my share of anxiety.

The attacks started when I was pregnant with LaShawndra. All through college and even now sometimes, I am seized with these overpowering floods of emotion. I can feel myself just spiraling into a deep and dark and smoky chasm of self-doubt, uncertainty, and fear.

It didn't seem to matter how many times my daddy told me that I was a special star in this constellation; I would just be plagued by worry and self-criticism. No matter how much I was up in their faces, my professors never seemed to take to me. And later I just knew that the beauticians and manicurists were talking about me when I went out to the mall to Lovejoy's 2 to get my hair done.

Nurse Bloom made a couple of sharp movements to draw my attention back to her. She was the kind of old woman who didn't have to say a word to get her feelings across. I could tell she was becoming restless.

"Just wait until you see this house," I said as I took the exit off the interstate connector that runs through Mulberry. It's so handy. "This property has a nice yard, and it's conveniently located near the Mulberry Mall."

I was determined to keep this on a purely professional level. However, when we drove past a billboard on the way that announced MULBERRY COUNTY FARMERS' MARKET—1 MILE, Nurse Bloom just started talking up a storm.

"Even though I've always been a workingwoman with no immediate family, I always found time to cook good, wholesome meals every day," she announced. "Long before the medical community started promoting healthy cooking, I was preparing my collard greens with onions and a little vegetable oil and no fatback bacon."

She went into this long discourse on exactly how she prepared each and every meal she ever cooked. How she boiled her eggs instead of frying them. How she steamed her cabbage instead of smothering it in fatback. How she used honey and molasses instead of white sugar.

I just put my mind and my face on automatic, the way I do so often with my clients, and they never know the difference. You can tell that by the fact that I had been the highest-grossing Realtor at Candace for the last three months. And you know all us black women do some business at Candace Realty. There are fifteen women working there, and I don't think there's one of us who is not a member of the million-dollar club.

I can still remember when I sold my *first* house. I was so excited and proud. And I had a date that night, too. So I felt as if I was shooting pretty good all the way around. But that dog of a man was just intimidated by my success. When I offered to pay for the dinner—hell, I had just sold a house—he got all manly and started talking loud in the restaurant about him being the man and he didn't need no woman taking care of him. It put such a damper on the evening. I ended up going home by myself and picking up LaShawndra from Mother's in the middle of the night so I wouldn't have to be alone. And she was too sleepy even to be excited for me and my news.

"Pull in here," Nurse Bloom ordered, as we came up on the dusty red road on the right that led to the outdoor market. I noticed she did not make suggestions; she issued orders!

"That's not the way to the house I want to show you, Nurse Bloom," I said pleasantly.

She paid me *no* attention.

"You gon' miss it!" she yelled, waving her arms across the steering wheel in front of my face.

I obeyed right quick, just to avoid an accident.

Even at eight in the morning on Saturday, the farmers' market was as busy as a hive. Farmers and their fat, corn-fed wives and children rushed here and there between the backs of their pickup trucks and the empty stalls, setting out crates and baskets of fresh produce.

Some of them even had baskets of early corn and Florida tomatoes for sale next to bins of collard greens and turnip greens and roots and spinach and snap peas and other spring crops.

And some enterprising farmers had produce for the more sophisticated chefs—shiitake mushrooms and herbs and arugula and asparagus.

"You come out here much?" Nurse Bloom asked, eyeing the farmers' goods hungrily from the Mercedes's passenger-side window as we crept by the stalls.

"Not that often," I said. "Being a workingwoman, I don't have that much time to cook. Especially from scratch."

I could just see myself trying to close an important deal and still running by the farmers' market for some fresh vegetables to cook that evening.

That's something my mother would do. Not me.

Nurse Bloom was looking at the food with such interest, like she hadn't seen fresh vegetables in years, that I thought she might be hungry. And anyway, *my* stomach was still growling softly.

"Are you hungry, Nurse Bloom?" I asked. "I could certainly use something to eat. You know, I missed breakfast this morning."

"No, thank you," she said. But still she kept hungrily eyeing the fresh produce we went by.

"Are you sure, Nurse Bloom?" I pressed her. The last thing I wanted was this old woman passing out on me. Even though she did look as robust as a horse.

"I said, 'No, thank you,' didn't I?" she responded to my kindness.

Well, then, starve to death, I thought. And then felt awful about it because I was fearing that she was some kind of mind-reader.

"I'mo get out and look around," Nurse Bloom said, doing just that

You Know Better

while we were still rolling to a stop, leaving the car door open to *ding, ding, ding* until I reached over and pulled it shut.

I brought the Mercedes to a complete stop and parked adjacent to the middle set of stalls. Nurse Bloom stuck her big head back in the car window.

"You wanna come?" she asked.

I declined and used the private time to enjoy a little respite from her and to call home to check my messages. I was waiting for a call from Pastor to see if our weekend trip to the Bible conference in Atlanta was still on for the next week.

Unfortunately, he had not called. But even more unfortunately, there was an anonymous call from somebody—it was a girl's voice— saying, "I thought you'd want to know. A man broke into your daughter's house last night and somebody got hurt, 'cause there was an ambulance outside." Then *click*.

Nurse Bloom got back into the car just as I hung up. I guess she could see the look on my face.

"Bad news?" she asked.

"I don't know yet," I said as I dialed directory assistance for the number to the Mulberry Medical Center. I get all kinds of anonymous calls like that about LaShawndra.

"Your daughter better leave my man alone, or she gon' regret it." Or "I seen some naked pictures of your daughter, LaShawndra. You want some copies?" Or "I bet you don't know where LaShawndra was last night." So I didn't know if there had been a break-in at LaShawndra's place or not.

I called the medical center because I just refuse to call the Mulberry Police Department looking for my daughter. I just refuse to do that.

The switchboard operator at the hospital gave me more information than I thought she would when I told her I was a relative. There was no one checked in by the name of LaShawndra Pines of Painted Bunting Lane. But there was another patient of that same address

who had been brought in by the emergency medical team. "A Crystal
Adamson," the operator said. "Are you a relative of hers, too?"

I lied. "Yes, I'm her sister."

She really opened up then. "Well, that's all the information I have
on her right now. That usually means she's in stable condition, or it
could mean she's worse off. The best thing to do is to come down here
and see 'bout your people for yourself."

She paused, then added, "Did you just call here a few minutes
ago?"

"No," I said.

"Well, you sound just like another girl who just called to ask about
that same robbery victim. But I didn't tell that other caller nothing,
'cause she said she wasn't a relative or nothing."

I just sucked my teeth and hung up. I had a good idea who that
"other caller" was.

Nurse Bloom's face was one big question mark.

"No, LaShawndra isn't in the hospital, but I think she just called
there. I need to go by there and check on her housemate," I explained
as we drove out of the market road and back into town.

I tried my best to avoid the Peach Blossom activity. But every
street I turned down seemed to be crowded with folks wearing peach-
colored dresses and suits and gowns, or floats covered with crepe-
paper peach blossoms. By the end of every festival I never want to see
that color again. When we finally made it to the medical center,
Nurse Bloom declined to go in with me.

"The only hospital I've ever been inside is St. Luke's, and I don't plan
to cross the threshold of any other!" And that was that. So I let down all
the windows—it was nearly nine o'clock by then and really getting
warm for April, even in middle Georgia. Then I went inside by myself.

It was a madhouse in that hospital.

The young woman at the reception desk—she wasn't anything
more than a girl herself—recognized me. "Ain't you Miz Pines's daughter?" she asked. And that got me all kinds of information.

"Yeah," she confirmed, "they brought Crystal in about five this morning. They thought she had suffered drama to the head. But now they just think she fainted. And she's okay."

That's what the girl said: "Drama to the head." Lord, help us all.

Unfortunately, the drama didn't end there.

When I walked into the waiting room, the first thing I heard was "When Aunt LaShawndra coming back? I want my *LaShawndra*! I want my *LaShawndra*! No, I don't want nobody else! When Auntie LaShawndra coming back?

"I want my Auntie La*Shawnnnnnndraaaaaa*!"

It was Crystal's little girl, and she was tussling with the social worker, a short, timid woman in a too-tight peach-colored polyester pantsuit—*quelle horreur*—who I knew from when we were in high school together. The woman was trying to quiet the little girl with one hand and hold a younger, sleeping boy in the crook of her other arm.

Before I could turn away, she handed the younger child to another woman and came running up to me, her peach stretch pants straining over her hips, forming a deep, wide V in front, with the older scream-ing child, still dressed in her pink-flowered pajamas, in her arms. All I could do was pray that the woman would not hand the child to me. I'm not the kind of woman who just automatically picks up a child.

But like most women in Mulberry, she was busy trying to impress my mother through me.

"Hi, Sandy. I haven't seen you in ages! What a mess, huh? Have you seen your daughter? Did you do something different with your hair? I called your mother and left a message on her machine—do you think she remembers me?—so she should be here soon, don't you think?"

I just smiled and shrugged, but to tell the truth, what I thought was, If this little girl doesn't stop screaming in my ear and calling for her "Aunt LaShawndra," I think I'm going to run out of this waiting room screaming and hollering just like that child.

Between that little girl's screaming and the thought of that tough old bird I had sitting out in the car waiting for me—impatiently, I knew—my nerves were frayed so raw you could hear them vibrating like violin strings.

One of the young candy stripers, a girl about LaShawndra's age, brought the child an ice cream sandwich from a vending machine down the hall from the waiting room, and that quieted her for about twenty seconds. But as soon as it was gone and she was good and sticky and messy, she started up again.

"I want my Auntie La*Shawnnnnnndraaaaaa*!"

I had to muster all my resolve not to walk over to her and say, "Shut up, child. Your 'Auntie LaShawnnnnndrraaaa' ain't nowhere to be found when you need her. And she the one who got your little ass and your mama's big ass up in this hospital in the first place."

Instead, I slipped out to go to the restroom. And of course, as Mother says, "you can't run from your own trouble. It'll hunt you down." While I was in one of the stalls, I heard some young girls about LaShawndra's age come into the bathroom. As they peed and primped in the mirror, they were just a-talking:

"Oooo-weee. Y'all hear 'bout LaShawndra Pines and how she might be hooked up in the break-in some kind of way?"

"Shoot, I wouldn't be surprised at *anything* she did. When you ever heard of her doing something good or something smart or something right, for that matter?"

"Uh, she such a little chickenhead. She make us *all* look bad. Now, my mom gon' be all up in my business, 'cause she say she don't want me going down that same road as LaShawndra."

"Like *that* could ever happen. Psst."

"I tried to tell my mom that LaShawndra Pines don't roll with us. She just did my makeup that one time."

"Yeah, the things she do, the trouble she gets herself into. She just makes us *all* look bad. She make people think we *all* little hoochie mamas like her."

I was too embarrassed to come out. I just pulled the lid down and waited in the stall until they left so I would not have to face them. I took a quick look in the mirror after I washed my hands real well and had to admit that even though my makeup was flawless—I have good skin; I get that from Mother—I did look a little thrown-together for my tastes. And I hate that, especially when I know people are talking about me for what LaShawndra is doing. I'm a Scorpio; I'm very private. I smoothed down my hair, reapplied my dark plum lipstick, and, opening the door with a paper towel, headed out.

Fortunately, I didn't have time to be embarrassed anymore. As soon as I had entered the waiting room, the doctor came in to tell us that apparently Crystal had not had "drama to her head." Instead, it seemed she was diabetic and had not been sticking to her diet.

In the middle of the burglary, she had passed out trying to protect her two little ones.

Well, you know I felt better on hearing that. But my feeling of well-being didn't last very long, because I then heard the girls from the bathroom talking over in a corner of the waiting room.

"You would think LaShawndra would have the decency to come up here and see about her friend," one said.

"Shoot," a second girl said, sucking her teeth in derision, "you know that hoochie mama is probably on her way up to Atlanta for Freaknik. You know she ain't gon' let nothing get between her and getting her sex on."

"Yeah, 'cause otherwise you *know* she'd be up here tryna be the center of attention."

"Everything LaShawndra Pines *does* is to get some attention," one said.

"Look at us now," another one added. "This is just what she wanted. Even though we're all up here in the Mulberry Medical Center waiting room worrying ourselves sick over poor Crystal in there, who is it that everybody is talking about?"

They answered in unison: "All together now—*LaShawndra*!"

I headed out of the building. LaShawndra had embarrassed me enough. Now I at least had a clue as to where she was—Freaknik. Humph! Where else would LaShawndra be? Black girls riding around in convertibles, flashing their bare breasts and being groped in public on Peachtree Street. You know it must be "end times" when that starts happening. Besides, I was a bit concerned about Nurse Bloom outside in the car by herself.

Nurse Bloom, however, had entertained herself just fine, thank you, by flipping on the ignition of the Mercedes and turning the radio on.

As soon as I got into the car, there it was on the local half-hour newsbreak between segments of *The Tom Joyner Show*.

"At the home of Crystal Adamson and LaShawndra Pines in the Mulberry community known as Bird City in the early-morning hours—"

I tried to switch stations quickly to some easy-listening music, but not before Nurse Bloom caught enough to be curious.

"Were they just talking about anybody related to you?"

Uh, I was so embarrassed I did not know what to do.

"Miss Pines, what do you think is going to become of our children if we continue to be ashamed of them?" Nurse Bloom asked.

This was getting spooky. It was like this old woman was inside my head. It was getting so I was afraid to think *anything*.

She was making me feel I *had* to defend myself.

"LaShawndra may be my daughter," I said, "but I cannot take responsibility for her. We are *nothing* alike! I was *never* that wild and irresponsible one day in my life. Not one day of my life.

"I'm ashamed to say it, but LaShawndra didn't even finish high school. My mother has done more than opened a few doors for LaShawndra. She has practically *kicked* down doors for her! But to no avail. My friends just stopped asking about her after a while, and I have to say I was glad when they did.

"I didn't *ever* have any good news to share about LaShawndra. We'd all sit around at lunch or at a staff meeting at Candace and talk about our children.

"This one's daughter had just won a scholarship to Spelman.

"That one's daughter was taking piano lessons, with a recital coming up.

"The other one was sending her firstborn off to officers' training school.

"And what could *I* say? 'Well, LaShawndra didn't stay out *all night* long last night.'"

I noticed Nurse Bloom wasn't replying. She just let me sit there and spill *my* guts, which is not something I ordinarily do.

I guess I was proving her point about being ashamed of LaShawndra. But there is so much to be embarrassed by or disappointed in with LaShawndra.

"LaShawndra's housemate is going to be just fine," I assured Nurse Bloom, filling her in with just enough information to keep her satisfied. It didn't work. She kept asking me a lot of technical medical questions I could not possibly answer.

So I excused myself, turned my face to the driver's-side window, and rang my mother's home.

I wanted to tell Mother that I had overheard that LaShawndra had probably taken off for Atlanta to go to that Freaknik party they have up there during spring break. Like LaShawndra has ever done anything she needs a break from. But I kept getting the funniest-sounding ring on Mother's phone, and no one picked up.

I hung up and just resolved that LaShawndra was not going to get me all upset and worried for nothing.

I was glad to relay good news to Nurse Bloom about Crystal. Crystal's not really a bad girl, but I still hated that LaShawndra would pick a two-time unwed mother who had not finished high school properly to be her best friend and housemate.

LaShawndra needs good-quality friends like Miss Bonnie's granddaughters. Or my colleague Brenda's daughter.

But, you know, LaShawndra *loves* street trash. She just loves any little girl who grew up on welfare or in foster care or who just about raised herself. And if she's not with one of those girls, then she's hanging around a bunch of boys. Just look for any group of boys—at the mall, at a party, on the school grounds, on the playground when she was eight years old—and that's where you'd find LaShawndra. The only girl in the middle of some little nappy-headed boys, pants-hanging-around-their-hips, joints-in-their-pockets, never-finished-high-school boys!

She's not interested in being friends with *nice, clean* girls, like the daughters of my colleagues or my mother's friends' granddaughters. Quality girls.

And I know for a fact that none of those nice girls want to hang out with LaShawndra. I heard one of my colleagues at Candace talking to her teenage daughter in the office next to mine one day. It was Brenda—she's more like a friend than a colleague—and she was trying to convince her teenage daughter—a lovely girl—to invite LaShawndra to some little party she was having. But the child was not having any of that!

Not that all those girls are pure as the driven snow either, you know. Most young girls now don't have the reputations my peers and I had. The way they dress. The way they talk. The way they dance. I could not even bring myself to chaperone LaShawndra's school parties because of what was going on out on the dance floor, to say nothing of what they were doing outside the gymnasium door in the breezeways and parking lots. The way they conduct themselves in school, in their cars, in movie theaters, in restaurants, in the mall. Shouting out obscenities and grabbing themselves and grabbing at girls' butts and titties.

Ooooh, I can't even stand to be around these young folks. Everything about them is so *vulgar*. Even what they think is sexy is really so vile and vulgar!

And the girls are so stupid they don't seem to know that the boys are really making fun of them and using them just to, as they say, get their sex on. And the girls comply—look at them on the videos, what *my* daughter wants to do. Look at them in their black leather skirts and halter tops, in nothing more than a bra and bikini panties, gyrating their butts and humping the air and thinking they're being seductive when all they are being is lewd for the camera. *Comme c'est vulgaire.*

Uh, I can't *stand* these young people.

Hell, I've seen LaShawndra walk out of the house at eight o'clock in the morning going to her job dressed like a dominatrix or something, no matter how many nice semiprofessional outfits she has hanging in her closet.

Hell, *I* ain't grown enough to dress like that!

I cringe every time she uses my bathroom. Well, I'm sorry, but I do. There's no telling where her little butt has been. Truly! When she comes out, I go in with a can of Lysol spray.

And even though I've had my share of experiences, I'm dating a preacher now. And church would really be out if I gave him something I picked up from using the toilet after LaShawndra. I don't think I'm rushing things to think Pastor might put a ring on my finger any day now.

I've never been married, which is not all that unusual among my peers. Of course, I've come close to it a couple of times, but most men nowadays are so reluctant to make a commitment. Sure, they'll bring a few things over to your house and shack up for a while. They'll let you struggle and be late for work expecting you to make them pancakes and bacon and eggs for breakfast when you're on the same fast track as they are. Of course, they'll take weekend trips to Callaway Gardens and down to Savannah with you. But make a commitment for *life?* No way.

But Pastor isn't like that. So the last thing I need is some embarrassing sexual problem to try to explain to the good reverend. You know? I've kind of gotten pleased with the idea of all the perks of the office of first lady. A lifetime pension from the church, whether or not he dies first. A beautiful rectory to live in for life. Courtesy dinners at the best restaurants. A churchful of women to at least pretend that they admire and look up to me.

My Pastor has a wonderful, Spirit-filled ministry right here in Mulberry, and I figure if my daughter's reputation or someone's bringing up my past has not sabotaged the relationship by now—it's been three months, a record for me—I don't want some STD to do it.

"Girls just go too fast nowadays," I explained to Nurse Bloom. I *knew* she had no idea how *hot* young girls are today. Don't get me wrong. It's not like I think I'm the Virgin Mary or anything. I've had my share of experiences. I'm nearly thirty-eight years old. I've lived and such. And so have my friends.

Shoot, I have a friend I work with and you have to hide your teenage sons from this woman. I mean it. Whenever I see a nice-looking young man going off to school with his books in his hand or a cute little bag boy at the Piggly Wiggly, I always think, Lord, don't let Patricia get a holda him!

She turned those boys every which way but loose. Tying 'em to the bed and teaching them all sorts of new techniques and positions. But she's a grown woman, old enough to have teenagers of her own. She's not some little hoochie mama without a job, a car, or a future.

"And I don't care what anybody says, Nurse Bloom, you cannot slow 'em down.

"Shoot, when I was a young girl, a preteen, and wanted to wear makeup like my friends, Mother gave me a stick of cocoa butter, a big jar of Vaseline, and a Revlon eyelash curler, and I was kinda satisfied. Mother can do that, make you feel satisfied with less than you thought you wanted."

"And as a teenager you were satisfied not painting your face?" Nurse Bloom asked—very suspiciously, I might add.

"Of course I was satisfied for a while, because I did look good. I used the cocoa butter all over my face and body—it even helped with blackheads and pimples. Then I used the Vaseline like a lip gloss and on my eyebrows to keep 'em smooth and dark and shiny. Then, after I curled my eyelashes, I put a little Vaseline on them, too, and it looked just like I had on mascara.

"Oh, it took me a while to get the hang of the eyelash curler."

I felt a little foolish at the personal leanings of my chattiness.

"You're probably the first person I ever told about that. You know, I don't believe in giving away my beauty secrets."

"Did you try the same thing with LaShawndra?" she wanted to know, all innocent.

"Shoot, what are you talking about? Ha! LaShawndra didn't take time for baby steps to the makeup. She went straight to the full stage makeup when she was ten or eleven. She used to sneak into my makeup drawer until she started saving her allowance for that purpose.

"Oh, I can't stop that girl! I never could!"

"Well, sometimes you can *show* a person quicker than you can *tell* them," Nurse Bloom said, using that even, relaxing tone I'm sure she employed when trying to calm agitated mental patients at St. Luke's.

"You must not be listening, Nurse Bloom. I tried *everything* with LaShawndra. It did not work!"

I could not believe how defensive Nurse Bloom was making me feel.

I needed to talk with someone who was not trying to make me feel all responsible for what LaShawndra—who is over eighteen years old—was doing. I said, "Excuse me, I'll be right back," to Nurse Bloom, and got out of the car. I tried my best not to slam the car door shut, but I could hear the nice comfortable thud a Mercedes door makes as I headed toward the hospital entrance. When I returned to the lobby of the hospital, I found a private corner over by a large rubber plant, flipped open my cell phone, and called my daddy.

I figured that Mother had not informed him of what was going on.

I have a wonderful father. I never could understand what was wrong with Mother's mind that she would let him go—not once but *twice*! If you ask me—and certainly no one did—Mother could have given Daddy another chance. He's such a good man and father. And Lord knows he loved Mother's dirty drawers. He still does, if you ask me. But, like I said, nobody did.

Mother acted as if something as small and petty as a few games of chance was grounds for divorce from a good man who loved her. Hell, it wasn't like he gambled away the deed to their house or the baby's milk money. It was *his* money he was gambling with anyway. And besides, he usually won. Sometimes my mother just tries to live on another plane.

I tell her you don't just throw away a good man for a little thing like gambling! Not in this time-space continuum. *Quelle folle!*

Anyway, I could tell by Daddy's voice that I had pulled her attention away from something important when I called. But he perked right up when he heard my voice. "Hey, baby," he said brightly, "what's goin' on?"

It was so good to hear his voice.

"You sound happy," I said. He did.

"Oh, do I?" he said innocently, and chuckled. Then he added, "I just talked with your mother."

"Really?" I said. "I've been trying to get her all morning." He didn't say anything, so I left it alone. I didn't want to talk about Mother anyway. I wanted to talk about *me*.

Daddy and I talk all the time. However, for some reason that day it seemed I had not heard his voice in *ages*! I told him everything I knew about the break-in—what little I knew—and about Crystal and LaShawndra and even Nurse Bloom and how she was tap-dancing on my nerves. And *he* didn't make me feel at all defensive.

"So don't be surprised if LaShawndra shows up on your doorstep,

Daddy," I said, ending the conversation with our customary "Love you—but you know that."

My daddy told me once he always envisioned that he and LaShawndra would be great old buddies. Real close. Great old buddies. But he said he felt that his being in the house, then out, then in, then out never gave them the chance for that to happen. He said, "I don't think I was the type of influence that your mother wanted for her."

I told him, "Oh, Daddy, that's not true! You're a *great* influence!" It still breaks my heart that he and Mother could not stay together. And I know Mother still has strong feelings for him. Even after two divorces Mother still wears the gold wedding band Daddy put on her finger almost forty years ago.

"Well, I love that little LaShawndra," he had said, "no matter what kinda influence I am."

I felt much better when I returned to the Mercedes and Nurse Bloom, who had tuned the radio back to the local news station.

I was so irritated I almost didn't ask her if she needed to use the restroom. But I couldn't be that mean.

"No." She almost barked her reply. Then, after a pause, she added, "Some days at St. Luke's when it was busy, I could hold my water *all day*." Then another pause and, "*I* was a *professional*."

As I pulled out of the hospital parking lot, I didn't say it, but I sure did think it.

Bitch!

11

Discovering that Crystal was okay and that LaShawndra, my little hoochie-mama daughter, was probably on her way up to Atlanta with one of her ghetto friends gave me a small sense of comfort. As comfortable as one can be when dealing with these screwed-up young people.

"If children are messed up in life, Miss Pines, it's usually because something done messed them up," Nurse Bloom said out of nowhere. "Even back in the fifties, when I was still a working nurse at St. Luke's, I saw all kinds of things come walking through that hospital door. Not just unwed mothers.

"You know, children don't take after strangers."

"That's just what my mother says," I replied, trying to ignore the fact that Nurse Bloom seemed to be wandering back through my head again, to say nothing of talking all up under my dress with the unwed-mother crack. I'm not a naturally deceitful person, so it was difficult for me to try to shield my thoughts.

I reached over to my car phone any number of times during that morning hour—it was about nine-fifteen when I first tried—and called my mother to tell her she was wasting her time calling around Mulberry and looking around Mulberry and worrying around Mulberry for LaShawndra.

LaShawndra always leaves whenever trouble comes up, and she's usually the one who has caused it. It's been that way her whole life. Now here she had done it again.

She was at the center of *another* mess, one that involved a break-in and hospitalization for her best friend. I still did not know how she was involved in the break-in. At the time I didn't think she would actually break into anyone's house, least of all her own. But LaShawndra was acting true to form: She made a mess, then got the hell out of Dodge.

And in the second place, that wild Freaknik was starting up in Atlanta. Although my mother refuses to believe it, with Atlanta less than three hours away, LaShawndra has gone a couple of years to that wild street party where there are accounts in the daily newspaper of black girls, *college girls*, flashing their breasts on Peachtree Street and open sex acts in public parks and the mauling of girls who misgauged the danger of a situation.

And that was where LaShawndra—my only daughter, the fruit of my womb, the only one on earth I had to carry on my name—was headed again.

I can't do anything with her.

LaShawndra is a little freak. That's how she sees herself: a girl who'll do anything with a man. She'd even tell me sometimes about all her misadventures in such detail that it would make the hairs on my arms stand up on end.

She even showed up at my office one afternoon just the year before in one of her hoochie-mama outfits—red jeans so tight you could see the V of her vagina—all out of breath and disheveled. I'm always so embarrassed when she comes around me and my associates looking that way.

"Sandra, can I hang out here awhile?" she asked, flopping onto my office sofa and throwing that big red leather bag of hers on the floor beside her.

"LaShawndra, this is an office," I told her. "I'm trying to work here. And besides, aren't *you* supposed to be at work?"

But she paid me no attention and proceeded to stretch out, with her big, thick-soled boots up on my quilted tapestry sofa.

"What kind of mess have you gotten yourself into now?" I asked her as I rose from my desk and closed the office door. "Talk fast. I don't have a lot of time for your foolishness today."

"Oh, it ain't nothing," she said, trying to sound casual as she dug through her makeup bag for her mirror and mascara. But I could smell her sweat all the way across the room.

"I just caught a ride with this guy out by the gate to our place, and just 'cause he bought me a Whopper and a tall Coke, he thought I shoulda been his girlfriend or something. So when we came to a stoplight not far from here, I just grabbed my bag, jumped out of the car, and made a run for it. I think I lost him in the park."

I thought, No wonder she's sweating like a horse.

I told her, "LaShawndra, don't even tell me about the crazy stuff you do!"

"Well, you tell *me* everything about *your business!*" she shot back, referring to the few times I had let her in on what was happening with me. Hell, I thought she would have appreciated being treated like an adult. Instead of having to sneak around in chests of drawers and trying to pry open locked boxes to find out things about her parents' lives the way I did, she heard it from me.

She might have been young, but I told her what kind of man her father was. I told her how hard and unpleasant it was to have a child at nineteen without a husband. I told her how the fun part of your life was over when you have a child out of wedlock the way I did. How difficult it is to find child care on a part-time salary. I tried to tell her her life was going to turn out worse than mine. I didn't try to hide things from her. Even when she was five and six, I came right out and told her when we didn't have enough money for the telephone, rent, *and* dental bills.

I can see the two of us now, sitting around the little kitchen table in our first apartment over near the Catholic school in Pleasant Hill. It was a new set of three duplexes that my daddy had helped to build. That's how I had been able to move in while I was still in college,

You Know Better

without a full-time job, just my part-time job at the Mulberry Telephone Company. LaShawndra and I would sit there, and she'd help me organize the bills into little stacks— She's always been smart. She just pretends not to be to make me crazy.

She'd try to tell me, "It's gonna be all right, Sandra." But what did she know? By then I had graduated from Fort Valley State College and been out there long enough to know that it was *not* going to be all right unless Mother or Daddy came and helped me out.

And sometimes I'd even tell her so. "You're just a child, LaShawndra. You don't know nothing." I'd try to tell her, "Things don't 'get right' just because you're wishing they would."

Then, when she started growing up and thinking she was grown and started smelling herself before she was even a teenager, she'd have the nerve to turn it back on me when I chastised her for messing up: "Well, you always said I don't know nothing." Then she'd twist on out of the room.

She did that one too many times to me, so one day just before her thirteenth birthday I grabbed her by the nape of her neck as she twisted off after calling herself getting me told about myself. She was wearing her hair in kind of a shag cut, and there was just enough hair in back for me to get a good hold of a handful and yank some sense into her head.

Of course, it didn't pull any sense into her head. But I did make her apologize for accusing me of being so neglectful and trifling. Because I *never* did that.

I always did the best I could. And still she turned out to be a little hoochie.

LaShawndra is like so many young women now: they seem to have such low self-esteem. I don't know *where* they get that from. I know that all my friends and I taught our daughters to respect themselves and not take any shit off these trifling men the way many of us did. Still, so many of the little girls nowadays define themselves by their vaginas. They call themselves "ho" and "bitch." They move like they're having an orgasm on the dance floor. They dress like they can be bought by the hour.

LaShawndra just seems *determined* to play to her lowest inclinations. My mother is always trying to get her to put her best foot forward and not be such a little ho. But after nineteen years all of Mother's encouragement and all of my hard work still has not done LaShawndra one bit of good.

I tried again to reach my mother, without success.

Turning to Nurse Bloom, who seemed content to sit there in the Mercedes and watch me, I said, "I can't imagine where Mother could be. Usually she carries her cell phone with her."

I was only trying to make pleasant conversation with the old biddy, but she just shrugged and looked out the window at the park across the street from the hospital. "You don't have to make conversation with me. I *enjoy* the quiet."

Good! I thought. And continued trying Mother's number.

I could tell from Mother's phone message the night before around midnight what was going on.

That late at night I hadn't even bothered to pick up the phone when Mother had called. Later I felt a little guilty about that. But she knew that LaShawndra was not at my house. LaShawndra avoids my place like the plague. Besides, even if she had come by there, Mother knows I don't open my door to *anybody* after ten o'clock at night. Not even to my own child. I live alone. I have to protect myself.

I kept calling Mother's home number and her cell phone.

I was trying to be a good daughter and keep her from wasting a whole day in a frustrating search for LaShawndra.

Mother has done that. Driven around Mulberry at all times of the day and night looking for LaShawndra. She pretends she doesn't, but she does. I won't. I simply refuse to do that. I just will not be seen riding up and down the streets of my hometown looking for one little hot-butt, bad-assed gal. Even if she is my own.

I can almost see my lovely, cultured mother right now, wearing an expensive wool suit and a string of fat pearls and matching earrings, turning off the lights of her big, wide Explorer and rolling up on some house party or nightclub in the middle of the night, looking for LaShawndra.

Uh, how common!

I know about how you have to roll up on a man's house sometimes to find out if he is truly living alone like he claims. With so many women—attractive workingwomen with something on the ball—looking for a stable relationship now, the pool of men who are not dogs is shrinking by the day. But I certainly don't want *my mother* being seen doing it!

Oh, I've done it once or twice when I was younger. When I heard that skinny yellow Negro was on leave, I sat outside LaShawn's folks' house out in the Sherwood Forest development many a night in the used Toyota my daddy gave me, with LaShawndra asleep in her carrier in the backseat. We nearly froze to death out there one night. It took me a few nights to realize that he wasn't going to see me out there and come running, overcome with guilt and remorse, begging me to take him back. So I could tell from the beginning that sneaking around in the night trying to catch some man in a lie was a losing battle. I *have* to get my eight hours of uninterrupted sleep at night, or I cannot face the kind of day I have and the kind of responsibilities I carry. I had to be realistic about it.

And besides, in a town as small as Mulberry, people recognize your car.

I was still getting that same funny noise on Mother's phones. When I hung up, I thought maybe it was for the best that I could not reach her.

My mother would just want me to try to get in touch with LaShawndra so we could tell her that her friend Crystal and her two children were okay. With LaShawndra somewhere between Mulberry and Atlanta, how could I have done that?

When I checked my own messages again, some girl had called—

anonymously—to tell me that LaShawndra had been seen sneaking around the crime scene at her place that morning. And she probably was.

I did not plan to tell Mother that. It would only have put her into high gear again and worried her about something she had no control over.

I was just grateful I had no messages on my machine at home or work from the police.

I never got into any kind of trouble like LaShawndra does.

When I was in college, my college chums and I might have done some pretty foolish things, silly things. But nothing as common and near-criminal as LaShawndra and her peers.

We *never* sold ourselves so cheaply, our sexuality so cheaply, as they seem to, the way they talk and dress and have wanton and unprotected sex.

Now, I'll admit that my college roommates and I would catch rides with some guys, older guys with jobs, and let them take us out to nice restaurants for a good meal. A steak or shrimp or something. But that was just when our money from home ran low. But we certainly did not sleep with them to pay them off for the meal and the couple of brandy Alexanders we drank.

We'd just give them fake names—mine was "Carmen"—and at the end of the evening—they weren't really "dates"—we'd have them drop us off at a fake address far from campus to throw them off the scent if they came back looking for us when they realized we had taken *them* for a ride instead of the other way around.

We never had sex with any of *those* guys. They were just meal tickets, and anyway they were old grown men in their thirties and forties who nobody wanted.

It was just a *little* dishonest.

We finally got caught when one of the guys came to the campus looking for us. And nobody made it easy on us. We had to apologize and everything.

My mother is always trying to make things easy for LaShawndra. That's part of LaShawndra's problem. Somebody is always making things easy for her.

I just say let her squirm for a while. It may do her some good to feel bad about some of the mess she's always causing. She thinks everything she gets herself into is going to be fixed.

Then, when it's me, Mother has the nerve to say, "Sometimes, Sandra, you just have to go through the fire."

Duh-huh. Like I haven't already had my share of going through the fire. Being left pregnant at nineteen and having to raise LaShawndra as a single parent and all, working two jobs when I was in my twenties and never having time for dates of my own.

Mother thinks I don't know, but she pays LaShawndra's rent nearly every month. And week after week, regular as clockwork, LaShawndra comes over and raids Mother's kitchen like it's the Piggly Wiggly. She takes detergent and paper towels and canned goods and toothpaste and lettuce and dishes of leftovers.

Of course, I may go by Mother's every now and then to see what's in her refrigerator. But that's different. It's not as if I go *shopping* in Mother's kitchen. I'm a single working mother with the responsibility of my own business. I need some help. Besides, Mother likes to cook. She says it relaxes her. Although I don't know *where* she finds the time.

But then, Mother has ways that defy science. Sometimes it seems like magic. While Mother was working on her dissertation at the university outside town, she was still finding time to sew and embroider little gifts for me and her friends to let us know she was thinking about us. When I was small, I used to think there wasn't anything my mother could not do. I guess I still believe it.

I can't even make it home in time to prepare a meal most days. And it's been that way since I can remember, certainly since I became a mother.

That's another reason I'm grateful for my mother. Mother *always* has something good to eat in *her* refrigerator. Personally, I don't know how she does it. I assume she's always just done everything. Kept house and worked on committees and advanced in her job—shoot, "advanced" isn't the word. She *shone* in her career! Even when she was married to Daddy, both times.

I told Nurse Bloom, "In most cases children may not take after strangers, but in LaShawndra's case she did. No one in our family is like LaShawndra. I tell her all the time, 'You don't take after Pines women.'"

LaShawndra is like lots of little hoochie mamas her age out there without a job, car, or future. I think LaShawndra needs to get up off her rusty dusty and get a real job or find some real direction in her life.

Now, Mulberry, Georgia, isn't any big exciting metropolis, but it is the kind of town where you can make some money. It's just a money-making town. Folks have tried and tried to get me and a number of my associates at Candace to move to a bigger city, to Atlanta or Dallas or even up north.

But you can't beat Mulberry for making money. And if you have a few connections and grew up here, it's not a bad place socially either. And if it's not in Mulberry—like foreign films or a Thai restaurant—it's less than three hours up the expressway in Atlanta. Not that I've had that much free time to pursue a social life. Between being a single mother and full partner at Candace Realty, my time has just been eaten up over the years.

But LaShawndra wouldn't even give it a chance by getting a good education or even a respectable trade or craft like my daddy, who is a master carpenter.

Oh, now she can do hair or makeup, look professional, too, but do you think she would settle down long enough to get a license or to even work on it as a career? No!

"You know what she wants to do for a living, Nurse Bloom?" I asked her as I made a sharp right on Oak to avoid the parade. "You want to know what she wants to do with her life?

"Get this—she wants to be a dancer.

"Not a ballerina. Not a contemporary modern dancer in a reputable dance troupe like Alvin Ailey. Not a hoofer on Broadway. Not a traditional dance instructor. Long story short . . ." I said.

"Too late!" Nurse Bloom interjected with a dry laugh.

Damn! I thought. She *cannot* stop yanking my chain. I ignored her and pressed on.

"She wants to be a dancer in a music video! *In a music video! Any music video!*"

I try to tell LaShawndra she may be young and fast, but she's not the only woman with a vagina.

Nurse Bloom didn't reply at all in the way I thought she would. I thought she would suck her big false teeth and roll her fiery black eyes at LaShawndra's foolishness. But instead she caught me looking at myself in the rearview mirror when I came to a stop sign. I had a new short haircut, and it did look cute.

She looked right at me as I raked the short hair at the nape of my neck down with my fingernails, and said, "Young women your age certainly are vain. Y'all seem to *stay* in the mirror."

She caught me so off guard I didn't have a chance to explain about getting used to my new haircut before she added, "When I was your age, I'd put on my nurse's cap in front of the looking glass in the morning and wouldn't glance in a mirror again the rest of the day."

I had to call on all my inner resolve to keep from responding, "When you were *my age*, Nurse Bloom, Moses was a pup! They probably didn't have mirrors!"

But I took the high road instead.

"Heck, Nurse Bloom, if you think *I'm* in the mirror a lot, you should see my daughter. She *lives* in front of the mirror."

"Oh, really?" Nurse Bloom said, as if I were lying.

"Really!" I said. "I try to tell LaShawndra she may look cute now, but that's not going to get her anything in this world without some hard work. Heck, I'm as cute as she is, and I've had to work plenty to excel the way I do. And her looks are not going to be something she can count on as the years roll by. Many's the time I've told her she had *nothing* to hold her in good stead."

When I was little, there was this old woman who lived next door to us on Oglethorpe Street. Miss Eliza Jane Dryer. She was the one who used to ask me about my dreams. She's long dead now. But I remember Mother telling me that when Miss Liza Jane was young, she was one of the most beautiful women in Mulberry. Mother said she was also a fast, fast, fast woman.

She used to hang out in honky-tonks and juke joints drinking and juking and dancing and hanging on to first one man and then another. Shaking her butt in everyone's face. Mother said she acted this way well into her sixties.

When Mother is referring to people who have no one in the world to care about them, she always says, "Like Miss Liza Jane Dryer used to say, 'I ain't got a child nor a chick.' "

I remember that Mother was always kind to Miss Liza Jane because she was so alone all the time. I can just see Mother taking her over a little blue-and-white china tureen of some good hearty soup she had made with vegetables from her garden. Mother can grow anything. Or some slices of a rich sweet-potato pie. Or she'd make me go over and take her a slice of one of my birthday cakes and a carton of milk and sit with her while she ate it. "If you can't spare a few minutes to go and visit with an old woman who doesn't have a child or a chick in this world . . . well, shame on your little butt!"

No one even showed up for that old lady's funeral. Mother made me put on one of my Sunday dresses on a school day and go to her sad little services, too. I was too young to own a black dress then—not like LaShawndra, who's been wearing women's colors for as long as she could get someone to take her to the mall—so I must have been about thirteen or so. They didn't even have the service at a church. I guess Miss Liza Jane didn't belong to any church. They had the service at Parkinson's Funeral Home in one of those little chapels there.

There really was no need to have a service at all, as it turned out. Mother and I were the only ones there. It was so sad.

Mother just wept all through the short service when she realized that no one else was going to turn up to put that old woman away. Mother said she hadn't planned to go to the interment, but we did.

"I can't let poor Miss Liza Jane go on her last ride all by herself" is what Mother said, tears streaming down her face as we drove behind the big, black, lonely hearse to Mulberry Public Cemetery.

I heard my mother say one time, "That's what happens to an old whore who doesn't have a family."

I hate to say it, but if LaShawndra isn't careful, she just might end up like that poor old woman, Miss Eliza Jane Dryer.

Alone with no children, no one man to care about her, no life's work, and no future.

LaShawndra has had the nerve to tell me to my face that I don't have to worry about *her* getting pregnant in her nineteenth year— she'll be nineteen in a few months—"the way Mama Mama and you did." I know that makes me nearly thirty-nine. But I'm hoping if I just keep saying I'm in my mid-thirties, nobody will notice. Almost forty! I can't even begin to deal with *that*!

If LaShawndra doesn't watch it, she's gonna end up just like Miss Eliza Jane Dryer—an over-the-hill, used-to-be-cute ho all alone in this world.

"Where are we headed now?" Nurse Bloom wanted to know. Actually, I was driving toward Spring Street so I could casually drive by Mount Calvary to see if Pastor's car was parked outside.

I lied.

"Well, Nurse Bloom," I said as I changed lanes to head across the Spring Street bridge. It was a good thing I was such an expert driver, because thinking about LaShawndra, trying to keep Nurse Bloom at bay, and negotiating Mulberry's morning traffic was quite a juggling act. "I thought we might head out toward Sherwood Forest. The homes there all have spacious backyards big enough for gardens."

I could tell from our visit to the farmers' market, she was a gardener. "And then I have this lovely place I want to show you out by the Ocawatchee."

She didn't say a thing about my plan or ask any questions about the houses. All she said was "Are those the bells of Mount Calvary I hear chiming ten o'clock already?"

I didn't answer. She was almost scaring me coming up with questions that seemed to flow from my thoughts. I began to suspect she might be an intuitive or something. She definitely wasn't any ordinary woman.

12.

I just decided to ignore the Mount Calvary dig. And it *was* a dig. I just knew it was. Nurse Bloom didn't seem to say *anything* that didn't have a point to it. And her comments always seemed to be motivated by what I had just been thinking. It was unnerving.

I made a mental note to ask Mother if Nurse Bloom was some kind of spiritualist or mind-reader or something.

I changed my plans right quick and turned sharply at the next intersection to avoid driving directly by the church.

"I was just thinking, Nurse Bloom, since we're over on this side of the river, I have one really lovely place to show you in a wonderful community called The Woods.

"It's not very far from here. Past Pleasant Hill. Not far from where my mother lives, in fact."

"Is that where your house is?" she asked.

"Oh, no, I don't have a house. I live in a condominium, but very upscale. Very high-class. *De rigueur.* I decorated it myself. It's out by Lake Peak on the edge of town. You might even want to look at a condo there that I know is available."

"Just let me take a look at your place," she said.

"My place? Oh, gosh, maybe on some other day. Not today! Today is kind of a mess, and so is my place. It's not usually like that. Because, even though I'm a single working mother, I pride myself on keeping a clean and neat house. But it's just today. There's so much going on with LaShawndra and *her* mess. And I had to get up unusually early for your 'appointment.' "

She just looked at me.

"Would you like some music?" I asked, trying to distract her.

Can you believe that old woman actually smacked my hand away from the stereo switch!?

"No," she said.

Damn, I thought, that means I'll have to talk.

"It's a good thing my daughter, LaShawndra, isn't riding with us this morning. She won't ride in any vehicle unless there's music playing."

No matter how hard I tried to push her out of my thoughts, all that seemed to be on my mind that morning was LaShawndra, my little hoochie-mama daughter.

"So we're headed for your place now?" Nurse Bloom just persisted.

"Oh, no, Nurse Bloom, I live on the other side of the river," I explained.

"Well, let's head over there, then."

"Oh, Nurse Bloom, I was in such a hurry to get here to you this morning, I left my home in kind of a mess," I tried to explain. I had the vents open, but it was getting hot in the car, at least to me. Maybe it was just the heat Nurse Bloom was putting on me to go to my home. I turned the AC on medium. I figured she might be a bit uncomfortable in the spring heat with that light wool cape over her crisp white uniform. I felt all wilted, but she looked as fresh and crisp as a new dollar bill. I guess she just commanded her body not to sweat. Then, when she looked at the vent and cut her eye back at me, I reached over and made sure the vent was not blowing directly on her.

I continued, trying to placate her, "But I bet we can see inside one of the models."

"No," she insisted. "I want to see *your* place."

She was about as stubborn as LaShawndra.

"Oh, Nurse Bloom—" I began.

She interrupted me with "I thought the customer was always right." I thought, Now, why would Mother send me this woman on a day like this? In fact, why would she send me this woman, period?

I certainly did not want to swing by my condo, but Nurse Bloom just sat there with her arms crossed over her big, solid breasts and a stern "I will not be moved" look on her face.

I tried just to keep driving and think of something to distract her from her plans, but she asked me, "Young lady, am I gonna have to *insist* that you show me what I want to see?"

I knew when I was beaten. I made the first right turn I could and headed for the Spring Street bridge.

Now that Nurse Bloom was getting her own way, she seemed suddenly to be in a better mood.

"The Ocawatchee River sure is high and clear today," she said pleasantly as we crossed.

"Um, you're right." I had not noticed. I really do hate that river. I know it sounds crazy of me, but every day when I cross it, I feel like it's taunting me with memories of my teenage years.

"Must be Cleer Flo' time," she offered.

I just said, "Um-huh," and didn't pursue that topic, because I've found that something as strange as a river suddenly turning from a muddy orange color to a clear green unnerved some clients. And the change was so sudden and unpredictable that it wasn't a true selling point.

I had found it best just to ignore the infrequent transformation of the Ocawatchee. Anyway, seeing as that was where I got pregnant with LaShawndra, I figured that the river had caused quite enough *transformation* already.

As we drove along Orange Highway, we could see Lake Peak from the road.

"This is a lovely recreational area, Nurse Bloom, if you're into nature," I said, settling back into my Realtor's mode.

"Humph, I'm 'into nature,' all right," she said with a dry laugh. Then, as I was about to launch into my Lake Peak historic spiel, she stopped me with "When I was young, colored folks couldn't even come around Lake Peak unless you was caring for some white woman's baby for the day. Now here y'all are *living* around it!"

Tina McElroy Ansa

When we pulled into the garage underneath my place, I was still trying to convince her not to go in—the Sherwood Arms Condominium is actually three stories tall, with a secured, private entrance inside the two-car garage on the ground floor, so you don't have to get out of your vehicle until you are safely inside your own building.

I pointed out this feature to Nurse Bloom.

She informed me, "I don't have a car."

It wasn't even half past ten in the morning yet, and I was so sick of this imperious old woman I didn't know what to do.

As soon as I put the key in my door and pushed it open, I realized something was amiss. The security alarm did not beep three times as usual.

"Oh, God!" I said under my breath.

The burglar alarm had been turned off from the security pad right inside the front door. No wires were clipped and exposed. So I knew it had been deactivated by the code. And Mother and I were the only two people who had the code. I thought.

"Hold on a minute, Nurse Bloom," I said softly, stopping her at the doorway of the condo.

"Mother!" I called. No response, no sound from within the condo. "Mother!" I called again. Again, no response.

I looked in. The entry hall and living room looked the same. And there was nothing disturbed in the dining room, where I had boxes of books and work-related materials stacked up against the far accent wall. I had that wall painted a deeper shade of rose to give the room more depth.

But you know how you know your own house. I could tell someone had been in there.

I tried to be cool, but I was intent on checking the windows and doors for signs of forced entry. When I found none—no broken windows, no split doorjambs—I realized that the burglar had climbed in the tiny bathroom window over my bathtub with the whirlpool accessory that I sometimes forgot to lock. I saw two small dirty footprints in the bottom of the tub. This "burglar" also knew the code to my security system and how long it took to dash to the controls and turn it off before the authorities were alerted.

Oh, I didn't think for a minute that it had been a random burglar in there.

When I got to my bedroom and saw clothes and jewelry and shoes tossed about like a hurricane had hit, I knew what the deal was.

It was Hurricane LaShawndra who had hit my home.

That little ho had come into my home and just taken what she had wanted. I checked my closets and drawers hurriedly. I truly did not believe that she had hit her own mother's home!

None of my TVs or my VCR was taken. None of my antique perfume bottles on my bedside table was disturbed. My computer, scanner, and printer were still connected and humming in my home office. But what was missing was an armful of my cutest, skimpiest outfits, my red leather wraparound dress, my dusty blue doeskin miniskirt, my little white eyelet retro halter top—I don't care that a few of them were a trifle snug on me right then. I planned to start on my Tae-Bo tapes the next week.

After I checked my closet and bedroom, something told me to check the refrigerator. I don't usually listen to that little voice inside because mine is wrong so often, but I went into the kitchen and opened the big black side-by-side. Sure enough, the three bottles of spring water I had put in there the night before were gone.

Then I ran back to the closet and checked. LaShawndra had also taken my good leather garment bag, two nylon overnight bags, and, even worse, my new animal-print overnight bag. I had not even used that giraffe-print bag yet. It still had a tag on it! I was saving it for a weekend trip I had hoped to take with Pastor to the Woman, Thou Art Loosed Conference in Atlanta in July. He had assured me we would have separate rooms and everything.

When I realized that no money was taken and then I checked the medicine cabinet and none of my prescription drugs were touched—

my doctor had given me some Valium for the stressful times in my life a few years ago and I still took them from time to time—I knew for certain it was no ordinary burglar.

This "burglar" only took cute little clothes—as if I'm not ever going to be able to fit back into them one day—and a couple of pairs of my most expensive sandals and some of my good underwear and new cotton panties with the tags still on them. And sure enough, I checked, and missing from my jewelry box were the big, heavy gold hoops that I knew LaShawndra coveted. This second-story girl was definitely LaShawndra, my daughter.

I was angry and ashamed and hurt and pissed off all at the same time. This was the thanks I got for letting her pick her own clothes since she was ten years old: She came and stole mine.

I picked up the portable phone in the bedroom to call the police. But I only got to the nine before I clicked it off and threw it on the bed. It bounced one time, careened off the coral-colored wall, and clattered to the floor in three pieces. That pissed me off, too.

I should have called the police anyway. But I knew Mother would never have forgiven me if I had gotten LaShawndra into even more trouble than she was already in with the break-in at her and Crystal's house.

I was so disgusted with LaShawndra that I just threw my head back and screamed like some bad actress in a B movie as I walked out of the bedroom. I hardly made it down the hall. I sat down on an ottoman in the living room—I had sent the sofa and chairs and table back to the store, but I did like the green suede ottoman that came with the set. I sat down there and cried like a baby for ten or fifteen minutes.

"What kind of person have I raised who would steal from her own mother?" I cried aloud. "LaShawndra *knows* better!"

I completely forgot that Nurse Bloom was standing there in the doorway of the living room, peeking into my empty dining room, her navy blue purse hanging over her folded arms.

Finally my sobs slowed down, and Nurse Bloom spoke, scaring me to death.

"The child stole your furniture?" she asked.

I started to lie. Then I thought better of it. I knew by now that Nurse Bloom could see right through my lies.

"No," I answered truthfully. "She took my good clothes and my new animal-print bag and a pair of my gold earrings. But not the furniture. I haven't had a chance to decorate and furnish completely in here," I said, sobbing.

"Well" is all Nurse Bloom said.

It seemed that LaShawndra's actions had even left Nurse Bloom speechless.

"I've never seen anything like this. Not in *my* family. LaShawndra don't care *nothing* about me, her own mother!" I was *too* embarrassed.

Nurse Bloom thought for a while and then said matter-of-factly— she didn't seem to have any other kind of tone of voice but strict and matter-of-fact—"It's not your concern whether or not she cares for you. The question is, Do you care for her?"

I couldn't stop myself. "That little thief!?" I cried. "Care for *her*? Care for *her*! Besides Mother, I'm the only one who has really *ever* cared for her! And anyway, who has she ever cared for but herself?

"Mother says all the time, 'People can change, Sandra. Young folks can make a turnaround.' But that's just the educator talking. She has to believe that to get up and put her efforts into the public-school system. But I know better. And this *proves* it!

"You talk about a lost generation. This one is. And, sad to say, my own daughter is at the head of that crowd."

Now she was stealing from her own mother!

"She doesn't need to *steal*, Nurse Bloom. She doesn't need to. Mother and Daddy and I give her everything she needs! Mother got her a job, although she didn't even finish high school."

"Well, she need *some'um!*" Nurse Bloom said.

"Well, hell, I ain't got it!"

I caught sight of a family portrait of Mother, LaShawndra, and me on the mantel over the fireplace—a real working fireplace. I had scheduled the photo session the spring before as a Mother's Day gift to Mother.

Now, looking at the three smiling faces in the photograph, I felt like such a fool. I jumped up and stormed across the room. Taking no thought for my injury, I smashed the frame against the white-brick hearth, sending glass shards flying everywhere. When the photograph fell away from the frame, I dropped the brass frame at my feet, picked up the picture, and tore it in three, ripping LaShawndra's image from those of my mother and me. Then I threw LaShawndra's section into the cold fireplace.

"You can throw her out of your life, but I promise you, you won't be able to throw her out of your heart." Nurse Bloom sounded like a totally different woman now.

"Watch me!" I said, almost hissing at her.

I stumbled over to the ottoman again, tripping over two large Spanish terra-cotta pots of dying orange and crimson bromeliads I had gotten from Mother and couldn't get to flourish the way hers did to save my life, and sank onto it.

Nurse Bloom came over to me, silent as the Ocawatchee River fog, and sat beside me on the big ottoman.

"I know lots of girls who would have given *anything* to have Lily Pines for a grandmother—a beautiful, loving, and *involved* grand-mother—and to be raised in the kind of home she was offered through a hardworking single mother like me," I said as I sobbed.

"But LaShawndra wasn't one of them."

LaShawndra didn't appreciate that every girl in Mulberry did not have home training the way she had.

For all the good it did.

"And to make matters worse, Nurse Bloom," I said, "Mother and LaShawndra will gang up on me in a *minute!*"

We'd all be together—the three of us—at Mother's house, sitting around the kitchen table, looking out at Mother's beautiful backyard and little babbling stream. Just like a family. And the next thing I know, I would be referred to as "the middle child." They team up and act as if Mother is the eldest, responsible one and LaShawndra is accepted as the baby, the spoiled one. And I'm "the problem child."

Nurse Bloom actually put her hand on my shoulder in a stiff, comforting gesture. She was trying to pat me on the shoulder, but in fact, what she did was hit me pretty hard. I think she was aiming for "Now, now, it's gonna be okay." Instead, it felt more like "Hey, buck up!"

I think it was the best she could do.

I know it's hard to believe, but I was beginning to find myself softening up to this old woman, who said just what was on her mind. She certainly was having an influence on me.

I had opened up to her in a way I had not even done to some of my best girlfriends who think they know *everything* about me.

Perhaps it was because she was like one of those overachieving older sisters who made no bones about the fact that she was judging you. So I was as honest with her as I had been with anybody in my life.

Nurse Bloom didn't seem to think too highly of me and my generation of women to begin with. With her, I felt as if I had gone to confession. I always envied Catholics, who could go into a small enclosure not much bigger than a telephone booth, unburden themselves, and come out washed clean. I hadn't felt clean in years. Nineteen to be exact.

"Maybe I just wasn't cut out to be a mother, Nurse Bloom. Every woman isn't, you know," I confessed to her.

"When LaShawndra wasn't but a few weeks old, I'd sit on my bed in the house on Oglethorpe Street and watch Mother hold and rock her so naturally. Mother would be singing and cooing, 'This a mama's angel, this a mama's *heartstring* here. This a mama's little baby girl here.' And I would think, Now, how does Mother do that? Does she really feel that way? Does she really *mean* those things? I don't think I *ever* said things like that to LaShawndra.

"If I did, I know the words got caught in my throat before they could come out.

"Mother thought it was postpartum depression, but I don't think it was. It never lifted.

"Now, here I am. Sitting in the biggest mess in the world. La-Shawndra has robbed her own mother. She's probably had something to do with the break-in at her own home. Her best and only friend is laying up at Mulberry Medical Center. And she's taken off without telling anyone for a hoochie-mama party in Atlanta.

"I tell you, Nurse Bloom, I'm sitting up in the biggest mess of my life."

Nurse Bloom tapped my shoulder again. It *really hurt* this time. But it got my attention.

"Sandra," she said, using my first name for the first time all morning, "*you* ain't in a mess. *LaShawndra* is."

When I looked up at her face, I could have sworn that she *was* a different woman. Her face, which had seemed so stern and disapproving before, with its furrowed brow and pursed lips, was now so gentle and accepting that I started to cry again.

When she spoke, her voice was so soft and sweet that it almost scared me. Where was that gruff, curt tone that I had come to expect from her? It was nowhere in these words.

"Young woman, when I say you can't throw somebody out your heart, I mean it. Back when I was a young girl, just about your La-Shawndra's age, the same thing happen to me that happened to you and your mama."

I swung my head up as I heard a gasp. Then I realized it was me.

"Yeah, Nurse Bloom ain't always been this upright, dried-up, over-the-hill old woman you see before you."

I had to look away for a second, because those were just some of the words I had been using in my mind to describe her. She gave a dry, sad little ironic chuckle and continued.

"I was living in the country with my grandmother before the First

World War, still just a skinny little flat-chested girl without one curve on my entire body, when I 'broke a leg,' as the old folks used to say. Grandmama's the one who raised me, because my mama had gone up north to Detroit to get a job at one of the factories there. What some folks called 'good jobs.' She went up there and never did come back for me.

"My grandmama, she was the community's midwife, so I had been watching babies developing in their mama's stomachs and babies being born all my life. So when I came up late in my cycle, I knew right away I was pregnant. And I also had been around enough women who was late, and heard the crazy stuff they had done and the homemade potions they had drunk to get rid of the baby to know what would work and what would kill you.

"They would come running to my grandmama for her to fix them up after they had messed their insides up with some concoction they drank. Grandmama was so kindhearted she hardly ever fussed at them for what they had tried to do.

"I didn't have no husband or no prospects, just this boy named Amos who I'd been messing around with since I was about sixteen. But I had plans. I wanted to go off and study to be a real nurse. I was a bright student, and Grandmama was so proud of me. Always bragging to her women and the white folks about how smart I was. She had been saving up her little egg and chicken and ironing money all my life for my nurse's training. I didn't want to make my grandmama shamed."

I was afraid to breathe and disturb the scene. I almost reached over and took Nurse Bloom's wrinkled old hands in mine. But I could feel her back stiffen as I moved toward her. So I just dried my tears, sat back, and let her talk.

"I screwed up my courage, waited for my Grandmama to be called off in the middle of the night to a woman having a bad time birthing, and took care of it myself. Hardest thing I ever did, drinking that nasty-tasting greenish concoction I had made. It made me sick, too.

"Grandmama was gone for three days and nights. And I was sick as a dog that whole time. Thought I *was* gon' die. But I didn't. And when Grandmama returned, I was well enough to pretend to be okay, doing my regular chores feeding the hens, hanging out clothes to dry, cooking our meals—and sitting up reading the Bible to Grandmama before bed and asking about her women patients.

"When I couldn't stand the thought of what I had done, I'd say I was gon' walk into town to the general store for some goods and go way out somewhere and lay in a ditch and cry."

I could hardly believe that Nurse Bloom was telling me all this, just the two of us sitting on my green suede ottoman in my living room, me hugging my knees to my chest. I didn't know what to say or do. But even in that vulnerable state, Nurse Bloom was in charge. I didn't have to say anything. She just kept on talking.

"After about four or five days I still had a big old lump in my throat all the time, but I wasn't going out to cry in a ditch no more. And Grandmama hadn't said nothing, so I figured she hadn't noticed. But the next night when I knelt at the foot of her old pine rocker to rub her tired feet, she looked down at me and asked, 'Where you get titties from?' And I just broke down crying.

"I wasn't with child no more, but my body had changed. And of course Grandmama saw it.

"I cried all that night in my grandmama's arms. She kept saying, 'You didn't have to do that, Joanna. You didn't have to go and do that.' Grandmama was crushed.

"It was that night back before 1920 that I decided to be a midwife. I devoted myself to that profession. I didn't get my nursing certificate until much later.

"I brought countless babies into this world, in and out of a hospital—

you was one of them. But I never forgot the one I didn't have. And I never did become a mother."

She stopped speaking for a while, and I just sort of looked down at my hands, now folded in my lap.

I couldn't bring myself to look up into Nurse Bloom's eyes.

"That's why I loved helping Dr. Williams to deliver babies at St. Luke's," she continued. "Every baby I brought into this world reminded me of the one that I didn't. And I know I did some good on this earth. I know it. But I could never throw that unborn child, my unborn child, out my heart."

13

Sitting on that soft suede ottoman in the middle of my nearly empty living room, I was as confused as I had been when LaShawn just up and deserted me when I was stuck out to there, as my grandmother, Mother's mother, had said over and over whenever I would waddle into a room. "Bless her heart. Look at her. She stuck out to there."

I tried to imagine Nurse Bloom young. I tried to picture her lying down naked in some Georgia country field with "Amos." I tried to imagine her afraid and at her wits' end, then full of relief and remorse. But all I could see was this stern old woman sitting next to me in a pristine nurse's uniform.

Sitting there in my invaded apartment, I felt the weight of Nurse Bloom's story and of the previous nineteen years like a ton of bricks on my heart.

I guess Nurse Bloom was right. I could not throw LaShawndra out of my heart. It *was* LaShawndra who was in a mess. But from where I sat, I felt I was in the middle of the mess right along with her. And the thought of taking on any of the responsibility for the both of us being there scared me worse than the memory of being in that delivery room without LaShawn and with all that blood and pain.

"Oh, Nurse Bloom, I don't think I can even begin to think about how I might have had something to do with the way LaShawndra is.

"I just don't know which way to turn," I told Nurse Bloom. And I was being truthful, because I had *no idea* just what I was going to do with that child.

"And now it seems as if you're making me see too much all at once."

"Maybe you should look at it one little bit at a time," she suggested.

I tried. I really did try. But as I sat there with my eyes closed, LaShawndra's whole life and my whole life came flooding back on me in too many scenes I wanted to erase forever:

Me at nineteen throwing myself down Mother's front staircase trying to make myself bleed the mistake out of my body.

LaShawndra at four months lying in her crib screaming her lungs out, and me standing there beside her frozen, the scent of Johnson's baby powder wafting around us, unable to take her in my arms, not *wanting* to take her in my arms.

LaShawndra at age eight getting up early one morning to try to fix me breakfast and burning up my only good Calphalon omelet pan. I could still hear the pain in her voice as she slammed into the bathroom muttering, "I was just tryna *please* you!"

Me at a fair at Mother's school pretending I didn't know who LaShawndra was when one of the other mothers pointed at her and said, "My God, look at that little one over there dressed just like a prostitute! Why would her mother let her come out of the house looking like that?"

"Oh, it's too late for this!" I cried in frustration, shaking my head until I almost became dizzy. "LaShawndra doesn't have a prayer," I told her.

Nurse Bloom gave me one of those looks of hers and said, "How you know? You ain't never prayed for her."

And I had to drop my head, because as many times as I had knelt down with Pastor, him clasping my tiny hand in his big one and raising them both to heaven, talking with God, I had never once thought to pray a true, fervent prayer for LaShawndra that did not include the words "Please, Lord, don't let that girl embarrass me today."

Nurse Bloom gave me a long, very thoughtful look—I don't think she had any other kind—and made a suggestion.

"Have you thought about calling your reverend friend?"

"Pastor? Call Pastor? Lord have mercy, Nurse Bloom, you have *got* to be kidding! I couldn't tell *him* about all of this! That my child is a thief and a liar and a little hoochie-mama whore. Hell, I been trying to keep all of *my* past from him as much as I can. I sure don't want him to know how much my daughter has messed up. What would I look like going to him telling him all my business?

"He preaches all the time on 'generational curses,' how the sins of the father are visited on the child and continue on from generation to generation.

"Mother says, 'Children don't take after strangers.' And I sure don't want Pastor thinking LaShawndra may have taken after me!"

"But if he is a man of God, pastoring a flock, don't you think he has heard it all?" she asked. "And if he is as good as you claim he is, what makes you think he's gon' condemn you?

"You got to have more faith in folks you love, and you got to have more hope for your child than faith," she said.

"What you gon' do? Just let her go down the drain like so much dirty bathwater?"

And I so wished she hadn't used that analogy, because then I could just see LaShawndra swirling down a filthy drain full of hair and scum and dead roaches, struggling for life and fighting for breath.

It was a terrible image, an image I felt I had seen and tried to forget before. I dropped my face in my hands and just wept some more.

I heard Nurse Bloom suck her teeth sharply and say, "Buck up, girl!"

And that just made me cry all the harder. I put up a good front, but I can't stand people to be mean to me. Then she softened.

"You know," Nurse Bloom offered, "in this life you gotta *fight* to live. You got to fight for every moment of life in this world. You got to fight for every breath you take. And I know what I'm talking 'bout."

When Nurse Bloom said that, I got a picture in my head of the first time I had seen LaShawndra. It was in the delivery room at the Mulberry Medical Center. She was lying in the doctor's gloved hands, covered in blood and mucus, struggling, struggling with all her little might to breathe. I was pretty drugged up, but it looked to me that there was something over her face hampering her breath. I had truly wanted to reach out and help. I think I even raised my right arm from the side of the delivery table. But then I recalled the last time I had seen LaShawn and felt the sharp hurt again of seeing him duck into the doorway of a religious bookstore—like he was going to be out at the Mulberry Mall buying a Bible—when he had caught sight of me coming toward him. I felt that hurt in my gut right where LaShawn-dra had been, and I quickly withdrew my hand.

"But every once in a while you truly need somebody in your corner to fight for you, too," Nurse Bloom continued.

"Some of us can do it all alone, and some of us can't. That's why we got each other."

I was going to remind her that *I* was a single mother and had done it all alone, but, as Mother says, "When you taking something out the lion's mouth, you don't yank your hand out. You *eeeeeease* it out." And that morning I certainly had gotten a lot from this particular lion named Nurse Bloom.

Then she tossed off one of those dismissive waves of hers and didn't give me a chance. Anyway, by then I had realized two things: I hadn't done it all alone. And I hadn't done that good a job with what I *had* done.

"Come on," she said, looking at the clock on the mantelpiece, "it's going on twelve. Get up, wipe your face, and take me back to town."

When I stood, I was so drained that my knees buckled under me. I had to steady myself by holding on to the walls of the hall as I wobbled to the bathroom. As I splashed cold water on my face, I noticed a thick damp peach velour towel the "burglar" had used and thrown in the direction of the clothes hamper and missed. It was just lying on the floor. Since I could still see her dirty shoe marks in the tub where she had broken in the window, I assumed she had only taken a whore's bath in the sink. And somehow that was as sad as her breaking into my apartment. But I was too exhausted to rail about that *and* still deal with Nurse Bloom.

I thought, Lord, now where is this old woman going to make me drive her? I just did not have the strength. Even though she had told me she was on a schedule, I could just see her ordering me around Mulberry until dark, looking for someplace called "Greenwood Bottom." But when we got in the car, she straightened the white nurse's cap on her head and said, "Take me back to the site of old St. Luke's Hospital. Somebody'll be by there for me at noon."

I started up the Mercedes and steeled myself for a lecture all the way back to Pleasant Hill. But she didn't say a word. She leaned her head back on the padded headrest and closed her eyes.

She didn't look nearly so old with her face in repose, her slack skin falling back smoothly toward her gray hairline. I thought, Uh, this old woman was there at St. Luke's when I was born. I tried to do the math to calculate her approximate age. Now, if she was nineteen before World War I, I thought as I pulled onto Orange Highway, how old would that make her now? I did the math, but then just dismissed my figures. Oh, that must be wrong, I thought. She *can't* be *that old*! She must have gotten her dates mixed up.

I could hear her snoring softly. I guess she wasn't as tough as she thought, because it seemed that the morning had worn her out. I know it had worn *me* out. Between Mother's early-morning call and the trip to the medical center and the break-in at my house and the burglary at Crystal's and Nurse Bloom's confession, I felt as if I could just crawl into a hole for a couple of weeks and pull the top in after me.

But in spite of my best attempts to distance myself from all that had happened that morning, Nurse Bloom had gotten me to thinking. I hate that. *Je déteste ça!*

It took me a couple of minutes to get up the nerve to disturb her. "Nurse Bloom?" I said softly.

She didn't stir. I said it again, a little louder this time.

"Nurse Bloom!"

"I ain't 'sleep," she said with her eyes still closed. "I ain't slept in the middle of the day since I was a baby. I was just resting my eyes for the trip back to my home."

It dawned on me I had not asked her what part of town she was living in or even if she was residing in Mulberry at the moment. But I decided not to go there. I had other things on my mind.

When she lifted her head from the headrest, I almost giggled, because her nurse's cap was pushed forward at a comical, jaunty tilt, like a sailor's on a weekend leave.

She straightened the cap and looked over at me as I continued to drive back down Orange Highway.

"What is it?" she asked.

I realized that my mouth was as dry as a powdered doughnut, so dry you would have thought I was taking my Realtor's exam for the first time. I swallowed hard, hoping she wouldn't hear the parched sound I made.

"I've been thinking..." I began.

"Oh?" she said. I mean, that old woman *could not* pass up an opportunity to be sarcastic with me. *Mon Dieu!*

However, once I had gotten my nerve up, I was not going to turn back. After all, I *am* Lily Paine Pines's daughter.

I forged on.

"I was thinking, Nurse Bloom, that when we finally find LaShawndra and she comes back and we get all this mess straightened out, maybe I ought to sit down and have a talk with her about myself a little bit, and about her, too."

All she did was lift one old eyebrow at me.

"Not that I haven't tried to talk to her before—Lord knows I've tried a million times to—"

She cut me off, "All right now, don't take one step forward and then turn around and run three backward.

"After all, you *are* Lily Paine Pines's daughter."

I didn't know if she was making fun of me or not. Considering our six-hour track record together, I figured she probably was. But I felt in my heart that I was onto something.

She didn't say anything for a while as I continued across the Ocawatchee River and toward the top of Pleasant Hill. I figured there wasn't anything else to say. I needed some quiet time myself, just to think. I believe that for the first time in her life, I truly longed to see LaShawndra's little face and wished she wasn't off somewhere, like at Freaknik.

"See, young woman," Nurse Bloom said after a few minutes of silence, almost with pride, "there is some hope for you yet." And that was it.

When we pulled up to the empty lot where St. Luke's Hospital had stood, there wasn't a car in sight. And I began to feel a little uncomfortable about her plans.

"Are you sure you'll be okay here by yourself until your ride comes?" I asked as I tried to help her from the car. She wouldn't let me take her arm.

"Course I'll be all right," she said snappishly, getting out of the car by herself. "It's almost noon now, isn't it?"

She stood on the sidewalk by the empty building site, squinted her black eyes at the hot noonday sun, and shaded them with her hand like an old farming woman, as if the digital watch had never been invented. I could just imagine her back at her grandmother's place in the country, chopping weeds in a little kitchen garden by the back door, looking up at the blazing sun to tell the time of day. I was beginning to sweat a bit myself in my St. John knit.

"I don't need you to be hanging around me like I'm a old invalid. *I* used to take care of invalids. Besides, I want a little private time here at the hospital site, if you don't mind."

I have to admit I was so glad to get that dear old exasperating demanding woman out of my car, I didn't know what to do. But I was also almost missing her already. Go figure!

"Well," I said, still hesitant to leave her there by herself.

"Go!" she said. "Go!"

When I kept standing there like a fool, unable to move, she added, "Maybe I'll give you a call sometime if I want anything."

I had almost forgotten for a moment that she was supposed to be looking for property. I assumed she hadn't seen anything that interested her, except the intimate details of *my life*.

I held out my hand, hoping she would ignore it and give me a hug. But she grabbed my hand, shook it firmly, and let it go.

Then she said, "You know, Miss Pines, you ought to think of giving your daughter your blessing sometime instead of always giving a curse."

"My *blessing?*" I said. I swear I had no idea what she meant.

"I mean, give her what *you* have been blessed with. You say your mother gave you herself—her time, her experiences, her handmade Halloween costumes, her strength. Don't you think she was blessing you with what she was blessed with?"

I thought about what she had said and nodded slowly.

"Well, give *your* daughter the blessing of what you have to offer. You claim you such a good businesswoman, why don't you bless your daughter with some good business sense?"

"Oh, Nurse Bloom, I've tried any number of times to get her interested in selling real estate. I've told her how much money she could make and all the things she could buy herself." I had to defend myself.

"No, Sandra, I mean bless her with some sense in *whatever* business she decide to go into. It ain't got to be *your* business. But she gon' need some business sense no matter what she do, ain't she?"

I stood there for a moment and nodded like a schoolgirl.

"Stand over her when she ain't looking, and extend your hand over her head, and bless her with your sense of proper fashion."

I had to smile a little, because until then I thought Nurse Bloom thought I looked funny and was dressed inappropriately for the occasion. Lord knows that's what I thought about LaShawndra.

Tina McElroy Ansa

"Bless her with a knowledge of how to do her hair and her makeup properly. Bless her with your knowledge of how to take care of herself in a pinch. Don't be always cursing her with picking the wrong man or the wrong friends or always being in trouble. Don't pass on the curse of having a baby before she ready, while she still a baby herself. Don't pass on none of that stuff."

Nurse Bloom extended her own right hand toward me, and I flinched a bit because I thought she might strike me. But she didn't. Instead, she spread her wrinkled old fingers over my head and said, "Bless your child, Sandra!"

I swear to God, at that very moment my knees became so weak I thought I might just fall to the dusty red ground and ruin my suit. At the same time my eyes closed, and I felt warmth spread all over my body.

When I opened my eyes, I was standing there just swaying from side to side.

And Nurse Bloom stood before me—her feet planted solidly, her arms folded, her navy blue leather bag hanging from her left arm—looking in the direction of where St. Luke's Hospital had once stood.

I started to say something. I think I wanted to thank her, but before I could get any words together, she repeated her original command without even looking at me: "It's got to be almost noon. Go!"

There seemed nothing left for me to do but make my wobbly way back to the Mercedes, get in, and drive away, which is what I did.

I tried to keep her in my rearview mirror for a while, but by the time I reached the corner up by the park and turned, Nurse Bloom had disappeared from my sight.

I was tempted to drive back by the pastor's church to check on him. Well, really to have him check on me, because I didn't know whether I was coming or going. But as I neared the church, I heard the chimes playing "Take My Hand, Precious Lord," and I could almost hear Nurse Bloom saying in my ear, "Don't always go running to mankind, young woman. Go to the one who can help you," in that way she had. So I bypassed the church—Pastor's car wasn't there anyway—and said a little prayer instead. It had been a long time since I had done *that* and felt any relief. Then I picked up my cell phone and dialed my answering machine.

When I checked, Mother had left another message on my machine at work, not even mentioning Nurse Bloom and the full day—six hours—I had taken up with her, but letting me know she was headed for the hospital to see about Crystal and her children.

I was too exhausted to deal with that on an empty stomach. So I headed back home first to change into some comfortable clothes and get a bite to eat.

It was well after noon when I pulled into the garage under my condo. And although I did not recognize it at the time—I thought it was just hunger pangs—I felt something like a flicker of hope in the pit of my stomach.

But that small light went out completely when I checked my messages on the machine in the kitchen and there was a message from the Mulberry Police Department.

"Would you please call this number as soon as possible in connection with your daughter LaShawndra Pines's whereabouts? She is being sought for questioning in connection with the break-in at three o'clock this morning at 442 Painted Bunting Lane. Thank you."

part 3. LOVE

LaShawndra Pines

14.

Now, okay, I know nobody's gonna believe this, 'cause nobody don't *never* believe what *I* say. And I know some folks gon' laugh at me, 'cause they don't think no more a' me than I'm just a little small-town ho from Mulberry, Georgia. But this time I *swear to God* this is the truth. This is just what happened that day I was out by the side of Highway 90 trying to get a ride to Freaknik.

First of all, I ain't on no "spiritual journey" or nothing like Mama Mama is or like Sandra claim she is. I just read my horoscope ever' day. It's *all* I read in the newspaper besides the comics. And I call the psychic hot lines from time to time. But that morning I was standing out there by the highway praying my butt off! I just kept saying out loud, "Helpme, helpme, helpme, helpme, helpme, helpme." I needed some help, you hear me?

I couldn't get no ride to save my life. I had asked everybody I knew in Mulberry to drive me up to Atlanta. All them people I hang out with at The Club. All them brothers whose breaths wasn't completely fresh that I done kicked it with. All them hos I done lent my lipstick to in the bathroom of some club when I shouldn'ta had because I don't know *where* their lips had been. But no, now couldn't nobody with a ride of any kind help me out, couldn't nobody hook me up. Any other time niggas be driving up to the house honking their horns and yelling, "Lil' Bit, you wanna go for a ride?" But no, not that day. Not one somebody would give me a ride even after I *begged* 'em. So there I was out there on the edge of town by the side of the highway in the hot sun trying to hitch a ride out of town.

At first so many cars passed me by I was beginning to take it personal. It was like they didn't even see me. For real, I was beginning to think they were doing it on purpose to keep me from leaving Mulberry. A great big old RV nearly ran over me and my stuff. For real! I woulda took down their license number if I'da had a pen.

And I was so stressed out, 'cause there was a lot going on that day with me and my little life. I had just about sweated all my makeup off and all the little crispness out my outfit.

It was a good thing I had had enough money for cab fare from the Sherwood Arms Condominiums out to the old county highway and hadn't had to walk all the way out there! But it took *all* my money! I betcha I didn't have thirty-five cents left in my pocketbook. Shoot, all I wanted was a *ride*.

I bet I had been out there standing on that clump of weeds and that dusty red Georgia clay in the hot sun with all my stuff around me for more than an hour. For forever!

When I looked up into the sky, the sun was big and round and yellow as my toenail polish. It was right over my head and so hot I could feel my scalp burning. I stopped praying long enough to look at my watch—it look like a bracelet, but it's really a watch. Mama Mama gave it to me my last birthday—and it was twelve noon, straight up.

Then, all of a sudden, I felt things cool off, because this great big old fluffy cloud covered up the sun, and I saw this big old dust cloud thing moving toward me along the road. It was headed right for me, but I was so surprised by it I couldn't move a muscle. When the dust cleared, I saw a big black shiny car come up on me like outa *nowhere*—I mean, out of nowhere! One minute it wasn't there, and the next it was. Like a magic trick or something. It appeared like outa that cloud of dust or a puff a' smoke or something.

Oh, it like to scared me to death! I betcha I jumped ten feet in the air and almost fell over one of my travel bags. For real!

Then, real slow, the passenger-side window facing me rolled down like something in a spaceship or something. And this old old sister was sitting at the wheel.

I have no idea exactly how old she was. You know, I can't even go there 'bout getting old, 'cause I can't stand to even think of *my* body getting old and fat and saggy.

Miss Thing shoulda had gray hair or blue hair, but it wasn't either one. This old sister's hair was red! Okay? Almost blond! I think it was "Autumn Haze." I know hair colors 'cause I do hair sometimes, and I had just did this ho's hair from The Club that very same color a few weeks before 'cause she gave me a ride down to Jacksonville to a party after a Jaguars' game.

If the whole thing of her driving up so sudden hadn't scared me so bad, I woulda said, "Do it, girl!"

Her hair wasn't long and nappy like Mama Mama's, and it wasn't greasy and dead straight like it was done with a hot comb like some old folks'. Her hair was relaxed and laid to the side with soft finger waves all the way down the back and the sides.

Then there was her face. Miss Girl's face was *made up*! Not like a old lady's makeup either, with red spots on her cheeks and flat lipstick all around and outside her mouth.

No, somebody had *beat* Miss Lady's face, you hear me? I probably couldn'ta done a better job myself, and I'm a sort of semiprofessional makeup artist. Her base color matched her light-complected skin just right and was blended in perfect at her old neck without caking up in any of her wrinkles—and she had plenty of them—on her throat. Mama Mama say aging light-skinned women break like white women 'round their neck. She say they break like bone china. This old lady's blush was applied in a angle up her cheekbone that made it look real natural and—what's the word?—flattering. And her eye makeup was applied so you could hardly notice it—no blue shadow and raccoon eyes for *her*! It was all tan and dusty mauve.

Even I was impressed.

I couldn't see her whole outfit from where I was standing, but her jacket had ruffles around the neck and was so low-cut I could almost see her titties! For real. It was made out of some kinda light, light material that looked like cotton knit, and it was a kinda shiny pinkish beige that looked good with her skin.

She leaned forward, and I could really almost see her titties. Then she rested her right arm—it was kinda flabby up above the elbow—on the top of the steering wheel, lifted her big round brown sunglasses up on her forehead, and looked at me real hard, like she was trying to make sure who I was. But it wasn't a mean look. It was friendly, just real intense.

When she opened her mouth and said something, I jumped again. She didn't sound *nothing* like I expected her to. Her voice sounded like it came from the back of her throat, with little tiny Christmas bells attached. Like a young woman playing with you. Real sexy and pretty.

"Lil' Schoolgirl," she said, all serious and everything. "You old enough to be out here on Highway 90 thumbing a ride all by yourself?"

And even though my heart was pounding in my chest so hard I could hear it in my ears, I answered her right back. Mama Mama say I'm quick on my feet.

"Heck, yeah," I hollered back at her. "I'm almost nineteen, and you know that's 'bout forty-five in hoochie-mama years. Hee-hee.

"I just look real young 'cause I'm little and short."

She kind of laughed to herself and shook her head and said, "Well, get on in, then." And the door on the passenger's side just swung open.

I was so glad to just get a ride outa Mulberry I didn't think about that door just swinging open like that by itself until later on. And by then it was too late.

"Well, no matter how old I am, I sure do appreciate you picking me up and giving me a ride this morning," I told her as I started throwing all my stuff in that car. "You a angel."

But I did need to stop and catch my breath a couple of times. That car of hers appearing out of a cloud of dust like that had *scared* me.

"Wow," I told her as I kept on throwing my stuff in the car, the leather purse Mama Mama gave me first, "it looked like you came outa nowhere. Anyway, I sure am glad you did. I'm so ready to get outa Mulberry, Georgia, I don't know what to do!

"I ask you, what *is* America if a little ho like myself cannot get a ride all on her own just up the road to Atlanta for Freaknik?

"You *are* going all the way to Atlanta, right?" I stopped, 'cause I didn't feel like getting all my stuff out of her car and standing by the side of the road again trying to hitch another ride.

She nodded, and I was on it.

"How are you going to get back?" she asked.

"Oh, no, no, no, no, no," I told her. "I don't need no ride *back* to Mulberry! No way! This ride up there all I need."

Shoot, I figured I wasn't *never* coming back to Mulberry.

She offered to help me with my things, but I told her, "Oh, no, no, don't bother to get out the car. That's okay, I can get it."

But then I did need her to take my extra bottle of natural spring water for me. And then I asked her to pop the latch on her trunk so I could put my extra makeup bag in there. Then I had to ask her to be extra careful with the black-and-yellow animal-print bag.

"It belong to Sandra," I told her.

"Is that one of your friends?" she wanted to know as she turned and put it on the backseat behind her. She was pretty strong for a old lady.

"Naw, Sandra ain't no friend," I told her. "Sandra, she my mom. She spell it S-A-N-D-R-A, but she say it S-A-U-U-U-N-D-R-A. I can't *stand* her! She so *phony*! She call herself a expert in speaking foreign languages, so she throw in some French when she wants to talk about me to my face without me knowing what she's saying or when she's talking to somebody she trying to impress. She so, so phony!

"And she gon' have a fit when she find out I took her new giraffe-print bag to Freaknik."

It still had the tag on it.

"How 'bout hanging this dress bag in the back, you know, on that hook over the back door?" I asked as I almost came to the end of my bags.

"Is this *everything* you own in the world, Lil' Schoolgirl?" she asked me as I handed her my blue makeup bag through the door. I liked that, 'cause that's what Mama Mama used to call me sometimes. It's from a old blues song. I guessed that's why this old lady knew it. Even as stressed as I was that day, I couldn't help but smile. The thought of my grandmama always makes me smile.

"Naw, this ain't nowhere near everything I own. I guess it *does* look like that, though. I don't usually travel with alla this stuff. A little hoochie like me usually gotsta travel light!" I said as I continued handing her things. "I probably got more shorts and jeans and shoes and stuff here than I need, but I don't know how long I'm gon' be gone . . . this time. Even though I *do* like to change my look two or three times a day, a little hoochie don't *need* many clothes at Freaknik. With all them cute college girls running around in nothing but Daisy Dukes and lacy bras, the last thing a little ho like me need at Freaknik is extra clothes!"

She didn't say anything, but she kinda made a ugly face, so I figured she just didn't know what "Daisy Dukes" were. So I told her.

And all she said was "Um."

As I hopped in the car and settled into the soft, creamy leather seats—they were like *butter*—I got a good look at her whole outfit for the first time. I know my mouth was hanging open. Miss Thing's light pink skirt was so short I couldn't hardly believe it. Mama Mama would have said, "You could almost see 'possible.' " And she had her old feet stuffed in the prettiest pair of beige high-heeled sandals I think I ever seen!

She caught me looking at her legs, so I did some quick thinking—Mama Mama say I'm a quick little study sometimes—and covered real quick. "I like that suit," I said. "And that hat, too."

"I'll let you wear it sometime," she said, and with her fingers kinda touched the brim of her pink hat shaped like a man's hat with a big pink feather on it. I think I had seen Eve wear one like it in a magazine. Then she cranked up the car, which surprised me, 'cause I was almost sure it was already on, but I don't drive, so what did I know?

We was ready to roll when I looked around and realized something.

"Wait! Hold up! Hold up!" I didn't mean to, but I really screamed it. "Where my panda bag?! Where my panda bag?! Hold up! Hold up! My *daddy* gave me that bag! Where my bag?"

Then I saw it right there hanging on my shoulder. Huh-hee-hee. I showed it to her. "Never mind, here it is. See, it look like a stuffed panda bear, but it's really like a backpack.

"Sorry, my bad," I apologized. "I *was* almost bugging, huh?"

Whew! I almost lost it there for a minute. I was *so* stressed out!

"Okay, I'm ready when you are. Let's get *rolling*!"

But she stopped me, all correct and everything, stuck out her hand and introduced herself.

"How you do, baby? My name is Eliza Jane Dryer. You can call me Liza Jane."

When I took her hand, it was so soft. It felt like a velvet glove. And it looked like she just had a new French manicure. I used to go out to Lovejoy's 2 at the Mulberry Mall every week to get my nails did. But I don't anymore, and they still look good all the same.

Dang, it was just too much trouble and bother to try to get some nigga to pay for my beauty-shop run every week. Shoot, I just do my nails myself and save *that fuck*!

"Uh, Eliza Jane Dryer, that's a sweet name. Miss Eliza Jane Dryer. Sound like somebody in a old black-and-white movie. Nice to meet you, too. My name LaShawndra Pines."

But she looked at me with this little question-mark look on her face. So I had to do her like I do them hos down at The Club and at the recording studio up in Macon who pretend they can't understand a perfectly good name.

"I *said*...my name...La-Shawn-dra. Capital L, small a, capital S, small h, small a, small w, small n, small d, small r, small a. LaShawndra. You spell it just like it sound. My daddy's name LaShawn. My mama's name Sandra. My name's LaShawndra. LaShawndra Pines."

I *love* my name. It really *means* something to me, you know? It's like those stories they have on cable on everybody who blows up the spot. You know, like *Behind the Music*. I don't know why people name you something, then make fun of it. Psst! Sandra so phony.

"I do just fine, thank you. How do *you* do, Miss Liza Jane?"

I just couldn't call that old, old lady by her first name even though her skirt was almost shorter than the little green one I had on.

During the introductions I was trying not to stare at this old lady whose look was *tight* as mine, so I looked around the inside of her car.

Now, Miss Liza Jane had her a nice ride. Oooh. It felt so *good* up in there. It smelled good, too. Real sweet.

And it was cool, but not too cool. I couldn't even feel the AC blowing directly on me. It was just right.

"What this is?" I asked. "A Lexus?"

Miss Eliza Jane Dryer just pointed to the cat and the emblem on the dashboard.

"A Jaguar?!" I said. "A Jaguar?! Snap, it sho' is! Says so right here. And look, you still got the cat on the nose a' your car.

"*Dang!* I ain't never even *been* in one a' *these*." I had to rub my hand 'cross the dash and console. It was like butter, too.

"How I look? How I look? How I look sitting up in here in this Jag? How I look?" I asked her, striking one a' my best poses.

"You look just fine," Miss Liza Jane said without even looking over at me.

Shoot, I wished right then I'd brought a camera with me so she could take a picture of me sitting up there in that Jag. But I was just tryna grab up some stuff and get up outa Sandra's that morning.

This car was the *bomb*!

I looked around for the phone. "You ain't got no cell phone up in here?"

I was disappointed in Miss Thing having that Jag and everything. I thought she'd be more on point than that.

Miss Liza Jane shook her head. "You need one?" she asked.

"It's just that I need to make a kinda important phone call right soon," I explained. "It's to somebody in Mulberry. I can call from a pay phone as soon as we make a stop. We *are* gonna be stopping soon, huh? 'Cause I got tiny, tiny kidneys and I pee a *lot!* Mama Mama call me 'Tinkle Town.' Especially when I'm stressed out."

"I'm not in any hurry," she said. "We can stop as soon as you like."

I appreciated that. I don't never hardly get nothing my way.

I didn't get a chance to read my horoscope that morning—I'm a Scorpio—but never mind how it had started out, I just knew that this *was* meant to be a "rewarding" day as opposed to a "challenging" one.

"It's a lucky thing I waited for *you*," I told her. I'm lucky that way. Sandra call it "dumb luck." I get outa more scrapes than anybody I know. Things usually work out for me. Well, they had up until then.

Miss Liza Jane didn't seem in any hurry to put the Jag in drive and get off the side of the road and on to Atlanta. And since it was her ride, I didn't say nothing.

"Lil' Schoolgirl, do you think it's wise to be out here on this county road by yourself hitching a ride with people you don't know?" she asked, like I had all the time in the world to sit chitchatting.

"Sure it is," I said. "I pick my rides real careful! Contrary to what everybody tries to be saying about me, I do *not* get into just *any* car with just *anybody*. I pass up all kindsa raggedy, trashy vehicles to get a ride in a car that's slammin'.

"Shoot, I took a couple passes before you drove up and stopped for me. And I really *need* a ride. At first it looked like nobody would stop, then it look like *everybody* was stopping.

"A guy in a blue truck, ppsst—*a old pickup truck!*—and another boy in one of those cars that could be a police car—a Oldsmobile or a Pontiac or something—painted *brown* stopped, but I just sucked my teeth and looked the other way.

"*Then*—you not gon' believe this!—then a old brother in a hearse drove up. Yes! A hearse! I guess that's why it shook me so much when you drove up in this black Jaguar. At first I thought he was driving a big black shiny limo. And I perked all up and brushed myself off, 'cause, number one, I *love* me a limo, and, number two, you know you get dusty standing by the side a' the road, and a girl standing by the side of the road can't be too careful about her looks. But then that thing pulled up and I saw what it was! *A hearse!* I didn't even look at it good. I just covered my eyes like this with one hand and waved it on with the other!"

"Was anybody in the back?" Miss Liza Jane asked, all playful like it was funny.

"Shoot, I don't know! I told you I didn't look. I ain't exactly *scared* a' dead people. I just don't wanna ride all the way to Atlanta with one."

Miss Liza Jane laughed out loud this time.

"What's funny 'bout that?" I wanted to know. I was *serious*!

She just shook her head and told me, "Go on."

"Annnnyway, I didn't even have to *think* to pass on them losers! Shoot, getting a ride in those old-nothing cars—*and a hearse*—I might as well be taking the *Greyhound bus*.

"Some of the folks I know, Crystal an 'em—well, not Crystal this time, but the rest of them kept saying, 'Why don't you jump on a Greyhound bus and go to Atlanta? Why don't you just jump on a Greyhound bus?'

"Now, folks who know me know good as anything I don't ride no bus unless it's got a band and musical instruments on it. Shoot, I know some girls from little bitty towns around here in middle Georgia—towns smaller than Mulberry, like Cochran and Hawkinsville and Montezuma—those hos be using the Greyhound bus system like Carey limousine service.

Tina McElroy Ansa

"Them girls be getting on the bus in Milledgeville and getting off in Macon, getting on in Unadilla and getting off in Savannah to do some shopping. Then they get back on the bus and ride all the way down to Jacksonville, Florida, to party with the Jaguars. You know, the professional football team down there. Now, I done that. That's how I know how to spell 'Jaguar.'

"I've partied with some a' them football players. But I sho' didn't take *me* no *bus* down there to Jacksonville, Florida, to do it. I caught me a ride with a girl in exchange for doing her makeup. You can almost always find somebody going that way. Shoot, I know girls who *wear out* the NFL *and* the NBA. And they ain't no Toni Braxtons neither.

"Shoot, I know some hos who say they know *all* the Greyhound bus drivers' first and last names who got routes in middle Georgia. They say on Friday afternoon the buses be waiting for 'em at the little dinky country bus stations like limos outside a Wu-Tang concert."

Then I just shut up, because I caught myself talking too much again. Sandra always telling me, "You talk too much, LaShawndra, you make folks hate you." I think she just say that to shut me up, but I did notice that Miss Liza Jane was so busy listening to me she wasn't driving that car.

But after I shut up, she still just sat there looking at me like I was still telling her something. So I thought I'd drop a hint.

"I *know* we fixing to get rolling, but can I spread this little blue-and-white-striped outfit out on your backseat first?"

Miss Liza Jane nodded and watched me kneel on my seat and dig in one of my bags for the outfit, Sandra's outfit. Since I'm tryna tell the truth and everything, I have to admit that everything I had with me except my purse and my makeup bag that I carry *everywhere* with me belonged to Sandra, even the shoes on my feet.

"That's cute," she said when I finally dug it out.

"Thanks, but it's cotton, and if I keep it rolled up in this bag till I

You Know Better

get to Atlanta, it's gon' be all wrinkled, and I may not have no iron where I'm going."

"Where you going?" she asked.

I didn't know what to say, 'cause I didn't have *no* idea where I was heading. I just told everybody I was going to Freaknik, 'cause that's what folks expect from me. I tell folks all the time, I'm just a little freak. All I knew that day was I had to get the heck outa Mulberry. I was kinda making it up as I went along.

"Oh, I got a couple of plans," I lied. "My granddaddy, Charles, lives outside Atlanta, and I might call him," which was a *huge* lie, 'cause the last thing I wanted was to let anybody in my family know where I was. To tell the truth, my family was part of what I was running from. "I'm probably gon' crash with some brother or other. And you know niggas don't be having no iron and ironing board—unless they gay or a mama's boy. And I ain't gon' be staying with neither one of *them*!

"I know 'bout niggas, now. My brothers and my music, that's what I *know*!"

She kinda made a face and cleared her throat.

"I got some Life Savers in one a' these bags," I offered.

She just waved 'em away and asked, "Oh, so you're a musician?"

"Well, I'm not exactly what you'd call a musician, exactly. I don't really play a musical instrument or anything, other than like some cowbells or a triangle or something. But I got a foot in the music industry, sort of."

Miss Liza Jane leaned back in her soft, cream-colored leather driver's seat and gave me another one of those question-mark looks.

"That's kind of a joke," I explained. " 'Cause, you see, that's what I wanna do with my life. I want to get my foot in the door, to dance in a music video."

She didn't say nothing, but I paused for a second, 'cause I half expected her to say something outa place like most old folks do when

I tell them about my plans. So then she said all polite and everything, "Oh, a music video."

"Um-huh. That's what I said: dance in a music video. That's *my* dream. You know, be one of them girls who *have* to be in all the videos who be showing a lotta skin and shaking their butts and th'owing their hair around. Shoot! *I* could do *that*! And with these new contacts. See, I ain't really got aqua eyes. Shoot, *I* could be one of those girls with the big titties and the green eyes on videos.

"*And* I can really dance, too!"

Miss Liza Jane listened real serious and didn't make a face like Sandra and Mama Mama always do. So I felt good about going on.

"All I want to do is get my shot, in one or maybe even a coupla music videos that get played a lot on MTV or BET. Then, I figure, for a little ho like me, it'll be clear sailing.

"Then I could be seen all over the world and everything. I could blow up the spot if I could just get the chance. If I could just get my shot, just *one shot* in a Top Ten video that play everywhere in the whole world on TV and maybe win a award.

"And I could be all up onstage, and maybe they let me say a word.

"Shoot! That's what *I* want.

"I ain't no kinda chickenhead little ho. I got a ambition. I'mo show people I can be something other than a buncha trouble. I'mo show 'em.

"I am!"

I was so stressed out by everything, I was almost shouting at that good-looking old woman in her black Jaguar. But I meant every word of it. I felt real comfortable with her, but I didn't feel comfortable enough to tell her the whole truth. I didn't mention the words I was writing whenever I could think of it, lyrics to songs that played in my head all the time. They were my *real* heart's desire.

Miss Liza Jane looked at me hard and deep. She reached down on the console and opened a pack of Juicy Fruit lying there. Slowly, she unwrapped a stick of the gum and slid it under her nose a couple of times. I thought she was gonna slip it in her mouth, but she didn't. She just held it under her nose. Then she picked up another stick and handed it to me. That's when I realized my mouth was so dry I felt like I'd been smoking chronic all night. And I hadn't had a joint in days, 'cause it was making me so forgetful.

I folded the stick of gum in half and put it into my dry mouth. We sat there awhile, looking out the windshield and enjoying our Juicy Fruit.

But wasn't no music on or nothing. So I couldn't stand the quiet one minute longer.

"Excuse me, Miss Liza Jane," I said, "but can't we drive and chew gum at the same time?"

She looked at me real hard again, opened her window, and threw her stick of gum out.

"Yeah," she said, "if you think you ready."

I said, "Yeah. I *been* ready!"

"Well, buckle your seat belt, then."

I did. And she *finally* put the Jag in drive and pulled off onto Highway 90, heading north.

15

She didn't look like she would drive the way she did. Miss Liza Jane looked like she would have that foot with the sexy beige sandal all *up in* the gas tank. But she didn't.

She drove so sloooow. We hardly pulled off at all. It was more like we creeped off. She might not a' been dressed like a old lady, but she sure did drive like one. If I'da had a Jaguar and a real driver's license, which I don't have neither one of them, I woulda been in Atlanta in fifteen minutes! At the rate she was driving, I figured we wouldn't even make it to the Mulberry County line in a hour. And the thought of still being anywhere near Mulberry, Georgia, almost made me want to bust out crying.

For real, that's the truth. Although I was putting on what Mama Mama called a "big brave front," I was feeling so bad and low I couldn't hardly keep my mind on where we went or how long it took to get there.

For a long time I had felt like I was all alone in the world, no daddy and no real mama. But that day I felt more alone than I think I had ever felt in my whole life. Because I had done something so messed up that I didn't think I could ever have anybody on my side ever again.

I ain't never had that many friends ever, especially girlfriends. But for the last year things had been kinda different. I had been living with my *best* girlfriend, Crystal.

But saying that doesn't really tell the whole story. I didn't just *live* in the same place with Crystal and her two children, Davon and Baby Girl. We all lived *together*. They my family, too. When I walk into the room, Davon, the baby, just raise his little arms for me to pick him up. It just make my heart hurt to think about it.

Crystal even taught her children to call me "Auntie LaShawndra." And ain't *nobody* ever did that! Except for them and Mama Mama, I ain't nobody's *nothing*!

I was hoping *I* could be the kinda auntie that *I* ain't never had.

Oh, I got two aunts out in California and a aunt in Mulberry named Mildred, my daddy's sisters. The last time I saw her was almost a year ago out at Lovejoy's 2 at the mall. There's a Lovejoy's 1, too, but it's where mostly old sisters be going to get their hair and nails did. Mildred was at Lovejoy's 2 getting her hair cut and styled. She had the nerve to act like she didn't even *see me*. Then, when I caught her eye when she was under the dryer and she couldn't pretend no more that she didn't see me, she had the nerve to go, "LaShawndra!? Girl, is that *you*? I didn't know who you *was*!"

She knew good and doggone well who I "*was*." And she reached in her purse and pressed a twenty-dollar bill in my hand. But that wasn't but that one time. And a lotta times I sure coulda used more from her than twenty dollars.

Oh, don't get me wrong, a few dollars always come in handy, especially for a little ho like me who don't ever plan to work a regular paying job. But lotsa times, I don't know, I coulda used somebody to just listen to me or tell me something I could understand, rather than being all sweet up in my face 'cause they think people watching them. Then be talking 'bout me behind my back. Talking 'bout how I didn't take after *their* side of the family 'cause they ain't got no *wild folks* in *their* family tree.

My own auntie tryna pretend like she didn't even know me! You talk about *dissing* a sister! My daddy's whole family, they all act like they shamed of me or something.

I don't know why! Most times I ain't nothing to be shamed of. Most times anyway.

That's why I was hoping to be a good play auntie to Crystal's children—before I messed up so bad.

We all stay in a real nice three-bedroom apartment in a part of town called Bird City on Painted Bunting Road. It ain't all upscale like where Sandra live, but it's nice.

Shoot, when I first left Mama Mama's house, the *day* I turned eighteen, I slept all *over* Mulberry. With this "friend" and that "acquaintance," this one's cousin and that one's play sister. Folks let you stay with them for a while as long as you doing their hair or makeup or sucking their dick or something. But that don't last but a night or two. And brothers don't hardly want you to stay all night. So I was *happy* when Crystal asked if I wanted to share a home with her and the babies. And a stable one, too.

Crystal had been in foster care her whole life. And she told me she been planning what her own home was going to be like since she was four years old.

I mean for real, it's *nice.* Like Mama Mama's house. It just ain't as expensive and got as much good stuff as Mama Mama's, but it's still nice. Crystal painted all the rooms herself. Bright, happy colors. She painted the children's room with all kindsa flowers and trees and little brown fairies and bunnies and squirrels and stuff. Just like it was out-doors in a park. Then she went back and painted a sky and stars and the sun and the moon on the ceiling. Crystal a good artist. She can draw *and* paint.

My room is "Robin's Egg Blue." Crystal's is "Coral Pink." Crystal call my room the "Hot Box." I call her bedroom the "Ice Crystal Palace," 'cause 'cept for her babies' daddies, don't nobody hardly get in *there*. Crystal is like one of those old Bible folks they talk about on television preaching shows, folks who only do it when they want to make children and not just for sex. Psssta!

Mama Mama say 'bout me and Crystal, "Opposites attract."

Crystal got books on the shelves and magazines and newspapers and stuff laying around, and she read 'em and read 'em to her babies, too. Me, I try not to read too much, even though Mama Mama had me reading before I went to kindergarten. Brothers see you reading, they don't wanna be kicking it with you that much. And besides, niggas be all up on you, saying you must be smart or something if they see you with your face in a book. Sometimes they be asking you questions to see what you know, and I don't do well on tests. So...

It feel so good there at Crystal's, like music playing when ain't even no music on. It's a real snug little place. That's what Mama Mama call it. A "snug little place."

It's one of the few places anywhere in this world where I feel whole, like myself, all the parts of LaShawndra come together there.... Well, they used to. For real. I know that make it sound like I think I'm all that when I ain't nothing but a little ho from Mulberry, Georgia, but it's true.

I call the decorating style of my room "Early Inspirational," 'cause I got lots of pictures from magazine covers of Janet and Toni and Mary J. and Missy and Foxy—girls I like or who I want to be like in the business—all over the walls. And they are good inspiration.

And I got little stickers—stars and moons and bluebirds and hearts and rainbows and butterflies and flowers and angels—that I put on my pictures from time to time. You know, like, if I wake up hearing Mary J. singing in my ear, then I feel like I *have to* give my girl a gold star or a butterfly or something. And I start my day by giving some of my girls on the wall they props for the day. I go around my room and pick out two or three and put a gold star or something on they picture to boost 'em up.

I love my room at Crystal's place. It's just the way I want it. And Crystal don't *never* come sneaking around in my clothes and things the way Sandra used to. Sandra don't care nothing 'bout me, she just nosy. But that's just how Sandra do things. That's her B.O. Wait! I think it's M.O. Well, it's either B.O. or M.O. Anyway... When I would catch her with her hands in the pockets of my coat, she say something stupid like, "I was looking for a pair of pantyhose."

It do feel safe at Crystal's. It ought to with all those burglar bars she got on her windows and locks on the doors. Shoot, Crystal wouldn't let nothing invade her household if she could help it. And I wouldn't neither, not on purpose. Things can just happen sometime without you knowing you were a part of it. You know.

Crystal got the good kinda burglar bars that pop open from the inside when you touch a special button. Baby Girl know how to open them bars. Crystal take 'em through safety drills just like in school.

Our home is a nice place to be, but Crystal say I'm hardly ever there. She say I don't hardly need no key. I wish she hadn't never given me one. I'm so irresponsible sometimes. That's what *everybody* say. Well, everybody but Crystal. Crystal, she trust me.

But it ain't like she trust me so she don't have to be bothered the way Sandra do. "Oh, you just wear whatever you want to. I trust your judgment," Sandra'll say. And all she care about is clothes. Crystal different. She still always checks my bed in the morning and worries about me when I don't come home for two or three nights. So I try to call or something if I'm staying over at some nigga's crib. She's only known me two years, but it seem like she known me my whole life.

Me and Crystal, we like that.

And I guess we are opposites, 'cause Crystal got credit. *Good credit!* She got white-folks credit. Oh, Crystal got insurance and a driver's license and AAA and stuff. And she keep it that way, too. That's another reason I like living with her. No matter what happens, she get the bills paid on time and stuff. Even if I'm a little slack and ain't got my part of the rent, Crystal don't let that stop her, and she don't sit around being mad with me till I can settle up either.

Crystal a *good* friend.

None of that under-her-breath, under-the-table, under-your-dress talk 'bout how she can't buy the baby milk 'cause she had to come up with *all* the rent money this month.

Crystal ain't like that. For real, she treat me like a sister.

The more I thought about Crystal, the more I remembered why I was so frantic to get out of town. And had to keep myself from busting into tears.

"Uh, my stomach hurt a little bit. You got any Tagamet or any-thing? Oh, never mind. Here some Tums in the bottom of my panda bag. You want one?"

Miss Liza Jane shook her head and frowned. "You eat something that upset your stomach?"

"Naw, I didn't eat anything yet today. I've been having upset stom-achs since I was a little girl. Stress makes it worse. That's what the doctor Mama Mama took me to said.

"Hey, Miss Thirty-five MPH, do you always roll this slow?" I asked after I chewed on three tablets and put the Tums back in my bag.

We were just poking along on Highway 90 in that black Jaguar.

"I'm comfortable with this speed," Miss Liza Jane said. "Besides, I haven't been driving in a while. I have to get used to all these dials and gadgets and all again."

She touched a button on the console between us, and all of a sud-den my seat back fell back all the way to the back floor.

"Wooooooaaaa," I yelled as I fell back.

Miss Liza Jane let out a little "Oooops" and reached over to help me up.

When she did, the car swerved back and forth across the two-lane country road like crazy. It's a good thing wasn't no other cars coming.

"I'm okay, I'm okay!" I told her with my head in the backseat. "You drive, *I'm* okay!"

I may not know how to drive myself, but I know a bad driver when I see one. And Miss Liza Jane was a *bad driver*!

When I finally found a button on the side of my seat to raise it up again, we were back in our own lane, and Miss Liza Jane was creeping along like we didn't just almost run her Jag into the Ocawatchee River running 'longside the road.

"I held it in the road, didn't I?" she had the nerve to brag.

"Yeah, you sure did," I said, trying to sound encouraging, but I was thinking, It was a good thing nobody was *in* the road!

I figured with the Ocawatchee running right next to the road most of the way to Atlanta, I had better stay alert to Miss Liza Jane's zigging and zagging so we really didn't end up in the bottom of the river.

I sometimes fall asleep when I'm on long car trips more than a couple of hours. And in a smooth ride like her Jaguar—it was so smooth I figured I could even put on lip liner and not go outside my lips—I was likely to zone out anytime.

"Oh, I guess the speed limit *is* slower on this country road than it is on the interstate," I said as I pulled down the mirror behind the visor in front of me to put on some more lip liner and gloss. I had learned my lesson, so I shut up for a while about how fast we were going.

That Jaguar had a light-up mirror on the passenger's side. What they call it? Yeah, a vanity mirror, like in a bathroom. I was thinking, Shoot, if I had me a cell phone and a microwave up in there, I could *live* in this car.

But when I got a good look at myself in that lighted mirror, I couldn't hardly stand the sight of myself. Uh, I looked so stressed! And the mirror was so bright. It showed too much. You shoulda seen me searching through my big blue makeup bag. "Where my concealer? Where my highlighter?" I asked. "See, I put some a' this highlighter here under my eyes, and it take away that sad, droopy look. See?"

But it *didn't* take that sad, droopy look away. I tried some lipstick. I betcha I put on lipstick a million times a day. I lick my lips a lot—like L.L. Cool J—so I'm always eating it off.

I had on a shade called "Lemon Drops" that was the same color as the little yellow stretch halter top I was wearing that day.

"That's an interesting color of lipstick," Miss Liza Jane said.

I thanked her and felt a little better. It looked like Miss Liza Jane had a way of making me feel good.

I was wearing the same lemon yellow nail polish to match on my fingers and my toes. I thought it showed I do be thinking ahead sometimes.

"Sandra got this little aqua and lemon yellow satiny slip dress that's the same color, too. I got it with me so if I don't get a chance to change my nail color, I got something else to wear with it."

"You always call your mother 'Sandra'?" Miss Liza Jane asked, like she was really interested.

We were crossing over a part of the Ocawatchee River, and I noticed that the water was that funny-looking dark, dark green of Cleer Flo'. The last time I was down there, the summer before last, this boy named Derek threw me in with all my clothes on. Everybody thought it was funny, but it wasn't. It's a good thing I knew how to swim!

"Yeah, I always call Sandra 'Sandra,' unless sometimes when I'm out and trying to impress somebody with the fact that *I got a Mama, too,* and then I call Sandra 'my mom,' but that's just for show. Sometimes—I have to tell you on the serious side, Miss Liza Jane—I get kinda queasy-uneasy, 'cause I can almost just *feel* folks *knowing* she ain't really 'my mom' the way I say it. That she just 'Sandra.'

"Psst. Oops, my bad," I apologized. "I don't mean to suck my teeth so loud when I talk about Sandra."

"Well, it isn't very attractive," Miss Liza Jane said.

"For real? Then I'll work on it, 'cause I try to work on my little self. I'm all I got. But Sandra don't be wanting me to call her 'Mama' anyhow. She just as satisfied as she can be with the way things are. She too busy trying to get people to think she my sister to try to be my mama!"

She is. If we go to the mall or somewhere to eat, she always suck her teeth if I look cute and say, "Shoot, don't no men look at *me* when I'm with your little butt."

Oh, well.

"Really?" is all Miss Liza Jane said. But I could tell she was really listening, not like them hos in Lil' Sis who just be playing me, like they listening, 'cause I'm doing their hair and makeup.

"Yeah, Sandra want to be young all the time! And I guess she look okay to be almost forty, which she won't be for two more years and she already tripping about. But when she dance, she give her old self away. She still do the Cabbage Patch."

Miss Liza Jane looked at me with this question mark on her face.

"You don't know what the Cabbage Patch is? Dang! Okay, here it is."

And I leaned forward in my seat and bust a coupla moves for her.

"That's the Cabbage Patch. Old-timey dance from way back in the eighties. That's what Sandra do when she don't be doing the Bankhead Bounce, which is just as bad," I said, showing her that one, too. "Sandra make me so sick."

I felt my eyes rolling in my head at the thought of Sandra. Miss Liza Jane caught me.

"I know," I told her. "I've got in trouble all my life for rolling my eyes. And sometimes I'm not even rolling them for real, but it look like that 'cause I got big eyes. Regi, this boy I know from The Club, say when I roll my eyes, I *rolllllll* my eyes, like 'the sun going across the sky in the summertime.'"

"That's kinda nice, huh? 'Like the sun going across the sky in the summertime.' Regi nice. He just can't kick it like I like it."

"Kick it?" she asked.

"You know, sex me," I told her.

Her next question really threw me.

"How do you like it?" Miss Liza Jane asked.

"I don't think nobody has ever really asked me that, you know, even somebody I'm kicking it with. Uhmmm. I guess I have to think about it a little bit."

Then Miss Liza Jane got real quiet. And I realized that she was really waiting for me to think. Ain't that something?

After a little while she asked me, "You got an answer for me yet?"

"Naw, I ain't got a answer for you yet," I told her. I needed even more time to think on *that*. I just had *so much* on my mind that day.

So she kept quiet and gave me time to think. For me, kicking it is like eating Fritos. Now, I like Fritos, and I enjoy eating 'em while I'm chewing. But later on, when I'm finished with the whole bag, I can't remember what it was like other than they was salty and greasy. I liked 'em when I was eating 'em, and I guess I want some more, but they don't seem like too much when I'm looking back on 'em. I guess that's why you have to keep doing it, sexing it.

"So you're nothing like your mama, huh?" Miss Liza Jane asked.

"No, I don't look *nothing* like Sandra. At least, I don't think so.

"We both 'bout the same size. She's a *little* bit taller than me, but she small, too. Mama Mama say most Pines is tall and straight, 'like a Georgia pine,' but not us."

"Like these Georgia pines along this road?" Miss Liza Jane noticed everything 'bout that country road. She made me smile.

"We 'bout the same brown-skinned complexion, too. And she got these old heavy eyebrows."

"Like yours?" Miss Liza Jane asked.

"No, they ain't heavy like mine. Nothing like mine. They heavy in a different way. It's like my eyes. Sandra got big eyes, too, but they ain't like my eyes, though."

She's not really even like my mama when you really think about it. She's more like my sister. No, that's not right either. She more like a cousin I don't like. Maybe that's the problem. Maybe I just don't know *what* she is.

I got my hair cut short now. I think I look a little like Nia Peeples or Halle Berry. But I been thinking of getting some braids for the summer.

Now, if you know what you're doing, a girlie can work some braids. I learned a lot of that from dancing and throwing my hair around. When I got it.

I've done a little bit of *everything* to my hair. It's been blond and red and brown. It's been short and long and straight and braided and nappy. I been everything but bald! Sandra say it's a wonder I *ain't* bald! But if I was, I'd *work* that look, too.

Talking with Miss Liza Jane and having her pay attention to what I said, I got too comfortable in that Jaguar, and I caught myself doing something else that gets me in trouble.

"Uuuuhh, Miss Lady, 'scuse me, I'm sorry," I said, trying to wipe the red dirt from the panel in front of me with the palm of my hand. "I didn't mean to put my feet up on your dashboard. That's just one of my many bad habits: putting my feet up on folks' consoles. I don't know why I do it. I ain't got no car of my own. I put my feet up on *everybody's* console, and I don't want 'em to be thinking I just be dogging *they* stuff 'cause I ain't got no car of my own. It's just that putting my feet up like that is so comfortable and natural-feeling."

"You can keep them up there if you like," she said, slowing down to take a little bitty curve in the road. When she slowed down, we almost stopped rolling altogether.

"For real? On the dashboard of your *Jag*?! Well, thank *you*. I appreciate that, 'cause it seems on a long ride no matter how hard I try not to, I always find my feet back up on the dashboard. Even when I have on boots."

"But can't truck drivers and men in other cars see under your dress?" she asked.

"Well, for sure," I said. "See, that one we just passed tried to look. So?"

Sandra say that's why I do it.

"But I'll take my sandals off first this time. Okay?"

"You got cute little feet," she said.

"Oh, you think so? They look big to me. I wear a seven and a half medium. And these are eights. They belong to Sandra. But they are cute. I told you, Sandra the fashion police. See, that's better with my bare feet. This way I won't be scratching up your Jag's interior."

It was the first time that day I had looked down at myself. My legs were so ashy! I thought sure I had dropped some of Sandra's good lotion in one a' my bags. But I went through all the ones on the backseat and couldn't find none.

"Nice color on your toes," she said, looking at my sunny toenail polish. "It matches your top."

I smiled and wiggled my toes. Miss Liza Jane noticed *everything*.

As I looked a second time for the lotion, Miss Liza Jane asked me out of the clear blue what I did for a living. "You didn't have to go to work today?"

She looked down at the clock on the dash. It was just a little after twelve, which seemed slow to me, but when I looked down at my watch bracelet, it had stopped running at noon, which was real funny, 'cause it ran on a battery that wasn't ever supposed to give out.

"Oh, I got a little piece of a job at the office of the Board of Education that Mama Mama got for me," I told her. I had to make myself not suck my teeth again, since Miss Liza Jane had told me it was unattractive. "But it's Saturday, and I don't hardly never show up no way, 'cause it don't interest me and has *nothing* to do with my *real* ambition."

"Your real ambition?" she asked.

I couldn't believe she had forgotten already. "I told you, I am going to dance in a music video," I reminded her.

"That's how you're going to make a *living?*" she asked, and raised one of her arched eyebrows. I meant to ask her if she got them did professionally, 'cause there wasn't one single little hair outside that perfect arch, but I was talking 'bout my dancing, and when I'm doing that, I can't hardly think of nothing else.

"Well, naw, they don't exactly *pay* you to dance in the background of a video," I had to admit. "But don't nobody know that, so don't tell nobody, okay?"

She kinda laughed and promised, "I won't."

"But I think once I do a couple of videos in the background, then I can move up from there."

"What have you done to prepare yourself for that career?" she asked, all professional-sounding like a interviewer.

"Shoot, I been hanging 'round Lil' Sis for close to a year now. That's almost forever."

"Lil' Sis?" she said. "Are those strippers?"

I laughed out loud.

"Naw, why you think that?"

"Because when I was young," she explained, kinda smiling to herself, "folks used to call a girl's vagina 'Lil' Sis.' "

"For *real*?" I said. "That's what 'Lil' Sis' used to mean? Hee-hee. That's funny. That's 'bout what it still mean. When I showed Mama Mama a picture of them, she said they all look like they need a good douche." Then we both laughed. Mama Mama, she funny.

"Lil' Sis is this girl group that's fixing to cut a CD up in Macon. And I think they gon' blow up the spot. They a cross between Lil' Kim and TLC. Up in Macon they got studios and everything. I catch a ride up there sometimes, and I got to, you know, know some brothers in the business up there. You know, Macon, Georgia, ain't no great big town or nothing, but it's got *some'um* going on.

"Unlike *Mulberry*. It even *sound* country, don't it?

"*Mulberry, Georgia!*

"Sound like somewhere near Andy Griffin's hometown."

"And you dance with this Lil' Sis group?"

"Naw, I ain't done no real dancing yet, except by myself backstage while Lil' Sis performing and between the sheets with one of the producers at the studio who say he gon' help me get in the business. And those hos in Lil' Sis just let me hang around 'em 'cause sometimes I do their hair and makeup if they ain't got nobody else. Shoot, Sandra used to ask me to do *her* makeup when I wasn't even ten!

"But my *ambition* is to dance in a music video."

"You like that word 'ambition,' don't you?" Miss Liza Jane asked. She seemed to notice *everything* I said.

"Yeah, 'ambition,' that's my new word," I told her. "I saw it in a story in a *Vibe* magazine that Crystal bought for me last month. Did I use it right?"

Miss Liza Jane nodded her head as she slowed down for a in'ersection that didn't even have no stop sign or blinking yellow light.

"One of my last English teachers, Miss Sadie Tyler, used to say, 'LaShawndra, you got a good vocabulary. You know lotsa words, but you don't know what *half* of 'em mean.'

"Shoot, sometime it makes me wish I had stayed in school at least through lunchtime and English class. But I *never* planned to stay in school all day, even if I went, even when Mama Mama was still a principal at East Mulberry High School and drove me to the middle school there every morning. I used to get dressed in the morning to cut school. You know 'cutting-school clothes.' Something cute and short and little and tight."

"Your mother and grandmother let you dress that way?" she asked.

"Well, Mama Mama didn't exactly *let* me wear those clothes. Sandra didn't care that much what I wore as long as it was in style. She feel she has a 'fashion reputation' to uphold. But Mama Mama did. So after I'd finish dressing in, like, a short red tube skirt and black bra and sheer long-sleeve shirt, when I was at Mama Mama's I'd have to put on a big sweater or blouse and leggings or something that looked nice over it so Mama Mama wouldn't see everything I had on. Then, after I got to school, I'd go in 'my dressing room'—that's what I used to call the girls' bathroom in the gym—and get my *real look* together.

"Girls at school used to stand outside the bathroom door and say, 'Five minutes, Miss Pines, five minutes.' Like I was fixing to go onstage."

"Why did they do that?" she asked.

"Oh, they was making fun of me, but *I* liked it! I'd pretend I was really fixing to go out and perform onstage in front of a buncha people, so I'd finish up my makeup real quick and hike up my skirt or whatever and go out that bathroom door like I was somebody."

Tina McElroy Ansa

I used to stand in front of the full-length mirror on the back of the bathroom door in Sandra's place or the one at Mama Mama's and try to decide what folks, boys mostly, that I would be hanging out with would want to see me dressed in.

Me, I try to always come dressed to impress.

"Like looka here," I told her. "Let me reach this bag. See this little orange dress trimmed in bright yellow? Now, this look good on *me*! I know it just look like a little cotton stretch dress, but this thing expensive. Shoot, I ain't got no extra money for clothes. Mama Mama bought it for me.

"She buy a lot of my clothes. She always has. Mama Mama likes to, she does. That's what she said. Mama Mama buy almost *all* my stuff."

Just then I saw the sign that pointed to the I-75.

"Oh, look, here come the ramp for the in'erstate," I said, tryna be helpful. "Now we can speed up and get off this old country back road."

Miss Liza Jane just kept on rolling.

"Hey, wait! Hold up! Hold up! You just passed the exit for I-75! You missed the exit!"

"No, I didn't," she explained, keeping her eyes on the road. "I have no intention of taking the interstate."

"You mean you not gon' take the in'erstate? You gon' take the back road all the way to Atlanta? You gon' take old U.S. 90 all the way up there instead?"

She just nodded.

"For real?! Why? What for?"

"I like the scenery," she said. "I thought we'd take the scenic route."

"Don't nobody care nothing 'bout no *scenic route!*" I almost shouted at her. "I seen this scenery *my whole life!*"

"I like it" is all she said real, quiet-like.

"Oops, my bad," I said. I knew I had gone too far. Sandra say I live in a land called "Gone Too Far."

"This *is your* car, ain't it?"

She looked at me and smiled, but she just kept right on driving up U.S. 90.

"Well, if you change your mind, there's lotsa places you can just jump on the in'erstate. You don't have to drive seventy miles per hour, but you could speed up a little bit on I-75. And we'd be in Atlanta in no time!"

"I can't get outa Mulberry and surrounding areas fast enough."

I hadn't even got those words out of my mouth good before I looked in the side mirror of the Jag and saw something else that stressed me out a lot more than driving the scenic route to Atlanta.

"Hey!" I shouted at Miss Liza Jane. "Is that a cop car following us?"

"Where?" she asked, glancing in the rearview mirror.

"There it is right behind us! Right there, two cars back! Behind us!" Listen, I was *bugging*!

"Act natural! Act natural!" I told her as she slowed down even more than we were going, if that was possible. Then we went around a bend and I got a good look behind us. "Oh, wait a minute. That ain't no *police*. Psst.

"I'm just tripping. But it *did* look like one there for a minute. Didn't it? Whew!"

"Well, Lil' Schoolgirl, what was the problem?" she asked. "I wasn't speeding."

"I know *that*. We ain't never got to worry 'bout that with you."

"Do you have anything with you that's illegal?" she asked.

"No, I ain't got nothing on me, no drugs or nothing. Shoot, as broke as I am, I couldn't afford cigarettes if I smoked 'em, let alone a blunt."

"My goodness, Lil' Schoolgirl, you act like you running from the law or something," Miss Liza Jane said.

" 'Running from the *law*'? Ain't nobody 'running from the law'!" My heart started to race again. All that relieved feeling flew right out the window.

"Why you say that? Why you say that? I don't look like no *fugitive*
from the *law*!

"Do I?"

Miss Liza Jane took her eyes off the road for a second to look at me and swerved a little bit into the other lane, then pulled the car back real quick.

While she pulled the car back into the lane, I recovered, too.

"Oh, you just bugging!" I said, trying to lighten up the situation. "Ha-ha. I knew that. You so crazy! Just like me! Ha-ha!

"You almost had me there. Hee-hee."

I laughed again like it was a joke and everything and put my bare feet back up on the dashboard, but I could feel my heart racing, and a little dribble of sweat began to roll down between my titties as the white sedan with the two white men in the front seat looking straight ahead speeded up and passed us.

16.

As we drove along, I couldn't help but stare at Miss Thang. She didn't look like nobody I had ever seen in Mulberry. She looked kinda retro, like something out of one of those old black-and-white movies me and Mama Mama and Granddaddy Charles used to look at on TV late at night. But she also looked like she just stepped out of one of the stores at the Mulberry Mall.

I looked down at Miss Liza Jane's legs and noticed that she was wearing a thin gold anklet on her right leg, just like a young girl. I couldn't hardly believe it. I didn't think old folks like her even thought about wearing stuff like that, even though they do sell 'em on the Home Shopping Network.

I thought I was being all undercover and everything, but she caught me staring.

"You lose something over here?" she asked. But she kinda laughed, too.

"Oh, my bad," I told her. "Was I staring at you?"

"Yes, you were," she said. She was still driving so slow. The "scenic view" was just creeping by. "Why? Do I look funny to you?" Every-thing she said sounded like a joke only she understood. But it wasn't a mean joke like Sandra try to say on me, like "What LaShawndra don't know could fill a library" or "LaShawndra, she a menace to society."

I told Miss Liza Jane, "Oh, your look is tight, wearing that hat and a string of what look like real pearls and gloves and that anklet. And that good-smelling perfume. Um, your whole car smell like it. It smell so sweet, like cotton candy or that white fluffy candy with pecans in it you can get at Stuckey's inside a pecan roll. What kinda perfume is it?"

"Angel's Breath," she said, and kinda laughed under her own breath.

I just smiled with her, but I didn't get that joke either. And Mama Mama say I got a good sense of humor.

"Never heard of it. They sell it at the mall?" I asked her. She just shook her head a little. I shrugged and went on talking.

"You know, this Jag is *fulla* you. It seem fulla your Angel's Breath and your colors and your cleanness. And you don't smoke neither. I can tell by the way your ride smell.

"I bet you one of those 'big' women like Mama Mama, too. Not big in size. Mama Mama got a *good body*, she can wear some twelves. But big in everything else—how she act and what she know and everything. Granddaddy Charles used to say she was *too big*."

I know what he mean.

When I was little, 'bout five or six, Mama Mama used to drive up to Atlanta to go shopping at Lenox Square or to visit one of her friends from college who was coming through town. Now, you talk 'bout some *big women* getting together for tea at the Ritz-Carlton and stuff.

You know *big*—huge, block-out-the-sun, gigantica, humongousaroni, suck-up-all-the-air-in-the-room big. You know, women out there taking they place in the world, running schools and offices and stuff, on committees and doing yoga till they a hundred years old or at least till they fifty or sixty, which I guess is just like being a hundred. On television shows and radio call-in shows talking 'bout issues.

Shoot, even now I've seen some of those very women that's friends of Mama Mama's all over the country on C-SPAN at national meetings. Believe me when I say it, the most boring stuff in the *world* be on C-SPAN. You know, meetings in Washington, D.C., on gender and race and image and stuff.

Just thinking 'bout that boring stuff they have on C-SPAN and CNN and C-SPAN2 make my head hurt. And I love me some TV. I could look at it all day, and I do sometimes when I don't feel like going to work. I could watch videos 24/7. And contrary to what some people say, that ain't just slacking off neither. Watching videos good practice for my career.

I told Miss Liza Jane, "You ought to see Mama Mama when she have one of her big sit-down dinner parties with all her good china and glasses and stuff. She go to all that trouble cooking and seeing that the house is clean and everything, then she spend all evening making sure nobody feel funny if *they* don't know the right fork to use. So everybody come out feeling good.

"It's like magic. But Mama Mama say it ain't no magic. She say it's just hard work.

"I mean, she so upright and righteous and real."

I surprised my own self with those words, 'cause they sounded real good together, so I repeated 'em to myself three times. That's what I do when I don't have no pen and paper handy.

" 'Upright, righteous, and real. Upright, righteous, and real. Upright, righteous, and real.' I *know* I can use that in my lyrics," I said under my breath. But Miss Liza Jane heard me.

"What's that about lyrics?" she asked.

"Oh, nothing," I said real quick. "I don't mean nothing 'bout no lyrics. I'm just talking. You know me, I'm crazy."

And she just let it go.

I have this habit of rubbing my fingers over my head right at the temples when I'm tryna put something out of my mind, like Sandra telling me that time when I was crying for my daddy, "You ain't got no goddamn daddy!" or like that ho who sit at the front desk at the studio up in Macon talking on the phone in front of me about "chicken-heads" showing up for jobs they not "qualified for."

It may sound heartless, but that Saturday out on U.S. 90 what I was trying my best to forget was everything that I was leaving behind in Mulberry: my pretty robin's-egg blue room, the broken window over Sandra's bathtub, the smell of cookies baking in Crystal's kitchen. It wasn't like I was forgetting about my friend—my *bestest* friend—

Crystal and her little family and the mess I had caused by being stupid and a little ho, but I just couldn't stand to think about it.

"You got a headache?" Miss Liza Jane asked. She made it sound like she really cared if I did or not.

"Naw," I said without thinking, "I just got a lot on my mind."

And she asked me real quick, "What?"

She asked me so quick it caught me off guard, and I didn't know what to say, so I kinda told her a lie. I didn't mean to, but I had to say something. And I couldn't tell that good-looking, sweet-smelling sis-ter the kinda terrible worthless person I was. So I told her, "It's my girlfriend I live with, Crystal. She in the hospital. I didn't tell you that before? Um, I talk so much, I thought *sure* I told you *that*."

"No, you didn't," she said.

"Yeah, she got hurt and her two children, too. She was in a car crash a couple of days ago, with her children. That's what it was. It was a accident. And I guess I'm just thinking 'bout them. They're in the hospital."

It just came out of my mouth.

"And you're worried about her?" Miss Liza Jane asked.

"Well, *sure* I'm worried 'bout her! She my best friend! What kinda person you think I am? But I *had* to go to Atlanta for Freaknik. I mean, people were expecting me."

Miss Liza Jane just put her lips together real tight.

"That don't mean I don't care nothing 'bout my friend Crystal! Oh, I'm sorry. I'm yelling at you again. My bad. I'm so stressed."

Right on cue my stomach start cramping up on me.

"Whoo, I need some more Tums. I got some more in this bag somewhere."

When Miss Liza Jane didn't say anything, I just kept on talking.

"That's why I need to make a phone call to the hospital to check on her." Well, it was partly the truth.

"Let's not talk 'bout Crystal right now, okay?" I asked as I popped a couple more Tums. And I meant it, too.

She just kinda looked at me out the side of her face and kept driving.

After I told her my lie, it got so quiet in her Jaguar I couldn't hardly stand it. As Mama Mama say sometimes when she says something that cut too close to folks' feelings, it was so quiet you could hear a rat piss on cotton. Mama Mama said that's how it got in her office when she asked this girl in the ninth grade whose boyfriend was hitting her all upside her head if it was gon' still be love when he started hitting her little six-month-old baby. Mama Mama all correct and everything, but she can be real, too, when it's just the two of us talking. But that quiet time gave me too much space to think, and all I could think about was Crystal and her children.

"Hey, can I turn some music on up in here, then?" I asked as I reached in the backseat for my big red bag. I carry *everything* in my red bag—makeup, nail polish, tissues, my wallet, a pair a' scissors, some emery boards, a comb, another comb, two brushes, hair clips, hair spray, some more Tums, condoms, two disposable lighters, a can of Lysol spray. "I got some CDs in here. Where's your player?" I had my Discman CD player with me and my earphones around my neck, but I didn't have no batteries, so the earphones was more for looks than anything else.

Miss Liza Jane was still looking at me so funny I thought she was mad at me for something. But she answered, "I don't have anything but a radio."

"You ain't got no CD player up in this Jag?!" I was surprised, but then I realized I didn't have no batteries, no car, no radio, *or* no money, so I said real fast, "Oh, the radio is just fine." I was glad to have the buttons and knobs to play with. "There it is: WMUL. Usually I only listen to WASS, 'cause they play my sorta music, but I kinda want to hear some sounds and keep up with something on the news today."

"I wouldn't have thought you were a newshound," Miss Liza Jane said.

I didn't know what a "newshound" was exactly, but I was just glad she didn't still seem so upset with me about something. I really liked the way she got over stuff instead of letting it drag on and on like Sandra.

"No, I don't usually listen to the news— Hold up! Was that news report about a break-in in Mulberry? Dang! I missed it."

She reached over and touched a button on the dash, and the station came in clear as cable.

"Well, it is kinda important to me. Oh, don't let me forget, I want to make that phone call to the hospital. It's kinda important, too."

"I won't let you forget," she promised, and I felt real lucky to be riding to Atlanta with her, even if it was like traveling on the back of a snail.

Since it looked like we was gonna take that old country, "scenic" route all the way to Atlanta, I just tried to make myself satisfied with looking at that. And right when I did, I remembered we were gonna come up on a McDonald's soon, and I was lunchy.

"You hungry, Miss Liza Jane?" I asked, hoping she would take the hint.

"No, I don't care for anything to eat, thank you, but why don't we stop so you can run in and get yourself something. You probably got to pee anyway, don't you, Tinkletown?" she said with a smile.

I tell you, when that old lady smiled at me, it was like the sun coming out on a dark, rainy day.

"Oooh, you right. I got to go to the bathroom *bad*. And McDonald's and Hardy's and places like that *always* have clean bathrooms. You don't have to pee?"

She shook her head.

"Well, I sure do," I told her. "I try to drink eighteen glasses a' water a day like Tyra Banks and Naomi Campbell an' 'em say they do to keep their skin pretty."

"Eight," she said.

"What?" I asked her.

"*Eight* glasses of water."

"For real? No wonder I pee so much. I was getting kinda bloated tryna drink eighteen glasses a' water in one day! Annnyway, I can make my phone call while I'm in there, too."

"Need some money for the phone?" she asked me real thoughtful-like, pointing to a big stack of quarters on the console between us.

"Naw, that's real nice of you to ask, but Mama Mama make sure I have these phone cards so I can always call her for help.

"But I can use some of this change for a hamburger and fries," I told her as I took a few dollars in quarters. "Or else those bitches in there be cutting their eyes at me when I come out the bathroom without buying something.

"Little minimum-wage hos! And *them bitches* got the nerve to be tryna put *me* down with their little red polyester uniforms. I know just about everybody who work at this McDonald's coming up. I been there before. There's a little club down near the river a few miles from here where I go with this nigga and jam."

Miss Liza Jane pulled her ride over so sudden and slammed on the brakes so hard she threw me and all my stuff all over that Jag. It was a good thing she had made me put on my seat belt.

"Hold up! Hold up! I ain't got to go *that* bad!" I yelled, although she did almost make me pee on myself.

She threw the car into park and spun around in her seat to face me.

"I cannot stand this one minute more!" she shouted. "Do you talk like this to *everybody?*" she wanted to know.

I told her, "Well, *yeah*, I talk like this to everybody. How else am I gonna talk?"

Mama Mama say I sound like old folks' children sometime. You know how folks who wait until they're real old to have kids have children who don't ever seem like they was ever young themselves? You know, old folks' children.

Mama Mama say she guess I been 'round her so much I'm almost old folks' children myself, so I use words that most young people don't even know.

"You mean, like old folks' words?" I asked her.

"That's *not* what I'm talking about," she said, her jaws all tight.

"Oh, you must be talking 'bout how I sound. I know how I sound. I try not to talk country. Most folks say you couldn't hardly tell that I'm from a little old country town like Mulberry. First of all, Mama Mama can get right proper on you in a minute. She say she bilingual 'cause she can speak in proper formal English in a school board meeting and then like everybody else when she go to get her hair done at the old Lovejoy's in East Mulberry.

"And then there's ways she talks at home that I ain't never heard her talk like outside the house. Oh, like when she mad or disgusted with me."

"You *know* that's not what I mean," Miss Liza Jane said.

I gave her my wide-eyed Valley Girl white-girl stare, but she didn't laugh.

"Hee-hee. Psych!" I laughed, but she still didn't crack a smile.

"I'm just bugging. I started to act like I didn't know what you talking 'bout. But I know what you mean 'bout the way I talk. Mama Mama say it make her— Wait a minute, what's the word she use? It starts with a 'cr.' What is it?"

"Cringe?" she suggested.

"Yeah, that's it! 'Cringe.' I like the way it sounds. 'Cringe.' She say the way I talk make her cringe."

"Me, too," she said. "You call yourself and everybody else 'ho' or 'nigga' or 'bitch' like it's nothing."

"It ain't nothing."

"It *is* something. And I can't stand it!"

"Mama Mama say all my stuff on the outside. You know, all my stuff. Not my coochie. Although now that I think 'bout it, she *might* mean my coochie stuff!! Hee-hee.

"But she mean my stuff: my feelings and my insides and what I think 'bout myself and other people and stuff. How I live and, you know, like that.

"She say I say *anything*! She say I let all that stuff hang out for the world to see. She say she hates to think of me all day long just walking around with my stuff hanging out."

"Well, I agree with her, and you can't do it here."

I asked her, "What you mean, I can't do that here?"

"I mean, you can't stay in this Jaguar and continue to call yourself and every other person a 'ho' or a 'nigga.' "

"For *real*?" I was getting kinda nervous. "What you gon' do?" I asked her, tryna make a joke out of it. "Put me *out*? Hee-hee."

She didn't crack a smile. "Yes, ma'am," she said.

"Out on the highway in the middle of nowhere!? Out on U.S. 90 in the hot sun? You gon' put me out just 'cause I don't stop calling them hos behind the counter 'hos'!?"

She looked me dead in the eye and said, "I do not care where we are. I am not going to sit up here and let you say those words over and over in my car."

"But you can't expect me to stop saying some words altogether, can you?"

"Yes I can," she said.

"Oh" is all I could say. "Well, which ones bother you?"

She said, "All of them! 'Ho' and 'bitch' and 'nigga' and 'dick' and—"

"Dang," I told her. "Those some of my favorite words. Can I still say 'dang'?"

She just nodded.

"Well, thank you for 'dang'! But what I'mo say if I can't say 'niggas' and 'ho' and 'bitch'? That's just what I call people. I don't mean nothing by it.

"Shoot, that's what I call *myself*!" I told her.

"*That* is what I'm talking about," Miss Liza Jane said.

I told her, "Well, I don't know what else to say, 'cause that's what I am!"

"You sound as if you're proud to call yourself a 'ho,'" she said.

"I ain't exactly 'proud' of it," I told her. "But I ain't 'shamed of it neither. And it don't really mean nothing!

"And *everybody* say those words all the time! Everybody! Everybody even say 'em in videos and on the television and in movies and *everywhere*!"

"No, dear, not everybody," she said.

"Well, just about everybody *I* know," I told her.

"Does your grandmother?" she asked.

"Pssst, no, she don't," I had to admit. Even though I had heard Mama Mama say under her breath one time when she was cleaning up my room at her house, "Bless her heart, she ain't nothing but a ho." And I *know* she was talking 'bout me.

"Does Sandra?"

"No, she don't neither."

"What about your grandfather?"

"Granddaddy Charles? No, he don't neither."

"And what about your friend Crystal?"

"No, Crystal definitely don't." Crystal don't even allow me to say 'dang' at home around her little darlings or look at any of the talk shows like Jerry Springer or Ricki Lake. She says it creates a negative atmosphere for her children. And she don't allow *nothing* negative around her little ones.

"So!" Miss Liza Jane sounded like me then. 'Cause "so," that's *my* word!

"How you expect a little coochie like me to—"

"I don't want to hear you call yourself that word again either," she said.

"I can't say 'coochie' neither?!" I couldn't believe it. Miss Liza Jane was being way, way strict.

She shook her head real quick, and the long pink feather on her hat just danced.

"Dang!"

You Know Better

"I just can't stand your language anymore," she said.

"*You* say you can't stand it anymore? What about *me?* I don't think I can stand to stop! 'Cause that's how I talk!"

"Well, you're going to *have* to stop, Lil' Schoolgirl. Words are powerful. After a while, before you know it, you're going to start thinking that's all you and the people around you are: a ho, a bitch, a nigga. And that's not what you are."

I told her, "Uh-huh. Uh-huh. Uh-huh. I hear ya. Uh-huh, Miss Liza Jane. I really like how you talk with me and how we conversate together and—"

She stopped me in the middle of my sentence. " 'Conversate' is not a word," she said.

"I can't say 'conversate'?!"

"No," she said.

"Why not?!"

"It's *not* a word," she said calmly.

"Yes it is," I had to tell her. "Now, for real this time, *everybody* do say that word, on TV I heard Snoop Doggy Dogg say it in a interview, and even smart girls at school used to say it. For real."

"No," she said. "The word is 'talk.' You can 'converse.' You can 'have a conversation,' but you cannot 'conversate.' "

Before I could stop myself, I sucked my teeth, real loud.

And she repeated, "It's not a word."

I was 'bout frustrated with her—if "frustate" is a word. I was going to suck my teeth again. But instead, I just rolled my eyes out the window so she couldn't see me and went on with what I was saying.

"Annnnnyyway, I appreciate you laying that wisdom on me 'bout how it make me sound and how it make me feel 'bout myself whether I realize it now or not, Miss Sound Like a Preacher, but I just know myself. And even though sometimes I know better, I still can't seem to do no better."

I thought for sure she was gonna just let it go like Mama Mama eventually do. Instead, she asked, "Do you want to get together all your stuff you got spread out all over this car and in the trunk and get out by the side of the road again and try to get another ride?"

I got the message. "Well, I'll try," I said. "I still don't think nothing wrong with those words you don't want me to say no more in your presence." I had to say it.

"I don't want you to say them *at all*," she corrected me.

"I know, I know. But for now I'm just gon' aim at not saying 'em in front of *you*," I told her as I put my sandals on.

Miss Liza Jane bit her bottom lip and thought for a second. Then, as she pulled back on the road and headed for the McDonald's parking lot, she said, "Well, at least that's *something*."

17.

When I got back in the car with my burger and fries, Miss Liza Jane was waiting just as patient, looking out the window at a empty field across the road from the Mickey D's.

"You know, that's funny," I told her as I got myself settled back in the Jag. "Everywhere I go, guys usually be hitting on me! But as cute as I think I look today, didn't nobody in there say nothing to me! Well, at least I got a chance to pee. I really had to go. Want some fries? Help yourself. I got the big one."

"You were gone quite a while, Lil' Schoolgirl," she said as she shook her head and pulled back onto U.S. 90.

I reminded her, "I had to order, pee, and make my phone call. And they put me on hold at the hospital and still didn't tell me nothing. They still *screening* calls back in Mulberry. You know how folks are who think they important. And if you ain't all correct and everything, then you ain't worthy to get through.

"Pssst. Folks think they better than other folks just 'cause they ain't never been caught in a mistake. And it could be a *honest* mistake, too!

"And they probably trying to star-sixty-nine me. But ha! The joke's on them, 'cause they won't get nothing but a pay-phone number and they won't know *where* I am."

"You didn't tell anybody where you were going?" she asked. Mama Mama say I'm a "quick study," but Miss Liza Jane was too fast for me. Every little bit of information that I let slip led her to another lie or something I had told, and left me feeling all tangled and tied up like that brother had me who was all into S&M.

"Oh, yeah, I kinda left a message at Sandra's house." I was beginning to feel that Miss Liza Jane was just *making* me lie.

That eyebrow of hers went up again, and she pointed to my seat belt and said, "Buckle up."

I fastened my seat belt. "You really are a safety nut. I'll try the hospital later. You sure you don't want some a' these fries? They still hot."

She shook her head.

"Oh, okay, more for me."

Then, without any kinda warning, she pulled off the side of the road, slammed to a stop, and said, "Looka *yonder*!"

I looked over to where she was staring, expecting to see "a yonder," whatever that was, and I saw a field that was covered with red things. I thought "yonders" might be some kinda vegetable growing there, like tomatoes or something, but Miss Liza Jane said, "Look!" And as soon as she did, every one of those red things—musta been hundreds and hundreds of them—took off from the ground and just *covered* the sky. They were like a big bloodred cloud over us.

"Redbirds!" Miss Liza Jane said, sounding all amazed and out of breath. Actually, it *was* kinda breathtaking, seeing all them redbirds at one time fly off like that. I don't think I *ever* seen anything like that before.

They circled our car like in that movie *The Birds*. Then they flew off back in the direction of Mulberry.

I just sat there with my mouth hanging open.

"That's a lucky sign for us," Miss Liza Jane said. "You know what redbirds flying around you mean, don't you?"

"Naw, what?"

"They mean love," she said.

"For real? Well, it sho' must be a lotta love around *us*." But I thought about the mess I was in and added, "But then, that would have to be a *miracle*!"

She kinda shrugged real casual-like and said, "Miracles happen."

I didn't say nothing, but I thought, Shoot, I wish I could believe *that*! Miracles happen!

We both turned around in our soft leather seats and watched all them birds fly off until we couldn't see them no more. Then Miss Liza Jane said, "Well!" and pulled the Jag back on U.S. 90.

It got quiet in the car again, and I got to thinking 'bout these little barrettes shaped like redbirds that Crystal bought for both me and Baby Girl to put in our hair, 'cause Baby Girl and me like to play like we twins. Crystal don't hardly ever buy her babies some little plaything without getting some little thing for me, too. Crystal, she like that. I had to leave those barrettes back on the dresser at Painted Bunting Lane along with all my other stuff. It seemed every time it got quiet, my mind went back to Crystal, who I was trying not to think about so much 'cause it made me so sad and nervous.

"What's the matter? Your stomach still bothering you?" Miss Liza Jane asked me, and I betcha I jumped a mile. Miss Liza Jane's voice could sneak up on you like a ghost.

I looked down and realized I was playing with my gold navel ring. I had gotten my navel pierced the month before. It was just healed enough for me to turn the ring easy.

"That's my navel ring," I explained lifting up my top so she could see the gold hoop there better. I was real proud of it. "That's a new part of my look, my style. See, it matches my nose piercing. This a real diamond in my nose. It was Mama Mama's earring, but she lost the other one and gave this one to me. She don't approve of piercings, but she gave it to me anyway. I been thinking 'bout getting another piercing down there."

When I pointed to my coochie, she raised those eyebrows of hers almost up to her hairline.

"Down *where!?*" she asked.

"Down where you call Lil' Sis," and I laughed 'cause I thought

she'd be pleased that I remembered what she had just told me 'bout
Lil' Sis. Instead, she nearly lost it.

"You gon' let somebody *pierce your vagina*!?" It was as close as I
had heard her come to yelling. And she was weaving a little back and
forth across the road again.

"Well, yeah," I said, keeping my eye on the white line. "You sound
just like Mama Mama when I showed her my nose and navel. She say,
'You sho' ain't no Pines woman, 'cause we don't believe in mutilating
and manipulating ourselves.' That's why I don't plan to tell her 'bout
my coochie ring."

"Why would you *do* something like that?" Miss Liza Jane wanted
to know.

"Oh, it's a sexual thing. It's for the sensation. That's what this girl in
the bathroom at The Club told me."

"Jesus, keep me near the cross," she said, like a chant.

I told her, "Now you really sound like Mama Mama. She says that
to me all the time 'bout something she hear I done done. When she
came across my whatchacallit—my portcolio of nude photos of
myself, she just about lost it. You know in the music-video business,
you gotta have pictures."

Miss Liza Jane didn't say nothing, so I just kept on talking, you
know, tryna school the sister.

"Yeah, you know, like pictures in *Penthouse* and *Playboy*. And, you
know, even singers and well-known folks be taking their clothes off
for the camera. And, shoot, they put 'em on the *covers* of magazines,
Vibe and *Rolling Stone* and *Vanity Fair*. Sandra be reading *Vanity Fair*
and *Vogue* and everything. She think she so all that. Besides, I didn't
have no résumé like Mama Mama say I ought to have to get a job
anywhere. I had to have *something*.

"Then somebody told me I *had* to have some photographs of
myself to leave at studios and producers' offices and recording com-
panies. So I got this brother who got a studio and darkroom set up in
his mama's basement to take some naked pictures of me—he didn't

even charge me nothing, 'cause I ain't had no hundred and fifty dollars for no pictures! But he musta shown 'em to every one of his homeys and everybody else in Mulberry. 'Cause somebody made a anonymous call to Sandra's house and left a message on her machine that said they had seen her daughter naked in pictures. And of course she freaked. And not in a good way.

"But Sandra ain't nothing but a drama mama. And I always figured Sandra was just mad that she waited till she was too old and out of shape to take some naked pictures of her own. That's what I figured.

"Anyway, Mama Mama act so upset when she saw the pictures of me, you woulda thought she thought I was still a virgin or something."

Miss Liza Jane still didn't say nothing. She just kept driving realllll slow on that back-country road. But she had got me to thinking 'bout my sexual life.

Shoot, I been kicking it since I was twelve years old.

His name was Jerome. Jerome had been asking me for some nasty for a while already. Shoot, I was almost a teenager, and most of the girls I knew wasn't no virgins anyway, so . . .

That first time I didn't even know all what he was doing down there. I didn't know if the brother could drop a load or not, you know, really kick it. I had sucked his dick before and he had ate me out, but you know that don't really count. Shoot, boys and girls almost do that on the dance floor and under tables in the school lunchroom. We hadn't really done the real thing before.

We was in my room upstairs at Mama Mama's house. I knew that Mama Mama was in the house. But Jerome just climbed up the flower vine thing and came in my window like he had been doing for a while. We call ourselves being quiet.

Me and Jerome was real busy kicking it in the corner of my bed, so we didn't even hear anybody coming up the stairs. When Mama Mama stuck her head in the door to check on me the way she did every night—been doing every night since I'd come to stay with her sometimes—we both stopped hunching up on each other at the same time. And we lay there just as still as this deer I saw on one of those nature shows on television when a hunter came up on him in the woods.

I guess we thought if we didn't make no move or no noise, she wouldn't see us. Now, ain't that silly? But that's what we did. We stopped right in midstroke on my favorite sunflower sheets. His shoulders were still all hunched up and curved like he be seriously kicking it.

Then Mama Mama turned the light on.

Uh, it was the biggest mess in the world.

Mama Mama screamed, "Jesus, Jesus, Jesus!" And she stood there in the doorway shaking her head real hard. Then she yelled, "I raise my hand to Thee," and that's what she did.

I know I didn't have no business laughing at a time like that, getting caught and all, but I couldn't help thinking, Put your hands in the air and wave 'em like you just don't care. You know, old school.

Then I thought about how it looked like she was pumping it up. Like we do on the dance floor, with our hands pushing up in the air.

Then Mama Mama screamed at Jerome, "Get out LaShawndra's bed! Get out this bedroom! Get out my house! Get out!"

She chased him down the stairs and out the front door with that pretty cut glass in the top. She slammed the door so hard behind him I thought that glass was gonna shatter into a million pieces. Then she sat down on the floor in the downstairs hallway and just cried. It made me feel so bad to see her like that, that after a while I tried to go down there, pat her on the back, and say something to her.

I don't know *what* I was gon' say. But she just looked at me real long and hard. At first I thought she might even *hit me*! And Mama Mama ain't *never* hit me. I ain't never got no whipping. Sandra kinda tried to once or twice, but you know Sandra, she don't want to do nothing to get hot and sweaty and mess up her little hairstyle or break a nail.

You Know Better

Except for this one time. See, I don't really drink. I figure I have to be careful, 'cause you know children don't take after strangers, and Sandra drink too much. And I told her so, too.

"Shoot, you almost a damn alkie." That's the last thing I remember.

Sandra slapped me so hard I swear I can feel it right now. And that was four years ago. Shoot, almost five.

Right here on my left cheek. Uh, it still burns sometimes when I'm feeling bad, and I have to rub my face a little bit to take the sting away.

Things really changed after that, after she slapped me in my face. It ain't like we was ever close or anything. It was just that after she hit me, slapped me in my face, that was the first time she ever did that, slapped me in my face. No nigga had ever hit me in my face, at that time anyway. So things was different with us—me and Sandra—after that.

I was already living between Mama Mama's house and Sandra's. But after that I pretty much stayed at Mama Mama's till I turned eighteen.

I think 'bout those kids who turn they parents in for smoking a little marijuana, a little chronic, and I almost say a prayer for them to rest in peace, 'cause I know if I ever *even thought* about doing something like that to Sandra, she'd kill me. For real!

If Sandra slap me in my face for saying one little thing to her 'bout her drinking, what you think she do 'bout something like turning her in to the police for smoking dope?! Shoot, not that *she* wouldn't think 'bout doing the same thing to me, turning me in to the police.

Oh, yeah, she yanked me by my hair once, too. But those were the only times she ever laid her hands on me.

Finally, that time with Jerome, Mama Mama just waved me away and said, "Go put on some clothes, LaShawndra." I didn't even remember that I was standing there naked.

Then she looked at me real sad and said, "Uh, uh, uh, her little titties ain't even started to bud out yet."

Then she sat there and cried some more.

Poor Mama Mama, she cried most of the night.

I heard her through my bedroom door. Then, the next morning, Sandra shows up, tells me to get dressed, and takes me to my first OB-GYN appointment. She didn't say a word about Jerome. But every time I tried to say something in the car, she just say, "Shut up, LaShawndra! I think you have said and done enough."

So we don't never talk much 'bout my sex life.

If Miss Liza Jane hadn'ta started bugging 'bout a little body piercing, I was gonna ask *her* what she thought about this boy—well, he ain't no boy, 'cause he almost a full-time record producer—who wanted me to be a part of a threesome with him and his girlfriend.

I don't think he want a threesome as much as he want to watch me and his girlfriend together doing it. He say he saw it on a video and had been thinking 'bout it ever since. He didn't come out and promise to help me get on a video if I did it, but he kinda led me to believe that.

And this guy make it sound so natural, 'cause he saw it on his own TV and everything. But I didn't have anybody else to ask. So I was still thinking 'bout saying something to Miss Liza Jane about it when I heard her just muttering under her breath as she drove along.

"What you said?" I asked.

"I was just thinking, here I am worrying about what you *say*, and I ought to be worrying about what you *do*!"

I started to tell her, "That was what *I* was just tryna say," but she sounded so sad and almost wounded—like Mama Mama that time with Jerome—I didn't have the heart to be smart-ass with her right then.

Sandra say I'm always being a smart-ass, but she's the one who tries to be a smart-ass with me, putting me down and making fun of me at the same time, always trying to put the burden on me for everything that's gone wrong in her life.

She never had time to play the piano. It's LaShawndra's fault.

Her hair ain't as thick as it used to be. It's LaShawndra's fault.

You Know Better

Her voice ain't as strong as it used to be. It's LaShawndra's fault.

She can't keep no relationship going. It's LaShawndra's fault.

Shoot, you'd think the whole world would be just fine if it wasn't for LaShawndra!

Sandra even blame me for whatever is wrong with her body. She used to walk around her half-empty apartment in her bra and panties complaining that they weren't giving out no bikini cuts in 1979 at Mulberry Medical Center when I was born. And they just gave her whatever, that's what she says. "They just gave me whatever, and now I got this big old C-section scar running down the middle of my stomach!" She wave her hand toward her belly, and then she really get started.

She can't wear no two-piece bathing suit or exercise outfit.

She can't wear no hip-huggers.

She can't wear no revealing evening dress.

She can't wear no cut-out clothing at all.

She can't go naked in front of nobody.

She blame me for all of that.

Shoot, I don't care 'bout her little scar. She be blaming me for most things going wrong in her life. If somebody didn't speak to her at the mall, she'd blame me. She couldn't finish college with her own class 'cause of me. She never got out of Mulberry 'cause of me. She was blackballed by a sorority in Mulberry because she had me out of wedlock.

But I just didn't pay that no attention. That's what Mama Mama told me to do when I was little and used to cry sometimes when Sandra say that stuff.

Mama Mama would sit in Granddaddy Charles's favorite easy chair in their bedroom and take me in her lap and say, "Don't take that mess on as yours, lil' girl. Sandra don't mean it. She just ain't thinking."

I could feel my face frowning up just thinking about Sandra.

Just then, a real good-looking brother came flying by us in a red

Cherokee, and I *had* to roll down my window and yell, "Whoa, nice Jeep, brother! Beep, beep, who's got the keys, for real!" I knew he couldn't hear me, but I had to say it. Besides the fact he was fine, his car was the first one we had passed in a long time, and we had been driving for a while.

I knew it was the back road and everything, but I could almost count the number of cars we had met or passed so far.

I asked Miss Liza Jane about it, and she just shrugged, which looked kinda cute, 'cause when she did that, the ruffles of her suit kinda jiggled 'round her neck.

"Oh, well, I guess everybody ain't going to Atlanta like me." I told her that because the way she was slowpoking along, you woulda thought she had forgot I was headed somewhere.

Noticing what was going on around me made me kinda lose my thought. Then I remembered.

But I ain't got no more respect for Sandra than she got for herself.

"Sometimes, when she be talking to me, lecturing me 'bout some-thing—like she got the right to lecture *me*!—all I hear is a sound like *wa-wa-wa-wa-wa-wa*, like on a Peanuts cartoon, like *Come Home, Snoopy.* And what she say makes about just that much sense to me, too.

"Shoot, sometimes Sandra's stuff be so raggedy that even *I* feel sorry for her. Sandra say I don't know *nothing* 'considering all the time she put into me,' but to tell the truth, it's Sandra that don't know nothing. She got issues, now, Sandra got *serious* issues. Humm-huh. And she *know* better. She *know* Mama Mama the only one who put any time in me.

"Shoot, Sandra need to get *herself* together. Be talking 'bout me and what I need to do and what I need to learn and what I need to under-stand. She don't *ever* want *me* to express *myself*. She can kiss my butt."

Miss Liza Jane looked at me and raised her eyebrow.

" 'Scuse me," I told her. "But she *can*, 'cause she still a real work-in-progress herself.

You Know Better

"Mama Mama been calling me a 'work-in-progess' since I don't know when. Since like forever. She call me all kindsa things, but she say 'em with love.

"Shoot, Sandra ain't even no work-in-progress, but she act like she above it all. Heck, listen to this, this is a woman who had the entire back of her Toyota Corolla blown away by a shotgun blast in the middle of the night while we was upstairs sleeping.

"I was 'bout nine or ten and just sleeping away. And all of a sudden I heard this big old *KA-BLAMMM!!!!* And the next morning when we went out to the car, there it was. You could see right into the trunk!

"A big old *shotgun hole!* You could see the little holes in the gray paint around the big hole that the gun made!"

"Really?" Miss Liza Jane said.

"Oh, Sandra act like it was a random mistake drive-by shooting. Yeah, right, a drive-by shooting on a gray Toyota Corolla parked in a quiet garden-apartment complex in North Mulberry in the 1980s. Yeah, right.

"Shoot, it was probably the wife of some man Sandra was dating telling her to step off.

"So she ain't got *nothing* she can tell *me!*

"Shoot, Sandra so phony. When it happened, the only thing she was even worried about was the way the guys at the body shop acted when they saw her car."

"How did they act?"

"Oh, you know, like she was some gangsta! Serve her right! Sandra is Miss Always Tryna Be So Fine and High-Class, looking down her nose at me and my friends. You ought to hear how she used to answer the phone when I would get calls. She'd pick up the phone all proper and everything, even say '*Bonjour!*' sometimes. And as soon as she'd hear it was some brother for me, she'd drop the phone on the table and yell, 'LaShawndra! It's some ignorant person for you. You need to teach your friends how to talk on the phone.'

Tina McElroy Ansa

"So when she was all embarrassed about her car being shot up, I just laughed at her. Miss Wanna Act Like She Above It All, 'specially above *me*, being seen as a *gangsta girl*! She said they had the nerve at one shop she went to for an estimate to tell her that they prefer she went somewhere else 'cause 'they didn't want no trouble.' Can you believe it!? They didn't want *no trouble*!

"Ha! They didn't know how close they were to the truth. Sandra ain't nothing *but* trouble.

"That's why she can't keep no man.

"She say that about me, too, 'cause I ain't got no one real boyfriend. She say, 'I don't know what you're talking about me for, LaShawndra. You ain't got no boyfriend neither.' "

"She doesn't have a special person in her life?" Miss Liza Jane asked.

"Oh, she dating a preacher now. But that's like not having no man, 'cause I know for a fact they ain't kicking it, him being a preacher and all.

"But I tell her real quick that I ain't like her, looking for a man all the time. I may not have no boyfriend, but I got all the men *I* need.

"*That* shut her up—for a while anyway. 'Cause she know it's the truth. I always had a buncha boys around me since I was a little girl. That's just how it's always been."

"You wouldn't like to have a boyfriend, Lil' Schoolgirl?" Miss Liza Jane asked me.

"Oh, I don't want to be all tied down," I told her, but that wasn't the truth.

I'd like to have one all my own at least for a little while. Shoot, to know some homey gon' be calling you on Saturday night at the same time, can't wait to see you and stuff like in the soaps. That'd be nice, I guess.

But I told Miss Liza Jane, "A little ho like me ain't really cut out for that kinda life, being tied down and everything."

Miss Liza Jane gave me one of those looks.

"Did I say 'ho'? Sorry. I really will try not to use that word anymore. For real."

"Thank you," she said.

"You're welcome," I said.

And since we were being so polite and everything, I asked if we could please turn up the AC a little bit? I was *hot!* And she reached over and touched a button.

The cool air blowing on my face and up under my skirt felt so good I just sat there and enjoyed it for a while and looked out the window at the "scenery."

"Oh, yeah, Sandra come back and tell *me* she don't want no man till she get her stuff together. She say she working on herself first. Which she is not doing.

"Sandra be having all these books 'round her place. You know, those spiritual deep books like that sister with the hard name who writes about valleys. You know, Ilonia or Eye-vanna or Eulonia—naw, that's a little town in Georgia. I know a *fine* brother from there. We kicked it a couple of times. I wonder where he ended up?"

Miss Liza Jane said, "It seems like every boy you mention you 'done kicked it with him a couple of times.' Is there *anybody* you meet who you *don't* 'kick it with'?"

"Oh, sure," I said. But when I really thought about it, I couldn't come up with too many names. And at first that was kinda funny, but then when I looked in Miss Liza Jane's face, it kinda brought me down.

"Heck, Miss Liza Jane, you keep making me forget what I'm talking 'bout. I'm not talking 'bout me, I'm talking 'bout Sandra!

"Now, what's that in-the-valley sister's name? Abinsinia? Yvonna? Iyanla! Yeah! That's it!

"Well, Sandra got *all* her books and a full hardback set of that *Course in Miracles* and all that stuff and everything 'bout finding peace and love. But she ought to pile all them books and tapes up in the middle of the floor of her empty living room and set fire to 'em.

Tina McElroy Ansa

Yeah, set 'em on fire for all the good they do *her*. Peace!? Sandra?
Shoot! She the queen of the drama queens.

"And she got the nerve to say, 'LaShawndra, she a fucking lost cause.' "

Miss Liza Jane made a ugly face.

"That's not what *I* say. That's what *Sandra* say. She cuss all the time. Sandra got a dirty old mouth! You think you offended by the way *I* talk! Shoot, you ought to hear Sandra sometimes when she think ain't nobody she care nothing about around. She sound as bad as anybody she be talking 'bout on my videos.

" 'Scuse me, but 'shit' is Sandra's favorite word. 'Who left this shit here?' 'What's that shit you got on?' 'Oh, give me the shit and shut up!' If she was talking 'round you, Miss Liza Jane, they'd have to bleep out words like they do on the radio. I don't know *why* they do that. It just make us come up with the missing words.

"When she be talking that way 'bout me and my music and my dancing and stuff, I just tune her out. She can't tell me *nothing*!

"The problem is, she don't give *me* no props—for *nothing*! For real! She don't hardly give me nothing like Mama Mama gave *her*! I want to tell her, Hey, I'm out here in this world just like you tryna make it by myself.

"Shoot, Mama Mama *always* let Sandra know she was there for her. 'Cause she gave her and her upbringing some thought! I try to think 'bout people and their feelings. I care 'bout folks. I be thinking 'bout this while I'm sitting down in that little cuticle at the Board of Education."

Miss Liza Jane chuckled. "You mean 'cubicle,' " she said.

"Yeah, 'cubicle.' Annnnyyway, I always thought it would be a good idea if people, especially women, could give away some of their pain. You know, like a girl having a baby could give some of the birthing pains to the daddy or her good friend or somebody.

"I done thought about this. You wouldn't be able to just give it to anybody, like somebody you didn't like or something. The person would have to ask or agree to it."

"You're thinking about your friend Crystal again, huh?" Miss Liza Jane said, reading my mind, 'cause I *was* thinking 'bout Crystal. Uh, Crystal was on my mind that whole trip!

I woulda gladly took a couple of those pains for Crystal when she was having Davon or Baby Girl. I woulda! For real. Crystal just smile and nod her head like she saying, "You sho' are a good friend," when I told her that.

But one day I heard her talking to her Baby Girl while she was changing her. Oh, Crystal be talking to her children all the time. Telling 'em their ABCs and their numbers, even before they can talk. She say it's her responsibility to teach them as much as she can so they have some of the advantages that she didn't have, bouncing around in foster care the way she did.

Crystal didn't know I was in the house. If she hadda, she wouldn't have thought of saying anything to hurt my feelings. She's softhearted like that. But I heard her say to her baby, "Aunt LaShawndra say she woulda taken some of them pains I was having with you, I just shake my head at LaShawndra and smile. I want to say, 'Shoot, girl, you probably couldn't stand one of them contractions,' but LaShawndra sensitive 'bout all that. So we don't say it out loud. Okay, Baby Girl?"

I just went on out the house so Crystal wouldn't know I was there and heard her.

I wouldn't hurt her feelings for *nothing*! I wouldn't!

'Cause no matter how strong she act, Crystal ain't *never* had nobody to ever pat her on the shoulder and say, Yeah, yeah, baby, it's gon' be okay. Mama's here.

At least I always had Mama Mama.

"Miss Liza Jane, you sure do seem to know *me*. Yeah, I *was* thinking 'bout Crystal, but I was talking 'bout Sandra, wasn't I?"

She nodded, and I went on. It felt good to talk and not have people say, "Oh, LaShawndra, shut up!"

"When Sandra be waving her *Course in Miracles* books in the air and pulling her little purple *Acts of Faith* out her purse like she read it all the time to make a point, I just tune her out and think about what I'm gon' wear to The Club that night. She don't do nothing but carry those books around for *show*. You know, when she want to be seen by her friends and co-workers down at Candace Realty—they try to be all real spiritual and stuff down there—and have them think she all deep and everything. She be pulling it out to some section she's marked in yellow highlighter.

"Shoot, I think a lot of them women—especially them friends of Sandra's—who be swearing by all them self-help, power-in-the-spirit books ain't even *reading* that stuff, let alone living it.

" 'Cause if they was, the world would be a better place, and they wouldn't be so mean and selfish and bitchy all the time. They ought to take some of all that money they make and buy themselves a *clue*."

"Don't say 'bitchy,' Lil' Schoolgirl," Miss Liza Jane said. "It's the same as 'bitch.' "

"It is? Dang! If we don't get to Atlanta soon, I ain't gon' be able to say *nothing*! See, you got me biting my nails—well, biting the polish off my nails anyway. And I ain't done that in *years*!

"For *real*! Pssst! I'm just gon' sit here and keep quiet for a while."

And that's what I did.

18.

I know this is hard to believe, 'cause I was in the middle of all that stress and everything. But before I knew anything, I had gone right to sleep!

Right there in the passenger's side of Miss Liza Jane's black Jaguar, with my feet up on her dashboard and music playing real soft on the radio.

When I woke up, I didn't even know where I was.

I felt like I'd been sleeping for *hours*! It was still light outside, just a little after two. But it felt like it shoulda been dark.

"Hey, Sleeping Beauty," Miss Liza Jane said as I stretched and smacked my lips some more. "You get a good rest?"

I think I was still sorta groggy and half dreaming, 'cause when I looked over at Miss Liza Jane, for a minute it was almost like I could see right through her, and I thought I heard some rustling in the backseat among my bags.

"Is your clock right?" I asked her as I wiped the slobber from the corner of my mouth and the crusty sleep from my eyes, smearing my eyeliner and mascara and yellow shadow all over my face. When I pulled down the mirror in the flap in front of me, I looked just like a clown.

"Shoot," I said as I reached for my makeup bag and some makeup remover to clean my face and start all over again. It was a good thing that I put on a fresh face of makeup three and sometimes four times a day, or I wouldn't have had all my materials with me.

I felt right proud of that, 'cause Mama Mama always say, "Be prepared." And she raises three fingers on her hand like this. I don't know why. She's told me two or three times, but I can't never remember.

I looked around, and even though the "scenic route" looked the
same to me, I swear we were passing some big old pine trees and a
bend in the Ocawatchee River on one side of the road and a big old
field with some cows munching on grass on the other side that I
thought we had passed a while before I fell asleep. One of the cows
even looked up at me with his head tilted to the side the way he had
before. But I didn't pay it no attention, 'cause, like I said, everything
in the country look the same to me.

"How long I been sleep?" I asked.

Miss Liza Jane glanced down at the clock on the dash, which read
2:15, and said, "About fifteen minutes."

Which I couldn't hardly believe. "For real? Gawd! You sure?" I
didn't mean to sound like she was lying.

"Do you have to go to the bathroom again?" she asked me.

I thought a second and said, "No, so I guess it couldn'ta been *that*
long."

But it sure felt like it. I felt like I got two or three nights' sleep in
that little time. Whew, and I *needed* it. I hadn't got a full night's sleep
in three or four days, what with running the street and everything
happening to Crystal and everything.

Ever since I was little, I've been falling asleep on car trips, but I felt
kinda bad sleeping like that while my best friend mighta been up at
the Mulberry Medical Center fighting for her life.

"Something worrying you?" Miss Liza Jane asked.

"Why you say that? I look like I'm worried 'bout something? For
real? I'm looking frowny?"

"A little," she said.

"Oh, well, I'll think about something else. A little coochie
mama—oops!—like me can't be having no frown lines."

And Miss Liza Jane obliged me by changing the subject. She made
everything so easy. Not like me at all. "It sure is pretty along this
stretch between Mulberry and Macon, where there's these big
stretches of the Ocawatchee River peeking through the trees."

I ain't never really noticed. I don't care so much about all that out-door nature stuff. It's too hard on my nails and my hair.

"The water is so clear and green!" she went on.

"You know 'bout Cleer Flo', don't you?" I asked her as I put on another coat of mascara. "Gawd, you wouldn't *believe* what folks around Mulberry are doing with water from that river. I know girls who douche with it when they want their periods to come on. But it don't never work. 'Cause I hear women who *want* to get pregnant—don't ask me, I ain't one of 'em—drink it when *they* at that time a' month when you can get pregnant. I say take the Pill all the time, and then you don't have to be figuring anything out and take any chances."

Miss Liza Jane smiled a pretty little smile. "It was quiet as a tomb in here while you were sleep."

That sounded like something Mama Mama would say. When I used to have been out partying late on Saturday and didn't want to wake up the next morning, Mama Mama would bring me a big glass of orange juice and stretch her hands out over me and say in this big booming voice, "Lazarus, come forth!"

"You know your Bible stories, Lil' Schoolgirl?" Miss Liza Jane asked me, all surprised-sounding.

I told her, "Oh, I went to church enough to learn a few Bible stories. Wasn't Lazarus the one who came back from the dead? I always thought about him like in those old black-and-white mummy movies Mama Mama look at.

" 'Lazarus, come forth!' *Ooo*-wee! Used to scare me right there in Sunday school."

When I told Mama Mama and Mama Mama's friend Miss Joyce that, Miss Joyce said, "Uh-huh, it's *always* the *baddest* ones who get scared the worst."

And I guess that is the truth, 'cause I do get scared easy. Sometimes I don't even like to sleep by myself. I guess that's why I'm always curled up in somebody's bed, as long as it's a warm body.

Tina McElroy Ansa

Crystal say she feels the same way, but she just gets an extra pillow and hugs it real tight. She say she ain't never liked sleeping alone in her own bed. Crystal say lotsa times she would beg, just *beg* somebody at her school to let her sleep over at their house when she say she know good and well that the foster family she was with didn't allow her to go on no sleepovers.

I used to try to crawl into bed with Sandra when I was little, but Sandra's feet always like *ice!*

I used to sleep in Mama Mama's bed all the time after Grand-daddy Charles was gone. Shoot, in the middle of the day on Sunday or in the evening, I used to like to stretch out on Mama Mama's big king-size bed and look at TV or listen to music or just lay there and talk to Mama Mama. Even though I got my own place now, I still do that. Sometimes we don't even talk. I just lay there while Mama Mama read a magazine or a book.

Even Sandra sometimes will come up to Mama Mama's room and lay 'cross the bottom of her king-size bed. And all three of us be just laying there all peaceful. It's the only time I can think of when we all together and Sandra ain't dogging me out.

I looked up and felt a little happy, because we were coming up on another exit for I-75!

"Hey, we can get on right up there," I suggested, hoping Miss Liza Jane would pull on the ramp. "See, we can get on right here and shoot right on to Atlanta! See! There's the sign: ATLANTA—157 MILES! You can slow down right here and we can take this ramp right here! Save some time. We be in Atlanta in *no time!*

"If you take this . . . If you just . . . If you . . ."

But by that time we had passed it.

"Dang, we 'un passed it now. You still don't want to take the in'er-state?"

She shook her head.

"Yeah, I know. You still want to take the *scenic route.*" I had to bite my lip to keep from sucking my teeth.

Y o u   K n o w   B e t t e r

Even with the music on and the free ride in a Jaguar, I was getting restless, 'cause the scenic route was boring. And I couldn't stop looking over my shoulder no matter how hard I tried. When I wasn't looking in the side-view mirror for the police to roll up on us 'cause of what I'd done to Crystal and her home, I was sneaking a look in the backseat, 'cause a couple of times it felt like we wasn't alone in that Jag. Crazy as that sound. But it was a crazy kinda day.

So I did what I always do when I get a little nervous and restless. I worked on my look.

"Mind if I paint my nails?" I asked Miss Liza Jane.

"Again?" she said.

I took that as a okay and reached for my manicure bag inside my big red bag under Sandra's giraffe-print bag.

"This lemony color is getting kinda old to me," I explained. "I think I'll try the sky blue. That may lift my spirits."

"Thinking about your friend again, huh?"

I tried to change the subject as I put foam separators between my toes and a couple of tissues under my feet on her dash. "Don't worry, I'll be careful with the polish on your leather interior."

She just shrugged. But I still showed her the jar of nail-polish-remover pads I was using so she'd know I didn't have no bottle of liquid remover to splash all over her soft leather seats. I was tryna be on my best behavior with Miss Liza Jane.

I smiled as I started my pedicure. "Come on, LaShawndra! Put you *best foot* forward!" Mama Mama tell me all the time. "Shoot," I used to tell Mama Mama, "I *am* putting my best foot forward!" God! But it wasn't good enough either. It *wasn't*! For *real*! My best ain't *never* good enough with folks.

And it get confusing, 'cause one minute folks telling you to "speak up, express yourself," and as soon as you do, they be saying, "Uh, LaShawndra, LaShawndra, shut up! Don't talk like that!"

"So," I just finally said. "So?"

"Where are you gonna stay while you're in Atlanta, Lil' School-girl?" Miss Liza Jane asked. "You don't have any money."

"Oh, I'll be okay," I assured her as I blew on my toes. "See, I got a plan. Everybody say I don't, but I do. 'LaShawndra just going from pillow to post,' Sandra say. But what *she* know?

"See, this weekend I'mo find out where the parties are at and go to one and find me somebody there to crash with tonight—either some girl coeds with wheels and they daddy's credit card and a hotel room or some brother with a crib. Then, when I finish Freaknik in Atlanta, I'm gonna move on to Macon. This gon' be my big chance. This time I just *know* I'm gon' get my chance to really try out for a music video.

"I told you, I can always do some ho's—oops—some girl's makeup and hair, and no matter what, I always seem to land on my feet. I was thinking 'bout that this morning while I was waiting for a decent ride to come along. And there's a couple girls in Macon and a guy, too, who pretend to be my friends because they know they gon' need my services—makeup and hair and nails—who'll let me stay at they crib for a few nights. I bet I can make it there for a couple of weeks like that. I do believe I can find some somebody who wants to help out a little coochie like me. Don't you?

"Mama Mama say I'm being unrealistic whenever I talk anything about my goals and aspirations and getting a little help from some-body.

" 'LaShawndra, you know you know better than to think some man you don't even know is going to take care of you for nothing.'

"I tell her, 'Mama Mama, that's all you know. I got a lot to offer somebody.' So I ain't *exactly* what you call a gold digger like some of those girls I know. Matter of fact, I ain't nothing compared to them! Them bitches expect to find some nigga to buy them Tampax! Oops.

"It's gonna be just like in those made-for-TV movies they show on Sunday night. That's my night in. Ain't much going on out in the street and in the clubs. And folks be getting ready for their week.

"Yeah, in these TV movies the one person in the whole story who didn't nobody think was gon' amount to much is the one who comes out in the end with the man and the beautiful clothes and the shoes to match and a all-expense trip to L.A.

"That's my plan."

"You aren't planning to come back to Mulberry and your home with your friend Crystal?" she asked.

I had to stop and think for a moment, 'cause I was telling so many lies I was getting my stories mixed up.

"Well, in Mulberry everybody know everybody. Everybody be knowing your business before you even plan to do it! And don't do nothing just a little bit wrong. They just *turn* on you.

"Yeah, *as soon* as I get some work in the music-video business. Shoot, just *one job*. Then I'm heading back to Mulberry, just for a visit, to let them see I made something of myself.

"Yeah, I'll go see 'bout Crystal and the babies and visit Mama Mama and take her to lunch and go down to The Club and let 'em see me. The Club, that's one of my hangouts, up over this old, old, old bar—way past old school. It's for old folks. But they do have good fish sandwiches.

"I don't know the real name of the bar—well, it's a bar and liquor store and old-timey whatchacallit ... juke joint—but everybody call it The Place. Just like everybody call the club in the back alley The Club.

"It's probably been there *forever*. I bet it was there when you was young. But you so classy and correct you probably wouldn't even know nothing 'bout no *bar* or no juke joint or no *club*."

Miss Liza Jane said, "Oh, I know about The Place. I used to live in Mulberry. I been around."

That's how she said it, "I been around." And even though I didn't think she meant it the way I woulda meant it, it made me stop and look at her a little different.

And I told her so. "Well, Miss Liza Jane, you ain't been around like a little ho like me. Oops. Shoot, it's hard to come up with another word for *that*!"

Then Miss Liza Jane gave me a whole list of words to use instead of "ho."

"You could call yourself 'person' or 'girl' or 'woman' or 'dancer' or 'musician.'

"Or isn't your music important to you?" she asked.

"Why you ask *that*!?" I said, and I *did* almost spill the bottle of "Am I Blue?" nail polish. "Yeah, my music is important to me. You don't think I'm about nothing? I take it serious. Sandra say I don't respect nothing, but I do respect my music."

"I believe you," she said.

That made me feel good. As a matter a' fact, right then I respected Miss Liza Jane enough to bust something on her I hadn't *never* told nobody else.

"If I tell you something, you won't tell nobody?" I said, almost looking around the Jag like somebody was there to hear me.

"Who am I going to tell?" she asked.

"Okay, I want to tell you something. But I don't want you to tell anybody, okay?

"Okay, here I go." And then, to lighten things up a bit, I bust some of Salt-N-Pepa's "Shoop" on her:

Miss Liza Jane didn't say nothing, so I told her, "You supposed to yell, *'Men!'* That's Salt-N-Pepa. Anyway, here I go."

I took another big breath and just said it:

"I been writing some lyrics. Some song lyrics."

"Really?" she said.

"Well, I ain't been *writing* 'em exactly on paper. But I been writing 'em in my head. I'mo write 'em down one day. But for now I just repeat all of 'em every night before I go to bed so I don't forget 'em."

She warm my heart, 'cause instead of laughing at me the way Sandra and them hos in Lil' Sis woulda—I can't stand them hos in Lil' Sis—she said, "Oh, let me hear some."

"Well, I ain't ready to *share 'em* with nobody else yet," I told her. "Shoot, you the first person I ever even *told* about 'em.

"So what you think?"

She thought for a while. I loved that 'bout Miss Liza Jane. She really *thought* before she said anything 'bout what I said. Then she said, "Well, it's a lot different from dancing in the background of a music video."

I had to agree with her on that. And it was scary saying it out loud. But it felt good to say it, too.

"How'd it happen that you started writing lyrics?" she asked.

"I guess I done listened to WASS and TV videos for so long, those words from all those cuts playing in my head along with the VJ's voice, that I looked up one night in a club up in Macon and saw that I had wrote down some words of my own on a napkin with a phone number on the other side. I know nobody would think that a little coochie like me—oops, sorry, I mean a little *person* like me—would come up with some lyrics. Shoot, it even surprised me!

"I know 'bout the music industry. I know 'bout video shoots. I know 'bout mike checks. You know, mike check, one-two, one-two. It don't mean nothing just 'cause I don't be telling people that I write music—well, in my head, anyway. It's just my business.

"I can't read music or play no real musical instrument like the keyboard or anything. This girl I knew in school named Chiquita tried to teach me once. And you know, Mama Mama tried to get me to go to piano lessons for about three or four years when I was eight, nine, ten, eleven, like that.

"The lesson would always be on Saturday. A schoolteacher friend of Mama Mama's used to teach a whole bunch of children on Saturday at this building she rented next to the Catholic school and turned into a studio. Mama Mama would try to drive me there and drop me off, 'cause she always had somewhere to be, but, shoot, I'd just sneak out after she drove off."

"Sneak off and do what?" Miss Liza Jane asked.

"Oh, I'd get a ride out to the mall or hang out in the school playground or go play with some boys or something—the kinda stuff I still do. Mama Mama would come back in a couple of hours and find me. She say that I'd always be the only girl in the middle of a bunch of boys.

"If I'da known 'bout my ambition then, I guess I woulda gone to those lessons at least a couple times. Just to learn the keyboard.

"Can we turn the jam up on in here?" I asked, and Miss Liza Jane reached for the radio to turn the sound up a little.

"Oh, good, that's WASS-FM. That's my favorite station in Mulberry. Sandra say I have 'this damn music' on all the time. But Mama Mama likes all other kindsa music, 'specially jazz. Miles Davis's 'Stella by Starlight' and ' 'Round Midnight' and Sarah Vaughan and all that. That's all she used to play when I was little and staying at her house at night, 'cause Sandra had something else to do. But she don't like it loud. She say it get on her nerves now that she ain't eighteen no more.

"The first and last time Mama Mama took me and some girls I knew to a concert at the Mulberry Coliseum, shoot, she made *everybody* sitting on our row get up and leave in the middle of a jam. She *did*! Not just me and two of her little stuck-up friends' grandchildren, but *everybody* near her who was younger than her. She gathered us up with our coats and bags and stuff and got our butts outa there!

"The whole time she was saying to herself, 'Oh, my God, I can't believe these children listen to that. I can't believe it!' And kinda wringing her hands like in a old-timey movie. And hustling us out of there.

"Ooh, hold up! Did I miss the local news again?" I was talking so much I didn't know if they had said something about Crystal and the break-in or not. I promised myself to pay more attention so I could hear the next report even though usually I *never* listen to the news.

I have the television on one of the music stations that play videos all the time now that I live with Crystal. And she don't mind the noise if the babies can't hear it in their room, and Crystal's room is between theirs and mine.

I guess all that's changed now.

Other than BET *Video Vibrations* or *Planet Groove* or MTV and old movies, I look at TV for mindless entertainment. That's what I'm looking for when I ain't working on my music. And I try to be working or thinking 'bout my work all the time.

That's what I think of it as. When I be talking 'bout "my work," Sandra just curl her lips and try to get Mama Mama's eye. But Mama Mama, she always look away.

I don't even talk about my ambition of being in a music video around Sandra hardly no more, 'cause she talks so bad about the music industry. She don't know *nothing* 'bout how the business works. Don't know nothing, but she got a *million* reasons why I ain't gon' make it in the industry.

"Sandra's worse than Mama Mama 'bout my ambition. She always talking 'bout how I can't just jump up and be in a music video. Like they don't know I been hanging out 'round studios and bands and nightlife for *years!* Like they ain't noticed how much music in my life. Like they don't notice I dress *just like* them little hos—oops—on TV. I work on knowing the business.

"A guy I know in Mulberry named William—they call him Wee Willie—really laid some wisdom on me about that one night."

Miss Liza Jane asked, "He your boyfriend?"

"Naw," I said. "I told you, I ain't got no one boyfriend. Wee Willie and me, we never got that deep. He just a friend, you know, somebody who was just nice to me and always had a good uplifting word for me. I done kicked it with plenty a' brothers—see, I didn't say 'niggas'—but I ain't been with just one exclusive long enough for him to learn my menstrual cycle.

"One night at a party Wee Willie heard me say I didn't know who directed that TLC video I like. He looked at me and said, 'That's stupid, Lil' Bit.' Then he took my hand—he got big old hands. You know that means he got a nice package in his pants—and led me over to the TV and turned to MTV and made me stand there in front of the screen in the middle of the jam until that writing came on at the bottom of the screen. And he read it off for me: the name of the cut—you know, the song—the name of the artist, if the song was 'featuring' any other artists, the record company's name, and the name of the director.

"Then Wee Willie said, real serious and everything, 'Don't be going around saying stupid shit'—he said 'shit,' I didn't—'like "I don't know this and I don't know that." You call yourself wanting to be in the music business, then you *better know* your business!'

"And he wasn't trying to kick it with me or nothing. He was just tryna help me out.

"He was being so nice and everything and not all up on me. He a big tall brother, but he don't act like that. And he cute, too—dark curly hair and kinda golden brown. He used to shave his head, but he don't no more. I mean, he was so *nice*. I don't think no man had been that *nice* to me for no reason since Granddaddy Charles moved out of Mama Mama's the second time. So I said real cute-like, 'cause I thought I looked cute—I was wearing my black velvet pants and a bra, a black bra—"

"That's all?" Miss Liza Jane asked.

"Yeah, that's all. I don't even think I had on any panties, 'cause you coulda seen them through the velvet pants. They real tight. Oh, and I had a coat somewhere, but I had hung that up. You get chilly some-times just wearing underwear, but Sandra say, 'You can't be cute and comfortable, too!'

"So I said to him—and I thought I was being cute and every-thing—'Thank you for your help. Can I pay you back in trade?' I heard that in a old movie.

"He looked at me like I was speaking French like Sandra.

"So I moved up closer to him, 'cause it was like loud and every-thing with the party jamming, and I said real loud I'd give him some head if he wanted me to. You know, I'd go downtown on him. Then I told him I had some condoms in my bag if that was what was slowing him down. 'Cause there *are* brothers out there who don't do nothing without a raincoat!"

"And you do?" she asked.

"Oh, sometimes I do. Sometimes I don't. It depends. I don't know *nobody* who use one *all the time.* Some niggas say they won't kick it with you at all if they got to use one of them.

"I just thought the condom thing might make a difference to Wee Willie. I even started singing 'I'll Be Good to You.' And I ain't got no *real bad* voice. So I knew that wasn't the problem.

"You shoulda seen his face. He got so mad *at me* I thought he was gonna hit me. For real! And I ain't never seen Wee Willie hit *nobody.* He ain't that kinda brother. He real sweet, 'cause he always talking 'bout spirit and peace and stuff. And sometimes he bad as Mama Mama with all that Martin Luther King Jr. history and getting mad when kids say 'Malcolm the Tenth' and giving-back-to-the-community stuff.

"Shoot, I was just tryna be *nice* and say thank you and I appreciated his help and talking to me like I had some sense! And I tried to tell him so.

"But he wouldn't let me explain. All he said was 'So, what's up with that, LaShawndra? What the hell that make *you* now, Lil' Bit? A prostitute?'

"He was so mad or hurt or something, I thought he was gonna bust into tears right there in front a' me and everybody at the jam. And you know how homeys like to be all hard and everything. Shoot, I know lotsa girls who can't stand a nigga who cries in front of them. Tenisha suck her teeth and say 'Pussy' real nasty if a nigga cry on her.

"Shoot, them girls think niggas be bugging if they cry."

Miss Liza Jane kinda rubbed her head at the temples like I do when I have a headache, tossed her pink hat in the backseat, and ran her hands through her red hair. Then she muttered, "Lord, I don't even know where to begin."

She took a deep breath, and of course you know she slowed the Jag down even more. I didn't know what she was gon' say next. Then she said real slow, "First of all, do you know what's gonna happen if you say 'nigga' one more time in this car?"

I didn't even have to think 'bout that one.

"Get all my stuff together that I got spread out all in this car and get out of this Jaguar coupe right here in Monroe, Georgia, and find myself another ride to Atlanta?"

She nodded her head.

"I'll try harder," I promised. I didn't even want to think about having to leave Miss Liza Jane and her Jaguar. Not only had she give me a ride, but I felt like we had bonded. Shoot, I had told her more of my personal stuff in three hours than I had ever told Sandra in my *whole* life.

"My bad. I *do* know better. I just don't do it.

"Now, what was I saying? Oh, yeah, I was talking 'bout Wee Willie. I wasn't serious or nothing. You know, 'bout giving him some head in exchange for him being so nice and everything to me. Well, really, I *was* serious. Shoot, I woulda sucked his dick for *nothing!* He a good brother."

A blue truck behind us started blowing its horn at us because Miss Liza Jane had started weaving back and forth 'cross the lines there.

"Quick, quick, where the button to drop the window? Oh, here it is. 'Honk! Honk!' yourself! We see you! Don't be blowing your horn at Miss Big Black Luxury Car here! This here a *Jaguar*! People better recognize!"

The truck just speeded up and passed us, which kinda embarrassed me, 'cause it was a old, beat-up truck that probably couldn't do over fifty.

"Hey, Miss Liza Jane, you okay?" I asked her. Her face look kinda funny. Not ha-ha funny. Strange funny.

270

"That's the second thing," she said, "Lil' Schoolgirl! Talking about 'sucking dick' at the drop of a hat! And considering engaging in threesomes with some grown man who might advance your career. My God!"

I didn't know how she knew about the threesome idea, 'cause I didn't think I had told her.

She just blew out a big long breath and said, "Help 'em, Jesus. Help these children."

I was in serious need of some help that Saturday, but I didn't think it was the kind of help she was talking about. So I didn't say nothing else about Wee Willie.

I see him from time to time. He ain't never said nothing else about that night at the party. He just wave and shake his head at me when he see me. When he walk away, sometimes I hear him say, "Still nothing but a coochie." And the way he said it, it made *me* kinda sad. Wee Willie, he a nice guy. Which prove that I don't think all men's dogs the way Crystal say I do. Or the way Sandra really do.

"Umm," Miss Liza Jane said all of a sudden as she sat up a little straighter. "Uhhhh, look at this! We coming up on something here."

I didn't see what she was talking about, but I told her, "Don't slow *down*! Don't slow *down*! We going slow enough as it is." But it was too late. We drove right into a big old cloud of smoke from a fire in the trees by the side of the road. But it looked like something out a scary movie, and I was kinda glad she slowed down, 'cause it was so thick. And just then Coolio came up on the radio, rapping 'bout walking through the valley of the shadow of death like the music from a scary movie.

It's a wonder any of us young folks can make *any* music.

Sandra try to be all mad and everything 'bout hip-hop and rap and the words they use and the sexy dancing and the things they sing and rap about, like going down on folks and shooting. But all she really care about is *her stuff*. She say we just *take* her music: Stevie Wonder and Sly Stone 'n 'em and just use it.

She be talking 'bout "sampling," but she don't even know what it is. I think it's like a compliment. It ought to make the first singers from back in the day feel *good* that we want to use they music and words.

But you know what Sandra used to say when I tried to listen to my jams in my own room? She stand in the doorway with her arms crossed and complain, "Why don't y'all come up with your *own* *songs*?!" That's what she say to me.

We wasn't driving fast, but we did finally get through the smoky patch and came out right at a little store.

"Hey, can we stop again at this place?" I asked. I looked down at the clock on the dash, and it was already half past three. "I need to pee and try to make another phone call."

Besides, talkin' 'bout dick and everything had gave me a taste for some Fritos.

19.

I guess I looked kinda droopy when I got back in the car with my Big Gulp and my bag of Fritos, 'cause Miss Liza Jane knew I still hadn't got through at the hospital.

"Don't worry," she said as she pointed to my seat belt and pulled back on old U.S. 90. "I bet you get through the next time."

By then I had been in that Jag more than four hours with Miss Liza Jane, but I didn't ever know what she was gonna say or do. She was kinda like me in that.

When we came up on the Ocawatchee again, she turned to me and said, "Watch out for your arm. I'm going to drop the windows and turn the AC off."

"All the way off?" I couldn't believe it. "What for? It's hot outside. I been out there."

"I like the feel of fresh air on my face," she said. "I don't get that a lot."

"Even if it blows your hair?" I asked her as the wind rushed in, blowing my hair all over the place.

But she just shook her curls in the wind and laughed like she ain't felt the wind in years. Then she stuck her head out the window a little bit like a puppy and sucked in a lot of air. Then she pulled her head back in and sniffed the air again.

"It ain't me, is it?" I asked as I leaned forward and smelled between my legs.

I didn't have time to take a douche, but I took a quick wipe-off in the sink that Saturday morning before I had left out of Sandra's house. But I had been standing out by the side of the road in the hot sun for a couple of hours and been kinda stressed out that whole day, so I lifted my arms and smelled under there, too. I thought maybe I was offending.

"No," she said, taking another deep breath of the air. "I smell rain."

"How you smell *rain?* Rain don't smell!" I laughed.

"Sure it does. Take a deep breath," she told me.

I took a deep breath, but I still didn't smell anything. Just maybe like dust or something.

"Does it smell damp?" she asked.

How is the air gon' smell *damp?* I thought, but I tried again.

"I guess I do kinda smell something. That's rain coming? Um. Behind Mama Mama's house smell like that sometimes in the evening after she's watered her garden."

Mama Mama's house, it's at the top of a hill.... Oh, I guess that's why they call it Pleasant Hill, huh?

Mama Mama's house may be old, but it's real comfortable. There's not a hard chair in the whole house. From the outside it looks almost like all the other old houses on the street, but inside she done gutted it and almost rebuilt it. It's got a upstairs and a downstairs. She got three bedrooms, but she turned the downstairs one into a den and office with a patio that leads to the backyard.

I spent most of my life in Mama Mama's house. First Sandra moved into the duplex apartment on Elm Street. That's when I was still little and Sandra was working for the phone company and finishing college. About two or three years old.

Then we moved into a little house in East Mulberry. We were just renting it. But while we were there, Sandra got interested in real estate, and when I was about nine or ten, she started working at Candace Realty. Then, a little while after that, we moved to the place she in now, a condominium out by Sherwood Forest development. It's called Sherwood Arms Condominiums.

The only time I felt like I had a real home is when I was at Mama Mama's place. Till I moved in with Crystal. I guess God was watching over me.

"Look," I told Miss Liza Jane, "I was just thinking 'bout God, and look, somebody wrote JESUS DIED 4U on this overpass up here. I know there ain't no point in saying it, but here comes a ramp to I-75 up there. We could get on if we wanted to."

"No, thank you," she said. "I don't want to."

I didn't think so.

I guess God be watching over me a lot for me just to make it from day to day. I got my own phone line, 'cause Crystal say I be getting so many calls my phone be like a 900 number some nights. It do cost a lot. But I got lotsa business to be taking care of. I may just look like another little coochie, but I'm that and some, too.

Mama Mama help me out with the bills most months. Shoot, Mama Mama take care of me. She buy my clothes and my underwear and my shoes and stuff. Then I go by her house all the time for the rest of the stuff I need: Safeguard soap and toothpaste and toilet tissue and Kleenex and Crisco and cans a' Campbell's tomato soup— that's my favorite soup. I make it with milk. Sometimes I get the milk from Mama Mama's house, too.

Shoot, I leave out of Mama Mama's house all the time with Piggly Wiggly grocery store bags *fulla* stuff! Just like I been shopping. Mama Mama *always* got a buncha stuff in her cabinets and refrigerator and freezer.

Even though I lived with Crystal and her kids, I betcha I still went over to Mama Mama's house every other day.

Shoot, if it wasn't for her, I wouldn't be able to make it. I wouldn't be able to carry on my little lifestyle. That's what Mama Mama calls it: "your little lifestyle."

I was talking and thinking so much, I hadn't been paying too much attention to the scenery going by until something struck me.

"Is it just me, or does it feel like we ain't making *no progress* in getting to Atlanta?" I asked Miss Liza Jane. "It sorta seem like we going 'round in circles. This old raggedy barn we coming up on look just like the last raggedy barn that it seemed like we passed a hour ago.

"I guess all raggedy buildings look alike, huh?"

"Not really," Miss Liza Jane said, and she said it as if I had just called the house she lived in raggedy.

"Where you live, Miss Liza Jane?" I hadn't even thought to ask her that before. I don't know why. Mama Mama say I'm real nosy.

"Oh, I live with two ladies from Mulberry, Grace Moses and Joanna Bloom. You know 'em?" she asked.

"Uh-uh, I don't think so. Are they old ladies?" I asked.

She kinda chuckled.

"They're about my age," she said. "We do some things together, and we do some things apart. We give each other space, and we get along fine. Like you and your friend Crystal."

That is how me and Crystal are. But sometimes living with Crystal is like living with Mama Mama. She keep her house clean *and* neat. And if you live there, *you* got to be neat and clean, too.

And you can't get away with nothing with her.

Crystal tell me in a minute if I don't clean up the bathroom every now and then, and I try to tell her I couldn't find the cleaning products. She say, "LaShawndra, you know better than to try that with me. *Everybody* in the whole world who got a bathroom keep their Comet and rag under the bathroom sink."

And she don't want to hear nothing 'bout how washing and scrubbing mess up my nails, 'cause she know I do my nails three or four times a day.

Then she say, "Now, go on in there and wash them short curly hairs out the tub." She always talk real sweet, so it don't even hurt my feelings when she tell me that.

Crystal got her bathroom all done up in yellow—"Sunshine Yellow"—'cause she say it's a uplifting color for her children, their personalities. She has matching rugs and fuzzy toilet-seat covers and even little yellow lace curtains over the little ti-nichy window over the tub.

I couldn't hardly get that bright yellow color out my head.

Crystal do know how to make a "home."

"Can we close these windows now?" I asked Miss Liza Jane. I had had about all the "fresh air" I could take.

"Thank *you*," I said as she touched two buttons on the console between us, and I could finally fix my hair so it wasn't blown in a hundred directions.

I could just see me and Crystal laying 'cross her bed drinking Diet Cokes and eating chips after work when she always talking 'bout a "home life" and "family." Like a home life's gon' make some difference in what a girlie is.

Shoot, I know plenty girls who daddies doctors, some of their mamas, too, and they ain't doing no mo' than me. Shoot, lots of 'em ain't even doin' much as me. Still living off they got-money families, living in they little pink girl rooms with lacy curtains at the windows, pictures of puppy dogs on the wall. I been there. I seen 'em. Fanned those very curtains to get the strong smoky smell of a blunt out the air before their housekeeper came in and smelled it.

"You want some of these peanut butter cookies?" I offered Miss Liza Jane the Ziploc bag. "Crystal made 'em yesterday. She make cookies two or three times a week."

She shook her head.

"You must be on a diet like Crystal," I told her. "You don't eat nothing."

Whenever Crystal be packing the bags for her kids to take to the sitter's, she always drop stuff in my bag, too. Sometimes it's a piece a' fruit. She knows I like pears. Or some crackers and cheese. Or some almonds or walnuts. Never no junk food. *Always* something healthy. Crystal always tryna make a home life for us all.

I don't care nothing 'bout no gardens and stuff. But Crystal has her little garden in the square of yard by the front door of our place. She grow a few tomatoes and hot peppers and some herbs. She *love* to be cooking something and step outside her front door and bring some herbs in and drop 'em in the pots of stuff she cooking, spaghetti sauce or homemade soup or greens. She get that from watching Martha Stewart on TV.

Crystal like to cook. She ain't the best cook in the world like Mama Mama, but she cook every day. She don't 'low her children to have no McDonald's or Hardy's or pork barbecue.

Crystal was *born* to be a mama. She musta been *born grown-up.* She say all the time she want her children to have everything, 'cause she didn't *have* no childhood, being raised in foster care and everything.

Mama Mama say don't none of us—me and my friends—have no childhood no more. Shoot, people don't think nothing 'bout no *child.* They say they love they children and everything, especially black folks. Mama Mama and her friends are the last group a' people, black people, I seen who really put some love and thought in their children.

My friends' folks don't want us to have their music. Don't want us to have their names. Don't want us to have their drugs. Don't want us to have their games and fun and memories and stuff. Shoot, if it wasn't for Mama Mama, I wouldn't know nothing 'bout the past and stuff.

And, shoot, sometimes I'm just curious. And who else I got to turn to but Mama Mama? At least *she* be keeping it real and stuff.

The only past Sandra want to tell me about is what happened to her last night. Well, she don't do that no more now that I'm almost grown and everything, but when I was little, she used to wake me up at night after she done been out to tell me this time she think this the one. *This* the man who gon' be the one.

If I had a new pack of press-on nails for every time she told me she thought this man was gon' be the one, I wouldn't never need to go shopping again. And he ain't never the one.

Shoot, I don't know what Sandra talking 'bout how much better she is than me. I seen *her* run out the house at 3:00 A.M. after some man without even taking time to brush down her eyebrows or see if I was all right there alone.

And she can be as trifling as she say *I* am.

When she was going to school and working, it took Sandra half a year, *six months,* to remember to get a lightbulb for the 'frigerator. Heck, we got to the point that we'd just leave a old flashlight by the door and use it to peep in the back.

Every time she'd open the 'frigerator door, she say, "Um, um, um, can't ever remember to get that lightbulb. I'll do it today."

But she didn't. She'd forget it till the next time she opened the 'frigerator door and no light came on.

But we ain't *never* talked 'bout when she was little, growing up and everything. If it wasn't for Mama Mama, I wouldn't know nothing 'bout Sandra before I met her.

I feel kinda bad for them girls like Crystal who ain't even got a Mama Mama. Mama Mama *there* for me. Mama Mama would be the kind of grandmama who would take care of my baby if I ever had one. But I ain't one of those girls who want to have a baby to have someone to love and to love her forever. I don't plan to have no baby when I'm nineteen and by myself like Sandra.

Shoot, I *know* better. I seen the kind of life that can come out of that. I don't think we never did sit down to a meal at the table in Sandra's house unless we had company or she have a date and was trying to impress him with how she knew how to cook and set a table and do right, you know.

But at Mama Mama's house it was like at Crystal's. I got just what Sandra got when she was growing up. Mama Mama used to sit down with me for a meal at least once a day, even if it was breakfast, which it had to be, 'cause some days Mama Mama wouldn't see me all evening once I was out the house.

Shoot, I don't know how to cook nothing but spaghetti—from the can—and cream of tomato soup and frozen tortillas. I can use the microwave, but I don't like to, 'cause every time I do something seem to explode. Mama Mama can make something outa *nothing*! For real! She can make a meal outa a couple a' things from the refrigerator and a can from the cabinets. I'm not like that, make something outa nothing. Mama Mama and Sandra both be getting mad at me when I don't know how to cook something.

Sandra *and* Mama Mama be dogging me right in my face sometimes. Like I'm too stupid to understand what they be saying. Sometimes they bad as those bitches in Lil' Sis and at the studio in Macon. I can't stand them hos.

Mama Mama be so through with me. She say, "Good goodness, LaShawndra, you must have seen me cook this chicken or this rice or this whatever a million times. And you mean to tell me you don't know what ingredients to get out the cabinet to get started!?"

Or Sandra—with her no-cooking self—will come in Mama Mama's kitchen and start in on me, too. Talking 'bout "I may have only cooked on Sundays," which is a lie in itself. Sandra didn't do nothing more than go by Mama Mama's house and bring home some of her and Granddaddy's dinner to put on our plates, or she stopped by the Dixie Pig. To this day the smell of pork barbecue and coleslaw makes me sick to my stomach, like I'm gonna throw up. That and Chinese food. I done had enough a' *that* to last me forever!

And this same Sandra would have the nerve to say to me, "I may have only cooked on Sundays, Shawndra, but you know enough to wait until the water boil before putting the rice in. You *know* better, Shawndra."

I just look at her. I don't even know where to start. God! So I just look at her.

Anyway, it may not look like it, but I know what I'm doing. You learn how to cook and the homeys be expecting you to cook and sex 'em, too. Too much work for this little coochie.

Shoot, when homeys know you can cook, then they be expecting to slide by your crib every day to get something to eat. Shoot! What I look like, cooking for some nigga?

I be telling those girlies who think they gon' trap a man by cooking for 'em that after they cook a big old meal in the kitchen—

You Know Better

shrimp and salad and potatoes and stuff—they gon' be too tired to kick it in the bedroom. Which I think is deep. But, you know, don't nobody be listening to me.

It makes me kinda scared to think it sometimes, and I sho' ain't said it out loud to nobody, but brothers don't be liking us girls no more. For real! That's what I think.

Fellas much rather spend time with their boys than with their girl. And you only hear them laugh a certain way when they with other guys. You don't *never* hear 'em laughing like that when they out at a club or the park or anywhere they hanging out with females. I noticed.

Mama Mama say we done finally got to the point that men and women been heading to for quite some time. Mama Mama say black men and black women finally all-out hate each other. She say, "Just listen to what the young men say about you in their music!" And Mama Mama ain't never been one to dog a man out the way Sandra and her friends do all the time. All Sandra and her friends got to do is get a little wine on the table or a little blunt, and before they can get a decent buzz on, they dogging some brother.

Then they be wondering why *we* can't find no decent man or just be happy when we find somebody who want to kick it with *us*.

Sandra all the time be talking about the words to my music. She say that rap music is the reason all of *us*—meaning me and my friends—are the way we are—meaning little coochies. She especially hate the guys—the players. She say young black women like myself have not been respected and don't even respect ourselves enough to demand respect from our own young black men. That's why she say these men call themselves "dogs." Road dogs, home dog, dog dog, my dog. She hate that.

I say that all those years of Sandra and her friends calling men dogs their whole life right in front of their little boys and little girls is enough to turn 'em all into dogs. Then she got the nerve to be mad at something as everyday normal as Snoop Dogg's Dog Pound.

Tina McElroy Ansa

"Hey, Miss Prophesy," I said, "drop your window and smell out-side. What it smell like now?"

I was only messing with her, but Miss Liza Jane did just what I said. Of course, you know she had to slow down first. Then she opened her window and stuck her face out.

"Is it still smelling like rain?" I asked, laughing a little.

She pulled her head back in and said, real serious-like, "Smell dif-ferent now. Something worse than rain."

Her voice sounded so like something from a monster movie it wiped the smile right off my face, almost scared me, but then I remembered where I was, and said, "Oh, wait, we in a *luxury* vehicle. We'll be okay."

20.

Then it just started to pour down! I couldn't hardly believe it was raining at all, let alone like it was, in sheets! 'Cause it was all sunshine and bright when Miss Liza Jane picked me up, and then, a couple of hours later, it looked like we were gonna be washed away in a flood.

Miss Liza Jane was really driving slow now. "I told you I smelled rain," she said.

"I know you said that, but, no offense, I didn't think you really could. I forgot you one of those big women like Mama Mama who can do *anything*.

"Well, I sho' hope it don't rain out Freaknik. You know, most of Freaknik is done outside, riding up and down the street and in the park and stuff."

"I *like* the rain," Miss Liza Jane said.

"I *hate* when it rains! It makes my hair all short and frizzy. Mama Mama always sings at me when it rains:

" 'LaShawndra get the blues when it rainsss.'

"Heeeyyyy. Wait a minute! What's that I hear?"

It sounded like percussion. *Ratta, ratta, ratta.*

"Hold up! This ain't no rain. You hear that? Bam, bam, bam, bam, bam! It ain't raining, Miss Smell the Rain. *It's hailing!*"

It was! Hail big as marbles was just dancing 'cross the road and bouncing off the hood and windshield of Miss Liza Jane's Jaguar.

"Pull up here! Pull up here! Quick," I told her as we came to a underpass of I-75. We pulled to the side of the road and parked.

There are hailstorms in middle Georgia all the time, but I had never seen hail like that ever in my life. They looked like the bath beads that Mama Mama keeps in a tall, pretty jar in her bathroom.

"See, it's a good thing I-75 was so close, or else we wouldn't have no protection from this hail! See, this expressway overpass come in handy." Miss Liza Jane knew I was tryna get her to get on the freeway again, but she didn't say nothing.

"Is the whole car under here? Good. Don't want no dents in *this* finish, huh?" I said.

Miss Liza Jane and me and the Jag was safe under the overpass, but even with the motor on and the windows up, I could still hear the big hailstones hitting the road around us like bullets. It almost made me feel like I was under attack or something.

Mama Mama say when things get real bad for her, she just close her eyes and say, "Jesus, Jesus, Jesus." And things start getting better right away.

She say that there's somewhere in the Bible that says when you pray—*really*, for real pray—when you in a real tight jam, then angels start to moving right then to help make it better. I didn't know if I believed that for real, 'cause I don't go to church or nothing. And I ain't no good girl like Crystal, but I sure needed a angel that day.

I'd been fighting back tears ever since I had heard 'bout the break-in at Crystal's, but thinking 'bout what a good girl she was pushed me right over the edge. When Miss Liza Jane saw me wiping my eyes, I covered up.

"Naw, I ain't crying," I said. "It must just be my allergies kicking up again. Yeah, I'm allergic to a buncha stuff. They make my eyes watery and red like this. I think I got some OcuHist or some other eyedrops in one of these bags here." And I picked up the first bag I touched, and it was the panda bag my daddy had sent me, which made me want to cry some more.

He left Mulberry right after I was born. He didn't even come to the hospital. Then we heard he entered the army and got a new family with a Filipino woman and moved to Seattle, Washington. Sandra say he was tryna get as far from me as possible. Once in a while I'd hear from him on my birthday, but I could tell he was only doing it 'cause someone was telling him he was too good a man to just leave his daughter down there in that little Georgia town without some contact. So that's what he made. *Contact.*

Whenever he talked, he sound like it was a duty. Everything he say, I could tell he was scared I was gon' ask him for something.

"What you studying in school, LaShawndra?"

"What movies you seen lately, LaShawndra?"

"What you gon' do this summer, LaShawndra?"

But he'd hesitate after each question. I could tell he didn't care nothing 'bout me answering. He just stop for a while 'cause he think I'mo say something like "When you gon' come see me? Can I stay with you this summer?"

Sometimes I could just hear him getting himself up for the phone call to me at Mama Mama's house. He *refused* to call me at Sandra's place. Then, when I was about ten years old, he just kinda eased off, and when I was around fifteen, he just stopped calling altogether. I ain't heard from him much since then, except for the panda bag the year before.

I could see Miss Liza Jane watching me stroking my furry bag, but she didn't say nothing. She just handed me a tissue from the box on the console.

"Thank you, Miss Liza Jane. Ummm, even your Kleenex smell sweet." I stuffed the Kleenex in my panda bag so I'd have something to remember her by when I got to Atlanta.

Miss Liza Jane cut off the motor and rolled down her window. Then she turned to the side, put one knee up on the seat, and got comfortable, not saying a word. I knocked boots with a guy once who could sit quiet like that all night, not ignoring me but just being quiet. He's this guy with thick eyelashes and these wet, wounded Tupac eyes.

Even as sad as I was, I realized that was good, and I repeated it three times: "Wet, wounded Tupac eyes. Wet, wounded Tupac eyes. Wet, wounded Tupac eyes."

Since I had been talking with Miss Liza Jane 'bout what I thought
and wanted to do, my little lyrics writing seemed more important, a
little more possible. They did!

By then, with us sitting under the I-75 overpass with the road
above and around us, I could almost hear my words playing with
music and backup singers and stuff. At first I thought it was some jam
I was hearing on the radio, but then I noticed there was no music
playing, just the weather report.

"So it's the rainy weather making you sad, Lil' Schoolgirl?" Miss
Liza Jane asked me.

"What? Am I looking frowny again?" I asked. When I looked in my
mirror right quick, I was really disgusted with my silly self, 'cause my
eye makeup was all smudged from me getting misty and everything. I
reached for my makeup bag again. I told you I put on makeup a hundred times a day.

"Uh, don't even pay me no attention, Miss Liza Jane, you know,
I'm just bugging. I don't know why I'm so emotional today. I think I
must be coming on my period."

"Maybe you thinking about your friend in the hospital," she
offered.

"Yeah, I guess it is 'cause a' Crystal and worrying 'bout her and
everything. I guess that's what I'm feeling now. I need to make that
phone call again when we get a chance. If this hail ever stop."

By that time it was hailing *and raining* at the same time. Believe
me, it was some strange weather going on that day. But looking back
on it, that whole day was 'bout the strangest one I ever had.

I took a deep breath, and a big old shudder ran through my whole
body. I don't know where it came from. I shook so bad there for a
while, Miss Liza Jane looked at me like she thought I was fixing to go
into convulsions. I did that once or twice when I was little and had a
high fever.

"I'm okay," I told her, and I reached for a tissue to start taking off my makeup. "I'm just acting crazy, like I always do. Now, you know I got to fix my face again after my eyes run. I'll just take it all off and start over."

When I looked in the mirror again, it scared me a little, 'cause for a second there, without any eye makeup on, I looked just like Sandra when she got that little-lost-girl look on her face, which she have whenever something don't go her way. I started putting on some makeup right quick.

Just then I realized that WMUL was playing music again.

"Shoot, did we just miss another news report? Dang, I can't catch the news on the radio for *nothing*!"

"I think I heard them talking about a shooting in Mulberry," Miss Liza Jane said.

My heart skipped a beat.

"I think they said it happened in a public park, Mulberry Square Park, drug-related," she said.

My heart started beating regular again.

"Oh, yeah, even in a little town like Mulberry they be breaking in and gangbanging and shooting over drugs and stuff, just like in the city," I told her. "That's just the world."

Sandra and even Mama Mama, who has worked around young people, don't seem to know just how violent it is around us. Lotsa kids are scared all the time. Scared in their families, scared of the men they mamas bring home, scared in school, scared out on the street just talking and playing and stuff. Even Mama Mama make me sick sometimes, talking 'bout going to school like it's some kinda *safe zone*! Shoot, ain't no place safe for us!

Mama Mama and her friends be acting like we growing up in the same time and place and world they did a hundred million years ago.

It's just something else to make us feel bad 'bout ourselves. And right then I was feeling bad enough.

Ever since I'd been sitting in Miss Liza Jane's car, I think I'd been thinking 'bout stuff that make me feel kind of uncomfortable and guilty-itchy. Like for instance, I always been attracted to niggas who carry guns. You know, hard brothers packing a nine. To me there's just something about a man who is packing a tin.

When I told Mama Mama that, she clutched her chest and said I was crazy. With everything that was going on with the break-in at Crystal's, it did all of a sudden seem kinda stupid.

What makes it even crazier, I don't even like to be *around* guns. I think I'm scared of 'em. But I just don't want to say that, 'cause it sound so country and stupid. Afraid of a gun. In some places you better be scared *not* to have one. Everybody got a gun, even Sandra.

Now, it ain't like I'm one of those bitches who all tied up in death. You know, the shooting in the middle of a party, the excitement, the drive-bys, the funerals and the buying of the black dress that still makes you look good while you mourning. The having the daddy baby to live on, for a while anyway. Taking care of the brother in a wheelchair. Meet you at the crossroad, blood. And all that. I know lotsa girls who got to find some kind of time to get out to the county detention center to see they boyfriends before they go out on the weekend. Lots of young folks don't think there's anything more interesting than having a funeral and some attention and your surviving homeys talking about you forever. Shoot, I got some more living to do before I'm gone.

I ain't into all that death stuff. What I want is to just live and dance and meet guys and get in a music video and drink some champagne with a strawberry in it while I'm sitting in a outdoor Jacuzzi with my titties bobbing on the bubbles. That's what I'mo do. That's what *I believe in.*

Wait, that ain't true. I don't know what I believe sometimes. I can't think about one thing for too long, unless it's music or the lyrics to my songs, or I get dizzy. For real, I get dizzy. I start seeing bright lights, and things start to spin a little if I don't shake out of it. For real.

Sandra and Mama Mama claim they scared for me when they hear 'bout me liking guys who carry guns and 'bout who I been hanging out with. *I* feel like "the mama" myself sometimes, trying to explain to them that this a *dangerous* world out here no matter what you do. It ain't like it was back in the day with them! They ought to know it. They the ones who sat around and made it this way.

They did! *They* didn't have no world where you scared to walk down certain streets during the day, and scared to kick it with anybody you want to like they did 'cause of what you might catch that'll kill you, and drugs that ain't even fun. And having to watch what you drink at a party even if you don't take no pills or smoke or nothing.

So if this the world we got, then it don't make no difference whether you careful or not careful. Locking your doors and staying outa dark, drug-filled places and not taking rides from strangers. "Stranger danger! Stranger danger!"

Shoot, you may as well go on and die right now, to let Mama Mama and Sandra tell it. Or be scared all the time.

Just thinking 'bout all that—death and decisions and danger—made my mouth so dry.

"You sure you don't want some bottled water?" I asked Miss Liza Jane before I turned the bottle up. "You supposed to drink eighteen glasses a day."

"No, thank you," she said. "And it's *eight* glasses."

"Oh, eight? For real? Did you tell me that before?" I had so much on my mind that day, I couldn't remember *nothing*. "Good! But it supposed to be good for your skin, so you know me. A little sister like me gotta watch out for my looks."

"Your makeup looks good," she said. I was just about finished. "Real professional."

Miss Liza Jane could make me feel so good. Just like Mama Mama.

No matter what she say, I know Mama Mama always got my back. She be slipping me a couple twenties right regular, and if I'm *really* in a crunch, I know I can count on her. Always. Shoot, if it wasn't for Mama Mama, I would be a motherless child, like Mama

Mama's friend Miss Joyce be singing 'round her house when she cleaning and drinking.

It goes:

Sometimes I feel like a motherless child

A looooooong way from hoooommmmmmme.

"I think it finally stop hailing," Miss Liza Jane said. "Want to try it again?"

"Yeah, it is still raining. But it's not heavy. Yeah, and now it's a little foggy. It look like the side of the road's on fire, don't it?

"Hey, it's your ride. You decide. Uh, that rhymes. I gotta remember that! It's your ride. You decide. It's your ride. You decide. It's your ride. You decide. Okay! My seat belt's on! Let's get rolling, then!" I felt like I was really getting some work done on my lyrics.

"We can stop at the next little store or gas station you see so I can make my phone call. Okay?" I just couldn't get Crystal out of my head.

"Here's one right here off the highway," she said. "You better run in before it starts raining hard again."

"Well, you right," I said, looking up to the sky, which was a funny-looking purple color. "It is starting to cloud up real bad again."

When Miss Liza Jane pulled into a parking space right by the door, I took some more of her change and hopped out of the car, right into a big puddle of muddy water.

21

I skipped through them puddles of water and jumped back in that Jag like I didn't weigh nothing.

"Uh-huh, yes, yes, yes! As Mama Mama say, 'There *is* a God!' "

"Good news, Lil' Schoolgirl?" Miss Liza Jane asked.

"Yes!" I said. "Whew! I feel like the weight of the world been lifted from my shoulders. Whooooo!

"I finally got through to the hospital where *somebody* would tell me something without me giving them a whole lotta information first.

"Oh, I still couldn't get all the 411, but I found out Crystal gon' be okay. She wasn't shot like somebody said. She wasn't never shot. She just had passed out 'cause she had forgot to take her medication for diabetes. Did I tell you she was diabetic? That's why she need to lose some weight. And guess what?

"The babies weren't never even hurt. They was just scared to death, I know. But didn't nobody slam Davon against the wall of his pretty bedroom and try to molest little Baby Girl the way somebody told me. Dang, people always getting their stories wrong!

"God, I feel like I got another chance at life!"

Miss Liza Jane just put the car in reverse, looked both ways, and backed out onto the road. "Is that all you found out?" she asked.

"Well, after whoever broke in saw Crystal lying on the floor, he grabbed up some stuff and ran out. That's what this girl I know on the switchboard told me.

"They say Baby Girl and Davon in the waiting room at the hospital. So they must be with somebody responsible. I betcha it's Mama

Mama. I sure hope so. The girl on the switchboard say they were with that responsible person all the time at the hospital.

"But Davon okay. That's the important thing, he and Baby Girl okay. They weren't hurt at all, physically. I know they were probably scared to death having a stranger break in their house and seeing their mama fall out. But they okay otherwise."

I pulled off my wet sandals and put my feet up on the dash. I felt relaxed for the first time that day.

"I was lucky enough to get this girl on the hospital switchboard who I had done a favor for one time—I braided her hair one time—and she was happy to give me some good news."

Miss Liza Jane just held it in the road, as she would say, and didn't open her mouth.

"Why you not saying nothing?" I asked. "This the best news I had in a *long time*! Ain't you happy for me and Crystal and the babies?"

She glanced at me right quick and asked, "What happened to the car-crash story?"

"What car crash?" I had forgotten all about what I had told her. I do that sometimes, forget to get my lies straight. "Oh, yeah, the accident. Did I say it was a car crash? I can't remember."

"Well, *my* memory is just fine," she said.

"Oh," I said, and pulled out my makeup bag again. I was just praying she wouldn't push me about it. But she did.

"Either your friend and her babies were hurt in a car crash or not," she said.

"Well, yeah, you right, either it was a car crash or it wasn't, huh? That's right.

"I *did* say they was in a car accident, didn't I?"

"Was that a lie?" she asked. Miss Liza Jane was so straight up.

"Kind of," I said. Psst. Sandra say I'm a *big* liar. And I *hate* for her to be right. Dang!

"Oh, they also said Sandra was up there at the hospital seeing 'bout Crystal, which is the biggest surprise to me. 'Cause Sandra don't care nothing 'bout nobody hardly but herself. I woulda thought it woulda been Mama Mama up there to see 'bout them. But the girl I know on the switchboard said she saw her herself. She said she think she was holding Baby Girl. Which I *know* ain't the truth. 'Cause Miss Sandy sure don't want to get her designer clothes all wrinkled with a child in her arms."

"And the story about the car crash?" Miss Liza Jane asked. When Miss Liza Jane wanted to know something, she just didn't let it go. It made me think how easy I give up on things if it don't work out right away.

"For real, what I told you wasn't really a lie. It was more like a mis-understanding than a outright lie."

She cut her eyes at me again.

"It was!" I insisted. She didn't say nothing.

"Okay, it was like this: I had just got in your car and just met you and everything, and I didn't know you that good, and I didn't want to tell alla Crystal's business first thing. So that's why I told you Crystal and the babies was in a car accident."

"What *is* the truth?" she wanted to know, all serious-like. Wow, way to bring a room down, Miss Honesty! She sho' brought me down.

I started to yell at her, "*You can't handle the truth!*" like that guy in the movie, but I could see she wasn't in no mood for one of my little jokes, even though *I* felt a whole lot better.

"Well, okay, I'll tell you the truth, okay? Okay. Well, let's see.

"This is what happened. Well, this is what I was *told* happened. 'Cause I wasn't there. This is what people told me when I was sneak-ing around the crime scene. Wait a minute, that make it sound worse than it was. I wasn't really sneaking, and it wasn't really like a crime scene. Okay?

"I'mo tell you."

I waited for a while and took a sip of the Diet Coke I had just bought and licked my lips. My mouth and lips was so dry.

"Now, I wasn't there. I had a date last night. So I was over to this brother's crib when it happened."

I took a deep breath and jumped right in.

"There was a break-in at Crystal's house last night."

"Last night?" she asked. I was glad she was saying *something*.

"Oh, yeah, all this just happened last night. Dang, it seem like it was a million years ago. It does. Shoot, it seem like I been riding in this car *half* that long anyway."

I took another sip of my drink and went on.

"Okay. So there was a break-in at our house on Painted Bunting Lane, and Crystal and the babies was there, of course, 'cause it was 'round three or four in the morning, and Crystal musta heard 'em breaking in and thought it was me and got up, and when she saw it was somebody breaking into her house, she ran to her babies' room to try to protect them, and they saw her and got scared, but then she passed out 'cause she didn't take her medication the day before, 'cause, you know, she a diabetic...."

"God! My heart racing so fast just telling you 'bout it. Wow!"

"Go on," she said.

"Well, somebody next door heard all the noise or saw the burglar run out—I don't know which—and called the police, and then the am'alance came and...

"And I ain't got all the facts and everything, 'cause nobody won't tell me everything. I got to get bits and pieces of the story from here and there. I didn't talk with anybody official or anything."

"Why didn't you talk with anybody official?" she asked.

"Why?...'Cause I couldn't get through to nobody on the phone. You know that I just tried back there at that McDonald's."

"What about when you were still in town? The police didn't know anything?"

"Oh, yeah, while I was still in town. Well...

"Wait, you getting me confused. Let me tell you how it was my own way.

You Know Better

"I woke up in the middle of the night. Well, it was way after midnight this morning—remember I told you I had a date. It wasn't no planned date or nothing. It was with this guy I know. I hooked up with him at The Club.

"Annnnyway . . . I woke right up and sat straight up in bed. Well, it wasn't a bed, it was just a futon on the floor. Anyway . . . I woke right up like somebody had called my name, and, I swear, I just felt all hot and sweaty, and I felt like I should go home right then. So I did.

"Mama Mama say you can't never go wrong following your first mind, and I don't hardly never do that, but this time I did. I woke the brother up, the brother I had just kicked it with, and asked him to give me a ride home, but he said he was still 'sleep. So I took some money out his pants pockets and called me a cab.

"Well, then, when we turned into Painted Bunting—that's our street—you shoulda seen all the folks standing around in their pajamas and nightclothes, and cars and the police still there.

"You know how people come out when they hear a police siren and am'alance in their own neighborhood. But everything was over by then. The paramedics and am'alance and stuff had left."

"You couldn't tell anything by how the house looked?" Miss Liza Jane asked.

"Oh, I didn't go inside. I didn't have my key. No! Wait! That's not why. There was that yellow police crime-scene tape across the door, and I couldn't get in. I just talked to the people standing around. No, weren't no police around by then. Yeah, they were there when I got there, but by the time I finished talking with everybody standing around, the police had left. Yeah, they had left.

"So then I had to leave to try to catch me a ride to Atlanta for Freaknik. And then you picked me up."

I had been talking so much, tryna keep my story straight and everything, that my head was spinning. I was glad Miss Liza Jane was driving instead of me, 'cause I wouldn'ta been able to stay anywhere near inside the white line.

Tina McElroy Ansa

"And you left before you found out anything about your friend Crystal and her babies?" Miss Liza Jane sounded like she couldn't hardly believe that, because she slowed down so much next to this old trailer park, we almost rolled to a stop. "What were you running away from?"

"I ain't running away! Why you say that?! I just wasn't no help back in Mulberry. I was just making people mad. So I thought I'd do everybody a favor and give everybody a little space.

"I just make some folks mad when there's a lot going on and lotsa questions being asked."

Just thinking 'bout the questions made me dizzy and feel kinda sick. Where were you, LaShawndra? What was going on, LaShawndra? What you know, LaShawndra?

"And also I thought if I just went on with life like nothing wasn't wrong, if I went on to Freaknik like I planned to before, then I'd come back home in a few days and everything would be like it was, all all right.

"I did! That's what I thought. That's what I was doing."

There was a big rumble of thunder and a flash of lightning, and I nearly knocked over my cup of soda. Miss Liza Jane didn't flinch.

"Anyway," I told her, "you making me forget that I got something to be happy about. The babies are all right. And Crystal all right. They not hurt or anything, and I'mo be happy 'bout that!

"Boy! Way to bring down a Jaguar, Miss Liza Jane! God!" I know it was her ride, but I reached over and turned up the radio.

"Uh, listen. That's Crystal's favorite song. It's called 'All That I Got Is You' by Ghostface Killah featuring Mary J. Blige."

We just listened to Crystal's jam for a while and watched it get darker and darker.

"I guess I better turn on my headlights," Miss Liza Jane said. "It's starting to pour down again."

I don't think I had *ever* seen so much different weather on one little two-hundred-mile trip.

You Know Better

"Whooooooeee, look at this rain come down. It's like hard to even see. I got back in this Jag just in time before the bottom fell out."

"Check your seat belt, Lil' Schoolgirl," she said, and actually started to drive a little faster. "Let's see if we can make some progress now to Atlanta."

"Good!" I told her. "When I get up there, I can settle somewhere and find out 'bout Crystal and the babies for real.

"I think things gon' get better and better from now on."

Miss Liza Jane just raised that arched eyebrow of hers.

"I do!" I said, and started searching in Sandra's animal-print bag for some lotion for my feet.

22

I shoulda known better than to get too happy. I had got a ride—my first one—in a Jaguar. I had heard that Crystal and the babies were okay. Miss Liza Jane had listened to me talk like I had something to say. We had finally got a good ways away from Mulberry. My nails looked tight. Miss Liza Jane had got me to thinking serious about my music and lyrics. And even though it was raining like a special report on the Weather Channel, we had just passed a sign that said ATLANTA—80 MILES.

Everything was looking good.

I had just drunk half of my last bottle of water and was putting on some more lip liner when Miss Liza Jane said, "What's that up ahead on the road?"

I felt another little shudder.

I flipped up the mirror visor. "Don't ask me. I can't hardly see *nothing*! This rain is coming down so hard!"

"Why, it looks like a roadblock of some kind," she said, like it wasn't nothing.

My heart almost stopped.

"Where? Up ahead of us? Where?" It had got even darker and stormier all of a sudden. I couldn't see nothing!

"I better slow down," she said.

"Oh, God, don't slow *down*," I begged her. "We barely rolling now. Wait a minute! Oh, God. I think you right.

"I think this *is* a *roadblock* coming up here! I can't see good. This rain so heavy. It's almost like nighttime."

I told myself not to, but I started panicking. "I can't see! Is it a roadblock? Is it a roadblock!? Put your high beams on. They right there on the steering wheel," I told her. "Quick!"

She fumbled a little while and clicked them on.

"Oh, my God, you are right. Yeah, it's a roadblock, Miss Thing. It's a roadblock for sure! Don't you see them flashing blue lights and them red ones? And I think I can make out a couple of those wooden barriers stretched across the road."

She was squinting up her eyes and straining and acting like she couldn't see good.

That always happens. When you get to feeling all safe and secure, the way I was, something always happens to snap you back to reality. I told myself I shoulda known better than to relax and think I was gonna just glide through the mess I had caused back in Mulberry without a scrape with the law.

"Quick, quick, turn off your lights. Turn off your headlights! Maybe they didn't see us." By now I was really yelling at that old lady.

"Calm down," she told me. "Calm down. Why you so nervous?"

"Nervous? Nervous! The police setting up roadblocks, and I know it's for me. And you asking me why I'm *nervous*?!

"Yes, I'm *nervous*! I better be *nervous*!"

But Miss Liza Jane just kept on driving like she didn't even hear me.

"What's wrong with you? How come you not stopping this car?" I asked her.

"Stop the car! Turn it around! Turn this thing around! Quick! Before they see us! *Stop!*"

"Lil' Schoolgirl, are you serious? I'm not going to stop the car in the middle of the road."

"Yes, I'm serious!" I yelled back at her. Don't ask me why, but I started putting on my sandals and grabbing all my bags and stuff on the backseat. I guess I was getting ready to make a quick escape if I had to.

"Don't you see? They looking for *me*! The police looking for *me*! They been driving these back roads looking for *me*! They set up this roadblock in the middle of this big old rainstorm to look for *me*!

"You gotta help me! Help me make a run for it!"

"No!" she said, as if that was the craziest thing she ever heard.

I thought *she* was crazy. "No? No?!" I said. "What you mean, '*No!*'? If they stop us and search us and stuff and find out who I am, they gon' arrest me and take me back to Mulberry.

"And then I'mo go to *jail*. Oh, God help me!"

Miss Liza Jane started fumbling with the high beams and the steering wheel and hit the horn two times, drawing more attention to us.

"Oh, no, Miss Lady, don't turn into no little feeble-minded old lady on me *now!* I ain't going to no jail. Cute and little as I am, I wouldn't last a night in jail without being passed around like a joint! I didn't mean Crystal no harm. I didn't mean no harm. And I was real worried about her, but I ain't going to no jail for *nobody!*"

Just then a big old bolt of lightning flashed, and through the rain I saw a road that forked off toward the Ocawatchee River coming up before the roadblock. "Hey, wait, wait, wait. Quick! Turn off here! Turn off here to the right!

"I'm serious 'bout this. Turn off. Quick! Turn off. This our last chance. I said we gotta turn off!"

When she didn't make no move to turn, I was so freaked out I just reached over and grabbed that leather-covered steering wheel and pulled it hard in my direction.

Of course, she slammed on the brakes, and we went spinning like a ride at the Mulberry County Fair.

We both started screaming. "Ooooooooh. Whoooooaaa! Look out! Look out for that ditch! Hit the brake! No, wait, don't hit the brake!" I yelled. I couldn't remember which one you were supposed to do when you went into a spin.

Oh, no! I thought. God! This car ain't gon' never stop spinning.

I grabbed my head. I swear, my whole life just flashed before my eyes. It was not a pretty picture.

As that car spinned around and spinned around, all I could think of was, Don't let me die. Gi' me another chance, Jesus! I don't want to go down like this—getting killed in a accident I caused while I was running away from *another mess* I had caused, too! "Help me, Lord!"

And you know I'm the one who claim not to be so big on God and all that. Making fun of Mama Mama raising her hands to God and Sandra tryna play so holy 'cause she tryna hook a preacher.

It was just like Miss Joyce said: "It's always the baddest ones who scared the worst."

My heart was beating a hundred miles a minute!

It was all in slow motion, it seemed like. First the car started spinning and skidding in the mud, then the front tires hit a big old rock on the side of the road, and the car slowly flipped over altogether. Like in a action movie, it flipped over in slow motion. I could almost hear that fast scary *Psycho* music playing. If I hadn'ta had my seat belt on tight the way Miss Lady had made sure I did, I know I woulda been thrown all around that Jaguar and bumped my head and probably be dead now.

But it was almost that bad. 'Cause when the car finally stopped spinning and skidding and flipping and I caught my breath and saw that I wasn't dead, I looked over at Miss Liza Jane and saw that she was laying 'cross the steering wheel with a little stream of red, red blood running down her face.

Well, I thought I was gonna die right then. I reached up and clicked on the interior light.

And all them thoughts I had had since I was twelve or thirteen about what it would be like to die—to just not be around no more, to not have to put up with the way Sandra looked at me and not to have to feel so bad that I kept letting Mama Mama down, and how hopeless it was for me to think I wasn't never gon' get no boy to really love me the way Granddaddy Charles loved Mama Mama, and if any of them brothers I done kicked it with come to my funeral—all that went right out my head. 'Cause the last thing I wanted to do right then was die.

Oh, God!

"Miss Liza Jane, Miss Liza Jane!" I yelled at her. "You okay?"

She stirred a little bit and opened her eyes a little bit.

"Oh, God, I'm so sorry. Did you see me? I grabbed the steering wheel like I was crazy or something. I'm so sorry."

"Good God! I almost made you crash your Jaguar! I almost got us *both* killed!

"What's wrong with me? What am I? Am I the Dark Angel of Destruction or something?! Bad things just seem to *follow me*!"

Miss Liza Jane opened her eyes all the way and sat back against her seat, and then I could see it wasn't no blood at all around her mouth. It was just her red lipstick smeared down to her chin. And I raised *my hands* to God and said out loud, "Thank you!"

Well, I guess that prove I do believe in God, 'cause I was just calling for Him with everything I had! *Jesus* Christ!

Miss Liza Jane looked around, reached over slowly and patted my hand, and then turned around and checked in the backseat for some reason. "Everybody okay?" she asked.

"Yeah, I'm okay. I think." I looked down at myself for the first time, and although my skirt was twisted around backward and I had broke two nails and a strap on my sandals, I seemed to be all right. "Are *you* okay, Miss Liza Jane?"

"I'm fine," she said, taking a tissue from the box on the console and wiping the lipstick stain from her chin.

"You sure? You not hurting anywhere?" I asked, feeling her all over, her neck and her arms and her thighs and legs. "I can't believe a old person like you not hurt."

"Well, I'm not," she said.

"Thank God you didn't total your Jag. Humph, just something *else* for everybody to blame me for.

"I can't believe we finally getting away from Mulberry, Georgia, and here we are in the middle of a almost-fiery death crash."

"Nobody died," Miss Liza Jane said, real soothing-like.

"Yeah, I know we didn't die. But I don't see how not. Didn't you see how we was spinning on this wet, slick back road? How we flipped over! Now we stuck in a ditch down here by the river. What we gon' do? What we gon' do?"

"Maybe the police can help us," she suggested.

"Oh, God, the police! I forgot about the police. I forgot about the roadblock.

"They gon' be here in a minute. They got to come over here and investigate. Where they at? Where they at? I don't see 'em. I know this rain is heavy, but I don't see 'em no more. Do you?"

I looked every which way, 'cause after spinning so many times I didn't know which way was which. But I didn't see anything or any-body on the road in front of us or behind.

"What happened to the cop cars and the blue flashing lights I saw? They was right up there on the road.

"You saw 'em, didn't you? You saw 'em before I did! We couldn'ta just made that up, could we? Not both of us. I *know* I saw a roadblock. And I *know* it was for me."

Miss Liza Jane didn't even bother to look around. She was staring in her lighted visor mirror putting on that red, red lipstick of hers.

"Nope," she said, blotting her lips on a tissue. "I don't see them."

"Miss Liza Jane, I think I'm losing my little coochie mind! I'm really tripping. Maybe I hit my head or something." I felt all over my head but didn't find no bump or blood or nothing.

"Can a little nineteen-year-old coochie like me have a nervous breakdown?" I asked her. "That must be it. All this stress and stuff. I'm bugging for real.

"Grabbing the steering wheel and seeing flashing lights." I looked down at my hands, and they were shaking like leaves on one of Mama Mama's willow trees.

"How come you so calm and cool?" I couldn't believe she was sitting there fixing her hair in the mirror like she was a little hoochie mama like me.

I screamed at her, "The police after me 'cause I'm the one who's responsible for somebody coming into Crystal's in the middle of the night and robbing her house.

"I'm the one who to blame for Crystal laying up there in Mulberry Medical Center close to death.

"That's what that roadblock was about. That's what this car accident was about.

"God punishing me! God punishing me! For what I did in getting Crystal hurt and scaring the babies and being irresponsible. Oh, God punishing me, and he almost took *you* with me!"

"That's not how God works," Miss Liza Jane told me, all calm and everything.

"How *you* know?" I screamed. "Oh, I can't bear to think about my best friend laying up in a hospital room. Probably with needles and tubes and stuff sticking out her body. And not being able to even breathe without one of those air face masks like in planes.

"And everybody thinking I'm responsible. Shoot, I *am* responsible for it. And I wasn't even there to try and help Crystal and her family. If somebody hadn't called the police, Crystal coulda gone into a serious coma and died right there in front of her babies!

"I don't wanna go down like that."

"You can't blame yourself just because you weren't at home when some stranger broke into their house," she said.

"But I *am* responsible! Ain't you been listening to me? I'm the one who's to blame for strangers getting in Crystal's house in the first place."

I couldn't believe that there weren't any more cars on the road or that the police hadn't shown up.

"Oh, Miss Liza Jane, I know you ain't *never* been 'round anything like a crime scene. You shoulda seen our place this morning all wrapped around with that bright yellow plastic tape. It said 'Crime Scene—Do Not Cross' on it, just like on TV. All wrapped around Crystal's nice place—no, her *home*. The home she made for her children and for me.

"That tape the color of Crystal's bathroom was all around Crystal's house. Oh, God, I can't get that picture out of my head. I tried to get inside the house and see what was what, but there was police all over the place and news reporters, too.

"And I asked one of the neighbors what had happened. It was a man with a buncha children who work all the time, and he didn't know me. And he said someone had broke into our place. And some nigga broke in—well, he didn't have to *break in* 'cause he had a key, a *key*!"

She just looked at me with those innocent, young-looking eyes all wide and curious.

"Don't you hear what I said? He got in with a *key*! The break-in guy didn't even have to break in. He got in with a *key*! *My key*!"

I expected her to gasp or be all surprised, but she wasn't. She just said, "*Your* key?"

"Oh, Miss Lady, Miss Lady, Miss Lady, as soon as I heard the man from next door say that he heard a police officer say, 'Wasn't no signs of forcible entry,' I knew, I *knew* it was me! It was me and that *key*!"

Miss Liza Jane still had this calm look on her face that sent me bugging, 'cause I knew she understood what I was saying.

"The key, Miss Thing, the key! The key to Crystal's house, where she got her babies and everything. Why I give it to that nigga?? Why I give it to him? Why I do that? Why I give it to that nigga??

"Oh, I wasn't gon' say nigga no more. Oh, fuck it.

"I'm such a stupid little bitch. I ain't nothing but a little ho, just like Mama Mama and Sandra say. Oh, she gon' be so 'shamed of me. Mama Mama gon' be so '*shamed* of me!

"Sandra don't expect no more from me than this, but Mama Mama...

"She had such high hopes for me. And I was gonna show her that I deserved it. Her hopes and stuff. Now I done put my *best* friend and her family in danger. My *only* friend. And I can't even remember not to say 'nigga.' "

"Tell me what happened," Miss Liza Jane said. And she was so calm, I settled down a little, too.

"It was a guy at The Club. He *said* he had a car and was gon' take me to Atlanta this weekend. Today, he said he would take me to Atlanta today! He *said* he was going anyway and he was gon' gi' me a ride for nothing! That's what he said, I swear, that's what he said.

"He say he didn't have nowhere to crash last night. That's what he said. And I had planned to be there by the time he came by the house. That's why I woke up in the middle of the night—I remembered this nigga had the key to Crystal's front door, and I wasn't there. And this guy I gave the key to kinda led me to believe that he was in the music business and might be able to help me with my career."

"And you gave him the key." Miss Liza Jane didn't even say it like a question. It was like she knew all along.

"I wasn't thinking. You know how I am. I know better now that he was just saying that 'cause he knew how stupid I am.

"How was I supposed to know he was a thug and a robber and a thief and maybe a killer! Somebody told me the guy had a gun, too. Oh, Jesus, I done messed up.

"I raise my hand to God! I swear I didn't want Crystal and her children to suffer just 'cause I'm a little dumb coochie. A stupid little dancing ho!"

Miss Liza Jane had the nerve to try to reach over and pat my knee. "Oh, LaShawndra, don't call yourself that."

"Stop correcting me! Stop correcting me! I am, too, just a little ho. I ain't gon' get it right anyway. You know that! And it ain't gon' make no difference no way.

"They just gon' trace that key back to me and know that I was the one who gave it out. Ain't that a accessory? Ain't that somebody who had something to do with a crime who can be charged with a crime, too?"

She nodded her head.

"I always *used to like* a nigga with a gun! With a tin in his hand. *Am I crazy or what?!*

"Even Mama Mama told Crystal that I wasn't responsible. She didn't say it in front of me, but *I* heard her tell Crystal one time, 'I don't trust LaShawndra with *my keys*.' She say, 'LaShawndra's not responsible enough to be trusted with a key to somebody's house.'

"And, see, she was right. God, I done messed up *big time*! I couldn't even get in the house this morning.

"But I swear, Miss Liza Jane—I raise my hand to God, just like Mama Mama do—I ain't *never* been careless with that key before. I ain't. The whole time I been living with Crystal, I ain't *never* give that key out to nobody.

"I don't *know!* I don't know *why* I give it to him! I been thinking 'bout that ever since I did it. I have!

"I don't *know* why I gave him the key! I don't *know* why I did it. It was so stupid and unnecessary and stupid."

"Um-huh," Miss Liza Jane said.

"He just made me feel like I had to prove myself or something. He kept saying, 'Well, either it's your crib, too, or it ain't.' And 'Ain't you grown? You ain't even grown enough to let who you want stay in your own house.'

"He just kept messing with me and messing with me.

"It wasn't but one key on the whole key ring. You know, I ain't got no car, and neither Mama Mama or Sandra give me a key to *their* house. Shoot, they say *they* ain't crazy!

"I wasn't even with the guy I gave the key to. I don't know *where* he is. I don't know if he the one who broke in . . . well, came in. Or if he lost the key or threw it away or gave it to somebody. I don't even know his last name. I just don't know.

"I was with another nigga last night. It's like you say: I kick it with every brother I meet. And now look where it's got me.

"I swear I had forgot about giving that key away and stuff. I wouldn'ta stayed away from home for nothing if I had remembered that some nigga had the key to Crystal's and her babies' house and I wasn't gon' be there to meet him at the door and hustle him off to my room for the night.

"I done that before, met somebody at the door before they rang the bell, and brought them in my room for the night. I done it plenty times, and ain't *nothing* never happened before."

"You've done that, huh?" But she said it like she knew that I had.

"Miss Lady, what I'm gon' do? What I'm gon' do? I don't think I've ever messed up *this* bad ever before. And I done messed up before, you know? I know I done disappointed folks and let folks down sometimes, but I ain't *never* done nothing so serious.

"Oh, Crystal!" I cried. "Don't hate me. Please, don't hate me."

Miss Liza Jane tried to assure me. "Crystal will understand you made a mistake. She won't hate you."

"I told Crystal not to give me that key. But she tryna prove a point and show I can be trusted, not like Sandra and Mama Mama and everybody else in Mulberry say.

"Now look what happened. Now look what she got for trusting me!

"I don't know *who* got it now. The key! The key! I don't know who got the key now. And the police came, and folks looking for me, and I done messed up so bad. And there ain't no getting out of it.

"Crystal ain't gon' never forgive me. Crystal look strong 'cause she a big girl, but she real fragile. She real sensitive. And even though she wasn't shot, I bet she got tubes and wires coming out her nose and arms. Oh, I can't even think 'bout *that*. Oh, that's way too intense."

I couldn't hardly stand to think about it.

"Let's talk 'bout something else. Please, Miss Liza Jane, I know you ain't never done nothing wrong in your whole life. Please, let's talk 'bout something else."

"There's nothing else to talk about, LaShawndra," she said. And I knew she was right.

"I know, I know. But I swear I just can't face talking and thinking 'bout Crystal. The whole time we been driving up this country road, I been trying to push Crystal and what I've done out of my head.

"I been trying and trying. I know you was thinking I was talking too much, but I kinda thought if I just kept on talking 'bout something else, it just wouldn't be so bad.

"And then I didn't want *you* to know what a screw-up I am. You could *think* that, but I didn't want you to know it for real.

"I'm so 'shamed. I'm so 'shamed of myself, I don't know how I been looking at myself in your lighted vanity mirror long enough to put on lip gloss.

"I'm *so* 'shamed and scared, Miss Lady. I'm so 'shamed."

Miss Liza Jane was just as calm. "Lil' Schoolgirl, you're going to have to buck up and look at this the way it is. Your friend wasn't killed."

"But she coulda been killed. They all coulda been killed in their beds. I been irresponsible and let something happen to her home and her safety and in front of her children. Crystal ain't gon' *never* forgive me! And I don't even blame her."

"Well..." is all Miss Liza Jane said.

"And I ain't even told you everything," I said. I could feel the tears and snot falling off my face into my lap.

"After I saw I couldn't get in Crystal's house, I went over to Sandra's place in the same cab that brought me home. And I broke in her house. So I'm just as bad as the one who broke into Crystal's house. See, I told you I wasn't worth nothing. I'm a fool *and* a thief! I broke in Sandra's house and took her clothes and her giraffe-print bag and even some water from her refrigerator. I told myself I'd replace it and make up for it, but I ain't probably gon' ever get a chance to do that. You think Sandra hated me before—I *know* she really hate me now. I'm just what she says I am. God, Sandra right! I *ain't* nothing but a little ho. And a little worthless, irresponsible ho, too!"

23.

Miss Liza Jane let me sit there and cry for a good long time. Every once in a while she'd say, "Go on, Lil' Schoolgirl, a cry'll do you good." And "You been holding it in too long. Let it go." And that just made me cry more, her being sweet like that to me, 'cause I didn't feel like I deserved it.

So I just cried some more until I *couldn't* cry no more. I didn't even care how my makeup looked. I don't know how long I sat there crying for Crystal and myself and my little hoochie life. The clock on the dashboard was flashing 12:00 over and over, so I didn't know what time it was or how long we had been there in that black Jaguar, stuck in a ditch by the side of U.S. 90.

When the tears stopped, with just some hiccups bubbling up out of me every now and then, Miss Liza Jane handed me three or four tissues that still smelled like her.

"Here, now wipe your face and blow your nose and drink some of your water." She pointed to the big bottle lying on the floor.

I did what she said. I felt like the robot in those old *Lost in Space* TV shows on the Sci-Fi Channel when Dr. Smith would take out the robot's power pack—drained.

"Drink a little bit more," she said. And she waited for me to take a few more gulps.

Then she looked me in the eye and asked, "Well, what you gon' do?"

"What do you mean, what I'm going to do?" I said. "Now that I know that ain't no roadblock up there for me, I'm gon' try to get up out this muddy hole and back on the road to Atlanta. I'm getting out of here. *That's* what I'm going to do, Miss Eliza Jane Dryer."

With everything I had just told Miss Liza Jane, I knew I had to just keep running.

"Don't look at me like that, Miss Liza Jane," I pleaded. "You look just like Mama Mama when she used to say when I was a little girl, 'LaShawndra, look me right in my eye and tell me the truth. You know I can tell when you lying. Now, did you break this vase?'

"And I would break down and start crying, 'cause she right. I can't lie to Mama Mama right in her face looking her dead in her eye."

I couldn't bear to look that old sister in the face either.

"I'm such a nothing, Miss Liza Jane. I'm such a nothing. As nice as you been to me, I ain't been doing nothing but lying to you this whole day.

"I was lying just now when I said that the first time I was praying was out by the road this morning. To tell the truth, I been praying ever since the stroke a' midnight. I just *knew* something was wrong. That's why I got up and came back home to Crystal's. That's the first I really knew something funky had happened. When I saw that bright yellow tape, I knew this wasn't no little mess like getting stranded at a party or sleeping with a girl's boyfriend. This was serious.

"I didn't want none of this to happen. I didn't want my best friend and her babies to be threatened and hurt. I don't want to go to jail. I don't want nobody to know what I did. I don't want to have to look those babies in the face.

"They gon' hate me, too, when they find out what I let happen to their mama and to their nice safe home.

" 'Crystal,' I told her, 'don't give me that fucking key.' And don't say nothing to me about my language, Miss Liza Jane. I can't change how I talk no more than I can change all the messed-up stuff I've done. I'm such a *nothing*!"

I didn't mean to be like a drama queen or nothing, but I couldn't stop calling on Crystal's name.

"Oh, Crystal, Crystal, you knew who I was. You knew I wasn't

nothing but a little coochie from the start. Oh, Crystal. I'm so sorry.
Lord, make Crystal know I'm sorry.

"I ain't nothing, I ain't nothing!" I cried.

Miss Liza Jane was like a DJ's scratch. All she was saying was "Well, what you gon' do about it?" Like I could do something other than just get as far away from all the folks I had hurt as I could.

Mama Mama always say that you got to *fight* to live. You got to fight for every moment of life in this world. You got to fight for every breath you take. When I was little, she make me sit in front of the mirror and blow my breath on it and say, "See there, LaShawndra, that's *your* breath, *your* life there on that patch of foggy mirror. That came out of *you!*" She say it just like that: "That came out of *you!*" *Fullllla* drama. I guess that's where Sandra get it from. That's what Mama Mama say, and I guess she know what she talking about.

" 'Cause I feel like I been fighting just to take my next breath ever since I woke up this morning, before the sun came up and I remembered that key and *knew, just knew* something was wrong back at my house—Crystal's place.

"I guess it ain't my place no more. I don't deserve it. That's the truth: I don't deserve a nice home like Crystal made, 'cause I ain't nothing but a irresponsible little coochie who don't deserve a home. Who got my best friend hurt 'cause I ain't got no better sense than to give my house key out to anybody just 'cause he give me a little attention."

Miss Liza Jane patted my hand, but she was still being all serious with me.

"Well, what you gon' do?" she asked again.

"Miss Lady, I just been pretending all this time with you like I'm just a little coochie on my way to Freaknik. I just been pretending that everything's okay back in Mulberry.

"It ain't! Oh, it ain't! It ain't okay!

"It ain't never gon' be okay again. Ain't no way to fix this."

"There's always a way," Miss Liza Jane said. "If you willing to do it."

"Oh, you don't know nothing 'bout messing up or just being a little ho, Miss Lady. I can look at you and tell that. You ain't *never* messed up like me. Never!"

Miss Liza Jane said, "Hummph."

I said, "What you mean, 'Hummph'?"

Miss Liza Jane handed me a couple more tissues and settled back in her soft leather seat.

"You know that club where you say you hang out?" she said.

"You mean The Club downtown?" I didn't know where Miss Liza Jane was going with this. I thought maybe she did hit her head in the accident and was a little confused.

"Yeah, The Club. The juke joint underneath it. We called it 'The Place.' That used to be *my hangout.*"

"For real?" I couldn't imagine Miss Liza Jane hanging out at no juke joint, smelling like beer and cigarette smoke.

"I was known down on Broadway. I wasn't no real streetwalker, but I sure did walk the streets."

Then she start singing. And I *really* thought she was bugging.

"*Why don't you steal, Miss Liza, steal Liza Jane.*

"*That old man ain't got no wife.*

"*Can't get a wife to save his life.*

"*Steal, Liza Jane.*

"*Why don't you steal, Miss Liza, steal, Liza Jane.*

"When I would walk into The Place, men used to sing that to me. We used to sing it when I was a child. Probably when your grandmother was little, too. You'd stand around in a circle with your little friends and you clap your hands while you sing that song. It was a ring game."

"A ring game?" I asked. "I never heard of that."

"Hummm," Miss Liza Jane said. "Ask your grandmother sometime about ring games. I loved to play ring games when I was a little girl. Especially that one—'Steal, Miss Liza'—'cause everybody said it

was my song with my name in it. Years later, men sitting at the bar
and leaning against the jukebox at The Place would sing it as soon as
I hit the door. I was pretty much a regular there and in a couple of
other places up and down Broadway.

"And I'd stand in the door of The Place all big and bold and say,
'You ain't gotta *steal me*, you can have me!' And they'd all fall out
laughing."

And Miss Liza Jane clapped her hands and laughed out loud like
she was in a world all by herself.

"I was pretty and hot, and my folks had left me my own house up
on Pleasant Hill, a little piece of money from their savings and an
insurance policy. I used it to buy a barbershop downtown. It was just
a little two-chair operation, but you couldn't tell me *nothing*! I
thought I was hot stuff!

"I just didn't take no time to make no life for myself. I was too
busy juking to make no life. I thought that was my life.

"It wasn't." She wasn't laughing no more.

Listening to Miss Liza Jane's story, I almost forgot about myself
and my situation for a second. Which is saying something, 'cause my
stuff was deep *and* intense.

"I didn't make no friends, no real friends, 'cause I didn't know how
to treat them. Didn't know how to cherish them. I didn't make no
family. I opened my legs for many a man to come in, but I didn't
never open them for a child to come out.

"When I got tired of one man, I went to another. When one of my
running partners got on my nerves, I dropped her and found another
one. When you got a little piece a' change, your own car, your own
business, and your own house, one friend after another is easy to find.

"And it was good for a while, my little life. Juking and partying
and hanging. But it didn't stay that way.

"Just like bad times, good times don't last always," she said. And
she kinda chuckled, but it was a hard, dry sound. Not like Miss Liza
Jane at all.

You Know Better

"I didn't make no career. The barbershop was just something for me to live on. And when I didn't need it no more, I just closed it up. I don't know what happened to the two barbers who worked there. They worked for me for thirty years. And when I didn't need 'em no more to keep the place going, I just closed the shop and let 'em go.

"I still regret that," she said. "But I don't want you living with no regrets. You don't have to. I'm here to tell you you don't. 'Cause that ain't no way to live."

Then Miss Liza Jane looked sad, really sad, for the first time since I known her, sadder than when she was talking to me 'bout my language and stuff. And the smile she smiled almost made me want to bust out crying again, it was so sad.

"You know, you look just like your great-grandmama," she said, taking my chin in her hand and lifting it up for a better look at my face. "You never knew your grandmother's mother, did you?"

"Who? Mama Mama's mama? Naw, I don't remember her. She died right after I was born. You knew her?" I asked.

"Um-huh," she said. "We used to be friends, as much of a friend as I was to anybody, back when your grandmother was a child." I tell you, Miss Liza Jane was one surprise after another.

"One of the last times I spoke to your great-grandmother, she came to my front door early one morning. She woke me up. I'd been out late the night before juking, so I didn't feel like crawling out of bed to answer no door first thing in the morning. I know I was short with her.

"She needed a little piece of money. You don't need to know what it was for exactly, but suffice it to say your great-granddaddy, your grandmama's daddy, was a bit of a gambler, and he had got in a game over his head with some folks who were serious about their money. It wasn't much to me. I had it, and I could have given it to her. But I didn't feel like getting up and getting dressed and going downtown to the bank that early, so I told her I didn't have it.

"Just telling you about it makes me ashamed of myself. She hated to have to ask me for it. I can see her face now and how embarrassed she was, especially after I turned her down.

"She said something like 'Oh, that's all right' and hurried on off the porch. I went on back to bed like it wasn't nothing and didn't even think about it no more that day. But we didn't never speak no more after that. And I don't think she ever even told anybody about it. Nobody in your family ever treated me like they knew.

"But even then I knew it was a heartless, thoughtless thing to do to a friend. You know, if you don't even have any love in your heart and you don't show any to your friends, then you really *are* worthless. And I didn't have no love in my heart."

"I can't believe that, Miss Liza Jane. For real? Oh, I can't believe that."

"Believe it, Lil' Schoolgirl," she said. She stopped and looked around the car. "There it is," she said, and reached on the floor behind my seat. When she picked up her pink hat, it was crushed on one side and the feather was bent at the tip. It didn't seem to bother her a bit. She just punched it out on the side and straightened the long feather with two fingers and placed it on her head without looking in the mirror.

It looked good on her.

"I didn't care 'bout nobody but myself," she said.

"But you don't seem like that now," I told her. She didn't. She seemed like the kindest person I ever met. Then it came to me that in all the time I had been riding in her Jaguar, I hadn't even asked her where she was going and why.

"That's what I'm telling you, Lil' Schoolgirl. People can change."

All of a sudden it dawned on me what she was saying.

"You tryna tell me *I* should change?" I said. "Change! Change! Me?! Oh, Miss Liza Jane, you know better than that. You know I'm one little ho who can't change nothing, even when I want to."

"No, I don't believe that," she said. "Everybody can change."

"No, everybody *can't change*! Not me. I can't hardly do *nothing*, you know that!

"I ain't one of those *big* women. I can't do hard stuff like Mama Mama and Crystal and my teachers and you! I can't! It's too hard.

"I can't raise no two children by myself!

"I can't say I'm sorry and do something to make it better!

"I can't work no regular job and try to better myself!

"I can't get no job, period, without Mama Mama's help.

"I can't cook no real dinner.

"I can't get no one boyfriend.

"I can't stop calling myself a ho.

"Shoot, I can't stop being one.

"I can't do it! I can't!"

"I did," she said.

"You did it!? You changed your ways?"

She nodded, and her feather danced around.

"So what? You ain't *nothing* like me! I don't care what you did in your life, you ain't never been as screwed-up and wrong as me. I know it! I know it! I can tell by looking at you!"

Miss Liza Jane got so still it was like she was a statue. She didn't blink or nothing.

"I just told you I did."

"You just saying that stuff," I said. "And what's me changing my ways gon' do for Crystal and her babies traumatized back in Mulberry! What's me changing my little coochie ways gon' do to change that? Tell me that, Miss Liza Jane!"

She didn't even seem to have to think about it. "Well, for one thing, you'll be able to put your makeup on and really look yourself in the eye in the mirror."

I just ducked my head, 'cause she was right 'bout that.

"You the only one who's ever paid any attention to the real me. And now I done messed up. I messed up! I messed *up*! Ain't no way to fix it even if Crystal be okay, I done messed up so big time that can't nothing fix it."

"It could be okay. Sometimes you get a second chance."

"*No!* It *ain't* okay! It *ain't*! For real! It ain't okay! No! *No!* Can't *nothing* fix this. Can't! I'm such a little nothing. I'm such a little coochie! And that's all I'm ever gon' be!"

Miss Liza Jane reached over and took me in her arms. I ain't never been held like that before. Even by Mama Mama. It felt like God was holding me or something. She just held me and rocked me like I see Crystal doing with her babies.

"People change," she said real soft in my ear. I felt surrounded by that Angel's Breath perfume of hers. "You ever thought that the best thing would be to just go back to Mulberry?"

"Go back!?" I pulled away from her right quick.

"Shit! You can pop the trunk of this Jaguar right now and put me and all my stuff off on the side of the road right now, 'cause I got to say it: Bitch! Is you *bugging?!*"

"Sometimes you just have to face the music, LaShawndra."

"Go back and face the music? Is that supposed to be some kinda joke on me? Face the music?"

"I'm very serious," she said.

"*So am I!* Go back?! Go back?! You have got to be bugging! I don't *ever* plan to go back to that little old town again! *Never! Never! Never ever! Never!*

"I been trying to tell you what they all think 'bout me. I been telling you that ever since I got in this Jaguar!

"I'm just a little ho who ain't got the sense to hold on to her own house key and protect the only real friend she ever had.

"I don't want to go down like that, Miss Lady. I don't want to go down as somebody who put my only friend and her babies in danger 'cause I ain't nothing but a little ho."

But I couldn't pretend that I hadn't been thinking that same thing. That I *could change.*

"Miss Liza Jane, can I tell you something?" I wasn't tryna be all dramatic and everything. I just had to pause to get my nerve up.

"I want something for my life. It may not be what everybody—Mama Mama and Sandra an' 'em—see for me but something just for me, *my life!* And just 'cause people think I'm a little coochie who was so irresponsible that I let my only friend get hurt 'cause I was trying to impress some boy ain't got nothing to do with my life. Right?"

She nodded.

"Wait! Let me slow my own roll here a minute." I had to think.

"I may not be the smartest girl in the studio, but I know I'mo have to pay some kinda way for being involved with a break-in and a robbery.

"You ain't got to be no college graduate to know that.

"And I ain't going to jail. I ain't gon' go out like *that!* I'm over eighteen now, but—I'm sorry—I *still* can't be responsible for myself.

"I just can't. It's too hard."

"Life can be hard," Miss Liza Jane said.

"Yeah, but a little coochie like me can't handle that."

"People change, baby." She said it again, but stronger this time.

God, that woman made me think!

"You know what? Mama Mama would say that you ain't told me nothing today that she ain't been trying to say to me a hundred different ways since I came into this world. But with you it seem different and new and real and true. I wonder why that is?"

"Maybe you were just ready to hear it," she said.

"Mama Mama say I don't understand about life. About what a life is. How precious a life is. 'You gotsta *fight* to live.' That what she say. 'You got to *fight* to live. People slip off into death all the time. People die in they sleep. People get caught in the crossfire almost every day. You got to *respect* this life.' That's my problem. I ain't never even thought 'bout nobody I love dying.

"That's what she say my friends'—boys and girls—problem is now. That we don't even know what life is, let alone respect it.

"She say black boys wouldn't be killing each other, girls wouldn't be putting themselves in dangerous situations if they understood about what *life*, what *a life* really means. She say they ain't no way they could be so, so, so . . . casual about shooting into a car or across a park or into a house or over they shoulder as they leaving. They'd *know* that this life thing ain't no game!

"Oh, *life*! Life a big thing with Mama Mama."

"It ought to be with you, too," Miss Liza Jane said.

"I guess it is," I admitted. I had to keep talking before I lost my nerve. "Okay, I'mo trust you. I guess I gotta trust *somebody*.

"Well, here goes. I been thinking 'bout going back to Mulberry, too. I can say I'm sorry and do what I gotsta to make it right. It won't take for forever, will it?

"Sandra would keep running. I don't want to be like Sandra. I want to be like Mama Mama. I wanna be like Crystal. Or as close as I can get. I may not be no big woman, but I can still be a woman just the same, huh?"

"Yes you can," she said.

"Gawd, it's gon' be the biggest mess in Mulberry. The biggest mess since I was born. Oh, God!"

Then I started thinking.

"How I'mo get back to Mulberry?" I couldn't stand the idea of getting out that Jag and getting all my stuff in the wet rain and tryna hitch me another ride in a new direction.

"I was just wondering how I would get back if I decided to go back and say I was sorry and start making up for this some kinda way."

Miss Liza Jane reached over to the key in the ignition and switched it on. The motor under that shiny black hood turned right over and just purred.

"You mean you would turn your Jag around and take me back to Mulberry? All the way back to Mama Mama's house? For real?"

Miss Liza Jane nodded.

"You would do that for me?"

She smiled and nodded again.

"For real? Thank you. You a angel, for real."

"You know, you can always ask for forgiveness. I wish I'd had the chance to ask a bunch of folks to forgive me," Miss Liza Jane said.

"That might be a good idea. Let me think about it for a second," I said. Miss Liza Jane sat quietly while I thought.

"I think that *is* a good idea. When I get back and things have settled down one way or another, and Mama Mama and Crystal, maybe, are speaking to me, I'mo do what you say. I'mo ask for another chance with all of them, too. But what I'mo really ask for is their forgiveness.

"That's a *real good idea*. For real!"

Then I had to stop and take a deep breath, 'cause I knew what I was 'bout to say was big. Big like Mama Mama big.

"Let's turn around. I guess I'm just one coochie who gon' have to face the music."

And, like a miracle, Miss Liza Jane drove right out that ditch. I looked at the clock on the dash, and it was running again.

"Is your clock right? It's just six o'clock? Just six!? For real?" I couldn't hardly believe that. "Feel like we been in this car for years!"

I put my feet up on the dash. And before I knew anything, I had fallen asleep again.

Epilogue

SUMMER 1998

I never would have thought in a gazillion years that the three of us would be sitting around Mama Mama's kitchen table together again—ever!

But here we were: me, Sandra, and Mama Mama, sitting there eating some homemade vegetable soup and cornbread for lunch, making plans for Mama Mama's fifty-ninth-birthday party.

It's been a little more than a year since I messed up with Crystal and the key and everything. And the world ain't come to a end the way I thought it would. Don't get me wrong, now. It was a big mess when I got back to Mulberry last spring, with the police and Sandra involved. But I'm right proud of myself for coming back and facing the music the way Miss Liza Jane said. And you know I ain't never hardly ever been proud of myself for anything!

And get this: I think Sandra may even be a little proud of me for coming back and everything, too. She ain't my best friend or nothing, but now she always tryna put her hand on my head for some reason— messing with my hair, touching my earrings, rubbing my neck. And she ain't hardly never ever hardly touched me before. I don't know what *that's* about.

At first I thought she was tryna hit me. But she wasn't.

She ain't First Lady Mrs. Pastor, but she working on it.

I'm still on probation for that key thing back at Crystal's, 'cause even though the folks who mattered to me believed I didn't do nothing intentional, the courts didn't. They charged me as an accessory before the fact. You know Crystal forgave me before I forgave my own self. Crystal like that. And I'm still in my robin's-egg blue room on Painted Bunting Lane.

I got a year to go on my probation, but Mama Mama say it keep me honest. And she's probably right. She usually is.

When Granddaddy Charles came in the kitchen on his way to a neighborhood building project, Mama Mama smiled bigger than me and Sandra put together. He's in charge of building some new kinda housing for homeless people that he and Sandra came up with. And Mama Mama didn't even ask him if he was going by the gambling house on his way home when he kissed her good-bye. It's the strangest thing—she don't seem to care one bit about that anymore, now that they back together again and everything. Mama Mama say three times the charm. It kinda give me hope that I might get me one special man of my own one day.

I still ain't danced in no music video. But now I carry my pad and pen with me *everywhere* I go so I can write down my lyrics. My pad and pen have become part of my look. And I don't even care when the brothas be tryna front on me because of it either, saying, "Oh, LaShawndra, so you all into your words now and ain't got no time for a brotha no mo'." 'Cause I'm tryna be *'bout something*. And do something with my little life. My life's the only one I got.

I think about Miss Liza Jane sometimes. Right after she put me out in front of Mama Mama's house that Saturday back a year ago, she just waved and drove off like she was gon' see me that evening. Even though I keep looking for her to be riding around town one day in that Jaguar with her two old-lady roomies, I never have seen her again.

By the time I got around to mentioning her picking me up that day on U.S. 90 to Mama Mama, all she said was, "Eliza Jane *Dryer*?!" And I said, "Yeah." And she said, "Um." Like that: "Um." And she kinda smiled. Then she laughed out loud like I had told her a funny story. But I didn't know what was funny. Even Sandra giggled a little bit to herself when she heard what I said, and it wasn't a ugly-sounding giggle either.

I guess we all changed. It's like Miss Eliza Jane Dryer said: "People can change."